GW01605025

Daisy Field

Gabrielle McMaster

Lough View Publishing, LLC

First paperback edition June 2022

Paperback: 978-1-8384868-3-9

E-Book: 978-1-8384868-4-6

www.gabriellemcmaster.wordpress.com

Dedicated to my great-great uncle Samuel Sullivan who fought in the First World War. After surviving the Battle of the Somme, Samuel continued fighting until he lost his life in a German POW camp on 12th July 1918. His sacrifice is never forgotten.

July 1914

Chapter One

The July sun streamed in through the stained glass windows, creating dancing diamonds of colour on the tiled floor of the church. The dust twirled in particles of light as I listened to Reverend Mullan's voice drone on. I was almost certain that he would have put the congregation to sleep if he continued for much longer. I willed myself to keep my heavy eyelids open by tracing the diamonds of colour on the floor. Had it ever crossed Jesus' mind that the Gospel of John would have sent people to sleep? Church was meant to be inspiring people towards God. But the only thing Moaning Mullan was inspiring was a mass exodus. I desired to be anywhere else other than the stuffy, damp smelling church. A movement out of the corner of my eye caught my attention and I glanced down the pew.

Ross Mason smirked at me before yawning. He leant back, closing his eyelids together before pretending to jolt himself awake. He grinned at me with a playful glimmer in his hazel-green eyes. I bit my lip to cease the giggle which threatened to erupt from my mouth. Ross narrowed his eyes at me, before deciding to repeat the same behaviour. This time he misjudged the timing of the jolt and whacked his head on the pew in front.

I let out a snigger and instantly covered my mouth when it escaped. People in the pew in front of us turned around to glare as though they desired nothing more than to listen to Moaning Mullan. Their curling lips and dead eyes made me mask my laughing with a polite cough into my hand. The second they turned back to the front Ross winked at me. He wore his usual cheeky grin across his face despite rubbing his forehead which already had a red mark.

In the two years that Ross Mason and his family had lived in our village, he became well known quickly among the villagers. My father had taken a shine to Ross after he bought the farm down the road from us. It didn't take long until Ross employed my father as a farm labourer. Ross and his seven-year-old daughter, Eliza, always sat in the pew with Father and I every Sunday, allowing them to natter about farming the second the service ended.

Reverend Mullan finished off his sermon, leading us into the most mumbled version of *'O God Our Help'* known to humanity. The sunlight danced through the hats of the women as they stood up, creating a plethora of rainbow halos. Despite the loud echo of the organ music, grumbles of strained singing resounded in the stone building as though everyone had fallen asleep.

Eliza grinned up at me with a gap-toothed smile as soon as Reverend Mullan wished us on our way. Her happy, smiling face was the best visual representation of how we felt to finally be free. As Eliza and I made our way out, I watched as Moaning Mullan's appearance aged with his hunchback and fragility. Matched with his pure white hair, anyone would have placed him in his nineties; yet Mother swore to me that he was only in his seventies.

The sun warmed my skin as I stepped into the brightness of the churchyard. Eliza sprung from my hand to run over to where

Mother stood. She had congregated with Ross' wife, Margaret, and his son, Arthur. Eliza and Arthur were two years apart, but they were the only children that Ross and Margaret had. Margaret smiled as Eliza ran to her side, leaving me trailing behind by the oak doors of the church. The fragrance of summer became all-consuming as the aroma of pollinated flowers and fresh cut grass greeted me.

"Thank you for looking after her," Margaret said to me as she took Eliza's hand. For once her smile appeared to be genuine; much out of character for her. As much as I tried to claim to Mother that Margaret detested me, she refused to believe it.

"You're welcome. She's a pleasure to look after."

The chatter of the villagers increased as others poured out of the church, leaving Ross and Father still inside. Margaret continued her conversation with Mother as I gazed at the fields surrounding the church. Their colour illuminated under the sunlight which created a glow around us. When I was a child, I loved to roam the fields and explore every aspect of nature. I'd always hoped that if I ever got married, I would take a walk through the fields in my wedding dress with my husband. Yet I had no proposal of marriage quite yet. I wasn't sure if I ever would; not at twenty-five. The life of a spinster seemed destined to be mine despite how much I didn't want it.

Father's hearty laughter drew my attention back to our huddle as he joined us. It didn't take long for Father to switch the conversation to how wonderful the singing was this morning. Clearly Father hadn't a musical flare in his body. Every time he made a comment like that, it just confirmed my suspicions. A warm hand rested on the small of my back in a light touch. It was enough to make my breath catch in my throat and my whole body stiffened. Knowing who it was, I refused to give in to the heat radiating through to my flesh. I glanced to my side as Ross' eyes met mine. His hand never left my back as he smiled at me.

In the sunlight his russet beard appeared more ginger than brown. His eyes melted into pools of hazel-green in the golden rays of the sun. The tired lines of exhaustion around his eyes never stopped them sparkling, showing his cheeky side. It was the side to him that Margaret never approved of. Any time he attempted to joke or laugh with anyone, even about the simplest things, Margaret always shot him down. Her piercing glare would be the only warning Ross needed to stay in line.

As a comfortable silence descended, Ross winked at me before clearing his throat. "Fred, do you think if I talk to Isabelle nicely that she might allow me in early to see Doctor Henry tomorrow?" An unmistakable smirk played on his lips as Father laughed in response to his question.

Margaret tutted and pursed her lips at him. "Ross don't be so silly. We're outside a church for goodness sake."

It took every ounce of strength in me not to react to Margaret as my hands balled into fists by my sides. The pinching of my nails digging into my skin was the only form of resistance I had. I turned to Ross and smiled with an innocence uncommon to me. "No such luck I'm afraid Ross, especially after calling me Isabelle. You know that I insist on being called Belle."

"There's your answer Ross," Father told him with a chuckle.

Ross removed his hand from my back and looked away from me. I watched as his Adam's apple bobbed in his throat for a split second. Yet, a soft smile emerged across his lips as he kept his eyes fixated on Father. "I guess I'll have to try a bit harder to get those perks then."

We made our way towards our houses outside of the village in the countryside. The gravel crunched under my feet as I lagged behind my parents and the Masons. Eliza and Arthur ran on ahead, despite Margaret's protests to stay close to us. Dust blanketed at their feet as they sprinted down the road. Hearing Margaret's regimental parenting made me thankful to have the parents that I did. I was an only child, and many saw my upbringing as difficult, or worse, that I was spoilt, but I wasn't. Once I left school at fourteen, I had to learn my independence. Eventually, on my twenty-third birthday, I ended up as the secretary in the doctor's surgery, working for Doctor Michael Henry. Around the village, Michael was renowned for his good medical practices as well as being handsome. His ice blue eyes complimented his curly blonde locks which rested on his forehead and above his ears in a cascading motion. Every young woman in the village wanted to court him, but he showed no interest in any of them.

After the Masons hired me as their nanny, Ross began teasing me about Michael having feelings towards me. He swore he knew a 'lovestruck' man when he spotted one. I tried to ignore his jesting as best as I could. But Ross was the type of person that you couldn't ignore. His witty charm was something that I wished every man possessed, even if it meant I was the punchline of most of his jesting and jokes. The more time I spent with Ross, the less his jesting bothered me. I would never admit it to him, but I took some enjoyment in his teasing and humour.

The Mason's farmhouse came into view as we edged around the corner. The bricked building stood out among the gems of green fields, making any local farmer envious. In the sunlight, the wooden porch illuminated against the house, creating a homely atmosphere as though welcoming us back. The Masons had money and, despite everyone desiring to know where it came from, no one dared to ask. Aromas of roast dinner flooded the house the minute we opened the door, signalling that Margaret had begun the lunch for us before leaving for church. We hung up our jackets on the hooks by the door and I watched as my parents entered the living room. I smoothed down my white dress as someone leant close to me. Their breath brushed against my skin, sending my skin prickling with goosebumps. A shiver ran down my spine and I willed myself not to show any visible reaction.

"I heard that Doctor Henry loves white on you," Ross whispered in my ear.

I turned around to discover his face was a mere few inches from mine. I swallowed hard as he stood there with a smirk emerging on his lips. "If my father hears you, he'll believe your teasing."

Ross chuckled, completely unperturbed by the concern I had over my father. He stood back from me and made his way towards the doorway, stepping aside to let me walk in first. I refused to make eye contact with him as I walked past to sit down near the fire where Arthur and Eliza played. The burning logs gave a warm glow to the living room, and filled it with a rich, mellow smell. Mother discussed sewing and dress making with Margaret as they nattered together in the corner of the room. I had no interest in either topic, much to their dismay. I could sew if I needed to, but it wasn't a pastime that I relished in.

"I always adored your fireplace," Mother commented to Ross when Margaret left to check on the food. I glanced up as they smiled at each other. Ross' features softened in a humbleness he possessed too readily when it came to his skills. "The sheer design of it is magnificent."

The woodwork crafted cascading flowers down the sides of the mantlepiece. When the fire was lit, the flickering flames caused the flowers to dance in their places. Many people didn't know about Ross' love for carpentry and woodcraft. My parents had loved the design so much when Ross created it that they had asked him to make us one too. Our design consisted of autumn leaves falling down the woodwork, providing a consistent reminder of the eventual destruction of life and nature. Margaret was just as accomplished with her embroidery and sewing skills. The talents of the Mason family were intimidating, but it never ruined our friendship.

Margaret poked her head around the doorframe, drawing our attention to her. "Lunch is served, if you want to come to the kitchen."

An array of bowls of potatoes and vegetables were placed around the kitchen table for each of us to reach for whichever we desired. My hand reached forward to pull out my own chair. As my fingertips grazed the wood, Mother shot me a glare from the end of the table. I removed my hands immediately, knowing I would get a scolding at home if I didn't. Instead, I stood there, shuffling from one foot to the other, and wringing my hands. I reached my hand out to pull out my own chair in mere impatience when Ross walked around the table to me. He pulled out my chair and helped me in as Margaret's beady eyes surveyed every move the two of us made.

As we began to eat, Margaret looked across at me with every mouthful she ate. She followed everything I did with a precision only known to doctors performing surgery. I tried to ignore her gaze, but the mere knowledge of it made my skin prickle and a heat to form at my neck. Any second she would make a jab at me, and I would have to swallow it whole without biting back.

"So, Isabelle," she began, knowing the irritation which would arise from using my full name. I made no response to it; giving Margaret satisfaction only added to her smugness. "Our children have informed us that you're quite the storyteller."

"Yes, I do enjoy making up stories for the children. Mother keeps urging me to write them down, but I haven't had the chance to yet," I stated, glancing down at Mother with an appreciative smile. I turned back to Margaret, but she didn't smile. She just nodded, ensuring that her stare continued to bore into me.

"It must be difficult to find the time to do anything else when you have two jobs. I'm amazed you can even keep up with the housework. Some might say that you couldn't possibly balance so much," she remarked, placing a small piece of meat into her mouth. She chewed as though she had the world's deepest, darkest secret on her shoulders.

This was just another rude and sarcastic comment to add to Margaret's list. Everyone remained silent, wondering which of us would bite at the other. I shrugged, taking a sip of my water. The air hung heavy, threatening to suffocate us if someone didn't speak soon. Father cleared his throat and attempted to remove the awkwardness by commenting on the food. It may have diverted the topic for a few moments, but it didn't stop the sly looks Margaret shot my way every so often. Eliza and Arthur chattered away to each other as if nothing had happened. They were too young to notice the knives being fired by their mother towards me.

"It's a lovely day for a stroll," Mother suggested as we finished up our dinner.

Margaret placed the knife and fork down on the plate. She nodded, showing Mother a beaming smile. "You're right, Nancy. I think that's what we will do. The dishes can wait until later."

Ross sighed as he leant back in his chair and rubbed a hand over his face. "I wish I could join you, but I have to attend to the horses today. Please, don't let me stop you from enjoying your stroll. Feel free to go on without me."

We made our way into the hallway to fetch our jackets for a walk. I dared to pray for a miracle; a chance that I wouldn't have to go on this stroll. I reached my hand out, skimming the collar of my jacket, as Margaret gave me a look of discontentment. My arm went back to my side, leaving my jacket shivering in the emptiness. At least she didn't want me to go as much as I didn't want to be there. But she wouldn't admit it to anyone, not even herself.

"Ross promised to show me the horses," I announced, trying to conjure up the most believable lie. Ross stared at me as his eyebrows pulled together, scanning my eyes for an answer I couldn't give him out loud. A smile gradually appeared on his face, and he winked at me, settling my somersaulting stomach.

"Yes, that's right. If no one minds, I can show you them now, Belle." He glanced at my parents, awaiting their permission to go across the fields with me. I watched as Margaret's shoulder slumped in relief at not having to deal with me on the stroll.

With no objections from anyone, especially Margaret, the five of them left for a walk. I followed silently behind Ross towards the barn where he held his horses. Our footsteps on the pathway drowned out the noises of the animals as we walked past the pens. Everyone in the village questioned how the Masons could afford such an expanse of farmyard and lands. Our family soon learnt that Ross' uncle passed on, leaving him a large sum of money. With the small number of animals that he previously looked after he wanted a farm more than anything else. For once, Margaret agreed with a decision Ross made and they purchased the farm. At least, that's the story they spun to everyone. Whether it was true was another matter entirely.

The scent of fresh hay and horses wafted out to me as I stood at the entrance of the barn. I'd been in the barns many times before, but I had never been comfortable around the horses. Ross walked past me and over to the horses in their stables. They munched on the hay as he opened the door to one of them. I watched as Ross' face completely altered as he admired them. The scowl he wore when Margaret scolded him had caused wrinkles around his mouth and eyes. Now, his eyes glittered, and he wore a beaming smile as he stroked the mane of the horse and its coat glistened in the sunshine. Ross ran his hand down the side of the body of the horse. He gazed over at me and jerked his head to call me over.

"Don't be shy. They won't harm you, trust me."

My heels echoed against the concrete floor as I walked over to him. With a cautious hand I stroked the side of the yellow dun horse. My hand shook as beads of sweat dotted my forehead. The horse shook its jet-black mane, causing me to jump. I fumbled with my hands as I stared at Ross. Did I do something wrong? Had I hurt the horse somehow? Ross didn't laugh at me; instead, he gave me a reassuring smile.

"We can ride them if you'd like to?" Ross offered me. The tension which had started to ebb away, built up in a pulsing headache at the mention of riding a horse.

During my childhood I had learnt many things: I should be seen and not heard, how to ride a bicycle, how to care for others, and patience. But riding a horse hadn't crept up once. Mother and Father always told me that they would get Ross to teach me how to ride a horse. Now that I was going to complete the dreaded task, a small perspiration built up on my forehead and I resisted the urge to wipe it away. My eyes bulged as they took in the size of the two horses. I swallowed hard as nausea overcame me. Ross must have sensed my problem as he proceeded to show and tell me how to get on to the horse. While I didn't know how to ride, I knew I was expected to sit side-saddle. But every bone in my body wanted to throw a leg on either side in the most unladylike manner.

"Shall we head out?" Ross asked me once I got onto the horse. He locked eyes with me from his horse, making sure I could manage on my own. I nodded as Ross began to ride out of the barn.

The warm air of the afternoon breezed against my face as we exited the barn. The sun beamed down on us, creating a perspiration on my skin that wasn't only due to the stress of trying to ride. Ross rode on slightly in front of me across the farmyard to the field behind the house. The back yard of the farm was nothing to look at with barns and pens where he held pigs, cows, horses, and sheep. Beyond the back gate laid the most beautiful scenery known to man on this side of eternity. Rolling green fields of paradise stretched for miles against the azure horizon of the clear sky. Something about the vibrant colours under the summer sun made the fields feel like coming home. Everything to do with Margaret's sarcastic and rude comments washed away as the nature engulfed every aspect of my being.

"I'm sorry for my wife earlier," Ross said, dragging me out of my thoughts and back to the reality I wanted to forget.

I glanced at him, but he didn't look at me. His eyes remained fixated on the horizon, as though he were contemplating Margaret's comments over in his own mind. "Don't apologise – there's no need."

A sigh escaped his lips, and he shook his head. "Her snide remarks are uncalled for, but she seems to take too much pleasure in saying them. I don't want you offended by her."

"You're just trying to keep me sweet so that you can get your doctor's appointment tomorrow," I jested with a grin, knowing I had to try to lighten the mood between us.

Ross laughed at my harmless teasing, shooting me a beaming smile that could have stopped a thousand hearts. Anyone who had met Ross and Margaret knew that Ross was the most understanding. It was Ross who had given me the nanny job when he noticed how well I got on with the children. Margaret desired to have someone more educated, but he rejected her demands immediately. Eliza and Arthur had gotten on well despite my apparent 'uneducated influence'.

Ross lifted the latch of the gate into the next field and kicked it open with his foot. He moved to the side to let me go in first with the horse. As soon as I set eyes on the field, I froze as an audible gasp escaped from my lips. If daydreams could become a reality, I had stepped into one. I never knew anything like this could exist; perhaps in folksongs or folklore, but never in our small village or my wildest dreams. The immaculate emerald meadow was littered from end to end with pure white daisies. It was the most beautiful sight I'd ever laid my eyes upon. I cursed myself for not knowing this existed until now.

Ross stopped beside me, and his eyes willed me to turn around to him. But I couldn't move my gaze from the beauty of the meadow. "It's beautiful, isn't it?"

I nodded as though in a trance. "I didn't even know this field existed."

Finally, I glanced at him to find his eyes still on me. The edges of his mouth twitched in suppression of a smile. "I come out here when things get too much. It's a bit of a trot on the horses, but it's worth it. When you realise your mistakes, it's nice to escape to this small piece of paradise."

My eyebrows drew together as his words rang out. What did he desire to escape from so badly? Nothing he said made sense to me; he had the perfect family and land to make anyone envious. I didn't want to ask him what he meant, despite my concern. I bit my lip as my chest tightened. Ross wasn't the type of person to admit their feelings to anyone. I released my lip from my teeth and focused on the dancing daisies in field. My mind kept racing with questions I could ask Ross, but I had to try to realise that it wasn't any of my business.

Ross turned the horse around and glanced back at me to follow. I pulled the reins to turn the horse, wishing that I could stay in the field forever. It truly was paradise, but today it wasn't for Ross. For most of the journey, we remained in silence, lost in our own worlds which we would never speak about to the other. Every so often, Ross broke the quiet trance between us to ask if everything was okay. I resisted every urge inside me to point out the irony of him asking me that. He couldn't even look at me on the way back to the farm. He knew that I could tell something was bothering him. Yet Ross didn't want to address it, until I had enough.

"Is there something–"

"No… I'm fine," Ross interrupted me. My lips slammed shut in an instant and I fiddled with the reins in my hand.

He stopped his horse and gazed over his shoulder at me. My throat constricted as the sun hit off his eyes, melting them into the softest shades I'd ever seen. He blinked and forced an apologetic smile onto his lips. A sigh escaped into the air from his lungs as he turned back to get off his horse. I frowned as he walked over to me and reached up to take the reins.

"I'll walk us the rest of the way. It will give you a chance to relax."

I nodded, refusing to do anything that would annoy him anymore than he already was. By taking the reins, it was his way of making sure that I never asked him about it again. If he was trying to control two horses, he knew I wouldn't want to distract him. By the time we made it back to the house, the others hadn't returned from their stroll. Ross stopped the horses at the entrance to the barn and stood beside them to help me down. I laid my hands on his shoulders as he took my waist in his firm grasp. Before I could ask him anything, he took the horses inside to the stables. I walked around the barn, kicking up the loose pieces of straw on the concrete floor. Ross' heavy footsteps echoing around the barn caused my head to spin around. He walked towards me, smiling in his usual lazy, lop-sided manner.

"Thanks for keeping me company today. I know you didn't want to go for the stroll with the others, but I'm glad you enjoyed seeing the daisy field."

"I wasn't much company. I spoke very little," I admitted, crossing my arms, and fidgeting with my jacket sleeve in my fingers.

Ross chuckled, causing my shoulders to ease. He tilted his head as his eyes glittered in the splintering sunlight coming through the barn slates. "You've always been like that, since the first time I met you. But your presence and small talk were enough for me."

A warm flush rose from my neck up to my cheeks. He turned to walk out of the barn, expecting me to follow him. I stood, frozen in place, knowing if I didn't ask it now that I never would. "What was wrong in the daisy field?"

Ross halted in his path and his back straightened ever so slightly. After a few seconds, he turned around and began to walk back towards me. "It's nothing for you to worry about Belle. It's just… I thought I would get a different life from what I did. People keep lying to me and, every single time they do, it's a constant reminder of the mistake I made."

He beckoned me to follow him back towards the house as though our whole conversation didn't happen. As we approached the porch, the others walked down the path towards us from their stroll. I watched from a distance as Ross laughed and smiled with them. Everyone would have believed that nothing had ever upset or troubled him. It wasn't the man that I had witnessed in the daisy field. He was putting on a façade and I didn't know why. Ross built his walls so high that I thought it impossible to get through them. But I had to try.

Chapter Two

The morning sun created an orange hue across the village as I made my way towards the doctor's surgery. Every street was bustling with busy people going about their day as early as possible. The start of the week appeared the most active day for the village. A gentle breeze ruffled my long lilac dress as the surgery came into view. Doctor Michael Henry got out of his car with his briefcase in one hand and the keys to the surgery in the other. The curls of blonde reflected the sunlight like a halo on his head when he beamed at me.

"Good morning, Belle," he greeted warmly as he opened the surgery. The keys clanged in the breeze as they remained in the lock.

"Morning Doctor Henry," I replied, slowing off beside him.

He sighed and turned to me, cocking an eyebrow. "You know to call me Michael when we're not around patients."

He swung open the door and the familiar sight of the waiting area greeted us. The surgery wasn't a massive building, but it was enough for the small number of residents of the village. A warmth enveloped me as we opened the curtains, allowing streams of sunlight to brighten the room. I laid my belongings on my desk in the waiting room before Michael entered his office. I stood by the doorframe, wringing my hands, as Michael set his briefcase on the desk. I coughed lightly, grabbing his attention, as he put on his white doctor's coat.

"Would you like some tea?" I questioned, shuffling my feet on the wooden floor.

"That would be lovely, but please make yourself one too."

Many of the women in the village envied me for my position in the surgery because of how close I worked with Michael. He was only two years older than me, creating a trend of women around my age asking for appointments. These were merely attempts for them to flirt with him in the hopes of a courtship forming. It didn't take long for me and Michael to catch on to their flirtatious ways. Needless to say, Michael remained single, much to the dismay of the local women.

After making the tea in the kitchen, I carried the two steaming cups back to my desk. My pathway became blanketed in a trail of the sweet aroma. As I set down the cups, Michael came out of the room. He grinned as the sweetness overcame his senses. "That tea smells amazing!"

I lifted one of the cups and handed it to him. The steam created a barrier between the two of us. His soft fingertips brushed against mine as he took the tea from me. I didn't want to snatch my hand away, but his hand lingered on mine longer than it should have. He walked back into his room again with a click of the door. I sighed and closed my eyes for a brief second before turning around to sit at my desk. My body jumped as my hand flew to my chest to clutch my heart. Beneath my hand, my heart pounded against my ribcage, threatening to burst out.

"How long have you been standing there?" I questioned, pulling at my cardigan sleeves, and fixing my hair. Did Ross see

Michael's lingering hand on mine? I willed myself not to let a blush creep onto my cheeks as my hands grew clammy.

Ross stood there with a stone-cold expression. He raised an eyebrow and tilted his head to the side. "Long enough."

My cheeks grew warm as I stumbled into my seat to distract myself. Knowing that Ross had seen Michael's behaviour made me want to run out of the surgery and back home. But I couldn't do that on Michael. I flicked through the appointment book with a shaky hand to find Ross a free appointment.

"H-He's free after his nine o'clock appointment," I informed him. Ross' eyes bore into me, willing me to look up at him. But I kept my focus on the appointment book and my own cursive writing of villagers' names. "Take a seat and he'll see you in due course." I jotted down Ross' name in the book. His feet pounded on the floor as he took the chair closest to my desk.

Michael came out of his room and walked over to me as he sipped on his cup of tea. The air grew heavy and suffocating as he placed his hand gently on my shoulder. Without looking up, I knew Ross was watching his every move. Michael leaned over my shoulder to see the people due for appointments today. The sweet aroma of the tea mixed with the inviting woody tang of his aftershave.

"Good morning, Mr Mason," Michael greeted, causing me to finally raise my eyes to Ross. He nodded at Michael but maintained his stone expression. "Who's first today, Belle?"

"Helen Wallis is first. Then I've managed to put Mr Mason in afterwards before your appointment with Mr Carmichael."

He glanced over at Ross again and nodded, swiftly removing his hand from my shoulder. I tried to ignore the coldness of my skin without his touch. "Thank you very much. I'll be out at nine to see Miss Wallis."

When Michael's door closed behind him, Ross began to chuckle. I frowned, glancing over at him as he laid back against the chair. He folded his arms across his chest and held his grey flat cap in his hand. Ross wore a smirk with one eyebrow raised.

"Sorry?" I asked him as politely as I could muster.

Ross tilted his head and smiled at me. "You cannot possibly tell me that you don't see it too." At my silence and blank expression, Ross continued, "Doctor Henry is infatuated with you."

My mouth opened and closed several times. It wouldn't have been the first time that Ross suggested such a thing, but it was the first time he did so within Michael's hearing distance. "That's preposterous."

"Is it?"

My lips pulled into my mouth immediately and I glanced down at the table. Ross never pushed it further, letting the two of us wait in the suffocating silence. I flicked through the pages of the appointment book from start to finish and silently prayed that Michael would return soon. I didn't care who came into the surgery, I just needed someone to stop the air weighing so heavy on us.

"He'll probably ask to court you soon."

My head shot up to glare at him. "No, he won't Ross. Don't be so silly."

He nodded, and his eyes bore into me. "He will, trust me." I diverted my eyes away as a warm flush rose from my chest to my neck. "Once he proposes, he'll try to kiss you."

"Oh, hush Ross! Don't say such things," I hissed as the warmth appeared in a red glow on my cheeks.

I lifted my eyes from my desk as a snort escaped Ross' nose. His body jolted up and down, attempting to suppress the laughter which threatened to burst out of him at any given moment. He spluttered and met my eyes as the hearty sound of his laughter engulfed the room. I'd often heard Margaret talking about how she fell in love by that single sound. As it rang a melody around me, I couldn't deny how beautiful it was. I found myself giggling until tears began to roll down our cheeks in warm rivers.

I reached for my handkerchief in my sleeve and patted my tears away as Helen Wallis sauntered in. Her blonde ringlet hair flowed out of her headscarf as she removed it. Even though she lived in the manor house with her father, Helen expected to be treated like a princess from a children's fairy tale book. Everyone in the village thought she was beautiful, and, out of the corner of my eye, I noticed Ross gazing at her as one would watch a wondrous sunset. Helen's beauty had clearly not overshadowed Ross either.

"Ah, Miss Wallis, right this way," Michael said, causing me to jump. Helen flashed us a pageant smile as she walked past into Michael's room. The second the door closed behind them, I let out a sigh and glanced over at Ross. He twisted his cap in his hands and shuffled in his seat, avoiding eye contact with me.

My stare bore into him, willing him to just take one look at me. Finally, he glanced my way with pleading eyes. I didn't need to ask him what he was pleading with me. Anyone who knew me was aware of my quiet nature. In this case, I didn't want to ask about what I had witnessed. It wasn't my business, nor was it my place to say to Margaret either. The air grew heavier until Ross eventually spoke.

"Please don't say."

"I won't," I promised, keeping every question I had at bay from my tongue.

The surgery door clicked open, and the echo of heels signalled Helen's departure. She strutted out, ignoring us as though we were nothing but furniture in the room. Ross smiled over at me once she left, but it didn't remove the tension my shoulders stiffly held. Michael called Ross into his surgery from behind me. As much as I sought the time alone after the incident between us, it was impossible when more people started to pour into the surgery. While Michael was attending to Ross, I made my way into the storage room to retrieve the patients' files.

Ross' face appeared above the stack of files in my arms as he left Michael's room. He smiled at me as Michael called the next patient. "Good day, Miss Wilson. I'll speak to you later," Ross greeted before walking off. I nodded at him, suddenly unable to speak. Ross had never been formal in his life, even in the best company. Something wasn't right.

I watched him walk into the sunlight of the morning, willing him to turn around just once to let me understand what was wrong. The stack of files dropped on my desk, drawing the attention of the other people in the room. I smiled at them as I lifted Ross and Helen's files from my desk. When I took them to the storeroom, my fingers itched to peek inside Ross' file. There was no way he could have been there for an ordinary appointment. He didn't spend long enough in Michael's office to warrant it. I flicked open the pages of Ross' file and started to read what Michael had noted down.

"Stitches from a cut across his stomach taken out. Scar likely to form," I whispered as I followed Michael's handwriting with my fingertip.

Ross' accident was well known by the people in the village. Only a year after the Masons had arrived, Ross was out in the barn cutting wood for a new design when the saw slipped on him. The jagged metal cut across the skin on his stomach. As Margaret and the children weren't home at the time, Ross ran to our house as fast as he could. He clutched his bleeding stomach, hoping the blood would stop flowing by the time he reached us. Father was tending to the front garden when Ross stumbled down the road towards the house. He brought him inside and Mother ran to get a rag that he could hold against his wound. While I stayed with Ross, Father and Mother went to Doctor Henry's house to fetch him. I put as much pressure as I could on his wound. His hands sealed around mine to maintain the pressure to cease the blood flow.

"Ruddy saw," he chuckled with a smile.

I stifled a laugh as I shook my head at him. Ross always laughed and joked when he knew he shouldn't have. When Michael arrived with my parents, he disinfected and stitched the wound. I watched as Ross didn't whimper or even shuffle in pain. He took whatever life threw at him and never once complained how unfair it was. That was the one thing I'd always known about Ross – he never voiced his pain nor his feelings.

The day at the surgery flew in while my mind raced with the possibilities of Ross' appointment with Michael. I didn't dare to ask either man because they would never tell me the truth. I stared down at the appointment book as Michael left his office to close the surgery for the day. He stood by my desk while I readied myself to leave. My heart always longed for home, even though I still worked in the village.

"May I give you a lift?" Michael offered.

I glanced up at him as I tidied the desk. His eyes sparkled in anticipation of a 'yes.' "You don't have to. I'm more than okay to walk home from here."

"Nonsense."

After locking the surgery, Michael opened the car door for me and allowed to get in. The car ride back to my house descended into screaming silence. Michael made the odd comment here and there, but it did nothing to remove the static quiet which hung over our heads. I gazed out of the window as the village transitioned into the emerald countryside. A peace came over my body as I relaxed into the seat. There was nothing quite like returning home.

"I do apologise for not talking much," Michael spoke into the silence. I turned to him, now aware of how close we had come towards my house. Ross' fields started to come into view in the distance. "Are you enjoying nannying for the Mason children?"

"It is an excellent position. Ross and Margaret are always very good to me. But working with the children is the best part of the job."

Michael veered off the road, pulling in at the hedges which formed a guard of honour for the road. I looked over at him with my eyebrows pinched together. His hands clenched and unclenched against the steering wheel as his eyes remained fixed on the road in front of us.

"Michael?" I dared to ask to grab his attention.

He swallowed hard, and his gaze met mine as he turned his head slowly. The usual beaming smile he wore faded to the point of being invisible. "You must know that I've been in love with you from the moment of your first day in the surgery. Belle, you have captured my whole heart and soul. I understand if this is a shock to you and if your feelings are not the same as mine. But I cannot possibly hide my feelings for you any longer."

My mouth opened and closed several times, wondering what I could possibly say to escape the situation. My mind whirled at a thousand miles a second. Nothing made sense. Ross' incessant teasing came to the forefront of my mind. All along he had been telling the truth. But for him to tell me the truth, he had to have known about Michael's feelings long before I did. A heat flushed my body and a desire to breathe in any form of fresh air overcame my senses. My hands scrambled for my belongings as

I flung open the car door. Our eyes met as I climbed out of the car and I swore his orbs were fragile glass, waiting to break at any second.

"Thank you for the lift, but I think I'll walk from here. I'll see you tomorrow at the surgery," I informed him, before closing the door. I tried not to run as I walked down the road towards home.

Michael tried to call me back at the top of his voice, but I cut through the nearest field, out of his sight. When I shut the gate, I spun around to see the field littered with daisies. The emerald and snow field had imprinted itself into my memory from when Ross had shown me it. The heads of the daisies tickled my ankles with every step I took. The more I thought about Michael's feelings, the more I was in a world of my own, analysing everything to no end. A distant voice pulled me out of my thoughts, causing me to lift my head and cover my eyes with my hand.

"Belle? Is that you?" I gazed across the field as the silhouette walking towards me formed Ross' features. He led one of the horses behind him as I stopped to wait on him to catch up with me. The horse's mane glistened in the sunlight as it followed Ross obediently. "What are you doing here?"

I shrugged, refusing to confess everything that had happened between me and Michael. Part of me believed Ross would only gloat, telling me how he had been right this whole time. I wasn't in any mood to listen to his gloating – all I wanted was to go home to my parents and forget any of it happened. Throughout my life, I always dealt with everything by myself. My parents had enough to cope with without me adding my problems to their worries. I started to walk away but stopped when the thudding of footsteps followed me. Turning around, I jumped as warm breath engulfed my hair. I stifled a laugh and stroked the nose of the horse. Ross stood back, watching us in the sunlight.

"He follows you better than he follows me," Ross stated, taking the horse by the reins. "We'll walk back with you, if you don't mind."

I didn't protest, hoping that Ross and the horse would provide some form of distraction from my thoughts. A peaceful silence descended between us as we took the path back towards home. The dust created a grey hem of dirt on bottom of my dress, but I didn't care. I had more on my mind than the chore of washing my clothes. How did I not see Michael's feelings before? How could I have possibly missed them? A humming noise stopped my thoughts immediately. The humming turned into singing, pulling me away from all the thoughts I didn't want to have to think about anymore.

A grin formed on Ross' face when he felt my gaze upon him. His singing ceased as our eyes met. "It's your favourite, is it not?"

The first time I heard the song was at a community dance in the village hall. Our families had attended as my parents had hoped to introduce people to the Masons. I had sat down with my parents, Ross, and Margaret when the band began to sing the song that Ross had remembered.

"What song is this?" I asked, turning to my parents.

Mother smiled at me, clearly realising I was in love with the melody. "It's called *'Come Josephine,'* Dear."

There was something about the melody that made me want nothing more than to dance to it. Unlike the other young women in the village, I didn't have a partner to dance with. Ross must have known how much I desired to dance to it because he sprung up off his seat with a hand outstretched just for me.

I shook my head and blinked rapidly with the fading memory as we approached home. "Y-You remember the dance?"

Even Mother and Father didn't remember that *'Come Josephine'* was my favourite song and had been since the dance. Ross nodded and stopped directly outside the cottage. "You underestimate me and what I remember about you." He never took his hazel-green eyes off me as he spoke. A small smile played at the edges of his mouth as neither of us dared to look away. His face inched closer until every detail came into view – from the beauty spot on his cheek, to the small scar on his forehead. My breath hitched in my chest as I swallowed hard. "I'll see you at the house later, Belle."

He turned and wandered back up the pathway with the horse trailing behind him. The mumbled words of *'Come Josephine'* echoed in his track. Ross' singing began to get fainter until it became replaced by the melody of the birds. Only when it descended into birdsong did I will myself to finally go inside.

Chapter Three

The silver-blue moonlight guided my pathway to the Mason household. Above me the stars asserted their dominance in the universe against the fading blue sky. I gazed up and smiled, knowing that for one night I didn't have to worry about Michael. For the last few hours my mind had whirled through every option possible for dealing with the situation. One option was immediately ruled out: quitting the surgery. We needed the money to maintain the cottage. Ross paid Father all he could for his work, but my wage helped to tide us over. As much as I desired to forget the incident ever happened, I knew I couldn't. One look at Michael's face would flood back a tsunami of memories.

Birds sang as they settled down for the night, creating a sweet melody to calm my intrusive thoughts once more. No matter what happened between me and Michael, I would just have to keep going with my job. I needed to for Mother and Father. For that reason, I never told them what had happened. Mother would encourage the courtship, but Father would remain cautious until he trusted Michael would never hurt me. Did I want a courtship? I wasn't so sure; I'd never viewed Michael in that way.

I walked down the pathway to the Mason house and spotted a silhouette on the porch. A cigarette lit up the sunsetting darkness of the summer evening. A warm smile settled over my lips as I realised it was Ross waiting for me. The closer I got to the porch, the clearer Ross' smile came through the cloud of smoke which bellowed from his mouth.

"You're lucky," Ross stated as I approached him. He took another drag from his cigarette before crushing it beneath his foot. The lingering aroma of smoke tickled my nose.

My eyebrows pulled together as I stood in front of him. "Why would I be lucky?"

"Margaret has gone out, so you won't have her judgemental stares. The good Lord knows I've suffered enough being her husband. Drink and smoking are the only two vices I've ever had. They only became vices when I married her funnily enough."

I covered my mouth with my hand to hide the smirk which threatened to turn into a grin. No one dared to involve themselves in the bickering between Margaret and Ross, including Mother and Father. It simply wasn't worth it because no one ever knew who was in the right and who was in the wrong. Ross raised one eyebrow at me, clearly knowing what I was trying to hide, before opening the front door.

"Don't tell her I was smoking," he whispered as his warm breath caressed my ear. Every part of my body froze with how close he was to me. "I'm trusting you to keep it a secret."

"You can trust me." My voice was a mere whisper, afraid that if I spoke any louder the hidden truths in my heart would spill out in a split second.

He rested his hand on the small of my back, drawing me into reality. Ross held the door open and, as I passed under his arm, my heart thudded in my ears at an unexplainable volume. Before

I could speak, Arthur and Eliza ran straight to me. Their tiny arms engulfed my legs and I bent down to hug them.

"Belle, I thought you weren't coming," Eliza panicked, her eyes wide and watering.

I smiled and brushed stray hairs away from her forehead. "Don't be silly. How could I not see my favourite two people?"

Eliza giggled as I stood up and Arthur kept a hold of my hand. As long as I'd known the Masons, Arthur seemed to take his shyness after Margaret. Despite her snide remarks, Ross was the more outspoken and forward of the couple. Everyone said that Eliza was Ross' double. The more time I spent with the Mason children, the more I agreed with their observation.

Eliza and Arthur led me to their room. Despite having a farmhouse, the children shared the room, begging to question what the other rooms could possibly be used for. For the first few minutes, Eliza and Arthur told me what they had learnt from school that day. As I went over the topics, ensuring they had understood everything their teachers had taught them, I spotted Ross walking past the room. Every so often he would glance in and keep an eye on the children. Usually, it was Margaret who performed such a task to check on my teaching.

"Can we read a story with you?" Eliza questioned once we completed everything that I planned to do with them.

I grinned at her beaming face and nodded. "Of course, pack up your things and then we'll read a story."

The children sat on the rug in the middle of the room as I read them a fairy-tale from one of their books. Half-way through, I noticed Ross standing at the doorway. I didn't know how long he had been there for. Our eyes met and he smiled at me before walking off, allowing me to finish the story for the children. I pushed every questioning thought away from my mind and tried to focus on the mystical world of fairy-tales. With a gentle hand,

I closed the book and gazed at Eliza and Arthur. They laid on the rug, breathing heavily as they drifted off to sleep. I lifted them into bed and tucked them in, knowing, for one night, that Margaret would let them sleep in their clothes.

The warm light from the living room drifted into the hallway when I walked downstairs. I put my head around the doorframe as Ross bent over, scrubbing the polish into his boots. Margaret still hadn't returned yet – if she was in the house, Ross wouldn't have had the audacity to polish his boots in the living room. I knocked the doorframe to draw Ross' attention before intruding further into the room. His head shot up as a smile pulled at the edges of his mouth.

"May I come in?"

Ross nodded, pushing away the cloths and polish tin. "Of course, so long as you don't tell Margaret I'm polishing my boots in here. She insists I do them outside."

I stifled a laugh and took a seat beside him on the sofa. I watched as he finished off his boots, before wiping his black stained hands on a spare cloth. With a sigh, he let his back sink into the sofa and wiped the beads of sweat from his brow with his arm.

"How were the children this evening?" Ross enquired, as though he hadn't paced outside the room to check on us.

"They were very good and well behaved as usual. They dozed off, so I put them into bed with their clothes on. I hope Margaret won't mind."

"Of course, she won't." Ross smiled into the distance and his eyes glazed over. For a split second, I dared to believe I had never witnessed Ross, the broken man, in the daisy field. "They're my everything; I don't know what I would do without them. It makes putting up with Margaret slightly more bearable."

My parents always told me that when I had my own children, they would become my whole world. 'You would do anything for them. You'd rather see a knife spear your very soul than see your children hurting,' Mother would always insist. While I was an only child, I knew I was my parents' everything. They always wanted another child and sought in vain to fulfil their desire. But after a miscarriage and a stillbirth, Mother was irreversibly destroyed. A part of her remained heartbroken, yet she tried her best to smile every single day for me. I couldn't possibly begin to imagine the pain she went through. With Mother's experience in mind, I understood how Ross felt about Eliza and Arthur.

Ross stood up to put away his boots and polish equipment. Out of instinct, I got up from the sofa, ready to help him. He spun around at the click of my heels on the wooden floor. "You don't have to help me, honestly; sit and relax after the day you've had. I'll put these out in the kitchen."

I sighed and sat down when he left. My hands rested in my lap as I wrung them out of the need to do something while I waited for Ross. His footsteps thudded into the room, signalling his return. He flopped down beside me again and I glanced at the clock on the mantlepiece. "I must be getting back soon. Mother will need me to help her out before I retire to bed."

"Once Margaret is back, I'll drive you. You shouldn't be walking in the dark."

I nodded and sat back into the sofa, allowing a pleasant silence to descend between us. My shoulders slumped as the tension of everything that happened today escaped from my body. All day Michael had prayed on my mind, but since I arrived at the Mason house, he had faded to a mere speck.

Ross coughed gently to grab my attention. I turned my head to look at him, but he averted his eyes. "Why were you walking across the fields today?"

All I wanted was to forget everything from the car journey home. Had Michael desired a courtship? Or had he desired more than that? The questions raced behind my eyes until I closed them tightly. I couldn't tell Ross what happened earlier. I vowed to never tell him which meant I had to come up with a plausible lie and swiftly.

"Michael dropped me off. My head was pulsing, and I thought that the fresh air would do me good," I spoke as the lie slipped off my tongue. I opened my eyes and looked at Ross once more. His eyes met mine as he nodded, but from the way his stare bore into me, I knew he didn't believe a word of my lie.

He moved himself forward on the sofa, ready to question me. I swallowed hard and my hands instantly grew clammy. I promised myself I would never admit the truth to Ross, but, in that moment, I didn't think I had a choice. The front door flung open, causing my body to jump. My heart thudded against my ribcage, and I resisted the urge to clutch my pulsating chest. I glanced over my shoulder as Margaret poked her head through the doorway.

"Oh Belle, I didn't think you were still here. It's good to see you again," she greeted me with a tight smile. I wasn't quite sure whether it was in politeness or discomfort at my presence.

I stood up from the sofa and returned the smile. "It's good to see you too Margaret. I was just leaving, but I wanted to wait for you to let you know that the children are tucked up in bed with their clothes still on. They dozed off when I was reading a story to them earlier."

Ross and I went into the hallway to get ready to leave. Margaret stood staring at me as I pulled on my jacket. My eyes followed hers to the hem of my dress which now had a brown halo of mud caked to it. I glanced away as a red flush warmed my cheeks.

"Belle walked here," Ross stated, knowing what Margaret was staring at. I didn't dare look at either of them. I could only imagine the exchange going on between them. "So, I'm driving her back."

"Yes, I can definitely see that. I'll check on the children while you're away," she responded.

I couldn't help but take one last look at Margaret. She pursed her lips as Ross grabbed his jacket from the coat hooks by the door. As I walked out with him, I refused to make any comment to Margaret. I wasn't going to dignify her snide remarks anymore. Life was always easier when I didn't create more tension between us.

It wasn't a long drive back to my cottage, but it was more pleasant than tripping over my own feet in the darkness of the road. As we pulled up, I thanked Ross for his kindness when the engine halted. My hand reached for the door handle, but Ross took it gently in his calloused grip. I gazed at him, and he avoided my eyes with every ounce of restraint his body possessed. The vein in his neck throbbed as he willed himself not to cave into his human instinct. Instead, his eyes remained firmly placed on my hand enveloped in his. Darkness coated everything around us, except for our hands which were illuminated silver-blue by the glow of the moonlight above us.

"If Doctor Henry ever asks you something that you don't quite know how to respond to, just do what you did with me. Lie about it to avoid answering with the truth," he whispered. His gaze finally met mine, hitching my breath in my throat. His hazel-green orbs glistened like smoky quartz as the starlight captured them.

"How did you know I was lying to you?"

The corners of his lips tugged with a small smile as he moved a stray curl away from my face. His hand rested against my cheek, but I made no effort to push him away. "When you lie, your eyes change from chestnut to the fallen leaves of autumn; in the exact same way they do when the light leaves them."

I swallowed hard, attempting to come up with a reply. I opened and closed my mouth several times before anything coherent emerged. "I… I didn't know they did that."

Silence fell between us as we refused to glance away from each other. Our hands remained encased as his touch warmed my cheek. In the darkness, Ross moved closer, and his breath cascaded over my lips, caressing them. I drew in a sharp breath, expecting everything I shouldn't have ever dreamt of desiring.

"Ross, is that you?"

I looked out of the car as Father's slim figure strolled towards us in the distance. What would Father possibly think with Ross so close to me in the dark? He may have thought it innocent, so why did my skin prickle at the suggestion of Father seeing us? I turned back to Ross as our faces remained a mere few inches away from each other. We locked eyes in the briefest of moments before he sat back in his seat, letting go of my hand.

"Indeed, it is," Ross called back, waving a hand out of the window. "I thought I would leave Belle home to save her walking in the dark."

Father approached us, with his usual laidback smile, as he talked to Ross. One thing was for certain: he hadn't witnessed anything between us. I let out a shaky breath before quietly slipping out of the car. My heart raced beneath my breast, desperate to remind me of the possibilities of what might have happened. I touched the base of my neck as I made my way towards the cottage. Perhaps I had imagined the whole situation with Ross. But, if I did, why could I still see our hands in the moonlight? The illuminated alabaster encased in the sun-kissed warmth could never have come from my imagination. It was a mere moment of compassion between two people and nothing more. At least, that's what I made myself believe.

Chapter Four

There was no doubt in anyone's mind, nor mine, that a home had a distinct aroma of a bakery. The mouth-watering smell of sweet scones filled the kitchen as I cooked the last batch for Mother. I flung my apron over the chair in the kitchen and arranged the scones which were already cooked onto plates. Silhouettes of Mother hanging out the washing in the garden danced over the floor. Everything needed tended to before Mother or Father would even consider leaving for the church fair. Once every summer, Moaning Mullan would host a church fair to raise funds for the upkeep of the building and the community. The fair drew everyone from the village and its outskirts for one morning every year. My parents always went to the church early before the crowds arrived, which meant I'd been awake since dawn preparing scones for the bake sale stand with Mother.

Mother came into the kitchen to check on the scones. Strands of her hair poked up everywhere like a hedgehog's spikes. I tilted my head and smiled at her weary face.

"I'll hang the rest of the washing out," I assured her.

She brushed the stray hairs away from her face, smoothing them into place, as she glanced at the basket. "Are you sure, Belle? There's quite a lot to do and you need to check on the scones too."

"Of course, I'm sure."

Mother thanked me and kissed my forehead. For a second, she held my face in her hands as she had when I was a child. With her gentle thumbs, she wiped away the flour covered on my cheeks. We shared a small smile before she disappeared into the bedroom to get herself ready for the fair. It didn't take long for Father to come into the cottage with mud stained trousers from tending to the garden. He practically sprinted to the bedroom to make sure he was ready in time to leave for the fair.

The church fair was always a huge occasion for the village. For as long as I remembered, I went to the fair with my parents to support the church. Needless to say, Moaning Mullan was still the vicar, but he always beamed with pride at the turnout of support every single year. Stalls covered the lawn behind the church building where people sold cakes and bakes, books, or bric-a-brac to raise money. Some stalls had games for the children to keep them entertained for the morning. At the end of the fair, it became a tradition to have a huge game of tug of war for the children too – boys versus girls, of course.

Once my parents left, I began to hang the washing out. The sun scorched down on me, reminding me of the glorious summer days still ahead for us. Fresh grass soon replaced the aroma of home baking as I hung out the bedsheets. I grabbed two pegs from my pockets as I threw the bedsheet over the washing line Father made. A shadow cascaded itself onto the white material behind my own. I froze out of instinct until the formless black splodge moulded into the figure of a man. I spun around to see Ross standing there. He had already changed for the fair – his brown suit and flat-cap made him look as though he were heading to a church service.

"How are you?" he asked before I could utter a word. He took off his flat-cap and held it between his hands.

My eyebrows pinched together as I wordlessly stared at him. Instead of answering, I desired nothing more than to ask him why he was standing in my garden, but rudeness wasn't my second nature. "I'm fine, thank you."

Ross came over to me, saying nothing more, and reached into the basket to hang up another bedsheet beside the one that perfectly captured his shadow. Between the two of us, we finished the washing in a confused silence. I lifted the basket off the crisp grass which had long since lost its dew in the morning sunrise. As I made my way inside to the kitchen, Ross' heavy footsteps followed behind me.

"Do you need something?" I asked, throwing the basket on the table beside the scones. I turned to face him, highly aware of how rude I probably sounded. He glanced at me with a blank expression before blinking rapidly and shaking his head.

"Oh no, no I don't. I just wanted to talk to you before the fair."

"Well, I need to get Mother's scones ready, so could you wait in the living room for a few minutes?"

Ross nodded, wringing his cap between his hands, before walking off to the living room. My shoulders stiffened as I tried to concentrate on taking the scones off the tray and onto a plate. Why was Ross Mason standing in my living room? What was so urgent that he needed to talk to me about now rather than at the fair? Unanswerable questions flooded my mind as I put the basket away in the cupboard. Nothing made sense, much like the night in the car with Ross. Even though it had been a few days ago, it felt like only yesterday. Ross stood by the fireplace waiting on me in the living room. His gaze caught mine in the mirror and he walked over to me, looking deep into my eyes. My body jittered as my stomach churned over until nausea came to the forefront of my worries. Something wasn't right. We hadn't spoken since the night in the car, and, from the darting look of anxiety oozing from his eyes, I knew he was about to bring it up.

"T-The night in the car when I dropped you home… do you remember it?"

I swallowed hard, wishing for nothing more than to forget whatever my imagination had conjured up. Nevertheless, I nodded in reply. "Yes. You dropped me home." His eyes clouded over, and he stepped backwards ever so slightly. It wasn't the response he expected. The colour drained from my face as I realised it wasn't my imagination. "Something nearly happened between us."

I expected Ross to apologise for that night and tell me how it was a lapse of judgement. Instead, he stood in silence, rubbing his hand over his beard. "There's no easy way to say this, and I know you'll hate me for it once I do," Ross began, pacing the spot in the living room. He stopped in front of me and took my hands in his clammy grip. "I love you, Belle. And I know I shouldn't – you don't have to tell me how wrong this is because I've thought it through for over a year. But I love you against every sensible and coherent reasoning. How could I not? You're the most beautiful and kind woman I've ever met in my whole life. I've harboured these feelings for you for too long. You must have known I've felt this way towards you."

I didn't know. But now everything made sense – the teasing, the daisy field, and the car… This was what caused this nonsense. If we never had that moment in the car, Ross wouldn't be standing in my living room. I dropped his hand and gripped my head, trying to think straight. I didn't even know what to reply to Ross. What could I reply? Nothing seemed anywhere near sufficient. He stepped closer, taking my hand from its hooked grip on my head, and encasing it in his once again. My conscience willed me to back off, but I couldn't. Something held me there.

Ross' breath returned to my lips again, reminding me of what might have happened that night. This time, there was no one to stop it, except me. His lips gently grazed against mine. I let out a shaky breath as my body screamed for more. This was wrong. Ross was married to Margaret. I was the nanny to his children, not to mention Father working his land. This couldn't happen. Before he could kiss me, I moved my head to the side, causing him to stop in his path.

"Ross, this is wrong. You know that."

He moved away from me and searched my eyes for any signs of me changing my mind. "For ages, I realised I married the wrong person. I stayed for the children but… the moment I met you, I knew I could finally give my love to someone. Someone that I love the way I'm meant to love my wife."

"You're still married!" The heat rose in my body as my fiery breath resounded from my flared nostrils. I watched his mouth open, ready to reply to me. "Just get out!"

"Belle, please."

"Just go!"

Ross moved further away from me, sensing the anger building in my body, and walked past to leave the cottage. I didn't make any motion until the door clicked shut. I waited for Ross' feet to crunch across the stones outside our house before I let myself calm down. The pinching of my nails into the palms of my hands eased as the anger escaped my body. I didn't have time to think about Ross and his ludicrous thoughts of love. If I didn't leave now, I'd never make it to the fair in time. I raced to the kitchen and grabbed the plates of scones before making my way to the church.

How could Ross do this on Margaret? I may not have been her greatest admirer, but I wouldn't want my husband declaring love for another woman. Not to mention the impact on the children. People in the village had always gossiped about Ross and Margaret's marriage being sour, but I never once thought that Ross would consider having an affair. Let alone an affair with me of all people he could possibly choose from!

I should have seen it coming – all the touches, the whispers, the time alone. What would people think of me if they ever found out? My cheeks began to grow warm at the mere thought of what would have happened if I hadn't stopped Ross when I did. I glanced at every person who passed me, expecting them to chastise me as though they could read my thoughts. A desire built up inside me to wonder about every possibility of what might have happened, despite how wrong it was.

The stalls bustled with people when I arrived at the church fair. Children's laughter and chattering filled the air. I weaved my way through everyone, trying to find the bake sale stall where I knew Mother would be. Women had crowded into the stall to set up their tables, as though it were a competition rather than a sale. Among the women, Mother's yellow dress stood out as she ducked her head between the gaps to try to spot me. The minute our eyes met, she waved at me over the heads and hats of the other women.

"Belle," Mother greeted me in a hug. She held me at arm's length, studying my entire face. I swallowed hard and willed myself not to give any indication of the incident with Ross. "You look flushed, Dear. You shouldn't have rushed yourself."

I touched my cheeks with the back of my hand, hoping the coolness of my skin would calm the redness. "I didn't want to be any later than I already was."

I placed the plates of scones on the table when Mother put the red and white checked cloth over it. Other ladies soon joined me in placing their array of bakes down. There was everything from Victoria sponges to shortbread and jam. The Vicar's wife soon came along to take charge of the selling with her grey curls bouncing beneath her blue feathered hat.

Mother and I walked over to Father who was conversing with Moaning Mullan by the tug of war game. The children readied themselves to partake; boys lined themselves up on one side while the girls took the other. As I glanced across the field, I spotted Ross standing with Margaret. He had his arm around her while they laughed with another couple from the church. Arthur stood by Ross, watching his sister conversing with the rest of the girls for the tug of war game.

I tried to imagine myself standing with Ross; his arm around my waist, holding me close to him. The image never once repulsed me. In that moment, all I desired was to be in Margaret's position. Perhaps there truly was an underlying issue to the tension between me and Margaret. Or perhaps it was because, since Ross and I grew to know each other, all we subconsciously desired was to be together. Ross' eyes finally locked on mine, and I swallowed hard, desiring to look away. But I couldn't muster the courage. If he spoke words of honesty in the cottage, then why did he continue to behave as though he were in love with Margaret?

I glanced away from Ross, excusing myself from my parents and Moaning Mullan. My head spun with the need for sanctuary in a peaceful place. There was only one place I could go to without drawing attention. My feet rushed me inside the isolated church which screamed an eery silence the second the heavy wooden doors swung open. My heels clacked on the tiled floor and resounded among the empty pews as I walked to the front. I stared at the wooden cross on the table, trying to calm my newfound envious heart. I should have kissed him in the cottage. It was wrong in every sense of the word. But I desired nothing more. I willed myself to bury every feeling I had towards Ross, but I knew I couldn't do it for much longer.

"Belle?"

My eyes grew wide, and my throat clenched, knowing it had to be Moaning Mullan. But it wasn't his voice. I turned around as my breath hitched in my chest with one single look at him. Ross stood in the middle of the aisle with a sweat covered brow. The church doors behind him were shut as tight as I had left them. How he got into the church so quietly I would never know.

"Are you okay?" he questioned as his eyes clouded with concern. A crease formed between his eyebrows as he waited for my answer. "I'm sorry if what I said has upset you so much. I truly am. All I can do is ask for your forgiveness."

My heart clenched in my chest as my nails dug into my palms. His words flooded into white noise as I ran from the front of the church to where Ross stood. Before he could utter another syllable, I took his face in my hands and finally allowed our lips to meet. I didn't know what came over me to kiss him in such a manner. But, in that moment, every desire we had been holding inside for the two years we had known each other was fulfilled. The rush of passion and warmth was welcomed as he responded to every touch of my lips. He wrapped his arms around my waist, pulling me closer to him, as he kissed me without any hesitation. Hidden desires no longer had to be secret between us; that was enough for me. Wanting each other was enough for both of us.

Chapter Five

We rested our foreheads against each other, refusing to be further away than we needed to. Our breath echoed against the hollow walls of the church as we grinned at each other. There was no doubt in either of our minds that the kiss was something we both needed. The signs of our feelings for each other had been there for a year. Yet I refused to believe or even acknowledge them until now. Ross' eyes shone at me as he kept a hold of my trembling hands, playing with the tips of my fingers.

"You've no idea how I have longed for that to happen between us," he admitted to me in a hushed tone.

"I've tried to suppress everything I feel about you, but…" My breath caught in my throat, afraid to admit what my heart desired me to. "But I can't any longer."

The release of tension which accompanied the kiss soon replaced itself with my racing heartbeat, causing an overwhelming weakness in my legs. Ross gripped my waist as I stumbled slightly. I blinked rapidly and grasped his arm so tightly that my knuckles started to turn white. Anyone could find out, especially with where we were at that very moment. I'd become a laughingstock among the villagers if they found out. Falling in love with a married man – I must have been insane!

"No one will find out. We'll be careful, I promise," he reassured me, as though sensing my thoughts.

"Anyone would think you had been planning this for a while," I tried to half-heartedly ease my own fear. Ross chuckled and pulled me closer to him, allowing my head to rest against the comfort of his strong chest. Instead of responding, he kissed my forehead and smiled against my skin; giving me the answer. Our lips met one last time, knowing we had to return to our families before they suspected anything. The parting touch almost made me stay there for a few seconds longer.

The screams and laughter of the children filled our ears as soon as we opened the oak doors. Ross closed them behind us before pushing his back against them to remain out of sight. He kept a hold of my hand as I started to walk away, latching on to my finger to hold me there. I glanced over my shoulder and smiled at him as I refused to let go of him first. He nodded and finally our fingers unlatched from each other's as we made our way back out to the fair separately to avoid drawing any attention to us. Ross walked off in one direction while I took the other, towards Father who stood waiting for Mother from the bake sale stall.

"Where did you go off to then?" Father enquired when I finally approached him.

"I just went into the church to clear my head. The heat from the sun and the noise just got too much for my headache."

Father nodded and, thankfully, never pressed me any further. "Margaret invited us over for dinner. Your mother was over the moon when she heard; she's happy to have Margaret's company tonight again."

'Not as happy as I am,' I thought. The prospect of seeing Ross again created a warmth which radiated through my chest. Even though our families would be there, I knew Ross would find a way from us to have even a few minutes together. My lips tingled at the mere thought of Ross' touch against them once more.

A shadow made its way over to me, pulling me out of my improper thoughts. I shaded my eyes with my hand as the person's blonde curls caught the sunlight. A soft smile crept onto Michael's face as he stopped beside me. My stomach churned as I looked around, searching for Father before he made a remark about Michael. But he must have walked off into the bake sale stall while I was in my own daydream.

"Hello Belle."

"How are you, Michael?"

Michael shook his head and his eyes dropped down to his feet. A red flush spread across his cheeks as he stared at the grass below us. "I'm more concerned about how you are after the day I took you home. I came over to apologise for being so forward with you. I shouldn't have said what I did. I hope you can forgive me, but I would very much like it if we could act like nothing happened."

My shoulders slumped in absence of the tension they once held. It was as though the weight of the world was finally lifted from my thoughts. Working with Michael since his confession had a similar atmosphere to a morgue. Neither of us spoke to each other unless we had to and, if we did, it was like pulling hens teeth. The prospect of working under those conditions again made my stomach lurch.

"Consider it done," I informed him, smiling wider than I should have under the circumstances.

A shaky breath escaped Michael's lips. "Thank you."

As Michael and I talked about the week ahead in the surgery, I spotted Ross chatting to my parents outside the stall. Mother held her empty plates under her arm – a sure sign that her scones had proved to be a bestseller once again. She waved goodbye to Father and Ross before making her way across the graveyard to Margaret and the children. Ross' eyes met mine as they clouded over with one glance at Michael. Despite the distance between us, I could sense the questions running through Ross' mind as his brow creased.

"Doctor Henry, I wonder if I could speak with you for a moment," Moaning Mullan spoke, breaking my gaze away from Ross.

"Of course, Reverend." Michael turned to me with an apologetic smile. "I'll speak to you later, Belle."

I waited until they walked off before I made my way over to Father. My heart pounded in my ears as I edged closer to Ross. Every moment in the church replayed in my mind. The feel of his lips against mine. Ross pulling me closer to his chest. His grip on my hips, keeping me grounded. I prayed that a flush wouldn't give away my thoughts in front of Father.

"Doctor Henry looked very friendly," Father commented wearily, looking over my shoulder at Michael.

"Nothing for you to worry about, Father." His face relaxed as an anxious smile covered his lips. Although I had addressed Father, my eyes remained on Ross as I spoke. "We just had a misunderstanding, and he was clearing it up."

"I must go and tell the Vicar that we're leaving. Your mother is already at the Mason's car with Margaret and the children," Father informed me, before he made his way over to Moaning Mullan and Michael.

Ross and I left Father talking while we walked back towards the car together. With each step we took, Ross' fingertips grazed the back of my hand, sending sparks bursting through my body. Every touch of Ross' skin against mine turned my moral compass upside down. Everyone's moral compass pointed to true north, but mine forever pointed to Ross Mason. When we reached the top of the hill, I spotted Mother speaking into the car to Margaret through the church gates. We still had time… we had time to be alone with each other, if we dared.

Ross took my hand and pulled me over to the far side of the graveyard. It seemed we both had the same illicit thought about each other. There was a small gap between a stone tomb with ivy growing over it and the wall of the church boundary. Ross pulled me in between the gap, squishing us together. He wrapped his arms around my waist, pulling me closer to him, and my hands instinctively rested on his shoulders. Our breath mixed in a lustful desire for each other. Every single passionate thought flashed before his eyes as he caressed my cheek with the palm of his hand. His lips met mine, igniting a violent spark in our souls. Every fear of this love was erased in a single second, knowing how much being near Ross felt like coming home. How could I not cave into the passion when my heart cried out for his touch?

"We better get back before your father finishes talking to the Vicar," Ross whispered when we pulled away. I nodded in agreement, trying to steady my breathing. He cupped my chin, drawing me back to him, and pecked my lips.

I squeezed out of the gap first, making sure no one was about, before Ross swiftly followed. We dodged the hidden holes and headstones to get back to the gravel pathway. Either side of us grey graves that marked the end of a life well lived created an eery guard of honour for our love. The crunch of the gravel resounded in the small space between us. Perhaps there was silence because we couldn't be ourselves with each other in public. But I truly believed that it was because neither of us wanted to go back to the lives we led.

As we approached the end of the pathway, Ross edged closer to me. "I promise I'll get time to talk to you when we get to the house." He placed his hand on the small of my back, leading me through the iron gates.

As we waited for Father by the car, all I could think about was the next time that I could be alone with Ross. Every touch created a flame, reminding us of the dangerous game we were playing. People who started illicit affairs always ended up scorched and burnt. Ross' hazel-green eyes met mine, shining as they mirrored every feeling that I held deep inside me. In that second, I knew I would go down in flames for him, and he would dive headfirst into the fire just to be with me.

Chapter Six

The sunlight streaked golden rays across the floor of the Mason living room when we arrived back. From the scents coming from the kitchen, Margaret's elaborate lunches were on the menu once again. I stood by the doorframe, waiting for everyone to sit down. My whole body froze and stiffened as Mother and Father took a seat opposite Ross. Margaret smirked from her chair by the fire where the children played at her feet.

"Sit down Belle," Margaret coaxed, tilting her head at me. The only available space was beside Ross. I swallowed hard, refusing to respond or move. "I promise Ross won't bite."

Everyone laughed at her comment, and I smiled weakly as I took a seat beside him. I rested my hand in the space between us to steady myself. Soon, Ross' fingertips grazed the length of each of my fingers. My breath caught in my throat as my heart raced causing a dizziness to come over me. My gaze shot up, darting at everyone in the room to check if they noticed Ross' touch. I let out a shaky breath as I realised no one could possibly see our hands. We sat too close together for them to even get a glimpse.

"The Vicar tells us that war will be declared soon," Father announced, drawing our attention away from each other. "Tensions are increasing in Europe between Russia and Germany over Serbia and Austria."

Margaret gasped, laying a hand on her chest. "Oh, how awful! Ross shouldn't be expected to go; that's the luck of owning land and animals. You, Fred, would be older than the requirements surely. At least you're both safe if the worst happens."

Father nodded as the edges of his mouth pulled into a smile. "Indeed. I suppose that leaves us out then Ross."

"Seems so," Ross responded, staring into the unlit fire. "Everyone finds something ever so romantic about war. I can't imagine the… the horrific nature of it all."

My mind raced with every hair on my body raising in sync. The mere mention of war spurred adrenaline through my body. The romanticism about war created false images which preyed on the minds of young men. My father was assuredly safe from any possible recruitment. But, if it came to it, would Ross be as safe as Margaret supposed? After all, he was a suitable age for the army.

"Margaret, would you mind if I went to the kitchen for a glass of water?" I asked, trying to ignore the nausea.

For a second, her brow creased as she looked at me. Her mouth opened, ready to ask me what the matter was. But, instead, she only smiled at me. "Of course. Or would you like me to get you it?"

I shook my head, taking cautious steps towards the doorway. I needed to get out of the room. Stumbling towards the kitchen, the mumbles of everyone hushed with one simple sentence. "I'll fetch it for her."

When I reached the kitchen, I gripped the sink, hoping to regain some element of composure. A hand reached past me towards the cupboard. The calloused and scarred skin could only belong to one person. Ross filled the glass and willed it into my clenched hands, peeling them away from the sink. I sipped the liquid, letting the coolness calm every anxious bone in my body. I set the glass in the sink and dared a glance at Ross. The cloud of concern lifted from his eyes which swiftly replaced itself with a hunger that oozed out of his very heart. He pulled me close to him and I wrapped my hands around his neck, desiring nothing more than the touch of his lips against mine. Ross' beard grazed my cheek before his lips locked on mine with such a passion that I had never known from him.

This was the worst possible idea Ross ever had for us to be alone together. He had to have known that Margaret could walk in at any second. Yet, despite every knowledge of it, neither of us pulled away. I needed Ross as much as he needed me. As the kiss got deeper, heels clicked on wooden floorboards in the hallway, causing us to pull away from each other. I brushed a hand over my head, smoothing down any stray hairs from my bun. My hand shot down to my side as Margaret walked into the kitchen. Her eyes darted between me and Ross.

"Thank you," I spoke directly to Ross, before turning to Margaret. "Do you need any help with dinner?"

"I can manage, thank you."

Her lips pursed as she glared at Ross. Neither of them looked away from each other; if Ross glanced away first, she would presume him to be guilty of the crime he had committed. I made my way past Margaret and back into the hallway – the small refuge in a house of secrets. The mirror on the wall bounced back a reflection of truth. A red mark decorated my skin between my mouth and my cheek; marking where Ross' beard rubbed against the delicacy. There was no longer any doubt in my mind; Margaret knew about us and what we had just done. The game had only begun and already it was becoming too dangerous. I should have continued to refuse Ross, but I couldn't change my heart. If I could go back, I wouldn't have changed my mind either.

Once Margaret finally called us for dinner, she requested for me to sit in front of her as normal. If she suspected something, surely she would have placed me somewhere else. Ross helped me into the table after Margaret and poured me a glass of water. Her gaze tore through me from across the table. I shifted in my seat, willing my neck to cool down from the temperature which rose at a heightened speed. I didn't dare to glance at her, knowing it would make things worse. One glance would confirm every suspicion she had about me and Ross.

Margaret placed a forkful of mashed potato delicately into her mouth and smiled at me as she swallowed it. "Belle, I wonder if you would take a walk with me after dinner before you go home?"

Out of the corner of my eye, I noticed the vein in Ross' neck pulsing at the mere suggestion from Margaret. Bile crept up my throat, questioning if she would confront me. What would I say to her? What could I possibly say to defend mine and Ross' actions? There was nothing I could have said to change what had happened.

I smiled politely at her. "I would love to."

Ross kept glancing at me throughout dinner when Margaret talked to my parents. I didn't dare to look back at him, even when Margaret was distracted. Ross and I were playing a game of chess; Margaret had us at check. She couldn't complete checkmate if we knew our move ahead of her. That was exactly what I had to do – I had to play a few steps ahead.

When we finished our meal, Ross offered to do the dishes after putting the children to bed. Without a single thought of hesitation, Margaret agreed and called upon me to go for a walk with her. Ross' eyes bore into the backs of our heads as we left the house. The silence rested between us like the ground piling on top of a coffin. The gravel crunched, emphasising the echoing silence.

"Belle," she started, releasing us from the suffocation. "What's happening between you and Doctor Henry?"

I opened and closed my mouth a few times, unsure of how to respond. Since dinner I had waited for her to ask about 'her husband' rather than 'Doctor Henry'. I cleared my throat, attempting to display surprise rather than hesitation. "I'm not sure. He did tell me that he had feelings for me."

Margaret stopped in her tracks and turned to face me. I didn't know what possessed me to tell her such intimate details. I hadn't even spoken to Ross about Michael's confession. But the minute Margaret's complexion altered with a smile plastered over her face, every second-guess I held about my confession washed away. "Perhaps you should embrace his feelings for you. Doctor Henry could give you an amazing life. And if there is any truth to this talk of war, then you'd be better to find yourself someone. We all need a sweetheart to love during war. I'll talk to your parents and make sure they understand about Doctor Henry, especially your father."

Before I could protest, she sauntered off, back towards the house, beckoning me to follow her. She definitely knew something was going on between me and Ross. My confession about Michael's feelings had given her a chance to force me away from Ross. As we made our way back, Margaret continued to suggest ways in which I could strike up a conversation with Michael at work. Of course, it had to give him a gentle nudge that my feelings matched his. I had to agree with her; anything that wouldn't arouse her suspicions any more than they already were.

Mother and Father stood on the porch outside with Ross in the golden hour of the day. Ross' eyes flitted between me and Margaret, hoping to gain a sense of what had happened by a simple look. I glanced at the ground and swallowed hard. I didn't want to lead Michael on, but I wouldn't have a choice if it was left to Margaret. It was the only thing I could do to keep Ross and I safe.

"Would you mind if I just walked back?" I asked, finally looking up at my parents. Mother's eyebrows pinched together as Father ceased talking. "I'm feeling a bit under the weather. Perhaps I got too much sun today at the fair."

Mother approached me and put a cold hand to my forehead. "Well… okay. But only because you don't have a temperature. Otherwise, you wouldn't be going back alone. Take your time and be careful."

"I will."

I set off before Mother and Father left the Mason house. The golden hue reflecting against the colours of the fields attracted me to take a stroll over the emerald paradise instead of taking the usual road home. Everything rushed through my mind: Margaret, my parents, Michael, and Ross. This affair was a game that I could never win. Ross and I could never compete for the prize of a love worth the words of every poet. Was this lustful passion and desire for each other worth losing everything? Was Ross worth losing the respect of every person in the village? I knew the answer I should have told myself. But it wasn't the one my heart screamed.

When Ross and I were together, everything felt right. The world rested in a peaceful state every time we embraced each other. But when I thought about Ross, Margaret's words rang in my ears once more. *'We all need a sweetheart to love during war.'* If or when war broke out, Ross wouldn't be called up, but Michael would. My heart clenched at the mere thought of Michael's name among the dead or missing. I couldn't bear to lose either man.

As I finally made my way onto the path towards home, I let out a sigh and my shoulders slumped when I spotted the living room light on in the cottage. Mother and Father had gotten home before me. All I desired was to crawl into bed and fall asleep, hoping that tomorrow would be better. At least when I slept, I didn't have to work out what to do. Ross and I only admitted our feelings for each other today, and we had messed it up already.

Mother came straight over to me when I closed the door. She took my jacket off my shoulders, fussing over me needlessly. I didn't realise how long I had taken to get home until I saw the clouded worry in her eyes.

"You get yourself straight to bed. I'll be telling Doctor Henry that you won't be going to work in the morning," Mother informed me as she hung up my jacket.

I was too lost in my own thoughts to form a response or even argue with her. She led me to my room with a hand on the small of my back. I stepped inside and let out a frustrated breath when she left. Mother had my bed ready for me and she already pulled the curtains over, letting in just a slither of the remaining daylight from the crack where the thin material didn't quite meet. I closed the door over and changed into my nightdress, before crawling into bed. I welcomed the darkness of a peaceful sleep as I tried not to think about the whole situation. Yet, despite every sensible reasoning in my heart, I fell asleep with Ross' kiss replaying in my mind.

A thumping at the window jolted me awake. I had no idea how long I'd slept for, but the darkness of night coated the room. I swung my legs out of bed and grabbed my dressing gown, pulling it around me as I made my way over to the curtains. Flinging them open, my heart leaped out of my chest as Ross stood there, soaking from the rain which continually lashed down.

"Ross, what on earth are you doing?" I questioned when I opened my window.

He blinked through the rain on his eyelashes. "Can I come in?"

I had no choice but to let him climb through the cottage window. Every woman knew how improper it was to let a man into one's bedroom. But this was much worse; it was a married man. I walked over to my wardrobe and grabbed a spare towel for Ross to dry himself on. The rainwater dripped from his hair and cascaded down his face as he took the towel from me. His fingertips brushed against mine, reminding me of the situation we found ourselves in only hours earlier. As he ruffled the towel through his hair, I repeated my question.

He sighed, pulling the material away from his face. "Margaret was suspicious."

My eyebrows furrowed together as our eyes met. "You just said 'was.' What could have possibly changed in such a short space of time?"

"Well, she was convinced you wanted me, but apparently now she believes Doctor Henry will court you."

My mouth pulled into a stiff line at the mere thought of having to lead Michael on. Despite us agreeing to forget his admittance of love, I knew that if I showed the faintest interest in him, our agreement would be forgotten in an instance. Hurting Michael wasn't something I was prepared to do for the sake of an illicit affair. I cared too much about him to even consider it. But I couldn't tell Ross either or I'd hurt him just as much.

"How did you get away from the house?" I asked, desperate to change the subject from any deception.

His mouth tilted into a smile as his eyes glittered with his usual mischievousness. "I told Margaret I heard noises coming from the horses. As always, she wasn't interested and rolled back over to go to sleep."

I sighed and plunked myself down on the bed. Ross laid the towel on the wooden chair in the corner of my room before sitting himself beside me. My heart wanted, no, *desired* Ross but I didn't know if it was worth the risk.

"Ross, this is –"

"I know this is dangerous and that we're playing with fire. But I have never felt this way about anyone before. I'm willing to risk everything I have for you and that's bound to count for something."

Ross couldn't have been lying about how he felt; not when he was willing to risk everything for me. What was holding me back from him? There was only one thing causing me to second guess everything: losing the respect of everyone, especially my parents. I couldn't even begin to imagine the heart-breaking look on Michael's face when he found out that I rejected him for an affair with a married man. He would think himself a fool and I wouldn't allow that to happen – I respected him too much. I laid my head on Ross' shoulder as we stared out of the window, watching the raindrops race each other down the glass panes. The rain pattered against the roof, letting us believe that we were the only people in the world at that moment.

"I'm sorry that I've got us into this mess, but I promise it will be alright," Ross whispered. He planted a kiss on top of my head, leaving his lips there.

"What if we get caught?"

Ross lifted his head and took my hands in his, forcing me to look at him. "We won't, not if we're careful."

Even in the dim light of the night, I could see his eyes shining in the most wondrous way. His mouth twitched at the corners, suppressing a smile. If I ever had any doubt of his intentions towards me, one single look at his face silenced them all. He was in love with me – I couldn't deny it. A smile crept onto my lips as I leant forward to kiss him. His lips grazed against mine, as though to await gravity to push us together. But there was no greater thing in this world than to let actions speak what words couldn't possibly suffice. Ross cupped my face in his hands, pulling us closer together as our lips met in a passion which sealed every wound in my heart. He held me there for as long as possible, refusing to let us be parted once again. Our foreheads rested against each other's as we pulled away.

"I must go before Margaret suspects something, but remember that I… I love you. I never want to let you go."

He pecked my lips once more before we stood up to finally part. I opened the window, allowing the torrential night to echo into the soundless room. Ross stayed by the windowsill as he refused to move an inch further. Nothing could have moved him, not even the world turning upside down.

"You need to go," I whispered, despite the lump in my throat which willed him to stay. He nodded and glanced away, making both of our hearts easier with the parting.

I watched him climb out of the window and the moonlight glinted off his white shirt. He never even considered bringing a jacket. His urgency to see me proved greater than common sense. Ross turned to look at me once more, smiling despite the rain pouring down every inch of his body, before walking into the night. I waited until he was out of sight before closing the window and drawing the curtains. As I snuggled back into bed, my heart thudded in the silence. Perhaps my feelings for Ross were stronger than I let myself believe.

Chapter Seven

The deception of an illicit affair continued for a week without Margaret suspecting anything. Despite mine and Ross' weariness of getting caught, we still met every single night. The barn became the sacred sanctuary for our love when the moon greeted the Earth. No one attended to the horses except Ross, so we knew we were safe from prying eyes. The small touches, even when others surrounded us, were what I craved most from Ross. One single glance across a room told me about every desire in his soul for me. To know that in a crowd, I was on Ross' mind meant more to me than I cared to admit.

True to her word, Margaret had spoken to Michael. While neither forthrightly told me, it was obvious from the way he kept sneaking side glances at me, to the grazing of our hands when we exchanged patients' files. As the work week went on, Michael began to pay me more complements, make me tea, and offer to drive me home. Paying attention to them felt like a betrayal – a nail in the coffin of the fragile relationship I had begun with Ross. But I refused to give Margaret any reason to believe her suspicions. Thankfully, Ross understood when he spotted Michael taking me home.

I woke up early to meet Ross by the gate to our daisy field. It had become a daily ritual for us. Michael had offered to pick me up that morning for work. Against every belief I held in my heart, I had to agree to it so Margaret wouldn't suspect anything. She was watching everything Ross did, especially if it wasn't his usual behaviour. After breakfast, I bid my parents goodbye before setting off down the path towards the daisy field.

Ross' figure leant over the gate waiting on me as I approached. The sunlight caught his hair in a glistening bronze as the gentle breeze ruffled it like dandelion pappus. He stared down at the ground, his arms dangling over the top of the metal gate. The gravel crunched under my feet, causing his head to lift. Time froze as our eyes locked on each other's and a smile spread across his sculpted face. If my time was over on this Earth, I was certain Ross' face would pass before my eyes as I took my last breath.

Ross swung open the gate with an ear piercing squeak, allowing me to step into the field. Only then did I notice he already had his work attire on. The white shirt and braced trousers became everyday dress for his farming work. He wore his best work boots, ready for the animals and the muck of the fields. He laid his hands on my hips and pulled me close to him. Instinctively, I wrapped my arms around his neck. Our lips grazed against each other's, still unsure of the new territory we had so readily flung ourselves into. The passion and hunger in his kiss silenced the danger we felt a week ago. It was non-existent in this small peace we gave ourselves. We held each other close, refusing to let reality separate us once more.

He pulled away, resting his forehead against mine, and smiled at me. "I'm a bit envious that Doctor Henry gets to look at you for longer than I do every single day."

I stifled a laugh and watched as his eyes glittered at the sound of it. "Then perhaps you should employ me for more hours than you already do."

Ross took my hand in his and walked us over to the shade of the tree in the corner of the field. With calloused fingertips, he brushed stray strands which fell from my plaited hair away from my face. "We need to meet again tonight. I know you're not teaching the children later, but… I just… I want to see you."

Ross played with my fingers in the silence, poised and waiting on my reply. It was breaking our new boundaries. Diverting away from our plan created more problems than solutions. Margaret's suspicions were a testament to our mistakes and risks. I opened my mouth to respond to him, but no words came out. What could I possibly say to such a suggestion?

A car rumbled in the distance, drawing us away from each other. My shoulders slumped as we walked back to the gate. At least now I didn't have to answer Ross' preposterous idea. We agreed to keep our heads down and not arouse any suspicions, but this idea ruined everything we planned. I opened the gate and stepped onto the road as the car headed towards us.

"If you want to see me tonight, then meet me in the daisy field."

I glanced back at Ross and nodded. His eyes shone with a hopefulness I hadn't seen before. "I'm just worried in case we get caught."

As I stood by the gate, Ross' hand found mine, lacing our fingers together. "I'll do everything I can to make sure we don't. I promise you that."

Ross swiped his hand away from mine as the car pulled up to a stop across the road. The door swung open as Michael got out of the car, smiling at the two of us. He had absolutely no clue what was going on between me and Ross. I should have been happy that our secret was safe, but a stab shot through my heart for Michael. He loved me and could provide everything I had ever dreamt of. Yet my heart remained infatuated with Ross. I could never tell Michael the truth. It would break his heart into a thousand tiny pieces; never to return to its original state. All I could do was let Michael believe that he had a chance, no matter how cruel it seemed.

"Morning, Ross," Michael greeted, casting his eyes to the clear blue sky above us. "It looks like it will be a good day."

"Indeed, it does. Perfect day for getting the fields ploughed."

"Very much so." Michael gazed at me with a half-smile on his face. I willed myself not to crumble and show the forlornness my heart nursed at that moment. "Ready to go Belle?"

I nodded and began to walk towards the car with Michael. I dared a glance back, just to see Ross' smile once more. "I'll speak to you later Ross. Have a good day."

"You too Belle."

As Michael drove off, I turned my head to watch as Ross never moved from the gate until the car grew smaller in the distance. His face remained in my mind, as though never letting me forget the love he held for me. Every part of me longed for Ross, like a piece of my heart wasn't in the right place until he came back to me. How did people cope with this feeling of incomparable love?

Michael opened the surgery and let me go in first. Without a second thought, I made my way to the kitchen to have some solitude. I filled the kettle and let the water heat up for Michael's normal cup of tea. If I listened to Margaret's advice, Michael would give me the world. With him, our love would be an oath, not a lustrous secret. I glanced down at my hands as I set cups on the saucers. These hands were in Ross' hair and over his chest… These hands had felt desire, passion, and fire all at once. I could have a simple life with Michael. But Ross' love was becoming somewhat intoxicating.

"Need a hand?" I jumped as Michael spoke, knocking one of the cups. He reached over and caught it before it hit the floor. The blood rushed to my cheeks as he placed the cup back on the saucer. Michael lifted the kettle off the hob and poured the water over the tea infusers, into the two cups. "I don't mind making us tea during the day when I don't have any patients. It's a pleasure to do a simple task for someone who does so much for me."

I laid my hand on top of his and prayed he couldn't sense how much my body was shaking. "Thank you, Michael."

During the day, when Michael came out to call a patient, he placed his hand on my shoulder as if showing those waiting that he wasn't ashamed of me. I would be lying if I said that I didn't think of Ross and how much I wished that we could show people our love. A pain hit the back of my throat and my chest tightened as my mind drifted to all the people we were willingly deceiving: my parents, Margaret, Michael, and Ross' children. I would forever remain Ross' secret no matter how hard I fought for something different with him.

Michael came out of the surgery to close the doors for lunch. I smiled at him from my desk and stood up, stretching my back. The door flung open, spilling sunlight into the room. I squinted in the brightness of the day. A man stood in the doorway and Michael rushed over to him, presuming he needed help. But he didn't. The colour drained from my face as the echo of the church bells ringing resounded into the room.

"We're at war!"

The man waited on us to follow him into the village. Crowds of people had flocked to the main square to hear what was happening. The bells wouldn't stop ringing, alerting people even in the outskirts of the village. Men held up newspapers, allowing others to read them, and handed some out to other people. *'Britain declares war,'* screamed in large, bold letters across the front page. Across the solid mass of people, on the other side, I spotted Ross and Father, fresh off the fields. The sweat glistened on their brows as they tried to hear the latest on what this meant for us in our small community. Ross' eyes met mine and his lips gradually formed a smile. Not even a crowd as large as this could part us from each other.

"It is true that war has been declared," a man in the crowd announced. Everyone turned and glanced around them to try to spot who this man was. I drew my eyes away from Ross and towards the man in a military uniform in the middle of the crowd. How we never noticed him before was beyond my comprehension. "That means that we require men to fight. Do your country proud and be ready to sign up. After all, the ladies love a soldier." A path cleared from him as people stifled a laugh at his comment. "The volunteers' recruitment will be starting tonight in the village hall. All men aged eighteen to thirty five should be there. If you have land to tend to, you do not have to sign up unless you feel obliged to do so. Thank you."

The man smirked at us, tilting his moustache to one side as though he had control over every single man in the village. How many of these men had appeared in random villages throughout the country when they heard about war being declared? Michael's hand found mine and gripped it tightly. I wasn't the only one petrified of war judging by the shaking of his grasp. This was the moment Margaret had warned me about – Michael was eligible for recruitment. Some young men in the village stepped forward as the crowd began to disperse. From the grin on the soldier's face, it was clear they had signed up already. I couldn't imagine what their families would feel when they told them. Michael pulled me by the hand, dragging me away from the sight of the officer patting the backs of the young men. Neither Michael nor I spoke as we followed the crowd back into our work. But he stood close enough to me that no one would ever notice we were still holding hands. It wasn't until we closed the door behind us as we stepped into the surgery that he finally let go.

"Are you worried about enlisting?" I asked without any hesitation.

Michael's distant eyes softened the minute he spotted my lips trembling. "As much as it might be my duty to enlist, I'm a doctor and I have a duty to aid those injured in the war. I'm just not looking forward to telling my father that I'm joining."

"Is he against war?" Men in our village had often voiced their refusal to join the war if it ever broke out. People had frowned upon them, believing the objectors thought less of those who signed up.

"I suppose you could say that. When he heard the news that war could break out, he swore that I wouldn't be going."

I rushed forward and wrapped my arms around Michael. He stood still for a few moments, taken back at my sudden affections, but slowly his arms enveloped me. My fingers bunched his jacket into my fist as I blinked back the tears which threatened to fall.

"Please tell me you'll be safe as a doctor," I whispered. A single tear rolled down my cheek and plunked on Michael's jacket.

"I will." His mumbled voice told me he didn't mean it. No one could guarantee their safety nor survival when they left to fight in a war.

Not a lot of people came into the surgery after the chaos in the village. Some didn't turn up for their appointments which wasn't surprising. They had no doubt flocked home to be with their families with the outbreak of war. Many of the young men would have to discuss their options with their loved ones before signing up. Michael decided to close the surgery early, allowing him time to confront his father about his own choice. As we stood in the kitchen, washing and drying our cups, Michael talked about his role in the war.

"I have to start in a hospital on or near the coast. I'll be dealing with the worst injuries coming straight from France to the nearest hospital. Whenever they require more doctors in France, I'll be moved there to help the soldiers on the frontline."

"At least you can do something for the war effort," I mumbled. Something niggled at my mind every time Michael brought up what he could do to help the soldiers. My heart yearned to do something useful for the men going to fight in the war; many of which I would have grown up with.

"The hospitals will require voluntary nurses from all walks of life."

"I don't have any qualifications, Michael."

He set down the drying cloth and faced me. "They'll teach you everything you need to know, and you'll do the certificates with the hospital. I've taught you some first aid since you've worked with me, but the hospital will put you through it as soon as possible. I can get papers for you to volunteer and put in a good word for you. You could work in the same hospital as me." I gently bit my lip as my stomach fluttered. My efforts to help the men wasn't something done in vain. Despite my hesitation, every part of my mind screamed for me to go and help those in need. Michael became aware of my silence and took my hands in his. "You don't have to make your decision now but let me know soon. I'll be leaving to help as soon as I'm called."

Leaving for the war effort meant abandoning everything I knew and loved. The village, my parents, and Ross would fade to a distant memory in the busyness of the hospital chaos. A lump formed in my throat at the mere thought of leaving my life behind. I didn't know if I could do it. Would I have hesitated as much if I hadn't started a love affair with Ross? I couldn't admit it to myself, but the answer screamed in the silence of my mind. No, I wouldn't have hesitated for a single second.

When Michael dropped me back to the cottage, I assured him that I would talk to my parents about joining the war effort. The prospect of doing something good for others was the only persuasion I would need for my parents. Their only child leaving home would bring a heavy sadness into our cottage, but knowing it was for the right reasons would more than make up for it. I waved as Michael drove off before turning back down the laneway towards the daisy field. Ross waited for me every single day by the tree in the corner of the field, shielding himself from any prying eyes.

As I approached, the gate squeaked open, and Ross' lop-sided smile came into view. His eyes squinted in the afternoon sunlight, dimming the colour they possessed. He leant over and pecked my cheek as I walked into the field. The scent of the daisies filled my senses as we made our way over to the shade of the tree.

"I have a gift for you," Ross announced, digging into his trouser pocket. He pulled out a chain which glistened like starlight in the sun. A small spiral design swung from the end of the silver chain as he held it up from me to see. "I got the blacksmith to make the spiral for me. I said it was for Eliza; a gift for when she gets a bit older."

I reached my hand up and let the spiral's cold touch rest in the palm of my hand. Ross twirled his finger in the air, telling me to turn around to face away from him. He brushed my hair to one side, letting his rough fingertips dance on my neck. I shivered and willed the goosebumps to settle before appearing on my skin. He gently placed the necklace around my neck, resting the spiral at the top of my chest, before fastening the chain.

"This is so beautiful," I whispered, clutching the spiral in my hand. Ross' lips kissed every inch of the back of my neck and my eyes closed with uncontainable pleasure. A small sigh escaped from my mouth as his kisses ceased. "Thank you."

I turned around to him and the light cast a shadow over one side of his face. In our daisy field, the war didn't exist. This paradise didn't deserve the destruction war caused. Ross grinned and lifted me up, causing me to squeal. He spun me around and I laughed as the daisies danced around us in the summer afternoon. It didn't seem like the world was about to fall apart in a war. All that mattered to us was our love for each other.

Ross gently lowered me down to the ground. I cupped his face in my hands; his beard tickled my palms as I lost myself in a sea of hazel-green. The sunlight bursting through swaying leaves and branches in summer could never match the colours of his eyes. My eyelids fluttered closed, and I gently pressed my lips to his. He pulled me closer to him, refusing to let my hands leave his face. Ross deepened the kiss with a subtle passion unaccustomed to him. Perhaps he did love me; it wasn't just lust and desire for him. The flame we ignited when our affair began, burned with a deep longing for something more than merely wanting.

I pulled away from the kiss, taking a deep, shaking breath. Ross' eyelids fluttered open and, with one look at him, I knew he was in love. I leant my forehead against his as a grin came upon my lips. "I love you, Ross."

"I love you too," he admitted with a tremor in his voice. His eyes never left mine as he spoke. "I'll never leave you, Belle. Never. You mean far too much to me. Now that I'm able to love you, I never want to stop."

Perhaps it was my naivety or my lack of understanding about love, but I believed him. I put every ounce of trust I had in the world on Ross' promises. Deep down in my heart, I didn't know if I should have.

Chapter Eight

"Did you make your mind up yet?" Mother asked me as she plaited my hair for the dance. The church had organised a dance in the village hall for the men who had volunteered to fight in the war. In two days, they would leave for the frontline. Thankfully, Michael wasn't one of them yet.

I glanced down at my hands which rested in my lap. "I haven't, but I know I have to make my mind up soon. Michael will expect me to give him an answer on Monday."

Mother finished off my hair and laid her hands on my shoulders reassuringly. My gaze rose to meet hers in the mirror as she smiled at me. "Whatever you choose your father and I will support you; so will Michael."

We left my room and grabbed our jackets in the hallway before leaving for the village hall. Ross and Margaret were due to meet us there. I didn't know what Margaret had planned, but there was something. Mother kept grinning at me as we walked, as though she held the world's deepest, darkest secret. The Masons always gave us a lift into the village in the car for events, but tonight they decided not to. I pushed away any questioning of our secret being revealed with the weight of the necklace against my chest. I hadn't taken it off since he gave me it last week. Mother made no comment on where I had gotten the piece of jewellery from. Perhaps she hadn't spotted it, but, if she had, she didn't ask me about it.

"Mother, can we keep the nursing between us three?" I whispered to her as we approached the village. "I just don't want Ross and Margaret knowing. At least not until I decide."

"That's no problem at all, I'll let your father know. We are both well aware that your father tells Ross anything that comes to his mind."

I hadn't told Ross about the possibility of me joining the war effort. I'd never admit it to him, but he was the only reason why I hadn't made up my mind yet. I didn't know if I could leave him. After all, we had only started our love affair. But deep down I wished that it wasn't such a difficult decision. Every time I thought that I was ready to sign up, flashbacks of Ross and I in the daisy field flooded my memory.

By the time we made it to the village hall, Father had been well versed on not telling anyone, especially the Masons. Mother bent his ear so much about the subject that he tried pulling his cap around his ears to drown out the sound. It didn't feel right keeping a secret with Michael when Ross didn't know. I had played right into Margaret's trap, creating a divide between me and Ross. Margaret and Ross stood outside the hall talking when we spotted them. We greeted each other with small kisses on our cheeks and Ross shook Father's hand.

"Oh Belle, I have exciting news for you," Margaret announced. I frowned, my eyebrows pinching together in the middle, as she smirked at me. She did have something planned. Whatever it was, Mother knew about it too. "Michael is waiting on you inside. The two of you can spend some time together tonight. After all, we're here to chaperone you."

"He hasn't asked my permission," Father stated, removing his peek cap. He rubbed his short grey hair into place.

Margaret tutted and glanced at Father. "Don't you remember that I asked you on his behalf yesterday?"

He shook his head at his own forgetfulness. "Yes, I remember now."

I walked past them into the porch of the village hall. Michael sat on one of the chairs with a white rose balancing in his hands. His eyes met mine in a glimmer of pleasure and he shot up from the chair to greet me. I dared to imagine for just a single moment what it would be like to have Ross court me. I knew it was impossible; it always would be. But that didn't stop me from wondering the possibilities.

"Michael, this is a surprise," I greeted him as he kissed my cheeks.

"Yes, indeed. I hope that I can at least have the first dance with you." He handed me the white rose which shone like the first fall of snow under the lights. The coldness of the de-thorned rose stem stung my flesh.

"Of course, you can."

The hall bustled with people and the chattering along with the music created a raucous noise. Some men from the village had dressed in their army uniform, standing taller with their chests puffed out in a pride unaccustomed to them. They danced with women who lived in the village, or those from their families who had come to celebrate their stance in the war effort. Everyone smiled and laughed as they bathed in the joyfulness of the room. I hadn't witnessed anyone from the village so elated before. My heart warmed in my chest with one glance at everyone.

"Shall we?" Michael asked, reminding me of the reality Margaret had thrown me into.

I nodded and pulled off my jacket while trying to balance the rose in my grip. Margaret immediately appeared beside me, taking my jacket and the rose from my grasp. I thanked her, forcing a smile she didn't deserve onto my face. Ross and I may have tried to play Margaret, but her games smelt of revenge. I turned back to Michael and took his hand as we made our way among the other dancing couples.

His arm went around my waist as his other hand took mine. He pulled me closer, causing me to lay my palm on his hip. Out of the corner of my eye, I caught Ross' stare following us as we danced. It seemed Margaret's games weren't just bothering me tonight. This was her way of testing Ross and I to our limits. No matter how much we wanted to, we couldn't let her win.

"Ross is very protective of you," Michael commented. My gaze shot to him, and he raised an eyebrow, expecting a response I couldn't possibly give him. Every word froze in my mouth. "It's not a bad thing. In fact, it's quite a privilege to have people look out for you. When I told Ross about my intentions, he came to the surgery to warn me that if I ever hurt you, I'd have him to answer to."

My eyes bulged hearing Ross' forward actions towards Michael. It now made sense as to why Ross was in the surgery all those weeks ago. It was nothing to do with an injury or illness. He wanted to try to persuade Michael out of courting me. I didn't know Ross loved me then, but, even if I did, I would never have condoned him threatening Michael in such a manner.

"I never knew that."

Michael cocked his head as his mouth pulled at the edges. "He didn't want you to know why he was there that day. I didn't think it was right of me to tell you."

We broke away from each other when the music stopped playing to clap the band. People took the small break in the music to change partners. A woman came over to us, with glittering sapphire eyes and silky black hair tied in a bun, asking for the next dance with Michael.

"Is that okay?" he questioned, as if my opinion would influence his decision. The woman gazed at me expectantly.

I beamed at the two of them. "Of course."

I walked over to the wall behind my parents and watched as the partners got their stances ready to begin dancing. When the music started to play, my heart desired nothing more than to find myself dancing. *'Come Josephine'* resounded in the village hall, reminding me of the first time I ever heard it.

"Come on," Ross spoke to me as he watched my longing eyes taking in the couples dancing. Margaret's gaze immediately shot to us, and she pursed her lips. "It's your favourite song and I'm not having you miss dancing to it."

"Go on Belle," Mother encouraged, smiling at me. If she had noticed Margaret's fiery eyes, she never would have had the courage to tell me to go with Ross.

I took Ross' hand, aware of the trouble it would later cause with Margaret. In that moment, I dared to hold my head higher in a defiance for the love I felt. No one would ever control how I loved someone, no matter who it was. Love would always win and, as Ross weaved us in between the dancing couples, we proved our love would never be defeated. Ross wrapped his arm around my waist and pulled me closer, making my heart pound faster. As we danced to the first few bars of music, we gazed into each other's eyes. I swore I would never tire of the constellations in his starry orbs.

"You never told me about you warning Michael," I stated. My voice came off more bluntly than I had wanted it to.

Ross sighed and glanced away from me for a split second. "If I had have told you, you would have known that I felt something towards you. I should have been happy, but instead I was jealous of Michael. I'm sorry for what I did; I'm trying not to let my feelings towards you show. But when his arms are around you, all I can think of is how those arms should be mine. My fingers should be laced in yours to let people see the love I hold deep in my soul for you. Yet, it cannot be. This is the closest possible situation and… it hurts me… it kills me inside that I cannot make you mine."

I laid my head on his shoulder, not quite knowing what to respond to him. This love would tear us from limb to limb before we could ever show people the truth. No one would understand the love we held and the depth of our passion for each other. For as long as we lived, our love would remain an illicit secret, rather than the oath it deserved. Ross tilted his head to rest it on top of mine.

"I wish things were different," I mumbled, watching the other couples dance and kiss freely around us.

Ross gently squeezed my hand. "Me too Belle. It's all I ever wish for."

Margaret, unsurprisingly, requested the next dance from Ross and I quickly found Michael back at my side. Ross danced close to us, trying to maintain as much contact as possible to me. Margaret didn't seem to notice what he was playing at. But Ross' plan didn't always work as other couples danced between us, blocking the way.

"Have you decided about the nursing?" Michael enquired.

"Sort of. I think I've made my choice, but I just want to spend a little more time thinking about it."

"That's okay," he reassured me. His eyes softened as they met mine. "I know it's a big decision. If I cannot leave with you, then I'll understand. But if you join me at a later date, you will always be welcome. We'll need as many volunteers as we can once the fighting gets heavier. I can assure you that the training shouldn't be too long if you do decide to join."

"Thank you, Michael."

Once the song finished, I excused myself to go outside for some fresh air. The sun started to set, creating a golden glow across the village. I stared at the sky, praying for an answer to every dilemma in my heart. If I was so satisfied with my decision, why did I desire more time before telling Michael?

"You're joining the war?"

I spun around at the sound of someone's voice and paled as Ross stood there. He folded his arms across his waist-coated chest. In the golden hour of day, the light portrayed how handsome he was in his brown pinstriped suit. But now was not the time nor place to think about such frivolous things.

"I'm sorry?"

Ross stepped closer to me, keeping his eyes on the ground. His chest rose and fell as he took a deep breath before looking back at me. "Are you joining the war?"

"How did you know?"

"I heard you talking to Michael," Ross spat with bitterness.

I winced and tried not to let my face show the shock overcoming my body. "You, Ross Mason, were eavesdropping on my conversation that had absolutely nothing to do with you!"

His reasoning for dancing so close to me and Michael made sense now. It wasn't anything about desiring to be as close as possible to me. He wanted to hear what Michael told me. But he got more than he expected when he decided to eavesdrop. Did he not trust me around Michael? I didn't give him the satisfaction of asking such a question.

"Why on earth do you want to join and risk your life?"

I sighed, casting my eyes to the sky. He would never understand my reasoning for going. "I'm twenty-five, Ross. I have zero prospects and I am doing nothing to leave my mark on this world."

"But nursing won't leave any mark on this world Belle. Not if it costs you your life. Our love –"

"I'm not staying here just so I can be your dirty little secret."

"You're not that to me!" he raised his voice, drawing my eyes back to him. A vein throbbed in his neck as he stared at me. "I've told you how I feel about you."

"Yes, and you've done nothing but tell me."

Ross scoffed and shook his head. I bit my lip and my brow furrowed, waiting for him to say what he wanted to. "You're in love with him. That's why you want to go."

"I'm not going to dignify that by defending myself! I don't want to speak to you again tonight. Perhaps in the morning you will have come to your senses."

I stormed past him, but he grabbed my wrist, stopping me in my path. I snatched my body away from him, glowering at the face I willed myself not to run to. He dropped his gaze to the ground before I walked back into the porch of the village hall. Every part of my being shook as my hands balled into fists at my side. My raged breathing filled the air until I halted in my path. Margaret stood in front of me in the porch, staring down her nose, with a smirk plastered over her face. For once, I didn't care if she heard Ross and I arguing. Ross deserved the aggravation from Margaret for how he spoke to me. No man would ever speak to me in such a manner and dictate what I would do in life.

All I wanted to do was leave the dance for the night. Michael and my parents obliged my request, and we left the hall immediately. I never spoke to Ross as we said our goodbyes to the people at the dance. Nothing would make me calm down and forgive Ross for his resentment towards my nursing opportunity. I wanted to better myself and my life, but Ross didn't want me to. The worst part of it all was that I hadn't fully settled on my decision. My heart remained in two places, unable to find its way to one destination.

Chapter Nine

I tossed and turned all night, unable to get a single ounce of sleep. Ross tapped at my window for almost an hour during the night. No matter how hard he tried, I never let him in. Eventually, he gave up and went home, leaving me alone with my tears. Dawn started to draw forth when I finally reached the blissful slumber of sleep. But it didn't last long as Mother flung back the curtains, allowing the blazing sunlight to pour into my room.

I opened one eye and gazed up at Mother from my pillow. She sighed as she watched me with her hands on her hips. "I'm going to Margaret's for some tea. Do you want to join us? She'll be more than happy to see you."

I resisted the urge to scoff at her last comment. Instead, I sat up in bed and shook my head, pushing my curls away from my face. "No thank you. I'll just stay here today; I'm still not feeling the best. But you go on and have a good time."

Mother came over and bid me goodbye with a kiss on my head. I stayed still in bed, waiting to hear her feet crunch across the gravel outside the cottage, before getting dressed for the day. Saturdays meant I could take a peaceful walk around our village without being spotted by Ross. He would be too busy tending to the animals with Father today to worry about me and where I was.

I closed the cottage door behind me and breathed in the fresh air. I tried to let the anger escape from my body in hot waves of air, but my shoulders wouldn't lose their stiffness. It wasn't in my nature to hold grudges, especially towards those I loved. But Ross' comments last night had hurt me more than I wanted to admit. I took the pathway into one of the fields which overlooked the village. The pristine emerald shone in the rising sun as the daisy field caught my eye in the distance. I swallowed hard, playing back fond memories of me and Ross among the dancing white. As I stood there, I could still feel the freedom that laughing in his arms gave me. If I left for the war effort, I risked losing Ross and everything we had. But I had no prospects in this village. I couldn't stay here forever, even if I wanted to.

I made my way across the field and towards the road as the blades of grass tickled my ankles. The rusted gate opened with a tug, and I closed it behind me as a voice called my name. I spun around to see Father standing there with a stick in his hand. His white shirt stuck to his skin in the sweltering heat and the braces on his shoulders created creases of sweat. It could only mean one thing: he was taking animals into a field and he wouldn't be alone. I forced a smile onto my face, despite my heart clenching in my chest, as the clatter of hooves resounded from the sheep following Father.

"Could you leave that gate open for the sheep?"

I nodded and pushed the gate ajar with a shaking hand. I stood back as Father herded the sheep into the field. I watched as the blur of white ran in front of Father. The trail started to slow, and there at the back of the herd was Ross. I swallowed hard and stared at the ground, willing it to open to let me disappear. I didn't dare to take a single glance at Ross, knowing the ice between us would melt away.

Father walked into the field behind the sheep to make sure they were all present. Ross stopped beside me, and the ends of his boots flexed as he curled and unravelled his toes.

"I'm sorry," he whispered to me, trying to act inconspicuous. He sighed when I didn't respond to him. Saying sorry wasn't going to fix what happened between us. He had to have known that. "Can we meet at our usual time when your parents are both back home?"

I glanced at his face and his eyes searched mine. "Yes, I think we need to talk."

Ross opened his mouth to speak to me, but swiftly shut it when Father emerged from the field. He closed the gate with a crash and a squeak before turning to us. His eyebrows knitted together as he looked at me.

"Did you not visit Margaret with your mother?"

"I didn't want to," I admitted. I smiled sheepishly at him, brushing stray hairs away from my face which had caught the gentle breeze. "I slept very little last night so I just didn't feel up to it."

"Neither did Ross apparently," Father added, glancing to him. "Either you two are connected or you both just didn't like your sleep very much last night."

Ross and Father chuckled over his last comment. I dared to stifle a laugh for fear of Father sensing something was wrong. As we walked, my mind remained on Ross. If Father's comment proved true, then Ross had to have tried talking to me for most of the night. Margaret must have noticed his absence from the farm. When I tried to catch Ross' eye to confirm my suspicions, he refused to look near me. His silence settled every doubt in my mind; Margaret did notice. My mouth grew dry as my throat constricted, making it difficult to breathe steadily. Without a second thought, I bid Father and Ross goodbye to go into the village, refusing to stay anywhere near Ross or Margaret at this time.

Every woman in the village chattered about whose son had just signed up for the war and when they were due to leave for training. The beaming smiles and glowing faces became the defining symbol of pride. My chest tightened as I tried to understand why Ross wasn't proud of me for wanting to do my bit for the war effort. Even if he tried to tell me he was only worried about my safety or in case I ran away with Michael, it wouldn't make a difference to me. He either didn't trust Michael to keep me safe or he didn't believe how much I loved him. Both reasonings hurt and cut me to the very core of my soul.

As evening drew near, Mother returned home with Father from the Mason house. I plated the dinner as they sat at the table in utter silence. The air grew heavier as they refused to say a single word to me. Bile climbed up my throat in a burning, sour-tasting acid. Margaret must have said something to them. It was the only logical explanation. My stomach twisted and turned as my mind screamed that she had outed mine and Ross' affair. If that was the case, then we had been outed by the one person we had tried our best to fool. The knives and forks sliced against the plates in piercing squeals until finally we finished eating. Every mouthful of food felt as though it had been lodged in my throat. No matter how many sips of water I took from my glass, it didn't shift the lump. Mother stood up first, motioning for me to follow her into the living room. Father led the way into the room, and I tried to calm myself, refusing to give away that I knew what they were about to confront me with.

"Sit down Belle," Mother urged as she took a seat on the sofa. I watched as Father sat beside her before I dared to rest on the opposite side of the room. "As you know, I went to visit Margaret today and she's worried about you."

I frowned, tilting my head to the side. "Worried about me?"

"She's worried that, with how close you and Ross are, and how well you get on, that people might get the wrong idea." A dizziness came over me and I gripped the chair for some support. Margaret knew everything and she had convinced my parents to keep Ross and I apart over non-existent gossip. We had underestimated our opponent. "She thinks that perhaps we should create distance between you two."

"What about my job with the Masons?"

Father sighed, glancing at Mother before looking at me. "I'm sorry Belle, but she doesn't think it would be appropriate."

"So, I'm losing everything for no reason?" I asked, raising my voice louder than I intended to.

A gasp escaped my lips as I shook my head at my parents. This wasn't happening. I needed to see Ross and now. Before Mother or Father could say anything, I shot off the chair and walked straight out of the house without looking back. Rain pelted from the sky, cascading droplets down my face like a waterfall. I blinked away the water as I picked up my pace, causing my hair to fall from its bun and stick to my face. The second I knew my parents wouldn't see me anymore, I sprinted down the pathway towards the daisy field. My heart pounded in my throat and my breathing resounded over the pelting of the raindrops on the gravel.

A figure emerged from the daisy field gate, and they spun around rapidly, yelling my name when they spotted me. I halted for a split second as my stomach clenched with one single look at him. The rainwater caused his shirt to cling to his heaving chest. Even from this distance, we were both soaked to the skin in a desperation to see each other. His hair dripped with the rain, falling into his eyes, and he wiped it away with the back of his arm. He ran towards me and, before I could think through my actions, I lifted the bottom of my dress and sprinted to meet him. He opened his arms and I jumped into them as he enveloped me in his body. I held his face in my hands, wishing never to see a day where I wouldn't know the hazel-green soul which stared back at me.

"I won't stop seeing you," he panted, swallowing to try to get a breath. "I promised you that I would never leave you. Nothing and no one can make me change my oath."

He pressed his lips against mine, as if to stop anyone from parting us again. After everything we had been through in the last few days, this kiss was everything we needed. No one would ever get a chance to come between us. The urgency of his touch proved every oath he ever made to me. I kissed back, pouring every ounce of passion and desire into one single expression of love. The bristles of his russet beard brushed against my alabaster skin as my hands remained on his face. All that mattered to us was staying here in this moment; a world away from those who tried to part us from each other. We pulled away, breathless from the kiss, and Ross continued to hold me in his arms above the ground. Our eyes met in a burst of autumnal colours in the middle of a lightning storm.

"I promise you we will find a way. I won't ever leave you," he stated, lowering me slowly to the ground.

I pecked his lips in response, tasting the rainwater between our flesh. All I could do was believe his promise all over again, despite how much my conflicted heart cautioned me not to.

Chapter Ten

By the time Sunday rolled around, it was as though nothing had ever happened. Margaret had, once again, invited us back to the Mason's house for lunch. Seemingly Ross and I being in each other's company didn't matter to Margaret when it meant showing off her cooking. Mother promised me that she would try to reason with Margaret, knowing I would need the nanny job if I decided not to go to war. Even the most logical and sensible diplomat in the country wouldn't chance negotiating and reasoning with Margaret. I had less than twenty-fours to make up my mind about the nursing which plagued my thoughts all morning.

Ross and Margaret stood outside the church with the children waiting on us. Out of the corner of her eye, Margaret watched everything I did. When she turned her back to chat to Mother, Ross winked at me. I prayed the heat rising from my chest wouldn't colour my cheeks the warmth of guilt. As usual, Margaret, Arthur, and Mother went into a pew beside another family. Ross led the rest of us into an empty pew, with an air of confidence, making sure that we were in the middle beside each other. Neither Ross nor I looked near Margaret, knowing it would only draw attention to our sly tricks.

Moaning Mullan came out of his room and climbed the pulpit to begin the service. He announced the first hymn, and I fixed my gaze towards the front of the church as we sang. Margaret's eyes bore fire into my cheek, but I refused to acknowledge her actions. Reverend Mullan ordered us to sit down once the organ music ceased. As he preached, I rested my hand in the gap between Ross and I on the pew. The coldness of the oak caused my hand to jump slightly before it rested in a comfortable manner. Ross' hand edged closer until it found mine and he hooked his little finger with my small, delicate one. It was only a small act of affection between us, but one which we needed in the circumstances; a reminder of the oath we made to each other.

The service didn't seem to take as long with Ross at my side. Once Reverend Mullan said his final prayer, we rose in our seats, finally separating our link. Mullan descended the steps of the pulpit as everyone started to chatter. He floated down the aisle towards the doors but halted beside our pew. I turned to look at him and his creased face stared back with furrowed brows. A lump formed in my throat at the mere thought of Moaning Mullan knowing the 'apparent' gossip. Would Margaret really have got him involved to separate me and Ross?

"Could you two wait on me in my room?" he requested, glancing from me to Ross.

My breath hitched in my throat, and I willed myself not to show how much my heart raced in my chest. The Vicar knew about our affair; there wasn't any other explanation. Ross answered for us, and I closed my eyes to steady my breathing. I didn't trust myself to utter a single word in case the tremors came through. Father took Eliza by the hand over to Margaret. She didn't look near us as she left with my parents and the children. Perhaps she had gone to Mullan about us. Ross laid a hand on the small of my back, directing me to Moaning Mullan's room at the back of the church. He slammed the door behind us, causing my body to jolt.

"What is this about, Ross? Does he know about us?" I hissed and glowered at him as he turned around to face me.

He grinned as he walked towards me, pulling me to him by my hips. "He wants to speak to us about an idea we had for the men going off to war."

"But we don't have –"

My words ceased on my tongue as I realised what Ross had done. The lengths he would go to for our love would never fail to amaze me. My mouth fell open as spots clouded my vision. I blinked them away and shook my head as I glanced up at Ross' glowing face.

"You are one sly devil Ross Mason."

He kissed me gently, daring not to move a muscle in case we didn't hear someone coming towards the room. How could I possibly have left him when he did everything that he could for me? I wrapped my arms around his neck, deepening the kiss as his lips moved against mine. Footsteps echoed in the hallway, pulling us away from each other. Ross and I fixed ourselves to ensure Moaning Mullan didn't suspect anything untoward had happened between us. The oak door swung open, pouring sunlight into the room which illuminated the dust mites dancing in the air.

He smiled at the two of us as he took a seat at his desk. "Ross tells me that you two think the church should hold something for the soldiers leaving."

"Indeed, we do Reverend. We thought perhaps a dedication service, or a fair like we always have, would raise community spirits for the men. Any proceeds raised could go towards little packages for the men when they reach the front; socks and that sort," I suggested, praying he couldn't pick up on me stumbling over my words. He nodded along as though liking my suggestion. Ross started to discuss it more, building the most plausible lie we possibly could. At least Mullan believed our good intentions.

By the time we left the church, Margaret and my parents had left with the children, leaving the Mason's car stranded for Ross. We drove back to the house in a comfortable silence with his hand laced in mine. For once, we could finally pretend this was how our lives ended up. If only it could have stayed that way. Ross stopped the car beside the stables, out of direct sight of the windows in the house. He leant over and pressed his lips to mine. I allowed myself to believe everything was going to work out between us as I kissed him back. My naïve heart wouldn't let the possibility of hope go.

Aromas of glazed ham cooking filled my senses when I stepped into the house. Ross closed the door as gently as possible, but it did nothing to ease the suspicion Margaret held. She stood waiting for Ross in the middle of the living room; arms folded over her chest and her lips pursed, causing her jaw to square as she glared at him.

"Ross, I need to speak to you in the kitchen now," she demanded, storming out of the room. I stepped out of the way to avoid her knocking me down. It didn't take a fool to work out what she wanted to speak to him about. Ross laid a reassuring hand on my shoulder before following her. Nothing stopped my stomach knotting until nausea made me sit down by the window in the living room.

Boisterous, raised voices resounded in the house and I glanced at Mother who shrugged at me. She leant over on the sofa to whisper to Father about the Mason's argument; the latest on a long list. I trusted Ross not to crack under Margaret's pressure. He was a much stronger person than I ever could be. The voices silenced in the kitchen, and I dared a swift look at the doorway as footsteps echoed in the hallway. Ross filled the space in the frame with a relaxed, lop-sided smile on his face. Anyone who did so much as glance at him could tell it was fake. A sour taste filled my mouth and I tried, with little success, to swallow it away. Ross flumped himself down beside me with a heavy sigh. I shivered as his rough fingertips brushed against my knuckles – a simple symbol of our safety.

"It was a wonderful service today," Mother commented, trying to ease the growing tension in the house.

Ross nodded, forcing another smile upon his face. "Absolutely, Nancy. The hymns were a fantastic choice."

Father joined in as they discussed the sermon in more detail than I ever thought possible. I willed myself to make some comment to their talk, but I couldn't pay attention. With every trace of my knuckles, Ross sent my nerves shuttering as a warmth flooded every part of my body. I dared just one glance at the gap between us. Despite Margaret's interrogation, Ross continued to break the boundaries she set for us. We played a game of survival of the fittest, desperate to win against Margaret at all costs. But even my heart knew there was only so far that we could run before the hunter caught its pray.

Margaret popped her head around the doorframe to call us for lunch. Arthur and Eliza shot off the floor to run to her. As soon as I took my usual seat across from her at the table, she shot me a glare which could have slit my throat in a second.

"So, Belle," she began, plastering a fake, polite smile on her face. "I heard about the nursing from Ross. Are you still looking to go and join the war effort?"

Her comment was only half right; she'd heard about it from Ross and I arguing outside the village hall at the dance. I swallowed the food in my mouth and glanced up at her, remembering not to give anything away. "Well, after much deliberation, I've decided that I shall stay here instead of volunteering."

The smug smirk on Margaret's face gradually fell, as did the colour on her face. All this time she had hoped I would go with Michael next week and leave Ross alone. I wasn't giving up our love without a fight. She cleared her throat and blinked down at her plate. "What will you do here then? You don't have either of your two jobs now."

I shrugged, slicing the ham on my plate with a nonchalance I desired to possess every day. "I hope when someone replaces Doctor Henry at the surgery that they will continue my employment there. I'm sure Doctor Henry would put in a good word for me with his replacement."

No one mentioned anything more about my nursing venture or the fact that I was staying at home. The talk swiftly turned to the war instead; a topic which everyone aimlessly chattered about at any chance they got. I drowned out their voices until it turned to white noise. I had made my decision to stay for Ross, but I didn't know how to tell Michael I wasn't going with him. It didn't take a fool to work out that his heart would shatter once I admitted I had decided to stay.

After dinner, Margaret cut everything short, as though she were desperate to get me out of the house at all costs. But her plans never came to fruition as Father and Ross talked in the living room about what would happen to the farm and the animals as the war grew heavier. A hard tap landed on my shoulder, and I turned around as Margaret beckoned me towards the kitchen. For once, my throat didn't clam and clench at the mere thought of what she could confront me with. Right now, I held the upper hand in this childish game, and I needed to maintain it to survive here.

She closed the door quietly before speaking to me. "You know you're missing a fantastic opportunity with the nursing and Michael. Staying here in the village and leaving Michael for… for my husband is not right. Ross doesn't want you. Can't you see that?"

If I fought back against her accusations, she would have the proof she needed of an affair. Her hesitation before mentioning Ross gave me enough reason to continue the lies. I stifled a laugh and shook my head. "The choices I make are nothing to do with either Michael or Ross. Nothing is going on between me and them. I haven't the slightest inclination how you can accuse me of such things, especially with your husband."

"Don't treat me like a fool," she scoffed.

"Perhaps if you were not so insecure in your marriage you wouldn't accuse me of such nonsense."

Before she could respond, I stormed past her and swung open the kitchen door. It banged against the wall, but I didn't dare to look back. My parents and Ross called after me when I left the house. My attempt at remaining calm had failed miserably. But anyone not guilty of what I was rightfully accused of would have reacted the same. I didn't give Margaret a single ounce of proof that she could hang us with. Our secret was safe, but I doubted it would be for long.

By the time I reached the cottage after taking the long way around over the fields, my parents were already home. I sighed and opened the door, knowing the questions I would have to answer. Mother ran out of the kitchen and pulled me into her arms. I sunk into the warmth of her motherly love; missing the simpler times of a childhood long gone.

"Your father and I were so worried about you," Mother whispered in my ear. I swallowed hard and blinked back the tears which threatened to spill over. "Ross spoke to Margaret to find out what happened. He told us she made some very ill-judged remarks about you."

"I'm fine. I'd just like to go to my room."

She held me at arm's distance, trying to scan my face for any obvious signs of upset. I forced a weak smile onto my face. A defeated sigh escaped from her lips as she reluctantly let me go. I took off my jacket and hung it up by the door before dragging my feet towards my room. Mother's eyes bore into the back of my head as I trudged down the hallway. I desired nothing more than to lie down and sleep until the morning sun greeted the horizon. To add to my troubles, tomorrow I had to face Michael. I tried to push it out of my mind as my stomach churned over at the mere thought of it. Leaving him to join the war effort alone while I stayed at home and fawned over a married man had given me a new low to stoop to.

I flung myself down on the bed and let a groan erupt from my body. A loud thumping at my window jolted me upright. I glanced over at the window as Ross stood there, ducking out of sight of the front of the cottage. He let the corners of his mouth tease a smile as I opened the window.

"I'm going to sort this with Margaret. Meet me tonight, at the usual time, in the daisy field," he spoke rapidly with an urgency I hadn't heard in his tone before.

I sighed, casting my eyes to the floor for a split second, before meeting his again. "Will you bring good news?"

He grinned and took my face in his hands. I hadn't noticed how easily my face cupped in his large palms until now. It was as though two pieces of a lost item had finally met in a sea of hurt, betrayal, and adoration. "I'll try my hardest." Ross pecked my lips before he ran away from the cottage. We couldn't risk Mother and Father hearing or seeing him at my window. If they knew Margaret's accusations were right, they would never defend me again.

I laid in bed, replaying his words in my head, as I stared at the timbered ceiling. I ran my fingers slowly over my lips, already missing the weight of his on top of mine. I trusted Ross to try his hardest with Margaret. My stomach fluttered at the prospect of Ross making everything right once and for all. I trusted him more than my naïve heart should have and perhaps that became my greatest mistake.

~

Throughout dinner, Mother and Father kept exchanging worried glances at each other. As much I had sought to reassure them that I was fine, they didn't believe me. Knives and forks scratched in a piercing silence until we finished our meal. Father walked to the living room as Mother and I washed the dishes.

"What will you do tonight?" Mother asked as she took the final plate from my wet hands.

I smiled at her as I dried my hands on my apron. "I thought I would go to see Michael tonight to tell him my answer. It might be easier than telling him in work tomorrow morning before he leaves."

"What a good idea. You head on and I'll finish up here," she said, stacking the plates to put into the cupboard. "Tell your father you're going out."

I shouted into Father as he lounged in the living room while I donned my jacket. Little did they know, I had every intention of meeting Ross in the daisy field before going to Michael. I walked down the pathway towards the field as Ross' figure hanging over the gate came into view. He never looked up as my footsteps grew louder the closer that I came to him. His head eventually lifted to open the gate for me, but his eyes never met mine. A lump sat in my throat, trying its best to strangle me as I breathed. He bounced from one foot to the other as he glanced at the sky.

"Whatever is the matter?" I asked, ignoring the shaking of my hands.

Ross ran a hand through his hair as he let out a shaky breath. When I stepped forward, he took one step backwards, away from me. He glanced around the field as though someone was going to jump out of hiding. "I have made a huge mistake."

"A mistake? Did you tell Margaret the truth?"

"No, I didn't." Both of us fell silent as his words escaped, hanging in the air between us. The birdsong had ceased in the trees surrounding the field. Not even the animals dared to make a single sound. The whole world had frozen; holding its breath as it awaited Ross to utter another syllable. "I made a huge mistake about us."

The colour drained out of my body, flooding into the soil of the daisy field. My eyebrows lowered and pinched together. "You don't mean that. Only several hours ago you told me how much you loved me! What has changed?"

"I just realised the mistake I made by starting this… affair with you. I'm sorry, Belle. Truly I am."

I shook my head and clutched the top of it, glancing around in the hope of conjuring up a solution to whatever had happened. My breath grew erratic in my chest as my heart pulsed in my ears. This wasn't real. None of this could be happening; not after everything Ross promised me. When my eyes landed back on his face, he couldn't even look at me, despite the fact I stood right in front of him. He fixated his gaze on anywhere except for my face.

"This isn't you, Ross. We both know that you don't change your mind as irrationally as this. We made a promise – an oath!"

There was no doubt in my mind that Margaret was behind this. If Ross could manage to look me in my eyes and tell me that leaving us this way was his idea, then I would believe him. "If you mean what you just said, look me in my eyes and tell me it. Then walk away from me forever." For a few seconds, he said nothing and didn't move a muscle. I held my breath in the hope I had figured it out. His jaw twitched beneath his stubble as he stared off at the sunsetting sky. The glow of the horizon didn't seem to colour us in that moment. Perhaps even nature knew the truth.

Ross' head turned, and he stared at me, dead in the eyes. My heart shattered into a million pieces as every part of my world crashed down in a single heartbreak. "I made a mistake with us. I don't want this anymore and I don't want to see you again. I feel nothing for you. I'm sorry, but this ends here. Tonight," Ross spoke with no emotion or tone to his voice. I let out a shaky breath as he did what I thought he would never do. "I don't love you anymore Belle."

As his last sentence pushed the final dagger through my heart, he walked away back towards his house. I stood there, more broken than I could ever comprehend. I dared to imagine, dream even, that Ross still loved me. He promised me the world and his love. I fell for his empty love because I believed he would fulfil every oath he made to me. Yet he walked away from me as though I was nothing to him. In the short space of a month, we had gone through hell and back. Surviving it wasn't enough for him.

I wrapped my arms around myself as I fell to the ground on my knees. Heart wrenching sobs escaped my throat, tearing it raw until the noise wouldn't come out. I choked as I tried to calm my jolting body. I had altered my entire life and vowed to stay from the war effort for him. In a split second, Ross threw it back in my face without another thought. My nails dug into the grass beneath me, tearing up the mud to resist the urge to scream or throw something. I wanted to believe it was all just a bad dream, but as my legs wobbled when I stood up, I knew it wasn't.

My fuzzy mind made me lightheaded as I stumbled towards the gate, leaving the daisy field for the final time. I would never return there; not without Ross. I closed the gate with a squeak and glanced back at the dancing daisies among the emerald. Every kiss and touch meant nothing to Ross. The daisy field had never been ours. Ross had to have been using me to leave me in such a cruel way. I clenched the metal of the gate, allowing the coldness to draw me back to reality. My hand dropped to my side as I turned to walk away from the daisy field. With every step I took down the pathway, I walked further away from everything to do with Ross. My chest tightened, making my eyes water, but I had to go. The chain around my neck stayed there; a reminder of when Ross had loved me. Despite everything, I didn't want to believe his goodness had evaporated into thin air. I needed just one small reminder of his goodness and his love.

The more my mind travelled to Ross, the swifter my disbelief vanished as every muscle in my body quivered. My hands balled into fists by my sides, pinching the delicate skin. Ross played with my feelings and made me fall in love with him. He had the audacity to paint us a happy ending and then set it on fire in a second. For what reason, I would never know. My pulse fired adrenaline through my veins as my walking pace quickened. I knew exactly where I needed to go. I had to claw back at least a small part of who I was before he devasted my very being.

The door towered above me as I hammered the wood until someone flung it open. A man the same age as Father stared at me. My hair stuck out of my bun at all angles from my anguish, but I didn't dare draw attention to it. He glanced at my dress which had coloured itself in mud. He took the pipe out of his mouth, scratching his grey beard as he observed me.

"Can I help you?" he asked in a stronger Devon accent than I imagined him to have. Smoke popped out of his mouth in bubbles as he spoke.

"Is Doctor Henry available?"

"Yes, come in."

The man led me through the extravagant house to the kitchen where Michael sat at the table. He stood up, skidding his chair on the wooden floor, earning a wince from his father. My eye caught the nursing forms on the mahogany table as he greeted me. I swallowed hard as I stared at the forms. Michael's father left, closing the door over behind him. The snap of the latch meeting the wood caused my eyes to shoot back to Michael.

"I was just filling them out in case you decided to go. I'm not forcing you to sign them," Michael defended, thinking I had readied myself to shout at him. He picked them up to put them away, but I stopped him, resting my hand on his arm. He glanced at me as my hand shook against his sleeve.

"I'll be leaving with you."

I lifted the pencil and signed my name at the bottom of the forms, filling out every detail possible to make sure I wouldn't get rejected. I never regretted signing them, even as I laid in bed pondering everything over that night. The next morning, I told my parents about my decision, and they helped me to pack, ready to leave to save lives. I made them promise not to tell anyone I was leaving, especially the Masons, until I had gone with Michael. They swore not to divulge what hospital we had been assigned to, even after we had left the village. They kept that promise for me despite Ross asking them endlessly where I had gone to. In the end, my decision remained the right one for myself.

September 1914

Chapter Eleven

"I expect the highest level of obedience," Sister Mary, the ward sister, announced as she paced in front of us with her lips pursed. By now, I should have been used to her judgemental eyes, but it still caused a cold finger to run up my spine. Our first morning shift grew closer with each tick of the clock hand. Each VAD in the line-up had earned their certificates in first aid and home nursing. None of us were allowed to care for the men until we had achieved them. "Now that you all know the basics, I expect nothing less than high standards. You may be volunteers, but you still must fulfil each task given to you."

With a flick of her wrist, Sister Mary dismissed us to our assigned wards. The morning duties didn't consist of much strenuous work; dusting, tidying, food and drink carrying. However, Sister Mary made it clear that as the war continued, our duties would increase as more would then be required of us. As Michael promised, the Red Cross assigned us to the same hospital near to the coast in Poole. Never in my life had I lived so far away from home. Yet, the thoughts of the village only appeared when I received letters from Mother and Father. While

I missed them considerably, Sister Mary kept us too busy to consider the possibility of returning home anytime soon. As much as I tried to convince myself I didn't miss Ross, his face and love imprinted into my soul; becoming the constant reminder of what I once loved and left behind.

"Wilson, you're on breakfast duty today," Sister Mary called as we made our way towards the ward. "Go and collect the trolley from the kitchen."

"Yes Sister."

The trolley clattered and rattled over the tiles in the corridor as I pushed it towards my ward. The doors at the end of the corridor loomed over me in anticipation for what was to come. I pushed away the nausea which tried to fight against my sensible thoughts. I had proved to myself that I was more than capable of nursing. Now I had the chance to prove it to Sister Mary too. I pushed open the doors and sunlight illuminated the ward as the trolley clattered in. Sally ran over to help me distribute the breakfasts to the men. A strand of blonde hair fell from her hair covering, capturing the light in golden rays. She stuffed it back into her headdress, glancing around to make sure no one spotted her.

I greeted the men with a smiling, pleasant demeanour, never wanting to disappoint them. Many of the men who reached us had received treatment in France before being deemed fit enough to travel home. Sometimes the medics had patched them up just enough to make it back to Britain, which meant they required surgery when they got to the hospital. While here, they stayed for the remainder of their treatment and recovery.

"Good morning, Daniel," I spoke, checking the name of the man in the bed. He beamed at me and the bandage around his head tilted at an angle.

"Morning nurse. Fancy an afternoon chat with me today?"

"I wouldn't want to spend my afternoon any other way."

In the afternoons, visitors usually came to the hospital to see the men. Those who didn't have visitors were never alone as VADs sat with them and helped them to write home. Sister Mary had already versed us not to ask them about the war. From the resounding voices filling the ward, it seemed like the men chatted about anything other than the war. To them, it was another world that they didn't wish to bring home.

Once we handed out all the breakfasts, the next VADs entered the ward to wash the men before the doctor's rounds. Sally and I left the ward, clattering the trolley back to the kitchens. The next part of our morning routine was the one thing we had dreaded since waking up. When the doctor finished checking the men, their wounds needed disinfected and rebandaged, or stitches removed. During our training Sister Mary had allowed us to practice this on one of the soldiers who didn't possess a severe injury. Their wincing and crinkled face in utter pain had imprinted itself into my mind. Today I had to deal with more severe injuries and, therefore, increased pain to the men. None of us wished to hurt the men, but it needed done for their health.

My nose twitched with the overwhelming aroma of disinfectant in the sluice room. Sally went to the opposite side of the room as we grabbed the bandages, equipment, and disinfectant needed for the men. We placed each item on the new trolley in the room, making them easily accessible for the VADs. The rolls of bandages piled up until they almost toppled; Sally reached forward to grab them before they landed on the floor.

"If only this was less painful for them," Sally mumbled as we placed the empty metal bowls on the trolley.

I sighed, finally accepting my heavy heart at the mere thought of what we had to put some of them through in a few minutes. "I know, but this is less painful than what they've experienced out there."

She gazed at me with soft sapphire eyes. "Do you have a sweetheart fighting?"

"No, I don't have anyone fighting."

"I don't have a sweetheart, but my brother's out fighting in France."

The fact Sally didn't have a sweetheart wasn't in the least bit surprising for me. Since we started coming to the wards during our training, I had noticed her giving Michael a second glance when it was his turn to check the patients. As far as I could tell, Michael hadn't noticed her. Michael's mind remained focused on helping the men coming home from the front. Everyone knew the wards would get busier as the war went on. I hoped, just like everyone else, that it would be over by Christmas for the sake of the men fighting. In truth, I couldn't imagine how pushed for beds the hospital would be. Our wards were too small to house a massive influx of patients. The hospital had been preparing for an influx arriving from the front any day now. Beds were moved out into the corridors, lying on either side to make sure as many men could get treated as possible.

We pushed the trolley back through the doors of the ward as the male orderlies pulled back the screens on the beds. Everyone waited patiently for the doctor to arrive to inspect the men. Sally and I stood by the closest bed, awaiting further instructions once the rounds began. The doors swung open, and the sunlight caught the blonde curls I'd grown to know. Michael smiled over at us before attending to the first man. Sister Mary followed on his tail, explaining various things Michael already knew. Unlike the rest of us, Michael had learnt how to drown out her stern voice. I glanced at Sally who stared at Michael with glittering eyes and flushed cheeks. A lump formed in my throat as I recognised the first signs of love – ones I possessed not too long ago.

When Michael made his way to the opposite side of the room with Sister Mary, Sally and I began to work on the patients with the new instructions he had left. Sally took the soldier on the other side of me, ensuring we could complete the task as quick as possible. I didn't know if I would ever get used to the sight of wounds. Sister Mary had warned us the men arrived at the hospital smelling from the mud and chalk of the battlefields. But the most pungent scent of all remained from their wounds.

"Let's take a look at you," I greeted the first soldier. I tried to appear as cheerful as possible, knowing it would help the men. I read over the notes Michael left, detailing the man had sustained a wound to the upper left arm. I lifted the sleeve of the pyjama jacket to reveal the stitches which would surely leave a scar. "It's looking better already."

"So, the stitches helped?" he questioned, doubt oozing from his voice. He tilted his head to try to see the wound on his arm.

I nodded, running a finger over the bump of stitches. "I'd say so. Compared to what the doctor has detailed here when you first arrived, there's a lot of progress."

I wiped some disinfectant over the stitches to ease the redness around the wound. The fieriness of the colour had started to disappear into the paleness of his skin. It wouldn't be long until he left us to return to the frontline, or back home depending on what his orders were. From the notes, the only thing preventing him from leaving already was the persistent ringing in his ears. Sister Mary and Michael wanted to keep an eye on him to ensure the noise was only from grenades and guns, rather than from a piece of shrapnel lodged in his brain.

I kept the bandages off the arm and smiled once more as I pulled down his jacket sleeve. "There you go; good as new."

"If only I was." His laugh echoed around the ward, and I couldn't help but stifle one myself.

"Here, here," the soldier beside him agreed, holding up his left hand which only had three fingers thanks to an exploded grenade. The two men laughed between themselves, and I shook my head at their humour. My heart remained light in my chest despite the wounds I encountered. I pushed away all thoughts of Sally's lovesick look which plagued my soul's desire for Ross more than anything else.

The morning duties were complete with cleaning and attending to the men. Tomorrow, Sister Mary would assign Sally and I to cleaning duties, allowing for each VAD to experience every duty expected of them. The volunteering nurses passed around the men's lunches as we prepared the ward for the visitors. Everyone looked forward to the calmness the afternoon provided. Sister Mary allowed for each of us to leave the hospital for three hours in the afternoon, but I didn't know if I would ever take it off. After all, I didn't have anyone taking a trip to Poole to visit me.

"Do you think that there'll be letters from home soon?" Sally asked as we brushed the corridors.

"Of course, they should be here any day now."

She sighed, brushing the sweat away from her forehead with the back of her hand as she leant on the brush shaft. "I just know that once I help the soldiers write letters today it will make me wish for news from home."

"Are you not leaving today then?"

Sally shook her head, smiling at me as I glanced up at her. "No, I'm not. I think I'd prefer to spend my afternoon with the soldiers."

Sister Mary popped her head around the corner and called us for a meeting outside the ward doors. Regular nurses flocked into the ward to take over from the VADs. Sister Mary didn't meet our eyes as she paced along the line. My chest clamped as acid burnt my throat when I tried to swallow. I watched as Sister Mary's face grew redder, standing out against the white of the uniform, and her jaw squared as she ground her teeth together.

"We have received word that a shipment of men is on their way to the coast now. This is the largest shipment we have received to date, and it will be a strain for us all, but especially for you," Sister Mary informed us. Her breath coursed out of her flared nostrils, making as much of an echo as her pounding feet. "We will need all of you tomorrow to work to the highest standards possible under this pressure. The men are expected in the afternoon and more beds will have to be placed in the corridors." She recited times and duties we had to fulfil when the men got to the hospital. I tried to remember as much of it as I could, ignoring the knotting in my stomach. "For this reason, letters will be withheld until the end of your duty tomorrow. We need you to focus and be on top form for this. One slip and it could be detrimental to the men's lives."

From the trembling lips and limbs of the other VADs, it was clear I wasn't the only one who desired tomorrow to be over already. An influx of patients would make or break each of us. I had to make myself ready for the job to take care of the men. They were fighting for our country, and I had to help save their lives no matter how much it affected me.

Chapter Twelve

"Wilson, run and get more bandages!" Sister Mary screamed at me as she tried to stitch up one of the new soldiers in the chaos. Blood oozed over her hands, coating every inch of flesh visible. I tore my eyes away and ran to fetch more bandages from the nearest trolley.

Nothing could have prepared me for this. I jumped over people, discarded bandages, and soiled uniform in the corridor. The aroma of rotting flesh and burnt soil stung my nostrils, threatening to make me vomit at any given moment. It was enough to make even the strongest stomach lurch into convulsions. People pushed, shouted, and wept over the images they could never erase from their memories. Sister Mary's harsh attitude towards us made every ounce of sense – no one could remain the same after witnessing the horrors of what humans could inflict on others. The hospital had personified Armageddon which I'd only ever heard Moaning Mullan describing in church.

I grabbed the bandages and sprinted back to Sister Mary as fast as possible. She had managed to stitch the man's leg wound, but it did nothing to ease the pain he was in. His face contorted into various wrinkles and bared teeth.

"Disinfect the skin around the wound and bandage it up," she instructed, before running to another soldier lying on a bed in the corridor. I took a swift glance down the corridor which overflowed with men. Those who could stand without making themselves worse remained against the wall, awaiting the orderlies to make another bed in one of the corridors. We had severely underestimated the number of men in the influx.

"Nurse Wilson," someone yelled when I finished. I looked up as one of the nurses waved at me. "Get Doctor Henry and see if he's free for emergency surgery. This man won't make it if he doesn't get surgery soon!"

I just nodded before running into our normal ward where I knew Michael had stationed himself. I flung open the doors and realised the chaos had descended into the wards too. Nurses and VADs bustled around with blood and soil caked to their uniform. Not a lot of new men could fit in the ward due to patients already present. But it didn't stop them trying to squeeze as many in as possible. Michael stood in the middle of the room, trying to help the nurse stitch a deep wound on a man's shoulder.

"Michael," I said, grabbing his arm gently. He turned to face me, and I spotted how little of his white coat remained the glistening colour. Instead, dark red stains patterned the material. "We need emergency surgery."

The two of us ran back to the corridor where the man laid. Michael followed my lead as we turned corners and dodged people rushing about. Michael took one look at the man sprawled on the bed and shouted for the male orderlies to bring him to the theatre immediately. I couldn't watch as they carted him away with Michael running behind them. There were too many other soldiers needing attended to.

"Nurse."

My head spun around, desperate to find where the voice had come from. A soldier raised his hand as his piercing blue eyes spotted mine. I made my way over to him and knelt to speak. "Yes?"

"I-I'm cold," he mumbled, shivering in the draft from the open doors and windows. He laid there with only his uniformed trousers on; the rest had been cut away to attend to wounds. Involuntarily, my eyes glazed over the wounds he received on his shoulders and side. The bandages around his head had already seeped through with blood.

"I'll fetch you a blanket."

I pushed my way through people to reach the trolley with the blankets piled on. The rough wool brushed against my fingers as I grabbed one and rushed back to the man. I placed it over him, hoping to ease his discomfort as much as possible. He thanked me before I left him to find Sister Mary. The two of us were covered in mud, stains, and blood; forming a collage of horror and pain. I had never dreamt this war could cause such utter devastation until it landed right in front of me. I willed myself not to glance down at uniform, knowing I would end up vomiting on the spot.

"What shall I do now, Sister?" I asked, standing beside her.

Sister observed the corridor, nodding to herself as she took in the sights before her. "We're easing up now. The male orderlies will pick up the uniforms to wash them. We'll start to get the men dressed in their pyjamas. But the best thing you could do now, Wilson, is to take some of the bowls of soiled bandages to the bin and disinfect the bowls in the sluice room."

I lifted two of the bowls from the trolley which overflowed with used equipment. People had stacked bowls on top of one another to the point of near collapse. They were balanced as though it were a fine art, rather than medical supplies. The corridors had calmed down, with nurses and VADs doing the final bandaging on the men or putting them into the hospital pyjamas. Part of me hoped the sluice room would become a welcomed respite, but the further I got away from the corridors, the more the soiled bandages smelt. Without the other aromas to disguise the pungency, I gagged as I binned the bandages hygienically in the sluice room. I tried to breathe through my mouth instead of my nose to avoid the smell of rotting flesh and metallic, dried blood.

As I disinfected the bowls, other nurses came in with the rest of them on a trolley. I offered to clean them, wanting some time alone; the images of the soldiers in pain, the blood, the smell, the anguished cries… it was overwhelming. I hadn't seen anything like it before. My hands shook as I scrubbed a bowl clean, and my chest tightened, reminding me how much I was on the verge of tears. I dropped the bowl in the sink with a clatter as my vision blurred.

A hand landed on my shoulder with a warmth I hadn't encountered since arriving at Poole. I spun around as another VAD stood there with a weak smile plastering her lips. "It's okay you know. It does get overwhelming during your first influx. I was here when we got the first ever one a month or so ago. I reacted the same way as you." She took the sponge off me, taking over my cleaning to let me calm down. Her long brown hair cast a shadow against the white headdress. She turned to me for a split second and the sun streaming through the window caught her soft brown, almost black, eyes. "What's your name again?"

"Belle. Belle Wilson."

She flashed me a toothy grin before returning to the bowl. "Nice to meet you properly, Belle. I'm Harriet."

Harriet's face became familiar to me as I realised that she shared a room with me, Sally, and a few other VADs at the boarding house down the road from the hospital. This was the first time we had spoken to each other properly. Sister Mary had assigned Harriet to night duty since we arrived, while Sally and I had been on day shift instead. The hospital must have asked Harriet and others to come in to help with the influx. I couldn't have imagined the chaos if they hadn't.

"Do you ever get used to it?" I questioned. The distinct smell of disinfectant started to make my nose tingle as it twitched. Harriet glanced over at me, and her eyebrows knitted together. "The injuries... Do you ever get used to seeing them?"

She finished the last bowl and dried her hands before a sigh escaped from her lips. "Not really, you just learn how to cope with them better." I nodded and tried not to let the daunting prospect of attending to the wounds in the morning cloud my thoughts. Harriet gave me an amicable smile and helped me back to the ward to get our duties from Sister Mary.

~

By the end of our shift, our letters from home awaited us at the boarding house. I grabbed the two letters which had my name scribbled on the front of them, holding them close to my chest. I missed Mother and Father more than I wanted to admit to anyone, but their letters always helped me to feel close to them. Each of us took off our soiled uniforms before showering away the memories of today. The mud and blood caked to my fingernails as I scrubbed them until the water turned cold. I desired to try to erase the memories of today; forcing them down the drain with the red and brown river.

I dried myself and pulled on my nightdress, ready to welcome the slumber of sleep. Sally plaited her hair on the bed beside me as Harriet and I picked up our letters to read. Everyone who had chosen to help with the influx laid in their beds reading their letters from their parents or their sweethearts. I opened my letters one at a time, savouring the reminders of home. After today, the paradise and peace I lived in at home seemed a non-existent to what the world had turned into.

Mother wrote telling me how Margaret had gotten even friendlier with her since I left, but she had never forgiven her for what she did to me. Margaret received the blame for me changing my mind about leaving for the war effort. But my parents would never tell her their resentment to her face. If they rocked the relationship or I confessed about Ross, then Father wouldn't have a job and my family would struggle financially. I couldn't let that happen. I would have rather lost the job as the Mason children's nanny than let my family go without their basic needs.

I placed Mother's letter in the drawer of my bedside table, along with other letters from my parents. The stack had grown so much since I first arrived in Poole for my training. What had once been an oak bottom in a drawer became a papered symbol of love. The next letter sat on my bed, staring up at me from its place. Father must have sent a letter, no doubt complaining about Mother making him scrub his boots outside now that the rainier weather had come in. Mother hated the mud and muck coating the wooden floors in the cottage. Many times, I had spotted her making him clean the footprints off the floor while he mumbled under his breath mocking her or making barely audible swears. I tore open the envelope, longing to hear from Father once again. The letter shook in my hand as the colour drained from my face and my throat grew dry. Nothing around me moved except for the letter which fell like a feather to the blanket beneath me.

To my dearest Belle,
Your Father informed me that you had left a few days after your departure. No matter how many times I requested to know where you went, neither your father nor your mother would tell me. All I can do is hope that this letter is sent on to you from the Red Cross headquarters.

I know that it was easier for you to run after how I treated you. It breaks me to know that I was your main reason for joining the war. You have no idea how much it killed me. But I decided to write to you, even though I know that you won't want to hear from me. I wish I had as much discipline as you. No matter how much I try, I cannot stop feeling this way. I tried to before the day of the church fair when I confessed how I felt to you. I knew that letting you go would hurt. But no matter how much I try I would rather suffer this pain than no longer have you in my life. You mean everything to me, Belle.

I shan't ask you how you feel towards me, especially because I don't expect to hear back from you. But I want to make things right. Every single morning, I wake up with an aching in my bones; a searing pain through my heart. Belle, my love, I cannot live without you. I would give anything to hold you just once more in my arms. I cannot let you join the war alone. If I stand any chance of seeing you again, I need to play my part too. Your father took over the farm from me and I enlisted in the village hall. I leave the training camp next week to go to the front. I'll depart on a train to London first and then I'll begin my journey to France from there. Thursday next week shall be my last day in England for the foreseeable future. I don't expect to see you at the London station, but I hope that somewhere along the way in the war, I will find you once again, my love. I couldn't possibly stay at home knowing that you won't be waiting for me in the daisy field.

All my love,
Ross.

A warm tear cascaded down my cheek, caressing my skin in a painful memory of a life once lived. My bed dipped beside me, and the person's voice faded into white noise. I wasn't paying attention; the world around me ceased to exist in that moment. The only pieces that remained were me, the letter, and a remnant of a broken Ross Mason.

"Belle, what's wrong?" Sally's voice finally came through.

I swallowed hard and blinked several times to force myself back to my reality. My eyes met hers as I shook my head while tears continued to fall. "He's gone to war because of me."

Harriet flocked over to us, landing herself on the bottom of my bed. The women consoled me, telling me it wasn't my fault. They tried to convince me he would have went anyway. But they didn't know Ross or what he would have done. In truth, even I didn't know he would have went to war to find me again. Images of Ross lying on a battlefield with the injuries I had witnessed so far in the hospital flooded my mind.

When my sobs settled to mere gasps of air, I told Harriet and Sally everything about who Ross was and what he meant to me. From the attraction which lasted over a year and the confession of love, to Margaret's meddling and the way Ross left me in the daisy field.

I sighed as I knew I had to confess to Sally about Michael and what happened between us. I tried every way possible to make it clear that Michael and I were nothing but friends now. Sally's shoulders slumped and the smile returned to her face in silent relief. I didn't think about whether they would judge me or not. I just needed to confide my soul to someone, anyone, who would listen to everything I had been through.

When I finished, neither of them said anything to me. They cast their eyes to the blanket, fidgeting with their hands.

Embarrassment boiled in my stomach, heating my skin a flushed red. I placed the backs of my hands against my cheeks, willing the coldness to keep the warmth at bay.

A sigh escaped Sally's lips as she glanced up, meeting my eyes. "You have to go and see him off."

"This is a man that I had an affair with."

"He is clearly in love with you," she retorted with a shrug. The affair didn't matter to her; all that she cared about was the love he felt towards me. "No man would go to war to try to see you again if he felt absolutely nothing towards you Belle."

"You'll regret it if you don't," Harriet chipped in with a smile.

I chewed on my lower lip, wondering what to do about Ross. If I didn't go and see him off to the war, I would regret it – I knew I would without Harriet telling me. I couldn't have him believing I hated him while trying to fight for his survival in the inhumane lands of warfare. My gaze shifted from Harriet to Sally who sat waiting on my decision. "Will you two come with me?"

They grinned at me and nodded, simultaneously replying, "yes."

Chapter Thirteen

Sister Mary permitted me to have the afternoon off to see Ross at the station. Once she agreed, the anticipated countdown to Thursday began. Even when it did come around, my mundane morning tasks made the day drag in. The duster seemed to go at an extra slow pace as I cleaned the soldiers' bedside lockers. No matter how much I wanted the hand on the clock to reach two, it didn't desire to budge any more than it needed to. As I dusted the lockers, I conversed with the men, enjoying their humorous talk. For a moment, they distracted the crippling fear which pulled at my gut over Ross going to war. It was the most welcomed distraction in the ward.

I walked over to the next soldier and his piercing blue eyes greeted me once more, sending my mind back to when I first saw him at the influx. I placed a blanket over Tommy as he was cold in the corridor. He called me his 'Blue Angel,' not only because of what I did for him, but also because of the colour of my uniform dress. He greeted me with a cheeky smile, showing the dimples in his cheeks in the sunlight.

"My mother wrote to me asking how I'm holding up," he told me as I opened his locker to clean it. "I wrote back telling her 'the best I can be after getting a piece of shrapnel through me head and bullets to my shoulder and side.' Long gone, I should've been. Long gone. But you were one of the ones who helped me, Blue Angel."

"All I did was place a blanket over you." I turned to him and raised an eyebrow, reminding him of the only thing I did to help him.

He grinned at me, the bandages still around his head giving him a goofy appearance. "That kept me from getting frost bit. You know, I write to my mother about you in every letter. I tell her how seeing you makes my day and helps me to feel less scared in this place." Tommy reached out for my hand as I shut his locker. I allowed for him to take it and only glanced around as a second thought. No one was watching us, including Sister Mary who wasn't even in the ward. "You're special to me, Blue Angel… very special."

I reached a hand to his forehead and brushed away the strands of jet black hair which hung in his eyes. He blinked as the strands no longer disturbed his vision. "You're very special to me too Tommy."

He placed his lips on the back of my hand before giving it a gentle squeeze. I tried to ignore the fluttering in my stomach; many of the nurses warned us that the soldiers knew how to charm a lady. But Tommy didn't seem like a charmer or a flirt. His affection towards me was more than genuine. Sally attended to him not long after he entered the ward and he continued to ask for the Blue Angel who placed a blanket on him in the corridor. I'd offered to help him every time Sister Mary assigned me to day shift. Tommy let go of my hand, allowing me to carry out the rest of my morning duties.

I worked my way around the room, chatting to the men as I cleaned their lockers. At every turn of my head, I caught Tommy's sapphire eyes which reminded me of the sun glinting off the ocean. He pulled funny faces, winked, or simply beamed at me. Every time he did, a warmth rose from my neck to my cheeks. I prayed no one would notice the rose flush to my cheeks or, if they did, they would merely presume it was from the work I had carried out.

This morning my mind remained on Ross and what we had once possessed between us. The thought of seeing him today made every part of my body shiver and vibrate in an adrenaline rush of excitement. But the second I saw Tommy's face in the ward and started to chat to him, the images of Ross faded to a black haze. My feelings towards Ross had always persisted in a complicated web. Now, they became more tangled to an unintelligible emotion. He seemed like a distant memory that was about to come back and haunt me.

I took my cloths to the washroom to keep any infections at bay from the ward. The space away from Ross had always been my greatest fear, yet it became my most welcomed distraction. Now, I had no choice but to face him. With every tick of the clock, the prospect of touching his hand once more knotted my stomach. I walked back to the ward at a slow pace, hoping the exercise would ease the anxiety building. The doors swung open, and I averted my gaze from Tommy. Perhaps if I tried to avoid him, I could work out my feelings for Ross before I had to leave for the station.

Nurses attended to the men in the space between completing morning duties and lunchtime. They talked to the men, brought them water, and took bedpans whenever they required them. Approaching footsteps caused me to turn around as Sally came over, biting her lip in an attempt to conceal the smile which dotted her dimples.

"Tommy wants to speak to you. He says he has something to give you."

My eyebrows knitted together as I glanced over her shoulder. Tommy laid on the bed playing with his fingers before wringing his hands. "Any idea what it is?"

"I don't know. I did see a little parcel beside him on the bed though."

Despite the heat which rose in my body, I made my way over to Tommy's bed. I poked my tongue into my cheek as I walked, willing myself not to show any obvious signs of confusion. From Tommy's lack of colour and fidgeting hands, he didn't need me behaving in any manner to put him off giving me his gift.

As though sensing my approach, his head lifted, and a beaming smile came over his lips. The bandage around his head moved up when he smiled in an almost comical fashion. I took a seat on the bed beside him, filling the empty space where his visitors should have been every afternoon. Yet, he never received any. His mother hadn't got the means to travel extensively to always see him.

"I have something for you, Blue Angel," he informed me. He reached over to the other side of the bed and lifted a brown paper parcel, handing me it. "Go on, open it."

At his insistence, I opened the paper with ripping sounds echoing around the ward. A letter and a hardtack biscuit fell onto my lap with a thud. I set the paper to one side and lifted the biscuit to see the centre cut out of it, forming a small photo frame. The empty space held a photo of Tommy in his army uniform, beaming into the camera as he always did.

I glanced up at him, as a wave of heat came over me, making me slightly light-headed. Instinctively, I held the biscuit to my chest and swallowed hard. "Oh Tommy, this is wonderful. I… I can't even begin to tell you how much this means to me. Can I open the letter too?"

He shook his head, taking the letter away from me in case I was tempted. "Open the letter when you're on your way back to the hospital this evening." At my nod of agreement, he handed the letter back to me, brushing his fingertips against mine. "In the morning, can we go out into the garden?"

"Of course, we can. I'll clear it with Sister Mary tomorrow though."

I stood up, clutching the letter and photo to my chest as though someone might try to wrestle them away from me. Tommy motioned for me to come closer; he never spoke, and his darting eyes warned me not to speak either. I leant over the bed, expecting him to whisper something in my ear. Instead, his cold lips grazed my cheek in a fleeting peck of a kiss. I allowed myself to stay there for second more before straightening my back. We held our gazes for much longer than we should have until Sister Mary's voice resounded from the doors, calling me away to grab the lunch trolley for the men.

Sally and Harriet gushed about Tommy the whole way to London. My stomach chugged and halted as the train moved over the tracks. Nothing could have prepared me to see Ross again after the last time in the daisy field. Our parting cut me so deeply to the core that I desired nothing more than to slap him across the face. But it wasn't in my nature to act that way towards anyone I loved. The mere image of his face faded with the closer we got to London. The green fields washed before my eyes like a smudged painting of the English countryside. Tommy's letter weighed against my breast, along with the photo in the biscuit.

The small reminder of him made me long to arrive back in Poole to see him once more. My fingers itched to open the letter and take my mind away from my shaking limbs. Yet I resisted the urge only because of the promise I made to him.

"What did Tommy give you?" Sally questioned, dragging my gaze away from the window.

"A photo of him in one of the army hardtack biscuits and a letter."

Harriet and Sally's eyes widened and sparkled. Harriet leant forward in the carriage to speak. "Have you opened the letter?" I shook my head in response to her. The urge to rip open the envelope grew stronger. I sat on my hands to avoid any temptation to peek. "He's going to declare his love for you. I know he is."

I raised a sceptical eyebrow at her. "Isn't that slight counter-intuitive? I'm going to see a man who apparently loves me while another has possibly declared his love. I feel like such a jezebel." The two women sniggered, and I couldn't help but smile at my own judgemental self.

When we descended from the train and onto the platform, we found ourselves in the middle of huddles of soldiers. Each one looked alike in their uniform, making it near impossible to pick anyone out of the crowd. We squeezed through the bustling bodies of soldiers, their families, and their sweethearts. The aromas of coal and cigarette smoke bellowed into the air around us as the squeal of the train mixed with the voices of the people. Harriet led us down the steps to the ground floor of the station, hoping for a less busy area to spot Ross. Much to our dismay, the soldiers gathered around the steps on the ground floor too. Harriet took our hands and led us through the crowds to the front of the station building. The sun shone down on us as we got further away from the crowds, adding another sheer of glisten to my clammy skin.

"Excuse me," Harriet said to a small group of soldiers whose faces were blurred by the fog of the cigarette smoke billowing from their mouths. They turned around to her. "Do you know Ross Mason?"

"Sorry, no," they responded in sync, shaking their heads.

We asked several other groups but ended up with the same response. I walked towards a clearing and leant against the brick wall, enjoying the coolness against my clothes. I didn't want to give up, but visions of the entire trip to London amounting to nothing flashed before me.

"Belle?"

For a split second, I swore the familiar voice had spoken in my mind, until I glanced to my right. Ross Mason stood there in his woollen green uniform. Under the sunlight, his light brown hair appeared almost blonde. This didn't seem real. My head spun, reminding me how I thought I wouldn't see Ross again until the end of this war. Yet there he was, standing in front of me; a mere shadow of the man I once knew. He had shaved his beard off under army regulations, but it made him look younger without it. If it wasn't for the voice and the hazel-green eyes, I wouldn't have recognised that it was him.

"I didn't think you were going to show… or even receive my letter."

I swallowed hard against a lump which seemed stuck in my throat and steadied myself against the wall. My palms grazed the spikes of the red bricks. "I didn't want you going to war while we weren't on speaking terms."

We stood in silence for a few moments, neither of us moving or losing eye contact with the other. Finally, Ross glanced away towards the café in the corner of the station. "Would it be okay to go to the café to talk? It might be easier than shouting over the noise."

I looked over at Sally and Harriet who stood behind Ross. In this crowd, I knew I didn't stand a chance of finding them again when the rush happened. I swallowed hard and opened my mouth to respond, but Harriet spoke for me.

"We can come too; we'll just sit at a different table. If you don't mind, Ross."

His shoulders slumped ever so slightly as an easy smile spread on his face. "I don't mind at all."

Ross and I sat at a table by the window, watching the people rush past, with a cup of tea each. I glanced from the window back into my tea, willing myself not to fall for those autumn eyes. Ross reached across for my hand, but I snatched it away before he could even graze my skin. All around us soldiers said goodbye to their loved ones, yet we sat in a stubborn silence over a life long gone.

"Why did you ask to see me?" I questioned, finally meeting his eyes.

Ross sighed, running the edges of his fingers over the rim of the cup. "I was wrong to do what I did to you. Margaret said that she knew about our affair, and I didn't want it getting out. People in the village would judge us for feeling the way we do."

My hands clenched the cup in my palms, resisting the urge to storm off. Ross once again only thought of himself and his family's reputation. He didn't care if they found out about my infatuation; as long as he stayed safe. My breath burst through my flared nostrils as I gritted my teeth. "So, you're telling me that you left me to save your own reputation? What about mine?" Ross stayed silent and averting his gaze to the liquid swimming in the ceramic. I scoffed and shook my head, trying to understand his thinking. "If you truly love someone then you don't care about your reputation. You want to shout their love from the top of the world. You never wanted to do that for me… for us."

"I love you," Ross stated, meeting my eyes once again. I swallowed hard as the epitome of the colour of fallen leaves bore into me. He reached for my hand once again, lacing my fingers in his. This time, I didn't pull away from him. "I'm sorry for how we ended. Before you ask, I'm still with Margaret for the children's sake. But my heart is yours; it always will be."

I let his grip fall to the table as I took a sip of my tea. The warm liquid coursed through my body. "I'm not sure if I can do this."

Ross nodded, trying to smile, but failing miserably. "I understand. Until we meet again, please write to me while I'm at the front and consider being with me properly when the war is over."

I nodded, not wanting to disappoint him on his way to the most horrific experience man could ever walk into. He kissed the back of my hand and we descended into a peaceful silence between us. When everything was said and done, only one more goodbye awaited us. I looked into his eyes and spotted the glittering hopefulness of adventure every newly enlisted soldier held. I wanted to warn him about what he would face, but I knew it wouldn't have changed anything. He couldn't leave the army now he was trained and enlisted.

The shrill of the whistle caused everyone to jump from their seats. They flooded out of the café towards the train. Ross took my hand as we followed the crowds to the steps up to the platform. Sally and Harriet stood waiting at the bottom for me to return. The crowds pushed and shoved, threatening to break my hand from Ross'. In the mayhem, he pulled me into his strong side, wrapping an arm around me to stop us from ever getting separated. The train loomed over us, puffing jets of steam into the atmosphere with a hiss. This work of man was leading Ross to possible death or injury along with thousands of other men. My throat clenched as images of injuries flashed before my eyes. I tried to push them to the back of my mind as Ross meandered us through the crowds to an empty space on the platform. I didn't want to let him go. Not yet… not to the war.

"I'm sorry for what happened between us," Ross apologised over the noise of the crowds. He leant closer to my ear, making sure I heard every single word. "I really do love you. I understand that you want time to think this through. Just… please write to me."

"I will, I promise."

He smiled slightly and pulled me into his body in a hug. I wrapped my arms around his torso, gripping his woollen jacket between my fingers. He kissed the top of my head and I willed myself to remember this moment forever. If I shut my eyes tight enough, perhaps I would have been able to imprint this moment into my very soul. I pulled away from his embrace before he led me through the crowd to an open carriage. Ross turned to look at me one last time. My breath ceased in my throat as I watched his eyes searching mine. I couldn't let him walk away with any possible feeling that I might hate him for what he did to me. He needed to concentrate on his survival.

Before he could step up into the carriage, I grabbed his sleeve and pulled him towards me. He didn't get a chance to ask me what was wrong as I had my lips firmly planted on his. He engulfed me into his arms as we kissed, holding me as close as possible. Time had frozen still; the crowds silenced and stopped mindlessly pushing each other. It was just us, the way it had been back home, in what seemed like another lifetime. Ross tore his lips from mine as the conductor called for him to climb on. He pecked my lips once more before hopping onto the train just in time for the doors closing. The final glimpse I had of him was of his grinning face and autumn eyes. If anything happened, that was how I desired to remember him.

Chapter Fourteen

On the way home, Sally and Harriet told me they thought I did the right thing by kissing Ross under the circumstances. Their reassurance quieted the bubbling guilt in my stomach. As London distanced itself from us, the two women took the journey home as an opportunity to catch up on much needed sleep. I couldn't sleep with every part of my body tingling after the rush of feelings from seeing Ross. Every time I closed my eyes all I could picture was his face in a pool of anguish from an injury received. I had to trust he would stay safe, even if I couldn't do anything to ensure it.

I watched out of the window as the last of London faded into green fields of the countryside. What would France look like in the middle of this war? The countryside would have turned into a battlefield; stains of blood and piles of bodies coating the places which were once loved by farmers and labourers. If man couldn't be the same after a war, then how could the landscape? I wished to banish all thoughts of war from my mind, knowing it wouldn't calm the nausea building over Ross' departure. Instead, I pulled off my coat and felt for the letter, along with the biscuit in my pocket. My hands fumbled in my pockets until I managed to get the letter out. Tearing open the envelope, the letter greeted me in his staggered handwriting.

Blue Angel,

The moment that I met you, I adored you. When I came round it was night and all I wanted was to see your face to make sure that I hadn't dreamt you up in my mind. Your warm brown eyes made a distinct mark on my heart. The next morning, I kept asking for you, and I couldn't have been happier when you came over to tend to my wounds. I thought my heartbeat gave it away when you were attending to me. You are truly one of the most beautiful women I've ever laid eyes upon.

Getting to know you since I came in last week has been the best moment of my life. Your smile makes me feel like the war was worth fighting for because I got to meet you out of all the horrors I've witnessed. As you know, I can't take too much out of myself because of my head injury. But I want to end this letter off by telling you that the time we might end up getting together is never enough to express how much I have fallen for you in such a short space of time.

Blue Angel, Belle, you are a wonderful woman and every single day I wish that we could fall in love.

All my heart,
Your Tommy

The grin didn't leave my face as we finally left the train station to go back to the hospital. All I wanted was to see Tommy before the end of my shift at eight. Every sense of guilt about Ross had been firmly squashed. In that moment, there was only one person who my heart longed for the most. We hung our coats up in the staffroom and attached our headdresses. The three of us made our way into the ward as the male orderlies lifted the dinner plates from the men. We had made it back just in time.

Sister Mary spotted us coming in and walked towards us with a slumped posture unaccustomed to her.

"Good to see you all again. Unfortunately, one of the men died while you were away," she informed us, glancing at the empty bed placed only four beds away from Tommy. My heart shattered in my chest, knowing the man's laughter and joking would no longer resound against the walls of the ward ever again.

"Is there anything we can do, Sister?" I asked, desiring to do something to ease the discomfort and loneliness which descended like a blanket over the ward in our absence.

She smiled slightly, nodding at us. "I suppose chatting and comforting the men would be enough before they go to sleep in a couple of hours."

Sally, Harriet, and I took off in different directions around the ward. I decided to check on the men who had been on either side of the man who passed, but VADs were already attending to them. The brokenness of the loss squished their faces in an anguish-wrenched expression. I kept my head low out of respect for them. I followed my feet to the one bed I knew I needed to see. I lifted my head when I came closer to his bed and his eyes met mine. His piercing sapphire orbs tore into me with a solemn loss I never wanted to comprehend.

"Belle, my Blue Angel," he greeted me, forcing a smile onto his face. I sat on the edge of his bed and cupped his hand in mine. "Did you read the letter?"

"Yes, I did. You're a silly fool to feel such ways about someone like me. You hardly know me."

He grinned back at me, pushing away the forlorn expression which coated his features only a second ago. "We've spent a lot of time together – a week feels like forever in this war. I can't be the only one to have been a fool over you."

Tommy was right – he wasn't the only person to have been a fool over me. But I couldn't tell him that. Ross was the first person to have let himself be foolishly in love with me; from tricking the Vicar, to having late night rendezvous in my bedroom and joining the war. I didn't want anyone expect Sally and Harriet to know about Ross. He remained a lifetime away in my heart. I swore that it would forever remain like that until I needed to tell someone else.

"I wouldn't say that," I eventually responded to him. I glanced around, making sure no one had their eyes in our direction, before bringing his hand to my mouth and kissing it. Through my eyelashes I watched as the beaming smile returned to his face and I longed to peck his lips just to make his night.

Instead, we spent the final hour chatting about our lives, knowing anything more would catch the eyes of too many people. I described the cottage we lived in and the fields surrounding us, leaving out the daisy field. Tarnishing whatever Tommy and I might have with memories of Ross didn't seem right. I told him about how I worked for Michael in the doctor's surgery before the two of us came to work in Poole to help with the war effort. Tommy listened intently, nodding along to everything, and making the odd comment. Speaking of home no longer made my eyes sting with tears. As Tommy began to speak of his own upbringing, I watched as he looked into the distance with watery orbs. Homesickness in the soldiers didn't surprise me after my first week in the ward. So many of the men lived with it, letting it create a hollowness in their chests, until they returned to see their loved ones again.

Tommy described the work he did as a farmhand; gesturing animatedly about the different animals he looked after. I smiled, blinking away the memories of the Mason farm with every ounce of strength I had. He lifted a notebook from his bedside table as he told me how he desired nothing more than to be a writer when the war was over. The notebook had followed him through the last year of his life, specifically the war the world had entered. His mother, whom he lived with, always loved to read his poems.

"In a little cottage in the country," Tommy said, smiling fondly of the memories of home. "That's where me and Mother live. Father died when I was twelve, so it's just been us two. Devastated she was when I went to war. But she knew I had to. The letter I got today said that she wants to meet you when she visits in a few days."

In my mind, I tried to picture what Tommy's mother would look like. I imagined her with the same jet-black hair, but she would have possessed much softer blue eyes. Rather than sapphire, her eyes would have lingered with an azure like daylight. The only person who would have the same piercing sapphire orbs would be his father. I closed my mouth to try to cover the shock of having to meet his mother. He had told her so much about me that the mere notion of meeting her caused a knot to form in my throat. What if I didn't meet her expectations? What if she didn't like me at all?

"Is it almost time?" Tommy questioned. I glanced down at my watch and nodded as the hand grew closer to eight than either of us desired. Tommy's crestfallen face gazed back at me. "Could you fetch me a bedpan?"

I made my way over to the nearest nurse and asked her to fetch a bedpan. She left the ward while I pulled the screens around Tommy to give him privacy. I stood outside the screens, wanting nothing more than to take Tommy away from the war. The glittering in his eyes every time that he spoke of home showed a longing I'd never witnessed in any person. The doors swung open as the nurse returned with the bedpan for Tommy. I took it off her and entered the screens to give it to him. A smirk coated his lips as he set the bedpan down beside him and took my hands.

"I wanted to kiss you, but I didn't want you getting into trouble," he admitted with a mischievous grin.

My heart fluttered in my chest as I bit my lip. "You're a bad man Tommy Felton."

He pulled me towards him until my face remained inches from his. "I just want to kiss my Blue Angel."

The moment our lips met I knew it wasn't like any of the kisses that I had with Ross. This kiss wasn't filled with passion, lust, and danger the way his had remained in my mind. Instead, Tommy's symbolised the deeper and truer meaning of love. It didn't matter how little we had known each other – all that we cared about was taking this moment before the war made us believe love was no longer possible. His hand rested on the back of my head, deepening the kiss in a delicate manner. I dared to believe we weren't in a hospital ward in the middle of war; we could have been anywhere away from the destruction of mankind towards each other. In that moment, the war didn't matter any longer to Tommy. One simple kiss had given him the peace he desired. I pulled away and let my forehead rest against his for a moment. He grinned at me before pecking my cheek and letting me leave him.

When he finished with the bedpan, a male orderly came to take it away from him. I pulled back the screens to see Tommy laying down on the bed now. The skin under his eyes coloured a purple-black tone and he breathed heavily, struggling to keep his eyelids open. His energy had continued to dip every day since arriving at the hospital. Many of the men were the same, but it was due to the medication prescribed to them which seemed to take the most effect on their bodies. Sister Mary walked around the ward, dismissing us from our duties as the nightshift started to pour into the ward. I pulled the blanket around Tommy and brushed the hair away from his forehead as his eyelids fluttered open.

"Goodnight Blue Angel."

"Goodnight my Tommy."

Chapter Fifteen

The day before I switched to the nightshift finally came around. As much as I loved conversing with the men, many of the VADs talked about how peaceful the nightshift was. The men rarely woke up, except those who had nightmares or might have requested a bedpan. Those on duty tended to write letters home at the desk in the ward. However, what many of the nurses failed to mention, was that the night was when some of the soldiers passed away. The death of the man when I returned from seeing Ross was my first death at the hospital. I didn't wish to experience any more. My heart remained fragile from losing one of the men.

Sister Mary assigned Sally and I back to breakfast and wound duty for our final morning shift for a while. I handed out the breakfast to the men and glanced over my shoulder to smile at Tommy. His eyes were already on me, grinning in his cheeky way. If I thought about it for long enough, I could pick out many of Tommy's characteristics which reminded me of Ross; his cheeky grin, the naughty side which always sought to get me into trouble, and his ability to make me laugh at inappropriate moments. Yet there was something undeniably different about Tommy. He always put me first so selflessly without even realising he was doing it. The strangest thing about being close to Tommy was that it didn't feel like a secret or a dangerous game – despite the trouble I would get in with Sister Mary if she found out. Ross could never offer me such an open love.

Once the men finished their breakfast, Sally and I took a side each in the ward to attend to the men's wounds. As more men arrived with us every few days, we encountered more wounds which we hadn't even thought possible before. Tommy's wound became the first head injury I had to deal with. Needless to say, it wasn't my forte, and Sally usually made sure she took Tommy's side as she handled the wound much better than I did. Her hands were poised and delicate. Mine shook with the slightest element of concentration I tried to possess; it wasn't surprising that Michael had never called on me to help him with patients unless he was completely desperate.

"How are we this morning, James?" I asked one soldier around Ross' age. I read over his record in Michael's almost illegible handwriting. His leg stitches had to be removed and the skin around the wound cleaned.

"The usual, Nurse," he replied in a Scottish burr. The variety of accents always greeted my ears in the hospital. The recreational areas echoed with Devon, Cornwall, London, Scottish, Irish, and even Welsh accents. "I hear the stitches come out today."

"Indeed, but you won't feel a thing."

I walked over to the trolley to grab everything that I needed to take them out. He chatted away to me as I removed them, taking my time with as much of a steady hand as I could muster. Bruises, cuts, and scars decorated his legs from thigh to foot; constellations of the devastation of war. Yet I never once heard him complain of his injuries or of any pain he had. Every day

James asked a nurse to help him out to the hospital gardens to walk around. He wanted to strengthen his leg enough to go home to his family before returning to the frontline again. The sheer resilience and determination of the men never ceased to amaze me. James watched as I removed the final stitch from his leg, and I glanced up at him through my eyelashes. He leant over and inspected the wound as I stood up to disinfect the area.

"All done and not a wince out of you," I announced, grabbing a cloth and disinfectant.

"You know me, Nurse; nothing to wince about."

As I travelled around the room, attending to the other soldiers, every fibre in my body began to spark and tingle at the prospect of taking Tommy into the gardens. No one had taken him outside since he arrived at the hospital because of his head injury. Michael and Sister Mary wanted to monitor him for as long as possible before allowing him out of their sights. Some of the men didn't want to go out into the gardens; they simple couldn't cope with it. Every time they tried to step a single toe outside, the nurses had to bring them back in. Their minds fought against them, and we had to respect they would make their way outside in their own time.

My throat clenched as I approached the one bed every nurse tried their best to avoid. In the corner of the ward laid the one man the nurses were apprehensive about attending; dodging him at any possible cost. A heat prickled my skin with each step I took towards him. Some of the nurses called him 'difficult,' spending as little time with him as possible. Sally had attended to him every day until now. Most of the time, she treated him as the other VADs did – get the job done fast and don't speak to him. It was now my time to attend to the man who glanced into space; a world away from everyone else. I swallowed hard and made my way over to him, looking at his chart to know what to do. The wounds on his face needed the stitches removed and his hands needed re-bandaged. Before I set the chart back in its place, I glanced at his name: Stephen.

"Hello Stephen," I spoke softly, smiling as best as I could. He made no response to me, but I knew not to expect one. "I'm Belle. I'm going to take a look at your face first to take out the stitches."

I hummed the tune of *'Come Josephine'* as I worked on him. Part of me hoped it would calm him and give him an element of peace. Perhaps it might remind him of a time before this war broke the world. Stephen didn't move, blinking into the distance as the war flashed through his mind on repeat. The images and noises he must have seen and heard still plagued him. One look in his eyes showed the depth of how much the war haunted him. I tore my gaze away, knowing my heart would shatter into a million pieces for him. Sister Mary called it 'shell-shock' and Stephen was the first case of it in our hospital in Poole. We predicted many more men would return from the front with those haunted eyes.

"There you go," I announced, tidying up the bed from the hospital supplies. *Blink. Blink.* "Let's take a look at your hands."

I peeled the blanket back to attend to his hands which sat on his thighs. I stepped back into the wall, knocking over some of my used supplies. They clattered on the floor, and I willed myself to pick them up before I disturbed the whole ward. My hands shook as I placed them back on the end of the bed. There wasn't much left of either of his hands. His right had only his little and index fingers remaining, while his left still had his thumb, middle, and ring fingers. A grenade must have exploded in his hands as he threw it. It didn't take a doctor to tell me that he was lucky to be alive. His haunted eyes made much more sense now I understood part of what he had gone through. I'd heard of such things happening, but I'd never witnessed the aftermath until now. The stares of the other nurses and VADs bore into me as I attended to Stephen. They waited for me to cave in and say that I couldn't handle treating him.

I kept my focus on Stephen's hands, ignoring their stares as they desired for me to give up on him. How could I give up on someone who gave so much for me and my freedom? The skin on his hands was red raw and there were no nails on the remaining fingers. I grabbed the bandages and scissors, taking a seat beside him, and started to work on bandaging up his hands. I started with the right hand and took extra care when wrapping the fragile skin. I couldn't begin to imagine the pain he suffered.

"Let's get this one bandaged up for you," I said, placing his right hand back on his thigh and lifting the left. As I wrapped his hands, I hummed again, allowing the tune to transport me back to home. "That's you done." I stood up, tidying the supplies back to the trolley, before returning to his side. I combed the hair from his distant eyes and pulled the blanket back over him. I started to walk away when a voice spoke into the silence.

"*Come Josephine.*" I spun around, expecting the soldier beside Stephen to have recognised the tune. Instead, Stephen's eyes met mine in a pool of brown, murky water, haunted by the life he lived in France. My heart leapt in my chest as I realised that he talked for one of the first times since coming to the hospital.

"Sorry?"

"That's the song you were humming."

I smiled and nodded, blinking back the tears. "It was; it's my favourite."

He turned his head back around, returning to his normal self. I glanced at him one last time before finally leaving his side. Stephen's eyes stared out the window, unseeing the world around him. In that split second, I prayed Ross would never remain so haunted by the war, but no one could ever escape the horrors of such a brutal world.

~

I pushed the wheelchair into the ward for Tommy to go into the garden. Two nurses surrounded us, helping him to stand beside his bed. I watched as his legs shook, earning weary glances from the nurses. None of us wanted to take any risk with Tommy; he was still classed as a high-risk case due to his head injuries. Sister Mary always had a designated nurse watching him from afar in the ward to make sure there was nothing wrong – whether he knew it or not was another matter entirely.

The nurses aided me in seating Tommy into the wheelchair. I stood behind it, supporting his back as they lowered him. The wheelchair bounced against my thighs as I stopped it moving. One of the nurses grabbed a plaid blanket, placing it around Tommy's legs to keep him warm in the autumn weather. I expected Tommy to weigh much more than he did as I pushed him with ease – an unfortunate result of the lack of proper food at the front. Many of the men came to us with gaunt faces and their uniforms hanging off them. A nurse opened the garden doors for us as we made our way into the sunlight of the afternoon.

Compared with the lost summer days, the breeze nipped at our skin in a bitter cold. I couldn't have been more thankful for Tommy to have a blanket wrapped around him, especially in only his hospital pyjamas. Other VADs walked around with a soldier linked in the hook of their arms. Each soldier wore identical pyjamas, slippers, and dressing gown. Some had walking sticks with them to help them get around easier due to their injuries.

Tommy took in his surroundings, gazing all around him at the trees and flowers, as I wheeled him towards a bench in the grass. The birds sung sweet melodies of peace in the trees, earning the smiles of the soldiers. I watched as Tommy moved in the seat, craning his neck in all directions, as he endlessly searched for them. He sat back in the wheelchair as he spotted where they were in the trees near the bench we stopped at.

The wood's damp surface stuck to my dress as I sat down. Tommy nudged me and pointed out the birds resting on the branches of the trees. His eyes sparkled with excitement, like a child discovering something brand new. A heat radiated in my chest at the sight of Tommy finally possessing an element of happiness and peace since coming to the hospital.

"You seem excited about the birds," I stated, watching his face.

That was when his features returned to his solemn expression mirrored only by the other soldiers. His signature grin had vanished into thin air. "They don't appear or sing their hearts out at the front. This is the first real time I've heard them singing since I got sent to the front."

"I'm sorry," I whispered, afraid to disturb the birdsong echoing in the garden. If this was the only thing which brought Tommy peace, then I wouldn't ruin it for him.

Tommy reached over and cupped my hands inside his cold palms. Our hands moulded together in a pattern only an ancient artist could recreate. How could one person feel so much like home? Perhaps everyone was born with missing parts of their soul, and we spent forever trying to find the people who would fit into those pieces. If that was true, I knew Tommy had filled one of the missing parts of my soul. I glanced up at him through my eyelashes and allowed myself to dive into his sapphire sea.

"Don't be sorry," he said, shaking his head. I swallowed hard and tried to push away the lump of my mistake which rested heavily in my throat. "You weren't to know what it's like at the front. But I don't want you to ever know; I pray that this is as much as you'll ever see."

A comfortable silence descended between us as the birdsong filled the atmosphere. The enthusiasm of the soldiers to spend time in the gardens made so much sense when I finally sat there for long enough to appreciate the nature. The beauty of the gardens reminded them of what the battlefronts had once looked like before the world fell apart, despite the sheer destruction of nature at the front remaining in the forefronts of their minds. Tommy continued to look around the gardens, biting his lip as his hands shook against mine. His mother had arranged to come to see him tomorrow. For the first few days he hadn't wanted her to know he was in hospital because he didn't want to worry her. But from his distant eyes, I knew there was more to it than that.

"My mother didn't want me to go to war," Tommy admitted out of nowhere as we sat in the gardens. "Father died a few years earlier and she didn't want to be alone. I ignored her, enlisting against her wishes. We write all the time, but it's not the same. I feel like I've let her down."

"Of course, you haven't."

"I have," he insisted. His hands grew clammy against mine, building a barrier of sweat between our skin. I watched as his chin quivered against the sunlight. "I got injured and now I'll end up going back to the front again."

I pulled away from his grasp and moved over to engulf him in a hug as tears rolled down his cheeks. No one looked over in our direction; if they did, they ignored us or glanced away as fast as they could. At the hospital, no one paid attention when one of the men started to cry. It was a regular occurrence despite the men getting embarrassed at doing so. All that we, as nurses, could do was comfort them as best as possible. Tommy's tears plunked on my shoulder as his body jerked in uncontrollable sobs. I rubbed his back until his weeping settled into deep breaths, as though trying to breathe through the tears.

"Can you promise me one thing?" he whispered as his warm breath caressed my ear.

I pulled away and searched his eyes for an answer before I asked the question. "What is it?"

"If I don't come back from the war, please visit my mother. She'll know who you are when she meets you tomorrow. I just don't want her to be lonely without me anymore."

I refused to let myself think about the possibility of a world without Tommy. I didn't want to believe I would never see his ocean blue orbs or cheeky smile ever again. I blinked away the tears which threatened to roll down my cheeks at any second.

"I promise, Tommy."

Chapter Sixteen

At the end of my shift, I made my way over to Tommy to say goodnight to him as had become my routine since we admitted our feelings towards each other. He laid down on the bed with the blanket pulled up around his chin. His face poked out as he smiled at me when he spotted my figure towering over him. Tommy reached a hand out from under the material and clasped mine, making me sit down on the bed beside him. For a while, neither of us spoke and the chatter of the soldiers and nurses filled the silence between us.

"You've been the best thing about this war, Belle," he told me. His eyes bore into me, reaching my very soul with every ounce of love in his body. I swallowed hard and gripped his hand tighter, afraid that if I let go, he might escape from my grasp. "It won't be over by Christmas; trust me on that Blue Angel."

I shook my head as my eyes widened. "You can't think like that Tommy. You must be optimistic. It's the only way to get through this madness."

"I admire your optimism, but I cannot partake in such thoughts. I've seen what it's like out there in France. There's no hope of peace soon," he admitted with a small, sad smile coating his lips.

Before I had a chance to argue with him, Sister Mary came around to dismiss us from our shifts as the night staff entered the ward. I stood up but kept a firm grasp on Tommy's hand. The most difficult part of my shift was saying goodbye to him. My chest tightened at the mere thought of having to walk away from him for the evening. As though sensing my reluctance, he pulled my hand towards his lips and kissed it. Without a second thought, I leant down and kissed his forehead. I didn't care if I got caught by Sister Mary or another nurse. How could I possibly care when my heart screamed at me to show him my love and affection? His eyes fluttered closed, feeling my lips against his skin.

"Sleep tight, Tommy," I whispered, pulling away from him. His eyes darted around to make sure no one had noticed. I watched as his shoulders slumped in a sure sign that we hadn't been caught by anyone. He grinned at me, and his eyes shone with a love I could never imagine anyone else having on this Earth.

"You too, Blue Angel."

I shot up in bed as someone shook my body awake. I glanced around, presuming I had slept in, until I spotted Sally towering over me. Her knitted brow caused my throat and chest to instinctively clench in sync. It was impossible for me to have slept in when I was on the nightshift now. I peeled back the blanket and stood up beside her, expecting her to have donned her uniform for an emergency. Yet she wore only her nightie with her hair plaited over her shoulder.

"Sister Mary needs you immediately. She's asked for you to get dressed and meet her at the hospital," she informed me.

Without a single question or protest, I put on my nurse's uniform and pulled my hair back into a tight bun. Out of the corner of my eye, I spotted Sally watching me while wringing her hands. Anyone on the nightshift who had one of these emergencies normally ended up having a telegram about a loved one who was missing or who had died at the front. My stomach churned as I fastened my headdress before running out of the boarding house.

A nurse waited on me outside the hospital to direct me to Sister Mary. She ignored every question I had about what the matter was as she walked me in silence through the hospital. Nausea overcame me as I willed myself not to think of Ross and the possibility of something happening to him at the front. I wouldn't allow myself to believe it. My thoughts ceased as Sister Mary's forlorn face met my eyes as she stood outside the doors to the ward. A darkness descended over her features despite the daylight shining through the corridor. The other nurse touched my shoulder gently, sending a shiver down my spine, before she left me.

With a single motion of her head, Sister Mary beckoned me to follow her into the sluice room alone. The aroma of disinfectant made sickness work its way up my throat as my stomach twisted and turned at a painful rate. Sister Mary turned around to face me when the door closed with a click. The world seemed to freeze as the once emotionless woman had watery eyes which stared at me.

"I'm sorry Nurse Wilson to tell you this. A few hours ago, Tommy woke with a pain and a clicking in his head. We put the screens around him, but in minutes he was gone." Every breath I possessed escaped my lungs as she finished her sentence. There was no way that my smiling, mischievous Tommy wasn't on Earth anymore. I wasn't going to hear his laugh or look into his ocean blue eyes again. "I know that you were close to Tommy."

I snapped back to reality and my eyebrows pinched together as I looked at her. "You knew… But if you did, then why didn't you say anything?"

The edges of her mouth twitched with the hint of a smile trying to break through. "I suppose I'm not a heartless old bag after all. Doctor Henry and I both knew Tommy was on borrowed time. You made him happy, and I couldn't take that away from him. It could be because my brother died only last week in the war that I wanted Tommy to have that small element of happiness. I wish my brother's final moments would have been happy."

I opened and closed my mouth several times, not quite knowing what to say. Eventually, I thanked Sister Mary and swiftly requested to see Tommy. As the death didn't happen that long ago, he would have still been in the ward. She swallowed hard and nodded, taking me into the ward. As she pushed open the door, she tried to assure me it was a quick death, but it did little to remove the aching in my heart. I hadn't experienced any pain like this before. It was as though God had removed a piece of my heart and soul the second that he took Tommy from this Earth. The soldiers' eyes watched me as we made our way to his bed which had screens placed around it still.

Sister Mary stopped at the screens before walking off to leave me alone with Tommy. I took a shaky breath and pulled back one of the screens to go inside. A single tear rolled down my cheek in a warm sorrow as I looked at Tommy's body. He still had his cheeky smile, as if he knew that he would never see the frontline again. Despite his demeanour and behaviour, the war had haunted him more than he would ever tell me. How many would have preferred death over having to face the horrors of the battlefields again? The only consolation to his death was his freedom from the haunting memories and the fear of returning once more.

I sat down, taking my usual place on the side of his bed, and lifted his cold, lifeless hand in mine. Only when his flesh contrasted to mine did Tommy's loss finally hit me. I let out a breath as tears streamed down my cheeks, willing myself not to believe he was gone. How could someone so full of life only a few hours ago have left this Earth? It didn't make any sense to me. I sniffed and tried to smile for Tommy's sake as I cupped his hand in mine.

"I'm going to keep all my promises to you. And when I hear the birdsong, I know that it's you reminding me that you're still with me. You're finally free, Tommy; it's what you always wanted since going to war... I just hope that I gave you the best of the borrowed time God granted you."

My throat clammed, ceasing my words, as sobs screamed out of me in an anguish I never wished to experience again. The echoes of my cries resounded against the walls of the ward as I bent over Tommy. A hand rested on my shoulder, pulling me away from him. Their arms gripped me tightly to aid my movements as we left Tommy's side. I blinked away my tears and realised that Sister Mary was the one comforting me in my lifetime of grief. She held me up to stop my whole body collapsing on the floor in a pool of heartbreak. The male orderlies moved the screens to the side and pulled the blanket over Tommy as they moved his body out of the ward. I screamed into Sister Mary's shoulder as they wheeled his body away from me forever. She rubbed my back, but it did nothing to ease the nails which dug into my very soul. My hands balled her uniform between my fingers as my body trembled.

My sobs froze in gasps of air as a distant humming greeted my ears. I sniffed and wiped my tears away with the back of my hand as I turned to see where the humming came from. All the men had their heads turned towards Stephen in the corner of the ward. He continued to stare into the distance, as though not knowing what was going on. But part of him did. The tune was unmistakably *'Come Josephine'* – the exact song I hummed when I attended to him. Soon, the other men joined in with him when they realised what the song meant to me. I took shaky breaths to calm myself, gripping Sister Mary's hand to keep myself grounded. A single tear rolled down my cheek as a small smile coated my lips.

"It's my favourite song," I mumbled as much to myself as to Sister Mary. The nurses stopped their work to listen to the men of the ward. Even though I had just lost Tommy, the compassion of every single man that I had cared for meant everything to me in that moment.

Harriet and Sally waited on me at the boarding house to return. I caught my reflection in the glass panel on the door as I walked inside. My eyes had turned puffy and red bloodshot from my sobs. A throbbing in my head and heart became a constant reminder of the loss. In my whole life, I hadn't experienced a death until Tommy's. But I never expected my first death to be the man I fell in love with. Everyone would have told us we fell in love too quickly, but was there ever such a thing as 'swift love' in a war? Or did we just seek the love and passion of humanity to remind us of the life we should have had before this war?

"What happened?" Sally asked, scanning my eyes for any sign of what had occurred at the hospital. Harriet wrapped her arm around me, holding me close to her.

I took a shaky breath and swallowed hard, praying the sorrow would grow easier as the days went on. "I… I went to see Tommy. He died a few hours ago."

Without a warning, I burst into tears and the two women held me tightly. They took me into the recreational area we had in the boarding house. I welcomed the soft fabric of the sofas engulfing me in a comforting hug. I glanced at the clock on the wall, realising I had to return to the hospital for visiting hours. Today was the day I was meant to meet Tommy's mother. Only now, I had to face her alone and she didn't even know about her son's death yet. My heart shattered all over again for her. The women attempted to cheer me up by making me a cup of tea with biscuits, but nothing worked. The only thing I desired to do was sleep so I didn't have to experience the pain in my heart any longer. Eventually, Sally and Harriet helped me to our room where the other nurses still laid, fast asleep in their beds. I removed my nurse's uniform and pulled on my nightie, before crawling into the solace of my bed. A tear dried against my skin as I slipped into the numbness of sleep. The black abyss helped to ease the heart-wrenching pain of losing Tommy.

A dark cloud had descended over the hospital when I arrived to see Tommy's mother. Sister Mary waited on me by the doors to the ward to take me to where she was. Her solemn smile appeared the minute she spotted me coming towards her. With a gentle squeeze on my shoulder, Sister Mary led me to Tommy's mother. The room sat only a few doors away from the ward itself. The closer we came, the more my hands grew clammy, and I blinked rapidly. I needed the courage to face her for Tommy's sake. Sister Mary landed a deafening knock on the door before opening it just enough for me to squeeze through.

When Sister Mary closed the door with a click behind me, I spotted a woman with jet black hair rolled into a bun at the back of her head. When her eyes met mine, I realised she had the same sapphire orbs as Tommy which were flooding like a monsoon in summer.

"Belle?" she questioned as her eyebrows knitted together. Her voice came out soft and gentle as she spoke. Tommy and his mother looked so alike he could have been her double.

"Yes, that's me. You must be Tommy's mother." I forced a tight smile onto my face, but it did little good for either of us.

She nodded and sniffed, pulling out a handkerchief to wipe her nose. The dust particles in the stuffy room danced in the sunlight. Putting Mrs Felton in such a suffocating room after seeing her son's body had quite possible been the worst idea the hospital had ever came up with. On the desk in front of her laid the contents of Tommy's locker; his uniform, letters, and photographs from home, along with a few piles of papers and his notebook tied together with string. I approached the desk as though it were something dangerous, ready to pounce at me. Tommy's mother stood up as she watched me drag my feet across the floor with my eyes fixated on his belongings. She reached over and lifted the papers and notebook. I glanced at the first envelope on the pile. Tommy had written 'Belle' on it in his usual handwriting. She handed it to me, and I took it from her with tears slipping from my eyes.

"Mrs Felton," I spoke, hearing my own distraught voice rasping in the silence. "I'm sorry for your loss. Tommy was looking forward to seeing you today. His whole face shone when he talked about your visit yesterday in the gardens."

She took a deep, shaking breath, refusing to meet my gaze. "Did he know I was proud of him, Belle? He always wrote to me about how he thought he'd let me down by enlisting. He hadn't… my Tommy could never let me down."

I sat down beside her and took her hand. "He knew you were proud of him."

"I should have been coming to see him," she burst out in a sob. Her shoulders jerked and trembled when I wrapped her in a hug. "I suppose, something good came from my visit. I'm able to bring his belongings back with me and I got to meet the woman my son kept writing to me about."

"Me?" I asked in a high pitch as we pulled away from the hug. My eyes bulged as I thought back to all the times Tommy told me he wrote to his mother telling her about me. A part of me believed he lied to try to flirt with me, but he didn't.

She stifled a laugh and wiped her tears with the back of her hand. "His letters forever spoke of you since he came to the hospital. *'Belle my Blue Angel,'* he would write."

We spoke about Tommy for as long as possible during the visiting hours. Speaking of him seemed to help her with the shock of her loss as she became more animated when telling stories of him. Tales of childhood times and how he always looked after her became my favourite stories of the Tommy I should have had longer to know. I admitted to Mrs Felton how Tommy didn't want to go back to the war; wishing he never enlisted in the first place. Somehow, like me, his reluctance to go back to the front eased a little bit of the grief of her loss. As visiting time drew to an end, I helped Mrs Felton to package up Tommy's belongings in some brown paper wrapping Sister Mary had stored in the room. She pulled on her coat as I cast my eyes to the package of everything I once associated with Tommy, remembering the promise I made to him before his passing.

"Mrs Felton, I promised Tommy before he died that I would look after you if anything happened to him," I informed her. She opened her mouth and blinked several times, as though trying to process what Tommy had done for her, even beyond his own life. "Would it be okay if we wrote to each other?"

A smile slowly formed on her face as she hugged the package to her chest. "I'd like that; I'll write down my address for you before I leave and give it to the Sister. It's what Tommy would have wanted. After all, you were his Blue Angel."

Before I started nightshift, Sister Mary handed me the page Mrs Felton left with her address on it and a promise to tell me about the funeral details so I could attend. She had also left me Tommy's service hat, which she must have taken out of the package before leaving. For the rest of my time in the hospital, I kept his hat and the biscuit photo frame he gave me in my bedside table, swearing to never let his memory fade.

Chapter Seventeen

Returning to the hospital after Tommy's funeral didn't seem real. Knowing he wouldn't be there, waiting on me in his bed, smiling as I came through the doors, tore my heart into tiny pieces. Sister Mary had granted me two days leave for the funeral as I stayed with Mrs Felton the day before. During the service, Mrs Felton and I sat together, becoming a beacon of comfort for the other. She gripped my hand during the service, as if no amount of screaming or crying would ease her sorrow. I tried to remain strong for her, but eventually my rock exterior shattered. As Tommy's coffin lowered into the ground I broke in front of his whole village. My knees sunk into the grass beneath us, willing this to have been the worst nightmare I had ever experienced. Mrs Felton comforted me as we threw a white rose into the ground on top of his coffin. It became the last mark of affection I could give the man I loved in such a short space of time.

When I arrived back in Poole, Sister Mary had assigned me to nightshift, allowing me an extra amount of time to grieve. I couldn't let my sorrow hold me back from my duty much longer – I had to nurse my sorrowful heart while helping the men who needed me most. A letter I watched Mrs Felton write to me the night I stayed with her awaited me at the hospital when I got to the boarding house. We promised to keep in contact through letters until I could visit again. There was only one person I hadn't written to yet. Ross had sent me a letter from France before Tommy died, but I had never possessed the right mindset to respond to him until now. My own stubborn heart prevented me from picking up a pencil to write back to him. Deep down, I knew I couldn't cope if I lost him too.

The nightshift remained a sanctuary for me while still grieving. The men's heavy, slumbered breathing echoed against the walls of the ward as I did my round. I checked on each of them, pulling up blankets or tucking in dangling arms when needed, before sitting down at the nurses' desk. Every nurse sat with a page and a pencil scribbling away to their sweethearts or family members. I watched as Sally's hand travelled at an incomprehensible speed while leaning over to check what her brother had written to her. She turned her head and caught me staring over at her. A smile pulled gently at the corners of her mouth as she reached for a spare page.

"Would you like one?" she whispered, afraid of disturbing the men.

I hesitated for a moment before nodding. "Yes please." I took the paper from her and grabbed a spare pencil which rolled about on the table. This marked my first letter to Ross and the pressure to get it right weighed heavily against my chest.

Dearest Ross,
I apologise for not writing as promised. I lost one of my men, Tommy, with whom I was very close to. He died suddenly and, as much as I have tried to overcome his loss, it is a daily struggle. I hope this letter finds you well and

that you haven't gone to the frontline just yet. I want you to stay safe in this war; even if we don't work out, I will always care about you.

Sometimes at night I replay the moment that we parted in the daisy field over in my mind. I can still picture your figure disappearing away from me – completely out of my grasp. Whenever it fades, an overwhelming ache in my bones cries out for you. When I pray to desire you back, I swear the voices tell me that you will come back to me safely. I know that you'll tell me you feel the same, but how can you when you have Margaret?

This is not a simple situation, and I shan't act like it is. All I will say is that I haven't quite made my mind up yet about us. There's so much to consider and, after losing Tommy, I cannot dream of the future. Not in this war. They say it's set to get worse for us and France might need us if the war continues after Christmas.

Christmas won't be the same without you this year, but you'll be in my thoughts and prayers until we meet again.

Please stay safe.

Yours,

Belle.

I folded the page and placed it into the pocket of my apron until I found an envelope. The chair squeaked against the floor as I stood up, but none of the nurses glanced up. They were all too enraptured in writing their letters to pay attention. Footsteps pounding on the ward floor drew my attention to Harriet sprinting towards me. I watched as the muscle in her throat twitched as she tried to swallow.

"Stephen is having nightmares. He's asked for you," she informed me, trying to regain her breath. "I think this is the first time I've heard him speaking."

Without a single chance of hesitation, I ran towards the end of the ward where Stephen laid in his bed shaking. Sweat glistened and dripped from his forehead as the blanket started to fall to the floor. I caught it before it landed on the tiles and called over to Harriet to grab me a damp flannel. The daytime was bad enough for the men with shell-shock as memories played back in their minds. But the night-time became even worse for some as they lived out their nightmares of the front. Harriet slapped the damp flannel into my palm as she sped back to me. With a gentle hand, I wiped the sweat from Stephen's face, holding his cheek in my palm to try to settle him. His distant eyes met mine, gazing at me intently as though to see if I was real or part of the nightmare. He gripped my sleeve and dug his nails into my flesh, but I didn't move his hand. He needed to know I was real.

"It's okay. I'm here," I reassured him, wiping a dribble of sweat which swept down his eyelid. His grip loosened slightly, and the pinching of his nails eased from my skin. He kept his hand placed on my arm until I finished cooling down his forehead. I sat on the edge of his bed and placed the flannel on my lap. Stephen's breathing laboured as he settled down with every time my hand stroked the back of his bandage one. His hand shook and quivered beneath the bandages.

I started to sing *'Come Josephine'* to remind him of the better times of this world. His eyelids fluttered closed, and his head sunk into the pillow in a mellowed calmness. As I sang, my mind took me far away, back to the times of home. The times before I knew the searing pain of loss and before Ross became accustomed to the horrors of war. The simplicity of life back then wasn't lost on me as a longing filled the hollowness in my heart. I desired to go back to the summer of 1914 once more. Neither Ross nor I would be the same people again when the war was over. Stephen's gentle snoring silenced my song, and I laid his hand down by his side, before pulling the blanket over him.

I made my way to the sluice room with the damp flannel in my hand. Harriet's footsteps followed behind me, closing the door once she entered the room. I turned around as she bit her lip, focusing on the tiles beneath our feet.

"How do you do that?" she quizzed, finally meeting my gaze. My eyebrows furrowed and I tilted my head at her. "How do you remain so calm and comforting to Stephen? He never speaks or even moves when the rest of us are near him."

I smiled slightly and shrugged, throwing the flannel in the pile of towels ready for the washroom. "I just treat him like any of the other soldiers. He can't help his shell-shock and I dare say treating him like he can isn't going to help him in the slightest."

Harriet's eyes returned to her feet as a solemn expression fixed on her features. She played with her hands, wringing them tightly, as I walked over to her. "My husband is in the war, Belle. I look at these men and… I'm scared of how this war will change him. What if he comes back with shell-shock like Stephen?"

I laid my hand on her shoulder, causing her to look up at me. A sadness clouded her eyes as a small smile played on her lips. "You must remember, we hadn't seen or suffered half of what they have. We can't cast them aside when the fighting stops, no matter what they might suffer from as a result. They've gone to war for us and our country."

In the silence of the sluice room, Harriet's hard swallow reverberated. "Is that how you feel about Ross, even if the two of you don't rekindle a courtship?"

I cast my eyes to the window and spotted the thin crescent of the moon against the black sky. The stars shone dimly in competition with the silver-blue illumination of the moon. Its light elongated shadows on the tiles of the sluice room, reminding us of how small we were in comparison to everything in the universe. Echoes of loneliness against the darkness of the night touched my very soul. The letter in my apron pocket and the silver chain around my neck became heavy, weighing me down at the mere mention of Ross. While I didn't know how I felt about him in any romantic or emotional sense, I knew that if he wasn't well after the war, I would look after him as best as I could possibly muster.

"Yes, it is," I finally spoke, turning to face Harriet once more. "I've lost Tommy to the war. It's absolutely broken me beyond my own comprehension, so I wouldn't neglect Ross because of the war. Each one of us will become a victim to this conflict, just in different ways."

We made our way back to the ward, awaiting the sunrise to signal a new day. Eventually, its fiery orange glow coloured the ward, waking up many of the men in the process. The sunrise which once brought a smile to my face, only reminded me that I had to face another day without Tommy in my life. I wasn't sure how I had coped with the burdening sorrow in my heart, but I somehow had the strength to face each new day. The possibility of a peaceful new year kept me fighting the pain every single day.

Chapter Eighteen

My Dearest Belle,

I've been told we'll be at the front for Christmas. Everyone thought it would be over by then, yet here I am, stuck in a war during Christmastime. Out of everything that keeps me going, you are by far the greatest support. I keep your letter in my breast pocket, over my heart. When I'm scared, alone, or sad, your words comfort me. If I squeeze my eyes shut, it's like I can hear your voice speaking to me. I miss hearing your laughter and your voice; that beautiful melody will forever be stuck in my mind.

Tommy sounded like a wonderful chap! If he reminded you of me then he's definitely wonderful. I jest of course. But if it is any comfort to you, I know that you will have made his time so much brighter. Always remember that and hold that knowledge close to you.

I look forward to the time when we can meet again. We keep our spirits up by singing in whispers so the Hun can't hear us. I always make the lads sing 'Come Josephine' for you.

Always yours,

Ross.

I read the letter aloud to Stephen as I sat with him during visiting hours. He hadn't been doing very well today and I was trying my best not to break at seeing him struggle so much. I hated seeing him more distant and shaking than when I first helped him in the ward. Sister Mary tried to assure me it was normal for men with shell-shock. Yet it did nothing to ease the tightness in my throat knowing I couldn't do anything to help him.

I gazed around at the family members who came to visit some of the soldiers, wondering why no one ever came to visit Stephen. Did he have any family or was he on his own? If he did have a family, had they been informed he was here? A chill ran down my spine as I tried not to think of what would happen to him when he was discharged next week. He had finally learnt how to operate every aspect of daily life with his injured hands with the help and dedication of the hospital staff. But he needed a family to support him with his injuries and shell-shock.

I tucked the letter away into my pocket and took his hand which no longer had bandages over it. "Do you not have anyone that could come and visit?" He cast his eyes to me and shook his head. "Are you on your own then?"

"Mother," he stated, staring into the distance again. "I live with my mother, but she's too old to travel to come and see me."

I nodded and sat back in the chair, keeping a hold of his hand. We listened to the chatter of the room, allowing it to fill the silence Stephen so readily desired for himself. As his hand shook in mine, a lump formed in my throat as I pictured Ross lying in a muddied trench over Christmas. He shouldn't have been there; he should have been at home with his children. My stomach lurched at the mere thought of the injuries he could face before the new year even began.

I started to talk to Stephen again, hoping it would take away the images of Ross flashing through my mind. He let me natter on about anything to him and the comforting presence of a listener made me already miss him before Michael discharged him. Just having someone to listen to my stories of home, my feelings about losing Tommy, and even Ross meant a lot to me in the loneliness of the war. He might not have realised it, but Stephen kept more of my secrets than I dared to know. I trusted him with every single one of them.

When visiting ended, I asked Sister Mary if I could go to the garden for a few minutes. I had originally asked for this afternoon off, but I decided to stay with Stephen after the bad day he had. With a nod of her head, she granted me the small break and I made my way out to the bench where Tommy and I had last sat. The unopened letter from his mother pressed against my pocket as I sat down. The ripping of the envelope joined the birdsong, and I unfolded the letter in my lap, hoping for some reassuring words from her.

Dear Belle,
I buried Tommy's jacket in the garden. I hadn't got the courage to let him go; not that part of him anyway. If I'm being honest, I cannot tell you what changed me. All I knew was that it was time to bury it. I didn't want to keep it forever.

I was in the garden, a day after burying his jacket, and in the tree by the spot was a Blue Tit singing its heart out. Right then, I felt Tommy near me. Growing up he adored birds and read a book on the different types. I would go for walks with him in the forest near our house. As we walked, he would tell me what each bird was, learning their song off by heart. The moment he heard the Blue Tit, he told me it was his favourite. Tommy always said that if, when we die, we become animals, he wanted to come back as a Blue Tit. Now, when I wake up each morning, I look for Tommy among nature and the sounds that it produces. I know that he is near me with the birdsong of each dawn and dusk.

Oh Belle, I hope you hear the Blue Tit's song and feel that Tommy is with you too. A man will never leave where his heart lays – even in death. I know that he loved you for the short time you two had together. I pray that you know that deep in your heart.

All in all, I think that Tommy got his wish. The Blue Tit sings in approval.

Mrs Felton.

I sighed, folding the letter into the pocket with Ross'. I glanced to my side and saw Tommy sitting there in his wheelchair; his head wrapped up and his gaze turned towards the sky. He watched the birds flying into the trees, telling me which ones were which. With a shaky finger, he pointed them out to me as they cast their winged shadows against the blue sky. We descended into silence for a moment, listening for one of the birds to sing to us. Finally, the birdsong greeted our ears in a sweet melody of nature. Tommy grinned as he turned to look at me. If I ever had any doubts about Tommy being there, they ceased the second his gaze met mine. I would recognise his cheeky grin and those ocean sapphire eyes anywhere.

"It's the Blue Tit," he stated, casting his glance back to the trees.

I followed his gaze to spot the bird sitting on a branch. It's yellow and blue feathers stood out against every other dull colour of nature. It wasn't surprising why it had become Tommy's favourite – its sweet song and vibrant colours symbolised him in more ways than anything else ever could. I looked back at Tommy, just to see him once more, but he had faded into the atmosphere. My breath caught in my throat, and I blinked away the tears which built up, realising my own illusion of the man I loved. The birdsong continued as the Blue Tit refused to disappear as Tommy had.

"Hello Tommy," I spoke with a smile. A warmth filled my chest as I closed my eyes to listen to its song. The sunlight danced in patterns across my eyelids, reminding me of the times I laid in the daisy field under the sun. I waited for the bird to cease its singing before I decided to go back inside. Mrs Felton's words echoed in my mind as I finally left the gardens to return to my duty.

'A man will never leave where his heart lays – even in death.'

~

It had been almost a month since I last received a letter from Ross. Despite writing back to him immediately, the days had passed with letters from only my parents and Mrs Felton. Every day a quiver filled my stomach as I helped the men with their injuries, questioning what could have happened to Ross. I hadn't dared to read the newspapers for fear his name might be mentioned in the pages upon pages of lists for the missing as well as the dead. The longer the war went on, the longer the lists became in the papers. Nothing could possibly have prepared me to read his name in the paper amongst the hundreds of other men.

Before Stephen was discharged, he tried to encourage me to find out about Ross. But I still couldn't. Soon, the quiver in my stomach turned to loss of appetite. Sally and Harriet always exchanged worried glances at each other every mealtime over me. I would push my food around the plate and take small bites – enough to fill me for the shift until I let the abyss of sleep take over my body. Visiting hours didn't cheer me up or bring a smile to my face anymore as they once had. The only thing that would change me was hearing back from Ross, or to know that he wasn't missing or killed.

On my nightshift, I spotted a newspaper sitting on the nurses' desk from one of the visitors who had travelled from London that afternoon. My hand hovered over it for a few seconds before I pulled it back to my side. The orange glow of the lamp on the nurses' desk created the only illumination in the ward. If I started crying at the sight of Ross' name on one of the lists, no one would notice due to the darkness. As I reached for it one last time, a tap landed on my shoulder, jerking my hand away. I spun around as Harriet stood there. Her eyes cast to the newspaper and back to me, sensing what I had almost done.

"Doctor Henry is waiting outside the ward. He wants to speak to you before he signs off for the night," she informed me. I furrowed my brow but thanked her and left to see Michael standing outside the doors against the wall. He had already changed out of his doctor's jacket, ready to return to his own boarding house.

Without saying anything, Michael beckoned me to follow him to the gardens. My stomach churned as I tried to think of every possible reason for Michael to need to speak to me. There remained only one logical conclusion in my mind: Ross and what had truly happened to him. The blood drained from my face, creating a coldness over my body. I shivered as my throat dried in an instant. No matter how many breaths I took, the air escaped my lips in shaky and raspy gasps.

"I'm sorry that you haven't heard from Ross," Michael started as we sat down on the bench closest to the doors. "I've looked through all the recent papers and his name isn't listed. I know you two were close and cared greatly about each other."

I frowned and turned to him as my thoughts froze. He hadn't known about my affair with Ross and he still didn't have any clue to my knowledge. So how did he know about Ross writing to me? My body heat started to rise despite seeing my own breath fog in the night air. "How did you know?"

Michael sighed but smiled nervously at me. "Sally and I have been… seeing each other outside of work. That's why I wanted to speak to you. We have a bit of past back home before…"

"Before the world turned against itself," I filled in, casting my eyes to the ground. Tommy's face flashed before my eyes, and I blinked rapidly until he faded into the darkness once more. God had deemed Tommy too pure for such a horrific world. He needed someone to take him away from the war and God stepped in to give him peace.

"Exactly, and I wanted to know if you were fine with Sally and I courting."

While I couldn't deny how many women were attracted to Michael with his handsome features, there was nothing but friendship between us. A small smile pulled at the edges of my mouth as a heat radiated through my chest, realising that Sally had finally confessed her affections to Michael. There could be no denial that his feelings matched hers to an insurmountable amount.

"Of course, I'm fine with it," I reassured him. His shoulders dipped and I watched as his Adam's apple bobbed in his throat. "I pray that we'll maintain our friendship though."

Michael beamed at me, and, in the moonlight, his eyes glistened like starlight. "I thought you would never ask."

He engulfed me in a brief hug before turning the conversation back to Ross. As much as I tried to listen to him, my heartbeat thudded and quickened beneath my breast at the thought of Sally and Michael. They had found someone who they had a genuine connection to. I hadn't felt that with anyone since before the war… since I last allowed my heart to fall for Ross.

But everything had changed in a few months, and I no longer knew how I felt towards Ross. The war had complicated everything; causing more headache and heartache for humanity.

"You're very good with the men," Michael said, sensing my reluctance to speak of Ross. "You have so much patience, kindness, and love for them. They really need nurses like you. I know all about how you've been helping Stephen and… and how you helped Tommy."

I stifled a laugh and turned to him, cocking an eyebrow. "Did Sally tell you?"

He shook his head and a twinkle shone in his eye. "Sister Mary did; she told me on the day that Stephen was discharged. She thinks very highly of you, Belle."

"But I just treat the men like any other person."

We stood up together as the chill of the night caused goosebumps beneath my uniform. I shivered involuntarily and wrapped my arms around myself. Michael walked with me back to the ward, continuing to tell me about Sister Mary's compliments. "Exactly. Most nurses see injuries or conditions; you see humans. We all admire that about you, even Sister Mary. Don't forget that, Belle."

When Michael left the hospital to return to his boarding house, I made my way into the ward. I viewed myself as nothing more than another VAD who desired to aid the men in their darkest hour. But, to the other staff, I had stood out for my humanity and love towards each of the men. In a war, finding someone with humanity in their heart and soul grew more difficult by the day. It was difficult for many people to believe that the good of humanity still existed – especially those who had fought at the front and witnessed the horrors.

As I gazed around at the sleeping men in their beds, a darkness descended over the ward as the reality of the difficult

Christmas ahead hit me. Everyone would struggle this year in such extraordinary circumstances. We had to work through it together to support each other through the difficult times. All we had in the middle of a world war was each other. Somehow, that had to be enough for us.

Chapter Nineteen

My Dearest Belle,

I know you were worried about me, and I thoroughly apologise for it. I was sent to the front and hadn't got a chance to write until now. At night, the sky never seems to turn black. The horizon always glows with the fighting going on far away. Red, orange, and then light blue; as if the fighting ceases to welcome in the new dawn. We're silent when the dawn comes up. For a split second, everything freezes, and the world appears normal, until the firing begins again.

There are so many different people in our regiment – Irish, Scottish, Welsh, and English of course. I tell them of you most of the time. I talk of you so often that they know who I'm writing to, and who I'm dreaming about. When I look up at the sky with the sun shining down on me, they tell me that you're looking up at the sky, wondering if I'm okay. I want you to know that you are not far from my thoughts throughout the whole day.

It was pouring down a few days ago and the trenches are still flooded. I step through a flood and end up sleeping in it too. If you're able to buy socks, please send them to me. I don't have any new socks and holes are forming too quickly. The mud squelches beneath our boots when we slip off the wooden walk-ways. It's a peculiar feeling to some men, but normal to me because of the fields I once worked in.

I cannot wait to hold you in my arms sweet Belle. We'll be in the daisy field again; I'll be spinning you in my arms while you hold your head back and laugh. I keep every memory of you deep in my heart. I revisit them at night because it's the only thing that helps me get to sleep. The memories silence the resounding gunshots and blasts that go through my mind in the darkness.

Forever yours,

Ross.

Dear Ross,

You have no idea how wonderful it is to hear from you. As requested, I hope these socks are suitable for the weather. I sent two pairs to keep you going – hopefully someday I'll learn to knit them for you. As it is a few days to Christmas, consider it a present from me.

Oh, how different Christmas will be this year. I'm on day shift so I get to celebrate Christmas morning with the men which I'm looking forward to. I think of you and how I wish I was with you for the celebrations, but it's impossible. Perhaps next year if the world returns to normal. Please let me know what Christmas is like where you are.

I think of all the memories of us too. They get me through the tough days at the hospital. While I still don't have an answer, the memories of you soften my heart. I miss those times. It made life seem so much easier in the daisy field. I know we will be back there again someday. I promise you that.

We were putting up some Christmas decorations for the men today. We got a small tree to sit on the desk and each man picked a decoration that they liked to put onto it. We all feel like a family right now and I hope the men feel that way too. I just wish that Tommy was here to celebrate. Mrs Felton, Tommy's mother, has sent me a Christmas card, a letter, and a gift. I haven't opened the gift or the letter yet as I'm saving them for Christmas, along with my parents' package. But I sent them something small in return.

I'm not sure Christmas will ever be the same again for us who have experienced the horrors of this war.

I never want to lose you. When I think of you, I don't just remember us. I remember your laugh, your annoying whistling, and how you smile with your eyes as well as your mouth when you're truly happy. You brightened up even my darkest days and, for that, I am truly thankful. In my dreams you come back to me. I touch and kiss you; it feels so real. I don't want to wake up when I dream of you. Waking up means living another day wondering if you'll come back to me.

Please keep safe. Merry Christmas.

Your Belle.

Dearest Belle,

The socks were perfect! I am wearing both pairs on my feet as I write this. Perhaps they won't last as long as you thought, but these are the best Christmas present. You're making sure that nothing happens to my feet while I am out here. I've seen some pretty nasty sights of men's feet in the trenches!

You desire to know what Christmas was like for me, so I shall tell you. The guns fell silent. Honest they did! The Huns and us. Everyone stopped fighting on Christmas Day. We came out of our trenches and stayed with the Huns out on the battlefield. Rumour has it that all over the front this happened, at least on the Western side.

I climbed out of the trench with my friend Robert, and we shared a cigarette with some Germans. Between me and Robert, we didn't speak a word of German, but they spoke broken English. We laughed, made jokes, and spoke about anything other than the war. Believe it or not, they're just like us Belle.

One man told me that he had a wife and child at home, but his wife wasn't his true love. His heart belonged to another woman. I thought of me and you, then. So, I told the Fritz about us. One of them said, if I survive the war, I should come back and claim you as mine. I know you feel indifferent about me right now, but I hope that I can.

After we played a game of football, we decided to sing Silent Night. Us Tommys sang in English while the Fritz sang in German. I stopped singing to listen to the two coming together in a beautiful melody. The birdsong ceased that day too, as though all nature wanted to listen to us. The birds had only ever stopped singing because of the noise of the guns before that moment.

When we got back to our own trenches, we received a tin from Princess Mary. It's brass with a carving of her face on it and two Ms on either side. We opened them to find a packet of tobacco and a carton of cigarettes. We also had a photograph of Princess Mary as well as Christmas cards from the Princess and the King. Some of the men who don't smoke were given acid tablets and a writing case of pencil, paper, and envelopes.

Sadly, the next day we went back to fighting. When there's a war on, a ceasefire only lasts so long. As I'm writing this, a deep sorrow rests in my heart that I cannot give you anything for Christmas. So, I have an alternative. If you look at the top of the spiral on the necklace I gave you, I have engraved an R and an M on it. Hold it close dear Belle.

Merry Christmas to you too.

Ross.

To my Ross,

I'm glad you had a peaceful Christmas. I cannot believe that you spoke to a German, shared a cigarette, and a song with them too. I shall hold that letter close to my heart to give me hope when things get tough. To know that my present was of use to you brings joy to me. Thank you for the surprise of the necklace engraving. I examined the chain and found your initials. You planned so much for me and I'm beyond thankful. It's been the most beautiful Christmas present.

The men here received the same brass boxes. You should have seen their faces! It made them so happy to be thought of by the Princess. We sang songs with the men too before they went to sleep. Silent Night was the final song. After reading your letter, when I look back now, I feel connected to you through that hymn. It makes me feel like we were together during the moment that we shared from different ends of the world.

Mother and Father sent me a small tin of biscuits, chocolate, and some lace embroidered handkerchiefs. Mrs Felton sent me a beautiful small, silver framed photo of Tommy and some biscuits. I hope I can visit her soon when she can travel close to me. I miss seeing Mother and Father too. I wish I could visit you more than anything. I pray we will meet again soon.

Please come back to me.

Belle.

1915

Chapter Twenty

The government and medical services called for more VADs in January, with an anticipation of a call-up coming for field hospitals in France. The call wasn't the result of nurses leaving their duties; in fact, it was quite the opposite. As the months carried on, the war grew exceedingly worse, and more men came home injured from the conflict. Hospitals had opened over England, Scotland, Ireland, and Wales, but they filled up quicker than anyone anticipated. Sister Mary requested to speak with us about the changing circumstances before we began the day shift. The head staff had decided on a change to the hospital guidelines to accommodate the war, according to Harriet who had already been briefed on the nightshift.

Despite Michael's fears, Sally and I had grown closer after he told her that I knew about their courtship. Yet she never once talked about Michael to me; she respected me enough not to. Of course, she mentioned him, and I always sought to ask how things were between them. From every conversation we had about Michael, I knew he treated her like a lady – the way she deserved to have any man treat her. Deep down, I always suspected she pitied me on days when she heard me whispering to Tommy's picture. Her clenched half-smile and wincing every time a whisper reached her ears told me she didn't want me to continue in this cycle forever. She didn't seem to understand that talking to Tommy was the closest thing I had to remembering him. I couldn't visit his grave while my duty remained in Poole. The moments when I watched her narrow eyes fill with tears as I held his photo became a reminder never to tell her about the Blue Tit. She would readily think I'd gone off my rocker to believe in such things.

We lined up outside the ward doors as though in the army itself. Sister Mary appeared from the depth of the ward, swinging the doors behind her. The light breeze ruffled our headdresses and uniforms as she began pacing in front of us. I glanced up from the tiled floor as a tight smile rested on Sister Mary's lips. A shaky breath escaped from my lungs as I knew it wasn't entirely bad news.

"As you know, there has been a call up for more VADs and more hospitals have opened. Here, we have accommodated for more wards which will prove useful for the war effort," she explained, putting her hands behind her back, and marching along the line. "Sadly, some other hospitals might not be able to hold as many men as we do. This will meant that the overflow will be sent to us. The number of officers able to go to specific officers' hospitals will be reduced, especially if they are in a bad way. This means we will be more than likely taking officers throughout the war now. We are one of the closest hospitals to the coast, so officers who are in the overflow or badly wounded will have to come to us."

A flush of warmth prickled at my skin with the prospect of dealing with more men. The war wasn't going to end any time soon and the mere thought of Ross staying in danger caused a dizziness to come over me. I rested one hand against the wall behind me, letting the coldness of the plaster steady me. Sister Mary dismissed us with a flick of her wrist to let us do our usual routine. A mourning silence fell over the VADs as the reality of the devastation of the war hit us. Most of the nurses and VADs had someone out in France, Belgium, or further afield, fighting in the war. Knowing the horrors of the conflict grew worse every day wasn't something our hearts desired to process. As I changed the bandages on one of the men's legs my mind kept drifting to Ross and every possible danger that he could find himself in. I swallowed hard as I squeezed my eyes shut for a second to block out every image which flashed in my imagination.

The hospital hadn't received a huge influx of soldiers in a while, so we expected one any day now. It didn't come as a surprise that the hospital guidelines changed in preparation for it. As much as I loved and cared for every single man in the ward, I swore I would never get as close to any of them as I had with Tommy. The debilitating ache of sorrow in my chest became a constant reminder of the pain of losing him. It had never faded or gone away with time as many people tried to tell me. I couldn't go through that pain all over again.

Once we attended to the wounds, Sally and I made our way to the sluice room to disinfect everything we had used. A forlornness coated Sally's features, creating unsmiling eyes which were not accustomed to her. I glanced over at her as we stacked everything which we had to disinfect. Her expressionless face made my brow instinctively furrow as I tilted my head, watching her.

"Is something the matter?" I finally asked, wishing her to know she could confide in me.

She sighed and placed down the bowl she started to disinfect. "Rumour has it they could call VADs to France very soon. Part of me feels as though it's my duty to go. But half the time I struggle with the injuries here. I constantly remind myself how the men have been treated to some extent before coming here." Sally and I clearly had the same stomach for war wounds. The more I experienced with each new injury, the more accustomed I became to coping with them. She glanced at me and smiled slightly. "I have a feeling that we'll be run off our feet soon enough. Apparently, the war is getting far worse."

"It's what we signed up for," I reminded her as much as myself. "Besides, the men are facing a much worse situation. Helping them with their wounds is the least we can do for them."

Sally wasn't the only one of us considering the move to France when the call-up came. Harriet and I had discussed it when she was on the same shift as us. In truth, I still hadn't decided if France was right for me for the very same reason as Sally. The variety of wounds, puss, and lost limbs never failed to either break my heart or cause nausea to spring to the surface of my worries. If I left for France, I would have to leave behind everything once again. Leaving my village might have been easy enough given the circumstances, but I couldn't possibly imagine leaving every trace of my time with Tommy behind. I decided to wait for the call-up before making the final decision.

We finished disinfecting and placed the items back in the cupboards and drawers where they belonged, before making our way back to the ward. Every week there were new injuries we hadn't seen before. The astonishment hadn't gone unnoticed by everyone when we received the first men who were suffering the after-effects of gas attacks. As if humanity couldn't destroy itself enough already, new weapons of war had been created to use on the battlefield. The men came to us with a usual injury, but they were either permanently or temporarily blinded from the gas too. Sister Mary informed us that their blindness depended on the amount of exposure they had to the gas. Sometimes, men arrived with bad lungs from the gas, but had been made to go on fighting at the front. As a result, they sustained a wound which brought them to us. In the ward, we currently had two men suffering as a direct result of a gas attack; one was permanently blind while the other had bad lungs. I couldn't begin to comprehend the pain each of them were in.

"You check on Jim, I'll check on Ralph," Sally instructed, heading in a different direction to me. I nodded in agreement and approached Jim's bed. The echo of my footsteps caused a smile to form on his face, knowing someone had come to see him. He reached out his hand, desperately searching for me. His grip clenched my hand as I laid my other hand against his cheek.

"Sally or Belle?"

"Unfortunately, it's Belle today, Jim."

He chuckled and let his grip on my hand fall. I tutted when I spotted the mess of his pyjama jacket collar. A small smile greeted my lips as I fixed the collar which stuck up in a somewhat mangled manner.

"Not impressed with the male orderlies dressing me then?" We both knew that the male orderlies let him put his own pyjama jacket on to help him get used to operating without his sight. As I adjusted the front of his jacket, the chest wound Jim sustained in the gas attack poked over the material. Before he arrived with us, the doctors in France had to operate on him to save his life, but there was nothing they could do for his sight.

"Somehow, I don't think it was the handy-work of the orderlies," I said, beaming at him despite myself.

Jim smirked at me and patted my hand in a friendly gesture. "Guilty as charged. Tell me, can you teach me how to fix it myself?"

I reached over, brushing my hands against his neck as I moved the collar back to the position it had been in. Jim lifted his hands to his collar, feeling the material against his shaking hands. "That's you," I encouraged as he folded the collar down around his neck. The second he finished he double-checked his handiwork before beaming at me with a puffed chest. "Now every time you do your buttons, check your collar to see if it needs fixed."

Every day since Jim arrived, he wanted me to describe something in the hospital to him. Yesterday he asked me to tell him every detail of the ward. He pointed out where he thought everything was and, much to my surprise, my descriptions had been enough for him to know. Today, he requested to know about the gardens of the hospital after Sally took him out there yesterday during visiting hours. He loved the sounds of the garden – the birdsong, crunching grass, flies buzzing around, and the chatter of the men – but now he wanted the descriptions to go along with them. As I sat on the edge of his bed, telling him every detail of the gardens, from the flowers and their colours to the birds in the trees, I spotted Sally running over to me. Her face grew red as she stopped beside Jim's bed. Her chest heaved as she tried to catch her breath before speaking to me.

"I… I've been called to go and help bring the influx to the hospital today. I need to leave immediately. Can you check on the men that I normally would?" Sally finally breathed out, resting her hands on her hips.

"Of course. Go on now and I'll see to them when I finish with Jim."

Sally ran out, leaving the doors swinging behind her, as I sat back down to spend more time with Jim before checking on Sally's men. I walked around the ward and spoke to the men to see if everything was alright with them. Out of the corner of my eye, I spotted one of the soldiers with their hand raised. I sprinted over to him as he crouched over in pain, clenching his stomach with his free hand. Before I could ask what was wrong, he vomited blood down his chin, staining his striped pyjama jacket. I yelled to the nearest nurse to fetch a sick pan, but she had already started to make her way to the door, evidently witnessing what had just happened.

"Someone get Doctor Henry," I shouted as the man groaned in pain. Another nurse left the ward to try to find him. The man retched as I tried to take off his jacket. The flow of blood dripped down me and, for once, it didn't affect me with the usual nausea. "You'll be okay," I reassured him, rubbing his back gently.

The first nurse ran into the ward with the sick pan outstretched for me to grab. I handed it to the soldier who immediately vomited into it before Michael appeared. His ice blue eyes bulged as the colour drained from his face when he witnessed the mess of the soldier.

"He didn't have internal injuries," Michael said to us as much as to himself. His eyes darted all over the man before landing on me. "Has he been eating?"

"He didn't eat breakfast; said he was feeling sick," the nurse who fetched Michael informed him.

Michael waited only a few seconds before nodding to confirm that he knew the problem. "He has a stomach ulcer. But it must be bleeding, causing him to vomit blood. They're usually the result of stress, which is hardly surprising given what this poor chap has faced. I may have to operate on the blood vessel if he continues to vomit. In the meantime, give him a blood transfusion and see how he is in an hour." The soldier stopped throwing up and lolled his head into the pillow with heavy eyelids decorating his face. He clutched the pan to his chest as he struggled to keep himself awake. "Anymore vomiting, call me immediately."

Michael walked off with a weary glance back at the soldier before leaving the ward again. I took the pan off the man to dispose of the vomit and disinfect it for reuse. As much as we cared about the health of the men, this added more worry and stress to the staff. On the day where plenty of emergency surgeries would likely have to take place from the influx, we didn't know how we would cope with an extra surgery. Despite every worry we might have had, we knew we would do everything to save every single man's life. I grabbed him a new pyjama jacket after disinfecting the pan and made my way back to the ward. The clean pan rested underneath my arm as I pushed open the doors.

A nurse had set up the blood transfusion for the man who laid limply in the bed. His face paled almost the colour of the gleaming white pillows beneath his head. I walked over to him, and his eyes lifted heavily to meet mine. He gave me an exhausted, weary smile as I set the pan beside him on the bed. A needle attached to tubing ran from the vein in the crease of his elbow to the bottle of blood which rested on a table by his bed.

"Sorry if I gave you a fright nurse," he apologised in a raspy and groggy voice.

I smiled and laid the new pyjama jacket over his legs on the bed. "Nothing to apologise for. You need to try to relax though; I'm sure you don't want more surgery." The man had come in with a piece of shrapnel needing removed from his leg in an emergency surgery. Trying to convince him to let us work on him was the hardest part of getting him into recovery mode.

I reached for his chart to jot down what Michael had said about the ulcer. The nurse had already made notes on the blood transfusion, including how much had been given from the bottle.

I spotted his name at the top of the chart before I placed it back at the bottom of the bed – Samuel. He chuckled as I set the chart back and I glanced at him with an arched eyebrow.

"What's so funny?"

"You telling me not to get stressed, Nurse. That's easier said than done when you see the world falling apart before your eyes. Knowing you played a small part of its descent into utter chaos tends to haunt you."

I sat on the edge of his bed, folding his pyjama jacket neatly for him. "Are you telling me that you feel guilty for joining the war?"

Samuel smirked, causing his deep brown eyes to twinkle in the sunlight which streamed through the window beside him. "If a man tells you that what he's seen out there hasn't changed him or made him question his own humanity, as well as others, then, My Dear, I question if they have a soul at all."

He didn't answer my question; at least, not directly. He wouldn't disrespect his country to say that he felt guilty for fighting for it. Loyalty to the others in their regiment and the country they fought for mattered the most to the men. Every single soldier in the wards around Great Britain and in the battlefields had volunteered to fight, many under a romanticised image of war. The romance and the disillusioned fantasies soon got kicked out of them in the most brutal way the moment they reached the trenches at the front. Samuel's words were right; every man had been changed by this war. But to what extent would Ross and I change because of everything we had gone through?

Chapter Twenty-One

"Someone get a doctor immediately!"

"I need a sick pan over here!"

All around me shouts from nurses and soldiers created an unbearable raucous in the whole hospital. This was, without a shadow of a doubt, the worst influx of patients we had experienced yet. I didn't know where to look or who to run to first. When Sally's voice reached my ears in a yell, I ran straight to her. Everyone seemed all over the place; my own mind was in a whirlwind to comprehend what needed done. I stared at the man lying on the bed in the corridor. His legs shook, eyes darting everywhere possible except the corridor itself, and his shoulders kept twitching mindlessly. *Shell-shock.*

"What's happening to him?" Sally asked, her voice shaking and high pitched. She tried to comfort the man, rubbing his arm and gripping his hand. "He won't speak, Belle."

I placed the blanket over him and stroked his face gently, trying to calm him down too. "Shell-shock – it's a severe case of it. There isn't much you can do right now except try to calm him and get him out of the uniform." We had received one case of shell-shock where the man became terrified of his own uniform.

Only by getting rid of it did we manage to calm him to a controllable level for himself.

Before either of us could say anything else, Michael shouted for me down the corridor. I patted Sally's shoulder and sprinted over to him at the sound of my name coming from his lips a second time. A man laid with a piece of shrapnel sticking out of his leg. Michael asked me to pull the screens over him to give the man some privacy. He briefed me on the injury; shrapnel trapped in the leg to an unknown degree. It needed removed before it caused infection, but if it wasn't removed properly, he could bleed to death. I glanced from the wound to the man's semi-conscious face. His eyes rolled in his head as his eyelids fluttered with heaviness. When Michael finished speaking, I froze and looked at him with little colour in my face.

"You want me to help you perform the surgery?" I questioned. My eyebrows knitted together as I shook my head. My heart thudded against my chest and a lump formed in my throat, sending the blood rushing to my ears.

Michael sighed, taking my hands in his to stop me backing away. "Emergency surgery is the only way to help this man. If I take out the shrapnel, it will more than likely rupture a blood vessel. By the time I take him to theatre he'll be dead. I need you, Belle. We need to save this officer's life."

Until that moment I hadn't laid eyes on an officer before. In the blur of everything I couldn't even focus on what he looked like. I blinked several times, trying to make myself come back to the reality of a life at stake. Michael asked again as he placed one of his hands on my shoulder. I glanced up at him and nodded in agreement, knowing I had already dealt with blood down me once today. Michael ran through the details with me, wanting me to pressure the wound to make sure the surgery would save the man rather than causing him to bleed out more. We readied ourselves to have to perform emergency blood transfusion in case the removal resulted in too much blood loss.

Michael gave me a nod before pulling out the shrapnel. Blood splattered over my hands and uniform as I pressured the wound. I pushed harder against the skin to stop the blood flow. A groan erupted from the officer's throat, and I glanced at him as his eyes shot open. His green orbs stared right into mine, before he fell unconscious against the pillow. Most of his blood had ended up on Michael and me; in our hair, over our faces, and down our uniforms. Michael stemmed the bleeding and stitched the wound but ordered me to put in a small amount of blood as the officer's face grew paler by the second. I fetched the correct amount needed and attached the needle to the bottle, before placing it gently into his vein. Michael's eyes met mine and he gave me an approving smile. I wasn't sure if it was for holding down the contents of my stomach or for being such a good help to him. Nevertheless, I returned the smile as we left the officer behind the screens to deal with the chaos of the rest of the hospital.

Just over three hours later, everything began to calm down in the hospital. We returned to our ward to allow some of the men to discharge before moving in some from the corridor. Sister Mary demanded that the officer became the first one moved into the ward. Once everyone was discharged or moved, she came in to see us in our ward. She glanced at the blood still down my uniform from Samuel's stomach ulcer and the officer's surgery.

"Wash that blood off you then return here," she instructed. She glanced around the ward as she spoke, as though checking everything was completed how she desired it. "We'll deal with the visitors and the soldiers in Ward One. In the morning, you'll be back in here and making visits to Ward One to help the soldiers you normally assist."

I made my way to the bathroom and washed the blood from everywhere possible, watching as the water in the sink swirled in a red spiral. The cold water sent shock waves through my body as I splashed it over my face to remove the blood from every aspect of my skin. As I dried off my face on a towel, I looked in the mirror, not even recognising myself. My blonde hair had dulled to a faded gold and my eyes no longer held their bold, deep brown which shone with caramel streaks in the sunlight. I had become a shell of the person I once was before this war. Every part of me had drained of life. Looking at my lifeless face in the mirror, I finally understood why the men were so changed by this war. A tear rolled a warm streak down my cheek as I swallowed hard. Tomorrow, we had even more patients coming in from the Western Front. I didn't know how much longer I could take the devastation man had inflicted on each other.

~

The shrill of the alarm clock did nothing to rouse me out of bed. My heart burdened the sorrow of losing two soldiers from their injuries before the end of my shift yesterday. While I hadn't dealt directly with them, their passing still weighed heavily on my conscience. I rolled over in bed and glanced across to see Sally lying in her bed, staring up at the ceiling. Her expressionless face had returned, and my throat clenched just watching her. I needed to be strong for everyone; Sally, Tommy, Michael, my parents… even for Ross too.

"Come on," I encouraged, forcing a smile onto my face as I flung back the blanket. Sally's gaze shot to me with the whooshing of the blanket sending a breeze towards her. "We must get going; these men need us."

Eventually, I managed to get Sally out of bed to head to the hospital. We washed ourselves, allowing the cold water to try to wake us up and remind us of our duties. As we put our uniforms on, neither of us spoke much, except asking each other if we were okay. Losing so many men in an influx always affected the nurses and VADs. We wanted to help every single man who came to us and save their lives. Losing one made me feel like a failure despite the many men I had managed to save.

Sally and I made our way to the hospital with the other VADs. No one spoke as though breaking the silence would bring us more bad luck than we seemed to already possess. The corridors created an eery silence which only broke with the clicking of heels and thumping of shoes against the tiles. The nightshift started to pour out of the wards and Harriet's sullen face greeted ours as we approached the ward.

"How many?" I dared to ask, knowing immediately what the issue was.

Harriet sighed and swallowed hard; the muscles in her throat fighting against the action. "Another two overnight."

Sister Mary hadn't informed me about the officer since I left the shift last night. By that stage, he had stabilised, but hearing Harriet's words sent a shiver down my spine. The unconscious body of the officer, lying under the sheet with nurses constantly checking on him, flooded my mind. "The officer, is he alright?"

For the first time since the influx, Harriet's mouth twitched as a small smile started to come through. My stomach fluttered as I dared to expect a hopeful answer from her. She nodded, releasing my burdens in one swift movement. "He's doing really well. He woke up during the night and asked where he was. But he's awake now, waiting on his breakfast and to see Doctor Henry."

I let out a shaky breath and Harriet squeezed my hands before leaving for the boarding house. Sally tried to smile, but her features contorted in a forced gesture. Her face paled as she stumbled when she walked. It would be impossible for her to get a half day off with the increased workload. Before we walked through the doors of the ward, I caught her arm.

"Perhaps you should tell Sister Mary that you're not feeling well. You don't look good at all," I offered her.

She cast her eyes to the floor and sighed. "She won't let me off with the work we have to do."

I shook my head, trying to remain positive for her sake. I took her head in my hands, making her look at me. "Go and try to speak to her while I get the breakfasts on the trolley for us."

With a reluctant nod, she entered the ward, and the sunlight engulfed her before the doors swung shut. By the time I brought the trolley with the breakfast dishes to the ward, Sally had finished speaking with Sister Mary. A tight smile formed across her lips, and she nodded at me, letting me know her requested had been granted. While I was glad for her, I couldn't help my insides quivering at the thought of Sally's workload being assigned to the rest of us. I pushed my worries to the back of my mind as another VAD helped me to pass out the breakfast to the men. Every so often, my eyes drifted to the bed in the corner where the officer laid awake. I reached for the next breakfast dish and made my way over to him. As with all the other men, he sat up in his bed, and I placed the tray on the bedtable. His inquisitive eyes studied me, and, out of instinct, I froze for a split second, unable to tear my gaze from his.

"You… you saved me," he stated before I could walk away from him.

I smiled slightly at his remembrance. "Yes, I did, along with Doctor Henry. How are you feeling today?"

He shrugged and stuck the spoon in the porridge. The metal handle glinted in the sunlight but stood upright in the mixture. The officer returned his gaze to me. "Helpless."

"I understand that, but you need to take it easy so you can recover quickly." I glanced over as Sister Mary walked into the ward, examining what each of us were doing. I bid the officer goodbye before leaving him to serve the rest of the soldiers their breakfasts. The last thing I needed was Sister Mary breathing fire down my neck for speaking too long with one of the men, even if he was an officer.

Once breakfast had been served and eaten, I gathered the dishes and returned the trolley back to the kitchens. Michael and Sister Mary already started their rounds when I returned with the new trolley piled high with bandages, disinfectant, and bowls. The second the wheels clattered over the tiles in the ward, Sister Mary walked over to me.

"Nurse Wilson, you're needed," she stated. My stomach twisted as I thought through every duty I had completed. Had I done something wrong? Or had I forgotten to complete a duty she needed me to?

"What happened?" I asked as another VAD came over to help with the wounds.

"Officer Blackwell won't have another nurse or VAD doing his wounds. He's requested to be treated by Doctor Henry or the nurse who aided him last night. Doctor Henry sent me to get you." I nodded and fetched everything from the trolley I would need. When the other VAD left to start their duties, Sister Mary leant into me. "We must try to accommodate Officer Blackwell as best as we can. They can't fit him into the Officers' Hospital yet, so he's staying with us for the foreseeable future."

Sister Mary walked over to Officer Blackwell's bed, carrying some of the equipment I needed to attend to his wound. She pulled the screens over to give us privacy before leaving me alone with him. Until then, I had no idea of his name or even the extent of his injuries. I reached for the notes and read how Michael wanted the wound disinfected on his leg and rebandaged to stop his pyjama bottoms catching on the stitches.

"Doctor Henry got me ready for you to clean the wound," he told me, snapping my attention back to him. I set the notes back on the end of the bed and peeled the blanket away. Michael had taken the officer's pyjama bottoms off and placed them over the top of his legs to cover his modesty.

The wound had happened on his right thigh and, as I looked down at it, I couldn't begin to imagine the pain he had been in. The skin around the wound had coloured red raw and a mere glance at it told me how sensitive the skin was. Crusts of blood decorated his thigh from where the blood poured out yesterday during the surgery. The officer's eyes bulging at me, staring right into my soul, as Michael pulled out the shrapnel flashed through my mind. I blinked it away and shook my head slightly to rid myself of the image.

"It looks sore," I finally mumbled, grabbing the flannel out of the bowl of water to wash his thigh.

Officer Blackwell chuckled. "It's not comfortable, let's put it that way."

I began to clean his thigh and around the wound, trying my best not to hurt him. He grunted every time the flannel brushed the raw skin around the stitches. I winced with every grunt which erupted from his throat. I'd never get used to hurting the men when I had to attend to them in the mornings. As I dried his thigh, he talked to me about a dream he had while he was unconscious.

"It was utterly beautiful, Nurse. I flew through the air, almost like I was one of the birds. I've never dreamt of anything like it before," he began, talking animatedly with his hands.

My thoughts drifted to Tommy and what Mrs Felton said about him desiring to become a bird when he passed. A small smile greeted my lips as I found myself talking back to Officer Blackwell. "What type of bird were you?"

"A Blue Tit."

Everything froze as my gaze immediately shot to him. He beamed at me, unknowing of what that bird meant to me. As I looked into his eyes, I couldn't help but smile back. The colours and vibrancy of his orbs captured my fascination. The sunlight streaming in through the window illuminated the halo of golden brown around his pupil which seemed to burst like nebula into the green. I'd never seen such beautiful orbs before; a unique and rare occasion where I had left myself speechless by something so simple. I couldn't help but stare at them. If I ever wanted to question if he minded my rudeness, I knew I couldn't when he never once tore his gaze from me.

"That's my favourite bird," I managed to finally say, still mesmerised by his eyes.

"Mine too. Mind you, I haven't exactly seen nor heard them in ages."

He blinked, causing me to dart my gaze away from him. A blush crept upon my cheeks in a red flush as I straightened myself and grabbed the disinfectant. "The garden here has one. It always sings in the trees."

He didn't say anything else as I placed a flannel covered in disinfectant on top of his wound. He winced, digging his teeth into his lip, as his hands gripped the bedsheet. The veins on the back of his hands started to pop to the surface as he squeezed the material between his fingers. I removed the flannel and watched as a bead of sweat ran down his forehead, travelling over his temple. I lifted the clean towel, wiping the sweat from his face, as his eyes fluttered open. Instinctively, I brushed his short black curls off his forehead which had stuck with the perspiration.

"Thank you, Nurse."

I smiled at him, not saying anything more, before wrapping a bandage securely around his thigh. He remained silent as his heavy breath tried to slow after the shock of the disinfectant. I secured the bandage in place and helped him into his pyjama bottoms again, before pulling the blanket over him. He flopped back into the pillow as I tidied everything I had used.

"There you go Officer Blackwell. You're all ready to go for the day," I told him, pulling back the screens.

"Call me Edward," he insisted as I made my way to the other side of the bed to move the rest. When I picked up my belongings to go, Edward spoke again. "What's your name? They call you Nurse Wilson."

I stifled a laugh and looked at him through my eyelashes. "Yes, that's right."

A grin pulled at the corners of his lips. "What is your Christian name Nurse Wilson?"

"Belle."

"Belle," he repeated, with a warmth radiating from his lips. A distinct glow glistened from his green orbs as the red flush appeared on my cheeks once more. "You have a beautiful name, Belle. Quite unforgettable."

Chapter Twenty-Two

The new influx didn't present us with much hope for the war settling down. While there were less patients than yesterday to try to fit into the beds in the corridors, they were just as badly injured. Everyone ran around the hospital, calling for extra help, more blankets, or to prepare for emergency surgery. With only Sally unavailable to help, we thought it would have been settled enough. We were sadly mistaken. After aiding only three patients, the front of my uniform had stained crimson with splatters of blood. The men arrived to us with their uniforms caked in chalk, mud and blood, causing the material to stick to their wounds by the time they got to the coast of England. We couldn't peel off the uniform as it would tear off a piece of their skin, giving them more pain than necessary. Most of the time, we had to cut the uniform off before we could even try to attend to the wound.

The nurses only asked Officer Blackwell if he wanted the screens over the bed to shield him from the chaos of the new influx. He plain bluntly refused, stating that he wanted to be treated as equal to his men. His lip curled in disgust as he spoke to them, as though he couldn't believe they had the audacity to ask him such a thing. Voices yelling caused me to flip my head around to try to help more people with the new patients.

"Nurse!"

"Help is needed over here!"

"Nurse Wilson!" Out of the corner of my eye, I caught Sister Mary calling for me. I ran over to her as she tried to calm down a patient who wouldn't stop shaking his head. His eyes rolled everywhere in his head, completely unseeing us, as though he were in another world. A world where the war still existed. Yet another case of shell-shock and no one knew how to handle it well. Sister Mary's posture slackened when I started to try to help.

"Nurse Wilson," she breathed out. "I think we may have to send him to a specialised hospital."

I frowned as I held the man's hand. "Why?"

"We cannot deal with this," she stated, gesturing towards the man shaking on the bed. "None of our nurses or VADs can manage this. This is the second one we've had in two days."

My breathing grew more rapid as it blew from my flared nostrils and my skin prickled with the rising heat in my body. "With all due respect Sister Mary, shell-shock, as you well know, is an injury. They cannot help it and we most certainly cannot reject them. We have a duty. They are human and we should damn well be treating them as such." My voice raised with every word I spoke to her. "This man is in our care, and we will look after him. If we cannot accept a shell-shocked man, then we cannot support the war effort. These men have fought on the front and witnessed things that we wouldn't even see in our wildest nightmares! What we see through injuries is only a small fraction of the horrors of this war. These men cannot cope or process what they have seen. Either help this man or let me help him!"

The whole ward seemed to fall silent as every pair of eyes bore into Sister Mary and me. They waited, holding their breath, to see what would happen between us; who would win to help this man or let him go elsewhere. Never in my life had I shouted at anyone in that way, let alone a figure of authority. The adrenaline caused my body to shake as the blood rushed in my ears, but I refused to give in to her. I watched as the muscles in Sister Mary's throat contracted as she swallowed. With a resigned nod, she stepped away from the man, placing all the medical instruments on the bed table, along with the man's pyjamas. She stood there for a split second before leaving me to it.

My chest clenched in a painful manner as the poor man's eyes darted everywhere possible on the ceiling. He still thought he was on the battlefield. This was truly the worst shell-shock case we had received since the start of the war. Despite the man's wound, I managed to start cutting his uniform off him and set it on the floor in a pile. His jacket had come off without a problem, but the trousers stuck to his skin by the blood of his wound. As carefully as I could muster, I cut his trousers off before scrubbing him down with a damp flannel. The wounds on his arm and leg needed stitched before they bled much more, risking becoming infected.

While I washed the dirt, blood, and sweat from him, a warm tear rolled down my cheek, prickling my skin. Since I started in the hospital, I had based my whole worth on how well I could or couldn't help the men. As I stared at the man's shaking limbs, a sense of failure clouded my mind. How did I help him with such a severe case? I couldn't give up on the man, despite his condition. I wouldn't want anyone to lose hope in me if I was in their situation. Tears continued to drip down my face and blur my vision as I questioned how I could possibly stitch his wounds and pull out pieces of shrapnel when he shook so badly.

"Let me help you with that," someone said. I blinked my tears away to see who spoke to me. I glanced up as Michael stood there with the needle and thread already in his hands. I nodded as silent sobs gasped from my lips.

Michael instructed me on how to aid him with the stitching and I swallowed back my sobs enough to focus. I held his leg and arm as still as possible while Michael removed shrapnel before stitching his wounds. I wiped the blood which spilled over from his leg and tidied all the equipment. When he finished the stitching, he stood by the bed as his eyes bore into me. He wanted me to make eye contact with him to see if I was alright. But I never allowed my gaze to meet his. How could I be alright when I failed to help the man? Eventually, Michael walked away, leaving me to finish getting the man ready for bed.

I took a deep breath and as I breathed out shakily, I wiped my stray tears away with the back of my hand. I willed myself to regain composure for the sake of my duty. I could always cry about it later at the boarding house, but not here in front of the men. I reached over and grabbed the man's pyjamas before pulling the screens around the bed. When I dressed him in his pyjamas, his shaking eased ever so slightly.

Sister Mary came over as I pushed the screens back into their place. She watched as the man didn't shake just as violently, despite the tremors still ever present. I ignored her as I pulled the blanket over his body, tucking him into the bed. Out of the corner of my eye, I watched as Sister Mary glanced from me to the soldier, and back again.

"Well done," she mumbled. I still didn't look at her; instead, busying myself with pushing the man's hair out of his eyes. "Perhaps you should take the rest of the day off. It's visiting time soon anyway."

Despite every exhausted bone in my body and the heaviness of my eyelids, I refused to take the offer. Sister Mary smiled slightly at my refusal, admiring my persistence. But it wasn't my love of nursing which caused such persistence to resonate from me. It was the love of the men under my care. Since coming here and leaving my parents at home, the men had become a family of sorts to me. No one ever gave up on their family, even when life got difficult. I wouldn't give up on any of them or take the easy route to avoid helping them.

I spent the rest of my day between the two wards, fighting back every yawn which desired to escape from my mouth. During visiting hours, I made my way to the other ward to see Jim. Once he gripped my hand, a grin formed over his lips as he realised it was me. He told me how much he missed me describing the gardens to him and, at his request, I recited what the gardens looked like. As I spoke, he mouthed along, remembering it word for word as though it were a tale told to a child to get them over to sleep. Every so often he would point or gesture in front of him, showing me where, in his mind, everything was placed. My eyebrows shot up every time he managed to accurately point to where things should be. At the end of my visit, Jim made a request he hadn't ever spoken of before.

"Can I feel your face?"

My eyebrows knitted together as I frowned. "Whatever for?"

He smiled at me, stifling a laugh. "To see what you look like." I reached for his hand and leant forward, bringing his fingertips to my face. Jim's fingers traced every part of my features; the point of my nose, the plump lips and cupid's bow, even my ears. I pulled out a strand of my blonde hair, allowing him to feel the curl which sprung back into place when he let go of it,

"Curly hair, just like my daughter's," he reminisced as tears brimmed his eyes. He pulled his hands away from my face and wiped the tears which overflowed. He knew he would never see his daughter again and that realisation clenched my heart until I held Jim as we sobbed together.

By the end of my shift, my eyelids threatened to shut with the heaviness attached to them. My whole body slumped as I tried to make it to the ward with the shell-shocked man I helped earlier in the influx. As I laid my hand on the doors, Sister Mary flung it open and asked if she could accompany me to see him. I shrugged, not making much comment on her lack of interest earlier, but I wouldn't overstep my position twice in one day. The man laid in bed, staring up at the ceiling, but his body shook very little now. Yet the blanket still quivered with every shake he made.

"The shaking starts violently if you touch him or move him," Sister Mary informed me. She tucked him in when his hand slipped out of the blanket, causing him to grow agitated. "You did a good job with him, Nurse Wilson. Also, the soldier with the stomach ulcer, Samuel, is healing well." When I didn't make a comment, she sighed and turned away. "Bid goodnight to Officer Blackwell and remember that you'll be dressing his wounds tomorrow."

She came with me as I made my way over to Officer Blackwell to say goodnight to him. She watched me as I checked his bandage and then left as he began chatting to me about tomorrow. When I finally reached the boarding house, I grabbed two letters which awaited me, and washed myself in the bathrooms. Sally already sat on her bed writing letters in her white nightdress. At the creak of the floorboard by my bed, she never lifted her head as she mindlessly scribbled on paper to her brother. I smiled at her as I settled down in my bed to read my own letters. The handwriting on the envelope sparked an adrenaline rush through my veins. I would recognise Ross' handwriting amongst a thousand different letters.

My Dearest Belle,
I'm glad Christmas was peaceful and everyone there is keeping their spirits up. The fighting continues yet all I can think of is how much I desire to have you in my arms again. At nights when I'm lonely I dream of you, and I hope that you're dreaming of me too. I miss you and, if it's the last thing you know, I truly do regret what I did to you, from the bottom of my heart. I pray one day you'll forgive me for it.

Do you think we'll ever see the daisy field again? I fear that it will always remain a distant hope and dream we once had – a fantasy we lived out. That only makes me regret what I did even more. My sweet Belle, you are an angel in every sense of the word. My heart yearns to kiss you and hold you just once more.

The war continues and we fear it will not end anytime soon. Please keep safe and hopeful. The men every night tell stories of waking up and the whole war being over in a flash. I cannot join in for I don't believe in fairy tales anymore.

I long to hear from you.
Love always,
Ross.

I smiled, folding the letter, and clutching it to my chest for a brief moment. If I shut my eyes tight enough, I could picture Ross holding me as though he were there in the room with me. But it was a mere fantasy – a life once lived as Ross reminded me. I opened my eyes and placed it to the side, knowing I needed to reply to him as soon as possible. But, before I did, I lifted my other letter and my brow crinkled. The envelope had no address on it, only my name, in handwriting I didn't recognise. I stared at it, trying to work out who it could be from. When I could wait no longer, my fingers tore the envelope in an impatient ripping.

Dear Nurse Belle Wilson,
If things have gone as planned, then you will have received this letter from Doctor Henry. I watched you stand up to the Ward Sister over the shell-shocked soldier. I haven't seen a VAD nor a nurse fight so powerfully against their superior and win the argument. I see why the men dote on you. You fight for what is right for them. Many admire you for that; I am one of those many admirers.

Yet, as you helped the poor chap, I noticed you crying. I wish I could have aided you, but I can't leave my bed yet. From watching you, I presume you have seen many awful things and it is all getting a bit much for you. I don't know what you've been through, but I can be a friendly ear to listen. Do not struggle alone. Most importantly never doubt the good you're doing for the men. Never doubt yourself, Belle.

I'm sure you know that the shell-shocked men will eventually have to be transferred to a specialist hospital. But take heart, you've done amazing things for them, and I hope you know that they do appreciate that.

Stay courageous,
Edward Blackwell.

I dropped the letter to the bed and folded my arms over my stomach. A gasp escaped my lips as I stared at the page resting on the blanket below me. I didn't want anyone seeing me cry in the ward, knowing they would scold me for such actions. Yet, Edward Blackwell didn't criticise me for struggling to cope. He encouraged me and praised me for continuing my duty. Edward reassured me that I wasn't failing at my job like I had presumed I had been because of the stress. I hadn't failed the men in Edward's eyes. In that moment, after the heart wrenching day I had, that was what I needed the most.

Chapter Twenty-Three

"Why do you have a smile on your face?" Sally questioned as we made our way to the hospital for our last day shift for a while.

I glanced at her as she stared at me with an eyebrow raised. I shrugged, trying to fight the smile pulling at my lips. "I got a letter from Ross."

She cocked her head, knowing full well that I wasn't telling her the truth. But I couldn't tell her about Edward's letter; she would presume something was going on between us when there wasn't. His words had helped me to rouse myself out of bed and look forward to my shift. My fingers tingled in anticipation for starting my shift as soon as possible. Much to my relief, Sally didn't mention my changed demeanour again as we entered the hospital.

After breakfast, Sally and I began to change the bandages on the men in the ward. I watched as an unmistakable glow flooded her face when she started to help the men. It was a far cry from how much she struggled to cope yesterday. Still, neither of us dared to mention France as we hadn't made up our minds yet. With a steady hand, I removed the stitches in a soldier's arm, and he winced with each pull of freedom his skin had. I blinked as I tried to focus on the stitches ignoring the green eyes which bore into me from the corner of the ward. No matter how much I desired to fidget or move around, I refused to turn to him. Edward was always the last man I attended to as Sister Mary always made sure no other nurse or VAD would see to him. It came as no surprise that Edward became known as 'Belle's Officer' to everyone in the ward.

Once I changed the water and grabbed a new flannel and towel, I made my way over to Edward's bed. He sat up, greeting me with a smile as I pulled the screens over. Edward gripped my shoulders as I helped to remove his pyjama bottoms to attend to the wound. Edward took the material from me and covered himself for privacy.

"So why the letter?" I asked him as I washed his stitched wound. Since receiving the letter last night, I had desired to know why he sent a letter to me.

A sigh escaped from his lips. "I watched you struggle, and I knew exactly how you felt. During the day you have so many distractions, but at night when you're meant to be sleeping… that's when the thoughts of failure come. At least that's how it is for me."

I rinsed out the flannel and glanced at him with furrowed eyebrows. "Why would you feel like a failure?"

"Look around you," he replied, gesturing with his hands to the ward just beyond the screens. "When you send men into battle, you're told to expect deaths. But I never expected so many deaths and injuries; some of which are life changing. These men are my men. The shell-shocked man, he's one of mine, and I wanted to thank you for looking after him."

"It's my duty to look after the men. It's nothing to thank me for," I reminded him, disinfecting the area. "You do realise you aren't a failure, don't you? You were simply carrying out your duty, just like I am. No one can blame you. You fought alongside your men in battle. You must try to remember that Off… I mean, Edward."

I wrapped his thigh in a new bandage as he chatted to me about his hopes for the future after the war. One thing I had always noticed about the men was how hopeful they were. Looking back, I think that was what kept them going in their darkest hours – the hope to achieve a future they had so desired in a world where a future seemed so unlikely.

"I want a family someday with the woman I marry. She'll be the woman of my dreams," he said whimsically.

I smiled at him as I secured the bandage on him. "So, you have a fiancée then?"

He chuckled and shook his head at me. "Chance would be a fine thing. My father thought it was a sin for a man of thirty-two to not have a woman to share my life with. But that's the thing, I believe in love, and I won't settle for anything less. Do you think I'm an idealist? A romanticist even?"

His eyes endlessly searched mine, hoping for an honest answer, and scanning for any traces of a lie. I stared back at him, still as fascinated by his eyes as the day I first laid mine upon them. "I think you're neither a romanticist nor an idealist. To me, you're a realist. Those who settle for less than love often find themselves unhappy. They seek to find that love, even if it means breaking every rule and reputation."

He nodded along, listening intently to every word I said to him, with a small crease between his eyebrows. I tore my eyes away from his and tidied up the supplies, before helping him into his pyjama bottoms once more. We pulled the material carefully over the wound, taking extra precaution around the stitches which would soon come out.

"Forgive me for being intrusive," Edward started as I moved to pull back the screens. My hand froze in place, and I turned to him. "Do you have a sweetheart or a fiancé?"

I thought of Ross out in France, but the memories of what he did to me and the question over what happened next with us loomed deeply in my mind. "Neither. Perhaps I'm more of a realist like you."

When visiting hours came around, I couldn't have been happier when Sister Mary told me to take a break. Wounds kept needing re-bandaged, lunches needed served, and medication had to be distributed to patients at certain times of the day. Running between two wards had created an aching in my feet and my head. Instead of the half day off, Sister Mary offered me an hour or two to myself, unless Officer Blackwell needed me. My whole body seemed to slump the second I took her offer. After grabbing some pages, envelopes, and a pencil from the nurse's desk, I informed Sister Mary I would be in the gardens in case Edward needed anything. Lately I hadn't had much time to spend in the gardens. My heart longed to hear the Blue Tit's song again, feeling closer to Tommy every time the melody greeted my ears. As I sat down on our bench, the birdsong started in the trees. A warmth filled my chest as my back rested against the wood. The edges of my mouth pulled into a smile as I closed my eyes to listen to the bird singing. I could almost picture Tommy sitting beside me as though he hadn't left this Earth at all. Part of me didn't want to open my eyes, knowing he wouldn't be there to beam at me with his ocean blue orbs. I let out a sigh and reluctantly let my eyelids flutter open against the sun. I reached for a page and began to write a letter back to Edward, seeking to distract my thoughts from Tommy.

Dear Edward,

I wanted to formally thank you for your letter. It helped me a great deal over the last few hours, giving me hope that my work does some good for the men after all.

I also wanted to tell you that you are not a failure either; not to your men nor to your father. I know more than anyone that it is difficult to see that you are not. But just look at all the men around you and those still on the battlefield. They are alive! You must try to be thankful for that. I know you have lost men; we all have. I miss my Tommy every single day that I wake and even when I'm in the slumber of sleep. The world shall not be the same without him, but life goes on. I have kept you alive and I think of that to give me hope on my darkest days. It's what you taught me to do after all.

You are by no means a failure to your father for being unmarried. When you marry for love and are happy, your father will see and understand why you waited. Always remember the happiness you will feel when your true love comes along.

Belle.

I put the letter in an envelope and sealed it after writing Edward's name on the front. As I picked up a page to begin Ross' letter, Sister Mary called me from across the garden. With shaking hands, I placed my writing utensils in the pocket of my apron and walked as fast as possible over to her. My heart thudded in my throat as my mind raced through everything that could possibly happen to Edward.

"Yes Sister?" I asked, hoping she couldn't sense the adrenaline of panic in my voice.

She smiled at me, easing the knot in my stomach. "One soldier would like to show you his progress by taking a stroll around the gardens with you, if that is alright?"

I nodded, despite my eyebrows knitting together, and she beckoned for someone to walk out from the hospital. A nurse appeared with a man on her arm in a dressing gown and slippers. A beaming smile altered my features as Jim walked out with the nurse. He grinned at me as he made his way over to us. I put my elbow out for Jim to take, allowing the nurse and Sister Mary to return inside.

"I want to see if I can guess where everything is," he said, his tone slightly higher than normal. My constant descriptions of the hospital gardens were leading to this moment for him, and I hadn't even realised it. Our feet echoed on the concreate slabs of the garden pathway as we walked around with Jim pointing out every single thing to me. A tingling surge flooded my body and my heart raced beneath my breast as I realised Jim had taken in everything from my descriptions. He could point out everything I had ever described to him in the exact spots they sat in the garden.

When he finished, I took him over to sit on my usual bench. As though sensing my return, the Blue Tit came back to sing its melody to us. I glanced in Jim's direction as his lips formed a smile, tilting his head towards the sun to soak in the atmosphere of the birdsong. He closed his eyes and breathed heavily with the warmth of the sun beating down on him. For the first time, in what I presumed months, he was at peace.

"Is it okay to listen for a while?" Jim whispered, not wanting to disturb the birdsong.

"Of course. Just let me know when you're ready to go back inside," I replied, taking out my writing utensils to respond to Ross' letter.

He gently squeezed my hand, not moving his head from the sunlight. "Thank you."

Dear Ross,

What can I say that will soothe your worries? If I say anything, will you believe it? Only you can answer those questions in your own mind. But I shall do my best to calm you. I feel certain that we shall see the daisy field again. We shall be reunited again before and after the war is over – I can promise you that. I know you cannot say much about what is happening over there. But all I desire to know is that you are not ill nor badly wounded. I think of you often and I just want you back on your farm where you were safe from all danger and harm. But you went to fight to try to return to me again. I cannot tell you that you were a fool for doing so, as I know how much the men that you're fighting with mean to you now. Perhaps the war might be over in a few months. When it is, we shall return to the daisy field once more.

Keep your memories of home close, knowing that you will return when this is over.

Your Belle.

By the time I finished the letter, Jim requested to go back inside the hospital. As we walked back inside, arm in arm, he asked if I could visit him tomorrow to walk outside in the afternoon. Despite Sister Mary assigning me to nightshift tomorrow, I agreed to his request without any hesitation. I wanted to try to help him adjust to his new situation and lifestyle. Taking him for walks was the least I could do and sacrifice for a man who sacrificed so much for our safety. For the rest of the visiting hours, I sat with Jim on the edge of his bed and talked with him until Sister Mary called me to help hand out the dinner to the men. With each smiling soldier I greeted, I realised that Edward was right in his letter. I wasn't a failure because the men seemed somewhat content here and the hospital needed my presence to make that possible for them.

Before I left for the night, I spoke to Edward to see how he was, checking his wound and any signs of a possible temperature on him. A temperature became a sure sign of an infected wound for the men since I arrived at the hospital. On my way out of the ward, I handed Edward the letter. He grinned at me the second he spotted his name on the front of the envelope in my cursive handwriting. Something about his glowing eyes and beaming smile made my chest fill with warmth. A small smile rested on my lips, and I discovered it was quite impossible to remove for the rest of the night.

Chapter Twenty-Four

Despite Sister Mary assigning me to nightshift for the last week, I still attended to Edward's wounds every morning. Once I finished at eight o'clock, Sister Mary called for me to go to Edward immediately before returning to the boarding house. I never complained about the amount of work. Sally and Harriet sat waiting for me to snap, but it would never happen because I needed to see Edward to exchange our letters. When I returned to the ward in the afternoon to take Jim for his walk, I would pop in to visit Edward in the other ward again. Like clockwork, he would always have a new letter waiting for me. Between attending the wards in the afternoon and going on duty at night, I always managed to get some sleep.

I placed Edward's letter in my bedside table and washed myself before taking off my uniform. The warm water relaxed every muscle in my body as it cascaded over my skin. I pulled my hair into a plait after donning my nightdress to crawl into bed. I'd never admit how much my eyelids desired to close when I attended the wards every afternoon. The men's smiling faces kept me going, especially seeing Jim's progress as he neared his time to get discharged by Michael. Sally breathed heavily in the bed beside me as I pulled the blanket over myself. I fell asleep as soon as my head hit the pillow with the resounding echoes of the women snoring in an exhausted slumber.

In the darkness of my dreams, Ross appeared to me out of the blackness. The daisy field came into focus as we stood in the middle of the emerald paradise. Ross took my hand, leading me back to the Mason farm. The sun poured its warmth down on us and I glanced at the back of his neck to see a collar of sweat building below his hairline. In that moment, all I desired to do was reach out and touch his skin. Soon, it would mark a year since I last saw him… or felt his skin against mine in a heat of passion. Ross led me into the haybarn which always remained our sanctuary, despite having to pull out threads of gold from our hair before we left. He closed the door with a snap and grinned at me. The longing which caused my heart to swell beneath my breast escaped my body in a sigh as we laid down on the hay. I gripped his suspenders between my fingers as his lips met mine in a heated embrace. We became one in breath and body with each passionate clash of our lips. This was the moment I had waited for since the train station. I pulled away from his lips, desiring to look into those hazel-green eyes just once more. I never wanted to forget those colours of autumn which had imprinted themselves into my very soul. My breath caught in my throat as Ross' face was no longer in front of me.

Edward smiled back at me as the sun streamed through his curls in rays of beauty. My lips parted as every nerve in my body fired in an adrenaline rush to my heart. Deep inside me, I longed to kiss him and know what it felt like to embrace him in my arms. Without a single hesitation, his lips met mine in a passion I hadn't been accustomed to. My chest fluttered in time with my stomach as he pulled me closer to him until there wasn't a chance for a slither of sunlight to seep through. I pulled away once more as he hovered over my body, staring down into my eyes. In my dreams, his eyes were still as beautiful, as if I had learnt them by memory. My hand reached up to his hair, letting my fingers lace themselves in the curls. The sunlight behind him illuminated the slight grey through his black locks. I watched as my hand travelled from his hair down his face, tracing his high cheekbones; learning his body for the first time. We shared a smile as my fingers started to unbutton his shirt, exposing the beads of sweat on his chest. The single sight of the hairs on his flesh caused a heat to build within me…

I woke with a jolt, flying up to a sitting position in bed. The moonlight swept through the room in a silver-blue illumination. In the silent room, my heavy breathing filled the air as sweat dripped down my temple. My skin grew warm with every passing second and I wiped the beads of sweat away from my forehead with the back of my hand. Every night my dreams had always consisted of Ross, Tommy, or home. No other man ever appeared in my dreams until now. I glanced at the clock ticking on my bedside table, realising I didn't have any time to work out what had caused such a dream of Edward. The nightshift would begin in an hour, and I had to get ready before leaving the hospital.

When we entered the ward, we separated in different directions to get the men ready for bed. With every possible excuse on the tip of my tongue, I avoided attending to Edward until Sister Mary barged into the ward requesting me. I suppressed a blush which threatened to break onto my cheeks in a warm red glow as I approached his bed. Sister Mary's eyes bore into me from the other side of the ward, making sure I attended to Edward without backing out once again. Edward's eyes lifted as my footsteps stopped at the end of his bed. He greeted me with a sleepy smile and my embarrassment seemed to drift away.

"Hello again," he said in a raspy voice. Despite his heavy eyelids willing sleep to come soon, he remained his usual suave self.

"Let's get you ready to settle down." He nodded and let me help him to lie down – adjusting pillows and blankets as needed. I checked that his bandages hadn't shifted from his wound before pulling the blanket over him. He watched everything I did with a precision I hadn't known from anyone. The hairs lifted on my flesh, creating a pattern of goosebumps over the flesh as he continued to stare at me. "What's wrong?"

A grin broke over his face as his eyes sparkled against the black circles under the eyelids. "I've been trying to walk during the days. Of course, I've been using crutches to help me. But I want to go outside when you visit tomorrow afternoon. I was just wondering if… if you'd take me?"

The happiness radiating from Edward was contagious as my own heart thudded against my chest and a beaming smile pulled at the edges of my mouth. "Of course I would! This is utterly fantastic news."

He shuffled in the bed until he was comfortable before looking up at me through his eyelashes. Visions of my dream flooded back, and I swallowed hard, blinking rapidly to remove them from my memory. "There's no one else I would like to share my news with. Goodnight Belle."

"Goodnight Edward."

When Edward had settled, I made my way over to the nurse's desk and sat with Sally as she wrote her letters. She reached over and opened a drawer with a squeak, pulling out blank pages for me to use. I thanked her and took my letters out of my apron pocket. Pencils rolled around the desk, breaking the heavy breathing and snoring of the men. I lifted a pencil and opened the first envelope from Mrs Felton.

Dear Belle,

I hope you're doing well. I have sent a photo of Tommy's grave with this letter and one of his flowers in the garden where his uniform is buried. I know these are not photos you may want to see all the time, but I want you to have them until you're able to visit again.

I think of you and hope that Tommy watches over you. The men that you look after are very lucky. From meeting you, and from Tommy's letters, you always put the men first with love and compassion in your heart. We need more people like you in the world, especially during a time like this.

I pray you're well and that I will hear from you soon.

Mrs Felton.

The small photos fell into the palm of my hand as a numbness came over me. The pain of losing Tommy hit me every now and again. Some days the pain seared my soul deeper than others and, as I stared at the photographs, the force of the sorrow came springing back. I blinked away tears as I took in the familiar sight of the graveyard. Mrs Felton had placed fresh flowers on top of the grave. Their shape had come out blurry in the photo as a breeze must have taken them. Daffodils grew out of the ground where Mrs Felton had buried Tommy's uniform in the other photograph. I ran my thumb across the surface, almost as though to check it was still real. Every day I waited to see Tommy's face when I came into the ward, but his inane grin would never be mine again. I released a shaky breath from my lips and placed the photographs into the pocket of my apron. I gripped the desk, wanting to feel something solid beneath my flesh to take me away from the clenching of my heart. Edward's letter caught my eye, and I unfolded my fingers from the wood to open the envelope. I needed something to distract me from losing Tommy. The person who started the rumour of time healing everything hadn't lost someone so close to them that it felt like their very soul had been torn in half.

Belle,

Here is yet another letter and I do not tire of writing to you. It is one of the simple pleasures I enjoy during this time of war. Our afternoon chats are the part of my day that I look forward to the most because I get to spend time with you. You and your stories keep me sane during this time. I long to hear more of them, even as I write this letter. The stories of riding horses in a daisy field are the stories that stay with me the most. You describe the experience with such love and emotion that I feel like I was there too. Perhaps someday I might see the emerald paradise you speak of with a special glimmer in your eye.

Thank you for helping me in my recovery. Without you I wouldn't be on my way to returning to the front. The only thing that saddens me about my recovery is that I will have to leave you. Forgive me for perhaps sounding foolish, but I don't want to leave you. Even if they paid me to leave everything behind for another life, I wouldn't take anything anyone offered me. I think of all the lives I could have lived, but I wouldn't want any other life where you're not in it. This life led me to you.

I promise we will meet again when I leave the hospital and before I return to the front. You have made my time here so much more bearable and enjoyable. The least I can do is return the favour.

I will see you when I wake up.

Edward.

A smile spread over my lips, altering my face, at the prospect of spending time away from this place with Edward. Heat radiated through my chest as my feet swung against the floor. I glanced once more at the letter and my feet froze in a swift movement. Edward was one of my patients. Nothing else. Hadn't I learnt from Tommy? Losing him had given me enough heartache without adding another one to it. What about Ross? I scolded myself as I folded the letter, placing it on top of Mrs Felton's. The smile fell from my face as I picked up my final letter from home.

The handwriting on the envelope was neither Mother's nor Father's. My head flinched back as I riffled through the people in the village who would possibly send me a letter. As much as I tried to come up with reasonable explanations, none of them made any sense. I stared at the envelope, feeling my chest tighten as I debated backwards and forwards whether to open it or not. Eventually, I tore the paper open, causing Sally's eyes to dart to me before returning to her letter. I scanned the bottom of the letter to find out who it was. The paper fell from my hands, cascading like a feather. My eyes glazed over the handwriting of someone I never expected to contact me from the moment I left the village. It couldn't be… but the evidence sat right in front of me.

Dear Belle,

By the time you get to the bottom of this letter, you will know who is writing to you. So, I shan't waste time explaining it now. I do not expect a reply from you, but I have heard the war is getting worse. Ross is out on the frontline, and he cannot guarantee his own safety. No soldier can. Yet I write to ask you to do all you can to keep him safe if he comes under your care.

I am well aware of what was happening between you and Ross. Do not try to deny it. While neither of you confessed, I knew he had feelings for you. You may blame yourself for him going to war, but I can tell you now that it was not your fault. I was not a loving wife to him. He would have rather taken his chances on a battlefield than spend another day as my husband. Please do not live in guilt because of the actions I caused.

Whether he survives and comes home to me, or whether he survives and comes home to you, please make sure he gets back here safely.

I truly wish you nothing but the best.
Margaret.

Sally's voice became white noise as I tried to process what I had just read. My hands shook as I folded the letter and made my way to the sluice room, desiring some form of fresh air away from the stuffy ward. The whole hospital seemed to enclose around me as the weight of the letter dragged my feet against the tiles. Before I closed the door to the sluice room, Sally put her hand out, forcing her way in. Her eyebrows pinched together as she scanned my eyes for an answer. When I avoided her stare, she took hold of my face and made me look at her.

"Belle, you're white as snow. What's happened?" she asked in the most forceful tone I had ever heard from her lips. Instead of answering her, I reached into the pocket of my apron and produced the letter for her to read. She took it off me with a cautious hand, reading it aloud as I paced the sluice room. Hearing Margaret's words resound in the room made everything more real. When she finished, my pacing feet was the only sound echoing off the walls. "Do you still have contact with Ross?"

"Yes. We write to each other but…" I trailed off wondering if I should admit something that I couldn't even admit to myself. I ran a hand over my headdress, desiring to twirl a curl around my finger. "I'm confused about my feelings towards him. One minute I think of him and the next… I think of someone else."

"Who? Tommy?" Sally questioned, handing me back the letter.

I folded the letter and placed it back in the envelope; a simple task to bide me time in confessing the one secret I swore I wouldn't. Sally's eyes bore into me, waiting for an answer. I sighed and glanced up at her through my eyelashes. "No, not

Tommy." My voice turned to a whisper as I finally spoke the truth. "Edward… Officer Blackwell."

Sally leant against the wall, staring at the ceiling as she attempted to process what I had just admitted. Her silence gave me the time I needed to realise what a mistake I made. Since starting my illicit affair with Ross, my life had filled itself with mistakes, and they seemed to keep getting worse as time continued. Tears blurred my vision, threatening to fall at any given moment. Once I took a deep breath, sobs erupted from my lips. Sally ran over to me and wrapped her arms around my shaking frame.

"Oh Belle. It's going to be okay," she cooed, rubbing my back in small circles.

"How is it?" I cried into her shoulder. "My whole life is a mess of love affairs and men I shouldn't be with. Nuns would turn me away at the doors of the convent if they heard my exploits."

Sally sniggered, and I lifted my head to look at her. Her sheepish smile lightened the weight of my heart. With gentle thumbs, she wiped away my fallen tears leaving damp streaks in their place. "Belle you would never get into a convent because you're the wrong religion." I stifled a laugh and sniffed as I shook my head at her humour. "Harriet told me that one of the VADs on her shift has a sweetheart out at the front while she's been having an affair with one of the male orderlies here." My eyes bulged at the news and Sally nodded her head, as though I never believed her. It didn't entirely surprise me that someone finally overstepped the mark. It had to happen at some point during the war. "Here's what you do: you write back to Margaret and your other letters. Jim is being discharged next week, so your time will be more focused on Edward until he leaves. See how things go and move from there. Trust me, Belle; at least, try to."

I sighed and glanced at the floor, weighing up every option in my mind. I didn't have any alternatives to Sally's suggestion. Time alone with Edward once Jim left wasn't something I revelled in after the dreams I had of him. A warmth began to flood through my body at the mere thought of the dream. I looked back at Sally as she searched my eyes for an answer. For the first time since Ross broke every ounce of trust I had in humanity, I found myself trusting someone all over again.

Chapter Twenty-Five

As Sally had promised, Jim left to go home to his family the following week. I sat with him until they came to bring him back home. His daughter ran to his side, and he wrapped his arms around her, his hands laced in her curls. Tears started to swell in his eyes as he held her close to him for the first time since he left for the front. Jim told his wife everything we did for him at the hospital; from the walks in the garden, to learning how to put his clothes on himself. His wife turned to me with watery blue eyes as she asked if I would visit Jim after the war was over and my duties had ceased. I didn't hesitate in agreeing to her request, knowing how close Jim and I had grown in his time in the hospital. She wrote down her address for safekeeping until I could finally make the journey.

Once Jim left, I put my attention into Edward upon the instruction of Sister Mary. I willed myself not to behave differently with him since my dream, but it was hard not to appear standoffish every time I found myself around him. Edward remained his usual suave self, which made it even more difficult, but he didn't seem to notice my change in attitude. Sister Mary assigned me back to dayshift with Sally and Harriet once Jim left. Edward and I had been out in the gardens every chance we got to help with his recovery. Every day, Edward grew stronger, and within a few days the crutches were changed to a walking stick. He still had days where he desired to sit inside and chat or write letters to our families together due to the pain in his leg.

Despite Sally and Harriet's pestering, I still hadn't mustered the courage to fully admit the truth about Ross and Tommy to Edward. They continually reminded me that I needed to, but I held off, praying the dreams of Edward would cease. Every night, he came to me in visions of daydreams and slumber. He became a continual reminder of the life I sought to run away from when I started an affair with Ross. After another dream, I woke with the resolution to finally tell Edward everything. If it turned his possible affections away from me, then it saved me a lot of anxiety and trouble. I had accepted he would turn me away before I even had a chance to plead my case of honesty to him.

I smiled at Edward as I pulled the screens around his bed to attend to his wounds. His curls stuck up, resembling a hedgehog's spikes. "How are you this morning?"

"I'm fine. I'm glad to see you," he responded. His eyes watched mine, hopeful for an answer I couldn't respond to.

Instead, I swallowed hard and helped him off with his pyjama bottoms; repeating what became a daily ritual since Edward arrived at the hospital. A new influx of patients was due soon, meaning I would have to take new men under my wing. I loved caring for the men, but I would end up losing time with Edward. If I didn't care if his affections were returned or not, then why did the prospect of less time with him clench my heart?

"Are you still okay to go outside today?" Edward asked after our silence lasted too long to be comfortable.

I nodded as I disinfected the wound which was quickly becoming a scar on his leg. My stomach fluttered as I knew what I had to do next. I couldn't keep putting it off forever – as much as I would have loved to. "E-Edward, can I talk to you about something… personal?"

"Of course."

His eyebrows knitted together as I took a seat on the chair by his bed, letting the disinfectant sink into Edward's skin. "I… I lied when you asked whether I had a sweetheart. Before the war began, I was having an affair with a friend of my family. His name was Ross and I decided to join the VAD when he told me he didn't love me anymore. I know how wrong it was for me to have an affair with a married man, but I couldn't help myself. He was good to me when things were secret. Perhaps I desired an oath rather than a secret from him. When he discovered I left to join up, he did the same thing, hoping to finally find me again in the war. He's currently on the frontline fighting… all because of me. Ross' wife wrote me a letter a few weeks back asking me to keep him safe if I ever came across him in the hospital. I haven't met him again since seeing him off at the train station before he made the journey to the front. But I wrote back to his wife, promising her that I would."

Edward remained silent as I bit my lip, waiting on a response or any sign he didn't judge me for what I had confessed. Refusing to wait a second longer, I stood up and wrapped the bandage around his leg. My skin prickled and the hairs rose along my flesh as the silence continued, weighing heavily on top of us in the most suffocating manner. Once I finished, I took his pyjama bottoms and helped him back into them without a single word shared between us. I pushed back the screens and gathered all the medical supplies to return them to the sluice room. I turned to walk away, but his hand gripping my sleeve caused me to freeze in my tracks.

"Do you still think of him?" Edward finally questioned.

I swallowed hard and spun around to face him. His beautiful eyes searched mine for any sign of an answer before I spoke. I nodded, knowing I had to keep telling the truth, and watched as his face fell. He dropped my sleeve and stared down at his lap, refusing to spend another moment looking at me. "I do... but every time I think of him, I end up thinking of you instead." Just as I turned to walk away, out of the corner of my eye, I saw Edward's head lifting. But our eyes never met as I made my way out of the ward, unsure as to whether I should have admitted the guiltiest secret my heart dared to possess.

For the rest of the morning, I had avoided Edward as much as I could to the extent where I ran all the errands and worked in the other assigned ward. With Harriet back on our shift again, Sally had someone in Edward's ward to help her with tasks Sister Mary requested her to complete. I didn't need someone to tell me that hiding became the most immature reaction to Edward's possible judgement. But it seemed the safest solution to me. I took some medical supplies which had been unused to the sluice room. The hairs on the back of my neck stood to attention as footsteps echoed behind me. I flung open the door and, once it slammed behind me, I spun around to see Sally and Harriet standing there.

"Why are you not working in our ward?" Harriet questioned, folding her arms across her chest.

"No reason," I replied, shrugging to try to remove their stares. It did little to stop their interrogation when Sally also folded her arms and both women raised an eyebrow at me. I sighed, knowing I had to tell them the truth. My jaw clenched several times before everything that happened with Edward spilled out of my mouth.

Sally stared at me with an open mouth. She blinked rapidly as though trying to understand why I would confess such a thing. "You… you told him?"

"Yes. He was clearly judging me for having an affair, so I admitted the truth to him about thinking of him every time I thought about Ross."

Harriet smirked, completely unphased by my brazen confession. "Well, let's not worry about it because it's visiting time."

"Why is that making you smirk?" I asked as a shiver ran down my spine.

"Visiting time is when you take Edward for his walk. Saying he's been asking for you all morning since that incident, I'd say it's about time you finally faced him."

A groan resounded from my lips, but I didn't protest, knowing it wouldn't matter even if I did. Harriet and Sally opened the door, forming a guard of honour as I walked out of the sluice room. They followed close beside me as we made our way to the ward. With them so close to me, I couldn't run even if I wanted to. Stepping into the sunlight of the ward crushed my chest, making it difficult to breathe. My eyes darted across the room until they met Edward's staring back at me. He sat up in bed and waited on me to come over to take him for a walk. I dragged my feet as Sally and Harriet escorted me over to his bed, leaving me there once he swung his legs over the side of the mattress. Without saying anything, I grabbed his dressing gown and put it on him, tying it at the waist.

"Ready?"

Edward nodded, standing up with the bed supporting his weight. I pulled his dressing gown down on him as he rested his hands on my shoulders. Sister Mary always maintained that every man should look well presented in the hospital, especially during the visiting hours. I reached to the chair beside his bed where his walking stick sat. He gripped it as we walked, arm in arm, towards the gardens.

"Belle, I…"

"Please, let's not talk about it," I pleaded, hoping he couldn't hear the shaking in my voice. Edward didn't argue with me, but his tightened grip on my arm settled my fluttering stomach. When we arrived out in the garden, the scent of fresh grass enveloped our senses. The sun shone down on us, creating a warmth sorely missed in winter. When I asked Edward where he wanted to walk to, he pointed straight to Tommy's bench.

I watched as Edward managed to sit down on the bench without my help. His recovery had improved at a rapid pace; a stark reminder of how short our time together would be when he finally got a space in the officer's hospital close by. As with all the men I looked after, I always revelled in the pride I felt for them as they continued to improve in their health. I sat down beside Edward, keeping a safe space between us, and silence rested over us for a few minutes before Edward spoke.

"I think you should know, saying that you were honest with your feelings, that I think you're beautiful. I would be lying if I told you that every time I thought of you, I didn't want to hold you in my arms or even just hold your hand. I do not and I cannot judge you for what you did when you were back home. I would be a hypocrite if I did."

I glanced over, meeting his eyes, and raised an eyebrow at him. "Are you telling me that you have done things you aren't proud of, Officer Blackwell?"

Edward chuckled as a red flush coated his cheeks with every sparkle in his eyes. "If you count having… *'relations'* with the vicar's wife behind his back then yes, I suppose so."

I glanced away from him, knowing my eyes bulged the minute he admitted it. My mouth opened and closed several times before I composed myself enough to speak again. "Why the vicar's wife?"

"Spur of the moment," he shrugged as though it meant nothing. "I thought that love was supposed to be wild and dangerous. I guess you could say I was naïve back then. But now I know better about what love is and what it definitely isn't."

A smile came over my lips as the muscles in my shoulders slackened from their tense posture. I wasn't the only person who had done something I knew was wrong in every sense of the word. Receiving Margaret's letter made me think about everything that happened and how things had changed between our families. A grimace took over my features every time I thought of how wrong my actions were. The tightness of guilt in my chest never left me since I read her letter. I closed my eyes, willing the pain to leave my body. The birdsong of the Blue Tit drew my attention to the trees behind the bench. I watched the Blue Tit sing for a moment until Edward's eyes bore into me.

I turned to him as the edges of his mouth pulled into a grin. "Why are you staring at me?"

"Because you're beautiful, Belle. I've seen war and the horrors that people wouldn't even dream of in their worst nightmares. So, I've learnt to appreciate the simple pleasure of looking at the beauty left around me. For it might be the last beautiful thing I see."

Something about the warmth of his words and his eyes made my entire body feel at peace. If this was the last peaceful moment I would get in this war, then I wanted to make it count with

Edward. I began to tell him about Tommy and how I had grown closer than I should have with him. He needed to know about him, and, for some reason, I wanted Edward to know everything which held a special place in my heart. Tears rolled down my face as I spoke the last words of Tommy's story. Edward reached into his pyjama pocket and pulled out his handkerchief, handing it to me.

"Tommy's okay. He's safe where he is and he's watching over you," Edward tried to comfort me.

I wiped my tears away with the silk material of the handkerchief and held it in my fist. "Tommy loved birds – the Blue Tit was always his favourite. His mother and I have this comforting thought that perhaps he's one now. It's always been around here since he died; right over there." I pointed to the Blue Tit which stood with a puffed chest singing his heart out in the tree.

Edward turned to look at the bird before facing me once again with a grin plastered over his features. "You see, he's still with you." A shiver came over him as we locked eyes for longer than we should have. I glanced away to stop a blush flooding my cheeks. "May we go inside now?"

"Of course."

I stood beside him, holding the walking stick for him while he got off the bench himself. He gripped my hand and the stick at the same time to balance himself with the pain of his wounded leg. He winced as he straightened himself, refusing to let go of my hand. I kept my gaze on our interlocked fingers, daring myself to imagine Edward as more than just one of the men I cared for. It was wrong to do so, especially after Tommy. But if it was wrong, I wasn't sure I wanted to be right. I looked up through my eyelashes to find Edward watching me. Did he know what I had thought? Did he know how wrong my desires towards him were and how much I scolded myself for such illicit imaginings?

"Promise me you will see me like we agreed; away from here, before I leave for the front again?" Edward pleaded with me as our eyes mixed in a sea of autumn colours.

"I promise."

The promise I made to Edward became the first one I had truly meant since the last time I spoke to Ross. As the Blue Tit's song resounded in the garden, I knew Tommy agreed with the feelings in my heart. He wanted this for me and, while I wasn't sure why he did, I had to trust my Tommy once more.

Chapter Twenty-Six

As the days passed by, Edward and I grew closer to each other. Neither of us made any advancement towards the other, but it never stopped the dreams of him which had become more vivid. The lingering looks between us and the small touches spoke words we could never say to each other. Perhaps the lack of understanding of what love was in our pasts prevented us from finally admitting the truth. Nevertheless, the small moments alone in crowded rooms gave us the most pleasant memories. I still wrote letters to Ross, knowing he needed someone to help him feel less alone at the front. But I didn't think of him in the ways which I previously had at home.

Towards the end of the week, Sister Mary called me over to inform me of the news neither Edward nor I desired to hear. The Officers' Hospital nearby had room for him to come to them for the rest of his recovery. He remained on his walking stick, but they wished to take him until he could fully walk unaided. I no longer had to do bandages on his leg after the stitches were removed, causing us to have less time together than before. No matter how little time we had each day, we still made up for it in other ways.

"It looks like it could rain," Sally commented as we eat our lunch.

I glanced out of the window and nodded as I watched the angry grey clouds drift overhead. I couldn't help but think of Edward and our usual afternoon walk when a black cloud appeared over the hospital. "It does, but hopefully Edward will still get his walk."

"I'm sure he will," she responded. Out of the corner of my eye, I spotted her looking at me. When I turned to Sally her mouth pulled into a tight smile which was more for my benefit than hers. "It'll be sad to see him leave us."

Edward and I never spoke of him leaving as though never speaking of it would change the circumstances that we would soon find ourselves in. It wasn't something either of us desired to think about, knowing the goodbye would tear our hearts apart. All we wanted to focus on was how to grow closer in the short time we had left.

Sally reached over and took my empty plate from me. She piled it on top of her own and sighed. "You better fetch Edward for his walk before it rains."

I made my way back to the ward as Edward sat up and waited for me to come to him. He pulled on his dressing gown as his walking stick rested on his bed. He glanced up at me as I walked over to help him. The heaviness of the air screamed for us to recognise how short the time was for whatever we might have had. Borrowed time in a war had become a sentence I loathed to hear, but it happened to be true all too often. I tied Edward's dressing gown for him with shaking hands as he reached for his walking stick.

"Ready to go before it starts to rain?" I double checked with him. The last thing I wanted to do was take him for a walk if his leg remained in too much pain.

He glanced at me and nodded. "Absolutely."

We made our way out to the gardens, arm in arm as we did every day. Other men were doing their daily walk while the rain held out. They smiled in greeting to us as we walked around the gardens before Edward asked to sit on Tommy's bench. Every time we sat there Edward always stared at the trees until he spotted the Blue Tit. Since I told him about Tommy, he always waited until he saw the bird in the trees or heard the melody of the birdsong. Without fail, it would always sit on a branch waiting on us to make an appearance before it started its song.

Edward sighed and fidgeted with his fingers in his lap. "I'm going to miss sitting here with you. It's so peaceful; all you can hear are the birds and their song. Compared to what I've seen, this is heaven."

"The Officers' Hospital will have gardens you can walk around too. Plus, there'll be other nurses to meet and spend time with."

He turned to me and the smile on my face fell with the forlorn expression he gave me. "But they won't be you." I opened my mouth to respond, but nothing would come out. I glanced down at my lap as my hands rested against my thighs. "Please look at me Belle." Reluctantly, I turned my head to meet the face I seemed to have memorised by heart. His clouded green eyes with their halo of gold shone at me, twinkling in such a way to send my stomach fluttering. "No matter how many nurses or women I might meet, rest assured, they will never compare to you."

Before I could respond, a rumble erupted from the clouds above us, and the heavens opened. The rain spurted from the sky, drenching us right through to our skin. Edward shot up, taking my hand to help me from the bench. He hobbled forward on his walking stick towards the hospital. I stumbled after him, not caring if someone spotted us holding hands. Instead of continuing to the hospital, he turned us around and went into the trees.

Edward never let go of my hand as he hobbled through the wooded area. His fingers laced in mine while the rain ran through the cracks between our flesh. We didn't go far into the forest when he stopped us. With a flick of his wrist, he let go of my hand, allowing it to fall in the force of gravity. He leant against the nearest tree, breathing heavily, and rubbing his thigh where his scar would soon decorate his skin.

"Why are we here?"

Edward's eyes flickered from the trees to my face and a smirk pulled at the edges of his mouth. "We would have been drenched going back inside the hospital. The forest here has better shelter for us."

I couldn't argue with him as only a few tiny drops of rain fell to the ground, plunking against the leaves underfoot. The fallen remnants of a winter once past crunched on the ground as I moved beside Edward. I closed my eyes, grateful for the peace of the rain falling. The bark indented the skin on my back as I leant against it. Leaves crunched on the ground once more as my eyes jolted open. Edward moved himself around to stand in front of me.

"Do you think we'll get in trouble?" he asked, blinking rapidly at me. He bit the inside of his lip as he waited for my answer.

"Don't worry, I'll think of something." He stood a few inches away from me and I swallowed hard as images of my dreams flooded my mind. "You worry too much about me."

He chuckled, shrugging at me as he gazed into my eyes. "I can't help it."

We stood beneath the shadows of the trees in the silence of our own breathing and the pattering of the rain falling to the forest floor. It was as if the whole world held its breath as we stared into each other's eyes. A mere few inches separated our faces while gravity dared us to take one move closer. Edward's hands reached my cheeks and cupped my face against his calloused skin as he pulled me towards him. Our lips met in a passion I hadn't experienced in my life. The heat rose in my body as I tugged him closer to me by his dressing gown. No amount of air could pass between us as we breathed in sync with our chests squashed together. We stumbled backwards until I found myself pressed against the tree.

Despite the rain easing off, we didn't pull away. We became one breath, one soul, in that moment – a feeling I could never transcribe to Ross. Edward's fingers toyed with the strands of hair which fell out of my headdress. I pulled away as my chest tightened. I had promised myself I would never fall for another patient after Tommy. Yet here I was, giving every piece of my sanity over to a desire for Edward. I moved away from him and resisted the rising panic of adrenaline in my veins.

"L-Let's go inside," I insisted, knowing Sister Mary could come looking for us at any moment. There was no plausible explanation I could give her if she found us coming out of the trees.

"Belle I'm sorry. I shouldn't have done that I –"

I shook my head, refusing to look at him. If I did, I would give over my heart once again. "We need to go Edward."

We walked back inside, drenched to the bone and not speaking to each other. Sister Mary ran to us when she spotted us coming up the corridor. She questioned us about where we had been when the rain started. Edward's eyes bore into me as I came up with the best possible explanation. I lied and told her we took shelter in the greenhouse. Her face slackened as relief washed over her. Without asking me anything more, she ordered us to go and dry off in one of the free rooms, assigning me to make sure Edward was dried and had new pyjamas.

I grabbed some towels and pyjamas in Edward's size from the sluice room before taking him into a spare room. I locked the door and helped him to dry off; neither of us spoke to each other as we worked together in a raucous silence. Edward put on his new pyjamas as I dried myself as best as I could without removing any of my uniform. I didn't have a change of clothes for myself. Edward struggled with the leg of his pyjama bottoms, and I walked over to help him. But he put his hand up, making me freeze in place. I turned away, unable to continue watching him struggle, and sat on the doctor's desk to wait on him finishing.

He brought his wet pyjamas and dressing gown over to me. The soggy pile weighed down my hands as I set them beside me on the desk. Edward continued to stand there, and I dared a glance up at him through my eyelashes. His eyes already rested on mine, waiting for me to say something… anything about what happened. A magnet pulled the two of us together as he stepped forward until he stood in front of my knees. Every promise I made to myself screamed at me to run. It would have been the bravest thing I ever did. But perhaps bravery meant caving into the desires of my heart. I took his hands in mine and pulled him closer until our lips met in a passion which ignited every fire in my soul. Promises always ended up broken. With the violent blaze between us with every touch of his lips, those promises melted into the flames. No space remained as Edward leant his hands on the desk, either side of me, to stay as close as possible.

Neither of us desired to break away, despite breathing heavily, because breaking away meant losing the spark we sought to extinguish only minutes earlier.

"Hello?" a voice resounded from the other side of the locked door.

We pulled away as quickly as we could muster, before unlocking the door. My hands shook as I fumbled with the lock. Edward stood close behind me, trying to help without arousing more suspicion. When the door flew open, Sally stood there with eyes darting between me and Edward. She cocked an eyebrow as she awaited an answer neither of us wished to give her. Edward announced he was going to sit in one of the recreational areas, leaving me alone with Sally's suspicions. I grabbed the towels, Edward's damp pyjamas, and his dressing gown to put in the laundry piles. Sally remained close on my heels as I made my way to the laundry room. I flung the door open, knowing there was little point in closing it.

Sally clicked the door shut behind us and drilled me with questions the second she stepped towards me. "What were you two doing?"

"Drying off after getting stuck in the rain. Edward needed somewhere to change his pyjamas in private," I responded, focusing on putting the clothes into the right piles. I turned around as Sally placed her hands on her hips.

"Do you expect me to believe that? The two of you were flushed when you opened the door and Edward couldn't even look at me."

My jaw clenched, shifting from side to side as I weighed up my possible options for an excuse. "I need to fetch Edward a new dressing gown."

Sally followed me through the door to the supply room where the pyjamas, hospital uniforms, and dressing gowns were stored. I grabbed a dressing gown for him from the stacks of new ones awaiting a soldier to take it in the new influx. Sally remained by my side, refusing to leave me alone after everything she saw. I walked around her and strolled back through the corridors until I edged towards the recreational area closest to Edward's ward. The dressing gown material hooked in my fingers as Sally's footsteps echoed behind me. Before I made my way into the area, she grabbed my arm, pulling me around towards her.

"I don't want you getting hurt," she finally admitted. Her eyes clouded with concern as she furrowed her brow. "It's all fine to have feelings now. But if you don't hear from him when he gets transferred next week, I don't want you heartbroken."

While I believed Edward when he told me we would still write to each other and meet after he was transferred, I couldn't help but question if it was all lies. The blood rushed to my ears, and I reached my hand out to steady myself against the wall. Fate hadn't remained on my side since I left for the war. Why would it decide to treat me fairly this time? Sally tried to talk to me, but my mind focused on the twisting of my stomach. I handed her Edward's dressing gown and walked towards the backdoors, leading to the gardens, to soak in the fresh air. I needed time to think about everything to do with Edward. The rain pattered against the ground, bouncing into the air like pixies dancing, as I opened one of the doors to let in the fresh air. A calmness descended over my body, settling the rising heat through my veins, when I listened to the rain.

I put my hand into my pocket and the rattling of paper drew my attention. Pulling out an envelope, I realised I hadn't read the letter Ross had sent me. In the haze of everything that happened with Edward, Ross had been so far from my mind that his letter remained untouched in my uniform. I tore open the envelope, disturbing the silence of the corridor, and unfolded the letter.

To my dearest Belle,
Everything you said soothed my worries. I cannot thank you enough for that. I just hope that what you said is right. Unfortunately, this letter might not be long as I am tired and cold out here. I can assure you that I'm not ill or badly wounded. I don't want to speak about what's happening here.

I promise I will keep safe so I can see you and the children again. I think of you every waking moment and even in my dreams. I want you to be with me again. I don't want to just see you in my dreams anymore. I need you in my arms again, holding you once more like we did in the daisy field. Every moment I get to hold you in my dreams, I keep close to me, replaying it over in my mind until I can see you again. I long to lie in the daisy field with your head on my lap, staring at the amber sunset. Perhaps someday soon we will once again.

I'll come back to you Belle. I promise I'll come back.

Your Ross.

I folded the letter as Sally's words drifted through my mind again. *'But if you don't hear from him… I don't want you heartbroken.'* Every day I dreaded the list of names in the newspaper in case one of them read Ross' name. Any woman with a man at the front behaved the same; darting their eyes towards the lists when they thought no one noticed them because they hadn't received a letter in ages. Would I be able to do the same for Edward and not panic if I never had contact with him? I knew the answer without having to tell myself it. A sigh escaped my lips, and I laid my head back against the wall, closing my eyes. The aroma of the rain on the pavements filled my senses.

"I thought I'd find you here." My eyes shot open, and I turned my head as Edward hobbled down the corridor on his walking stick. I pushed myself away from the wall, standing up straight to wait on him to reach me. He stood on the opposite side of the corridor and leant against the closed door. A slow, sad smile came over his lips as he gazed longingly at me. "I never want to hurt you, Belle."

"Did Sally speak to you?"

He stifled a laugh and shook his head before gazing back at me. "Speak or threaten. Most nurses are terrified to speak to officers; Sally doesn't seem to fall into that category." I couldn't help but smile. Sally wasn't going to let this go any time soon, not after what happened with Tommy and Ross. "She just cares too much."

"That's very clear. In fact, I had to persuade her that I would do right by you."

I diverted my eyes away from him, not knowing what to say, and focused my gaze outside the open door. The gardens resembled an old Irish folktale in the rain, coating everything in a mystical starlight. A hollowness filled my chest as I remembered the fields of home under the moonlit sky. What would it be like in the fields with Edward instead of Ross? Would it still feel the same with someone different, or did those fields belong to Ross and I?

Edward grabbed my hand, drawing me back to the hospital. I glanced down the corridor to check we were alone. The deserted hallways danced with the coldness of the souls who had left us too soon. I looked into Edward's eyes as he ran his calloused thumb across the back of my hand, tracing circles on the alabaster skin.

"I promise you that we will stay in contact constantly," Edward stated, never letting my eyes wander from his green sea. "You're just going to have to let me prove to you that I mean my promise."

"I'll try."

Edward pulled me into his arms, and I allowed myself to sink into his warm embrace. His head moved towards the other end of the corridor before separating us. His eyes drifted down to my lips as though questioning if the desires were worth the trouble that we might find ourselves in. He pulled me back to him until our lips met in a kiss filled with a longing passion for each other. I wrapped my arms around his neck, allowing not even the breeze to try to part us. It was only us in that moment – a world away from violence and loss. This moment became our peace and paradise in a world where blood stained soil. We held each other there, not wanting to let the war part us just when it had brought us together. We needed to believe that even if it forced us into a goodbye, it would bring us back together again. In war, believing and hoping were all we could do to face another day apart from those we loved.

Chapter Twenty-Seven

The day of Edward's departure to the Officers' Hospital came around quicker than either of us anticipated. Sister Mary had requested that I went with Edward to oversee his transfer as I had been by his side since day one. I tried to keep a smiling face as I dressed myself for dayshift, but Sally and Harriet's shared glances told me it didn't fool anyone. The Red Cross truck waited on Edward when we arrived at the hospital. I turned my eyes away from it, refusing to believe what I had to accept. Sally and I made our way to the sluice room to fetch our supplies for the men. While Sally attempted to distract me with small talk, my thoughts drifted to seeing Edward again when he was no longer one of my patients. Only then could we be whatever we wished without the judgement of other people.

"Are you feeling okay?" Sally questioned. The weariness echoed in the cracks of her voice, tempting herself not to overstep the line despite her concern.

I glanced over at her and shrugged. "I've gotten so used to saying goodbye to the men that it doesn't affect me as much as it did at the start." Every conversation I had with Edward always brought us back to the promises he insisted he would keep. Ross had broken me with his false promises, making it difficult for me to believe anyone else, even Edward.

Sally didn't push me further as we walked towards the ward to attend to the men. Out of instinct, my eyes travelled over to Edward's bed in the corner. The sapphire blue suit, red tie, and white shirt rested on his bed – the hospital uniform he needed to put on yet. His eyes met mine and a smile rested over his features. A warm glow crept onto my face as he winked at me. If Sister Mary did so much as glance at us, we would find ourselves in unimaginable trouble.

"There'll be no one to make you glow quite like that," Sally whispered in my ear. We grinned at each other, knowing humour was the only way to keep going in the darkest moments of our hearts. We picked up our supplies and went in different directions to begin working on the men.

From where I worked on one of the soldiers, Michael's voice drifted over as he gave Edward the go-ahead for his transfer to the Officer's Hospital. For so long we knew how final this moment would be. Yet, until Michael's words reached my ears, my heart hadn't the courage to accept the reality of the situation. I always knew Edward wouldn't remain with us as long as the other men, but that did nothing to remove the hope of his continued presence. Every touch and kiss between us didn't settle any doubt of the promises he made to me. His questioning stare and raised eyebrow told me that he knew I didn't believe him either.

"Nurse, have you heard about the war?" the solider I worked on asked as I readied myself to apply the bandage to his foot.

I furrowed my eyebrows and shook my head, trying to ignore the churning in my stomach. "No… why, what's happened?"

"Fighting in Belgium they are – heavy, very heavy fighting Nurse. Apparently, the French were overcome with gas; the Germans drove them back."

I fastened the bandage around his foot and straightened myself. "Where did you find this out?"

The man reached over and lifted a newspaper which sat on his bed table. He flicked through the pages until he found the article he talked about. He handed it over to me to read for myself. The article described the gas attack, stating the men recovered well from it. I had witnessed the effect of gas on the men first-hand; it wasn't a 'good recovery' like the newspaper article suggested. When I reached the end of the article, I thought back to Jim and how his life had changed from blindness caused by a gas attack. He had been one of the ones unfortunate enough to find themselves exposed to too much of it. My throat closed over, and I blinked away tears as I imagined what those French men went through. I handed the soldier back the newspaper and, before I could utter a single word of response, Sister Mary came over to me.

"Nurse Wilson, Officer Blackwell is ready to go. Nurse Smith will take over from you," she informed me. I nodded and placed the medical supplies back on the trolley. I glanced behind Sister Mary to see Harriet waiting to take over my duties for me. "Officer Blackwell has requested a bit of air before leaving, so you're relieved of your duty."

I fetched my coat from our cloakroom and found Edward outside the front doors of the hospital. He rested his head against the wall, closing his eyes against the sun beating down on his face. A content and peaceful smile rested over his lips, easing the tense muscles he wore so often on his features. The sun cast a shadow over his face, emphasising his high cheekbones more with each passing second. The sapphire of the hospital uniform complimented his skin and made it appear a sun-kissed texture I'd only ever known on one man before him.

"You seem to be happy to be leaving me."

Edward jumped at the sound of my voice as his eyes shot open. He stood at attention as though caught sleeping on sentry duty. "Quite the contrary, I can assure you," he replied, still wearing the easy smile across his lips. I raised an eyebrow at him, not believing a word he said. "I don't think I've ever been more at peace since meeting you. I'll take that peace, the contentment you give me, everywhere I go. I just hope you know I intend on keeping my promise."

I didn't respond, knowing he could tell the answer without me replying to him. Edward walked forward on his walking stick and took my hand in his. I stared down as he entwined our fingers together; two broken pieces finally finding what made their hollowness whole again. I glanced through my eyelashes as his face edged just inches from mine. We shouldn't have been so close with prying eyes everywhere, yet that logic utterly left our minds. Edward's eyes met mine in a sea of sunlight bursting through the trees and his warm breath cascaded over my lips, drawing me ever closer to him.

"Are you two ready to go?" the ambulance driver called. We pulled back from each other as he stubbed out his cigarette on the ground.

I nodded, reluctantly stepping further away from Edward. "Absolutely."

The driver helped Edward and I into the back of the ambulance before slamming the door behind us. He hopped into the driver's seat and the engine rumbled beneath our feet as he drove off. Edward rose off his seat, trying to move over beside me. My heart leapt into my throat as I gestured to him to stay where he was. He could have hurt his leg even more had he stood and fell over in a moving ambulance. I gripped the sides of the ambulance and tried to manoeuvre myself over beside him. His hands held my waist as I lowered myself down beside him.

Edward put his index finger to his lips and pointed to the square window which allowed for us to see the driver's seat. If we could see and hear him, the odds of him being able to do the same were very high. Edward's fingers laced with mine as he brought my hand to his lips, laying a gentle kiss on it.

"I'm going to miss our time together," he whispered in my ear. His warm breath against my skin sent a shiver down my spine.

"I'm going to miss you too; my days won't be the same without you constantly there. I just hope we'll see each other again."

Edward let out a slight laugh, shaking his head at me. "I knew you didn't believe my promise."

I turned my eyes to the floor of the ambulance, watching as it vibrated against the force of the engine. The edges of my mouth pulled into a tight smile as I refused to look at him. I couldn't admit to his face that I didn't believe him. He squeezed my hand, trying to make me look at him. Before either of us could do or say anything more, the ambulance came to an abrupt halt. I shuffled over to the other side of the vehicle before the driver opened the door. Sunlight poured into the darkened ambulance as the driver reached his hands in to help me out first.

The Officers' Hospital resembled a manor house, and I could easily see why it was maintained only for officers. The bitter taste of bile crept up my throat as I witnessed that class still mattered to people during a war. Men from all walks of life fought and died beside each other on the Western and Eastern Fronts. Yet people still cared about class divides in the worst violence to ever greet mankind. My hands balled into fists as the stones crunched with Edward walking over to me. His elongated shadow stood beside mine as we gazed at the hospital. My jaw and hands unclenched as Edward reach over to link our arms, using it as an excuse to touch me in the simplest way.

We made our way inside in silence as we revelled in the final touch that we would have between the two of us. I pushed open the door and Edward walked inside, refusing to let go of my arm. A nurse turned at the whooshing of the door and walked over to us. From the smile on her face, we knew she waited for him. I handed over Edward's belongings in his kitbag to her. She took it and slung it over her shoulder as though this were an everyday occurrence. Little did she know how much this final moment between Edward and I would make or break us.

"I'll let you say goodbye," she said, turning to leave his kitbag where his bed was waiting for him upstairs.

I turned to Edward and gazed deep into his swirling green eyes. Neither of us desired to utter anything similar to a goodbye. In a war, goodbye was too final of a word when parting ways. When I blinked, I found myself back in the train station in London seeing Ross off to war. This wasn't sending Edward off to war or saying farewell. This was parting until fate reunited us once again. Edward let out a shaky breath and pulled me into a tight hug. I relaxed against the grooves of his body as my head rested on his shoulder. Edward's breath cascaded over my ear as he leant his mouth close to me.

"It won't be long until we see each other again," he mumbled. I nodded, not wanting to argue with him over my disbelief in humanity's promises. I swallowed hard and breathed him in one final time before we parted. Edward pulled an envelope out of his hospital jacket and handed me it. I took it from him, refusing to let his eyes leave mine until they had to.

"Ready to go Officer Blackwell?" the nurse questioned.

Out of the corner of my eye, I noticed her standing facing us, but Edward and I were too busy staring at each other. He didn't respond to her, trying to stay even a second longer before we had to part. I blinked away tears and forced a smile onto my face to tell him it was time to go.

He nodded and finally turned to her. "Yes Nurse. Thank you for your help with my recovery Nurse Wilson."

The nurse led Edward towards the stairs, arm in arm as we had once done. I waited for him to fade into the busyness of the hospital, making my goodbye much easier than I knew it was meant to be. Edward froze for a moment before he glanced back and grinned at me. I raised my head and smiled back, knowing that one final glance at him was all I needed to walk away from the hospital.

The trip to the shore to fetch some of the influx wasn't long but remained a rickety reminder of the emptiness of the ambulance. Edward's absence descended over me in a heavy silence only contained by the chatter of the driver, as though he could sense my forlornness. I rattled the envelope, caressing it with my fingers, as I debated opening it or not. It marked the final parting of us; we would have to sit and watch what we would eventually become. Would his promises hold true, or would we remain a passing flicker of infatuation in this war?

Unable to contain my eager fingers any longer, I tore open the envelope and unfolded the letters with steady hands as though preserving it for future generations. As the paper straightened out, a photo of Edward in his officer uniform fell onto my lap. I picked it up and smiled at the face I'd grown a deep affection for in the time we had together. I tucked it back into the envelope with a cautious hand before reading the letter he wrote for me.

Dearest Belle,
We first started to get to know one another through letters. It was how we connected and how we were there for each other when we physically couldn't be. This is why you're reading this letter. I know you doubt whether I was sincere or not, so let this be a written assurance for you. Let letters between us be the connection, the invisible string, tying us together until we meet again. Whether we meet before I return to the front, or during the war, or even after it, these letters will forever connect us. We shall keep every single one – each letter keeping us together because we physically cannot be. Fate brought us together, so let words keep us together until fate brings us back to one another once again.

Remember, I cannot forget you Nurse Belle Wilson. You are quite unforgettable.

Forever Your Edward.

I pressed the letter against my chest, holding it by my heart, as I dared to believe Edward's promise. After a few seconds, I folded it and placed it back into the envelope with the photo I would treasure for a lifetime. Tucking it into my coat pocket, a tingling of adrenaline flooded my whole body with a hopefulness of seeing Edward again. I couldn't base Edward's promises on the empty oaths Ross made. Edward was nothing like the man who broke me into a million pieces in the daisy field.

I closed my eyes and Edward's face turning back to me one final time came into vision. A smile coated my lips as I remembered how it was all I needed. The Officers' Hospital screamed class divide when we glanced up at it on the grounds. It didn't take an aristocrat to tell me that Edward and I weren't in the same class. Edward had to have known that from the stories I told him of home and the daisy field. Yet it didn't seem to deter him from me if he did realise it. All that mattered to me was that society didn't divide us from each other. If it didn't matter to him what class society shoved us into, then perhaps we stood a chance. We couldn't let society part what fate had brought together.

"Ready to get some of the injured men needing our care?" the driver asked me through the window. Only when he spoke did I realise the ambulance had stopped. The shuttering under my feet ceased as he switched off the engine.

I glanced up at his grinning face. I couldn't mistake the cloud of concern which dimmed the amber colour of his eyes. A deep breath escaped my lips as I found myself returning his infectious gesture. "Definitely – let's save some lives."

No matter what darkened my heart, I had to keep going to save more men who did their duty for our freedom and country. It wasn't that long ago that I saved Edward from an horrific injury. Today I had to keep working to save more of his men. As he always reminded me on our walks when the Blue Tit sang, I had to continue living and working every single day for Tommy's sake. As I jumped down from the ambulance and landed my feet on the solid ground of the coast, that was exactly what I did as the boats came in with more men needing our urgent care.

Chapter Twenty-Eight

A week had passed since Edward left for the Officers' Hospital and, while the influx brought new faces into the ward, I still found myself missing his. I had written back to Edward when I reached the boarding house the night of leaving him off. Every day since, I checked for a new letter, anticipating his desire to meet against what my heart told me. No letter arrived from Edward. Ross' letters ceased their connection too; worrying me more than I ever cared to admit to anyone. As always, I had to push the twisting in my stomach away with the continued questions in my mind. My focus had to stay on the men and their care.

"We're getting more soldiers today," Sister Mary announced at around ten in the morning after she called us out of the ward. We stood in our usual line as she checked the watch around her thin wrist. Crinkles formed around her eyes as her frown deepened. "They will be here in a few hours. Make sure the corridor beds are ready for them when they get here."

It was no secret that the fighting in France was getting worse. The newspapers produced lists upon lists of the dead or missing which seemed to grow longer every day. Shipments of soldiers kept arriving at the coast with many of them in a worst condition than we had received before. As much as I desired not to think of Ross, I couldn't help but wonder how he was coping in the middle of it all. All I wanted to know was that he was safe wherever he happened to be. I made a promise to get him back home at the end of this war. No matter what, I always fulfilled my promises.

Upon Sister Mary's instructions, Harriet, Sally, and I began to prepare the beds in the corridors for the men coming into the hospital. The limited space from the men already placed in corridor beds caused us to exchange weary glances every so often. We would have to fit more men into the wards or corridors somehow to ensure each of them had a place in the hospital. We smiled at the men in the occupied corridor beds, making sure we kept them company. No one received special treatment at the hospital; it didn't matter if they were in a bed in the ward or the corridor.

"How are you coping?" Harriet asked me. I glanced over to her as we folded a blanket on one of the beds.

"Surprisingly well. I do miss him of course, but I know I'll see him soon. I'm due a letter sometime too."

When we passed any of the men lying on the beds, we joked and spoke with them; none of us wished to speak of the war. They didn't want to talk about it and neither did we, not with our loved ones out fighting. As we completed the final bed in the corridor, the influx arrived in full force. Sally called for us to come as quick as possible. Harriet grabbed my hand and pulled me towards the front of the hospital. We sprinted past the nurses helping some of the men inside until the sunlight drenched us in the reality of the war once again. All around us men bled through their uniforms and wounded men walked about looking for a nurse to aid them. The moment the men noticed us they began to approach in their dozens, each seeking help for their injuries. We laid our hands on them, trying to calm them down while male orderlies pushed men on stretchers past us to get them inside as soon as possible. From the injuries they had experienced, many were on their way for emergency surgery.

My eyes followed each stretcher which made its way past us and into the hospital. Every time we received an influx, I always swore it was the worst we had experienced. Yet, every single time the next one proved worse than the last. This one was truly the worst of them all… at least, at the minute. How could humanity do this to its fellow man? How could men take up arms against each other? The soldier speaking to me tapped my shoulder to alert my attention away from the stretchers. I finally tore my eyes away and looked at him as a light-headedness came over me the minute that I spotted his injury. He held a blood-soaked bandage over where his left eye should have been. In the last year at the hospital, I'd never come across an injury like this soldier's before. Nausea overwhelmed every inch of my body as I took the man inside to get him the help he needed.

Nurses, orderlies, and doctors bustled about like flies, pushing and shoving past each other to attend to as many men as possible. None of them seemed to stop or slow down as they continued on their way to fetch more men from the front of the hospital. Blood, soil, and chalk decorated the corridor floors. We could do nothing but walk and run through it, praying we didn't slip in the process. At the nearest free bed, I laid the man down and took in the sights before me. My mind drew back to the last horrific influx of men, when I first met Tommy in the corridor. Tears started to fall over the skin on my cheeks as I settled the man into a comfortable position on the bed.

I didn't know whether it was the memories of Tommy or whether it was the horrific wounds of the soldiers, but I couldn't contain my emotions any longer. I fetched one of the basins of water, a flannel, and bandages, knowing I had to clean the eye wound. The water dripped over the sides as I rushed back to him to make sure his wound didn't get infected. I dropped to my knees on the floor and reached for the flannel with shaking hands. Tears streamed down my face in silent sorrow for what the world had descended into. The soldier lifted the bandage off his eye, letting me know my thoughts were correct; no eye remained as the skin had grown over from an injury sustained.

The soldier's stare bore into me as I cleaned and disinfected his wound. With a shaky, bloody hand he reached out and held mine. His eyebrows knitted together as my lip quivered. "You okay, Nurse?"

I swallowed hard and let out a deep breath to steady my thudding heart. "Bad memories."

He nodded as if he understood exactly what I meant. He gave me a tight smile, crinkling the skin around his eyes, before letting my hand go. I dried my tears with the back of my hand and handed the soldier a bandage in case his wound started to bleed again. Michael walked down the corridor, checking on the men who rested on the beds after nurses attended to them. I stood up and ran to him, telling him about the soldier who lost an eye. His eyebrows shot up as he followed me to where he laid in bed. I had to leave Michael with him, knowing there were too many other soldiers needing help too.

I made my way back outside to the front of the hospital as the solid mass of soldiers had diminished to a trickle of men left over; all still unattended and injured to a lesser extent than the other men. A man limped over to me, leaving bloody footprints in his path. I took hold of his arm as he struggled for breath.

"Nurse, my foot is killing me," he told me. He gripped my arm as tight as possible as we walked over to the back of an ambulance. "I think something went through it; shrapnel or a bullet."

I sat him down on the edge of the back step of the ambulance. With a cautious hand, I removed the shoe which had blood coming out of it. The sole had worn thin from the war, with holes starting to form in the flimsiest parts. A bandage sported his injured foot with red stains across the top of it. I unwrapped it as blood continued to trickle out of his wound. It wasn't much, but it was enough to make the bandage stick to the skin of his foot. I tried to peel it away without taking the skin with it. The man winced as I separated the bandage to reveal the wound. A bullet hole to the top of his foot.

I glanced up at him through my eyelashes as tears clouded his vision. But it wasn't from the pain. He knew I had realised how he received the injury. I hadn't spotted it on any of the soldiers before – I had only heard about it from other nurses and in the newspapers. I diverted my eyes from his as I started to wrap his foot up again to get him inside.

I tried to give him my best, reassuring smile as I grabbed his shoe, knowing he couldn't possibly put it on until I had cleaned and disinfected the wound. "What's your name?"

"P-Paul. Paul Jenkins."

He snatched his shoe from me and put it on, despite my protests that it would cause the bandage to stick to the wound all over again. His eyes darted all around him and my eyebrows knitted together as he checked everywhere outside to see if any of the men had noticed his presence or his wound. When he was certain they hadn't spotted either his wound or himself, he allowed me to help him inside the hospital.

I laid him on a bed in the corridor and proceeded to clean the wound on his foot. As predicted, putting on his shoe had caused the bandage to stick. My jaws clenched together as I willed myself not to breath heavily through my flared nostrils. Once the skin separated from the bandage, a doctor came down the corridor towards us. He leant over my shoulder and examined the wound for himself.

"Did you clean the wound out?" he quizzed, never taking his eyes off the hole in Paul's foot. I nodded in response, and he took Paul's foot in his hand, gazing into the hole. "There's no damaged tissue from what I can see so far. So, use antiseptic, stitch it up, and he'll be fine."

The doctor took a second glance at Paul's face, shaking his head with an upturned lip, before walking off. I lifted the medical supplies needed off the nearest trolley and made my way back to Paul. He laid on the bed, facing the wall, away from everyone's prying eyes. Even when I reappeared and tried chatting to him, he never turned his face towards me. I disinfected the wound and, finally, he looked at me. The whites of his eyes were bloodshot and glazed with sorrow. I wasn't sure how long he had been crying for against the wall, but he was in a bad way with whatever had happened on the battlefield.

"You don't think what they all do, do you?" he asked. His eyes bore into me as I began to stitch the hole in his foot.

I frowned, trying to focus on each stitch. "I'm not sure what you mean."

Paul sighed, swallowing hard as though what he was about to say would change the way I thought of him. "They call me a coward."

"Why do they say that?" My voice raised slightly as I turned my gaze to his face. The stitch held steady in my hand as my fingers clenched the needle.

He glanced at his foot and then back at me. I watched as his Adam's apple bobbed in his throat. "They think I shot myself."

"Did you?"

Paul stifled a laughed and motioned for me to come closer. I leant into him until his breath tickled my ear. "You have no idea about the things you see over there. All… all I could do was try to stay sane until I found a way to get home. Don't say. Please, Nurse."

I sat back, trying not to let my eyebrows fly up or my eyes to bulge after what he admitted. He had shot himself in the foot just to get back home and away from the horrors of the frontline. A pain seared through my chest as I nodded in agreement to keep his secret. I had witnessed first-hand the trauma the soldiers experienced from what they had seen out in France and Belgium. I couldn't blame Paul for doing what he did. If I was in his position, I probably would end up doing the same thing. How could I possibly judge him for doing something over a war I had never experienced on a battlefield?

I didn't know back then, but if Paul's secret did get out to the higher command of the army, he would have faced court martial for cowardice in the face of the enemy. It became the only deterrent for the men who sought to run away from the images of destruction before them. Looking back, I was glad I agreed to keep his secret; it allowed for him to regain himself mentally to face another day in this war-torn world. That was what I desired most for Paul – a chance of making peace with his own mind. I managed to give it to him, for as long as he possibly had in this life.

~

At the end of my shift, my shoulders slackened as I reached the boarding house. My eyelids grew heavy, threatening to shut as I fetched my letters to read. The warm water descending over my skin in the washrooms did little to waken me up as the heat relaxed every tense muscle in my body. All I desired to do was read my letters and crawl under my blanket to welcome the dark slumber of sleep. I dried myself and plaited my hair before pulling on my nightdress. As always, our room filled with rustled paper as the women wrote letters home or read the letters from their sweethearts and families. I flumped down on my bed and tore open my first envelope.

Dear Belle,

I'm glad my letter reassured you and I hope this letter will manage to reassure you even further. I am allowed to go out without a nurse now and my first, but only, wish is to see you. Please let me know how you are faired to meet me next week. I want to take you along the coastline. I know the only times you have seen the coastline is to collect the men. But it is beautiful, and I want you to see it in all its beauty.

I miss you every day. If you miss me, just picture us in the trees. The one time we let ourselves feel everything that war seems to have stopped humanity from feeling. We defied the war then and we will continue to do so until it is over. The war will not drive us apart. Even in the darkest of battles, my heart and entire being, down to the depths of my very soul, will yearn for you.

All my love,

Edward.

Every fibre in my body tingled as I held Edward's letter close to my chest for a brief second. I nudged Sally on the bed beside me and passed her the letter to read. Edward had kept the most important promise he ever made to me. Perhaps not all men would treat me the way Ross did. Perhaps I had found the one true person who sought to give me every love I ever deserved. When Sally finished reading the letter, she passed it to Harriet's bed on the other side of her.

"You need to reply immediately," Harriet told me, handing me the letter back across the beds. I took it from her, and a small smile crept at the corners of my mouth as I rested it on the bed beside the envelope.

Sally grinned widely at me when I glanced back at them. "I guess I was wrong about him after all, Belle."

I cast my eyes back down to the letter and nodded as I ran my fingertips across his indented handwriting. "We both were wrong about him."

Before I pulled out the spare paper to reply to the letter, I tore open the other envelope. My heart clenched as my throat tightened, hoping and praying it was finally a response from Ross. Despite everything, I still cared deeply about him, and I didn't wish to spend another day with anxious eyes darting across hundreds of names in the papers to spot his.

My dearest Belle,
I had a dream of home last night. You were there in the daisy field with me, and I spun you around, allowing the daisies to dance with us. The chain I made you caught the sunlight and it glistened like starlight under the descending sun. I swore I was right there with you. I could touch every golden strand of your hair and the texture of curls remained on my fingertips. But when I woke up, I realised that it was just wishful thinking. I have a feeling, deep in my bones, that I shall see you again very soon. I'm not sure why or how, but it gives me hope and keeps me going during this time.

I'm glad to hear that you're enjoying your work at the hospital. The men are so very lucky to have a kind, caring, and loving woman like you to watch over them. You must be good at your job if they allowed for you to look after an officer until the Officers' Hospital could take him. They must know how special you are.

Belle, I know you will have seen sights you wish you didn't. You will have had to face up to tasks you never thought you would have been faced with. But know that I, and the men you look after, sympathise with you in this. This war has brought us unexpected challenges, but we shall complete every challenge that comes to us. We shall remain victorious at the end of this war – this battle for the goodness of humanity.

I miss you more than you can imagine. You are forever in my thoughts and heart. Please stay safe.

Your Ross.

I stared down at the two letters from the men who held love for me in their hearts. Later, I would end up replying to both letters, telling them I thought deeply of them every time I saw an injured man or the smile of a recovering soldier in the hospital. Everything I would write was true for my own feelings. But, deep down, I knew fate would pull me to either Ross or Edward. The war and fate would step in to direct the path of my life… of my love. Which one would it be?

Chapter Twenty-Nine

The day had arrived to meet Edward again for the first time since his transfer. I had requested the visiting hours off from Sister Mary, which had been gracefully granted. Of course, I never told her who I needed it off for – the lecture of the divide between patient and staff would never leave my ears if I told her the truth. Sally and Harriet helped me to pick out the appropriate dress to wear, stating my uniform wasn't appropriate to see him again in. Before the excitement could fill my veins in tingling anticipation, Sister Mary made me complete my morning shift before leaving in the afternoon.

"Are you nervous?" Harriet asked me in the sluice room as we put away all the supplies we used for the men after their lunch.

I shrugged as I placed disinfected bowls in their rightful cupboards. "I'm not really sure. I don't think I'm nervous. But, then again, I haven't seen him in a while."

Sally smiled as the heat in my cheeks grew to a rose flush. "I think he's the one for you, Belle."

I couldn't help myself as I let out a laugh at her comment. Those who knew Sally were aware of how much of a hopeless romantic she professed to be – constantly dreaming of happy, fairy tale endings. On the other hand, I was far more cynical about romance and so-called happy endings, especially since Ross. I didn't allow myself to believe in fairy tale endings anymore. Ross had crushed every possibility to dream of such things. But I'd be lying to myself if I said I didn't dare to believe in them, just once, when I thought about Edward.

"Ah yes, I forgot that you don't believe in happy endings," Harriet chirped in, mocking me with a grin on her lips. "But it looks like you're going to have to try to because it's almost time for you to go and meet Officer Blackwell."

I glanced at the watch on my wrist as it ticked down the minutes until I would finally set my eyes upon my new emerald paradise. I hurried out of the sluice room with Sally and Harriet close on my tail. Sister Mary stood in the corridor as we halted, causing her to turn her attention to us. She greeted us with her usual tight-lipped smile and stern, crinkled eyes.

"Have you put everything away?" she asked, already sensing I was on my way to leaving the hospital.

"Yes Sister," I responded, straightening myself to my full height as I pushed back my shoulders.

"Good," she replied, walking us towards the sluice room. She poked her head inside, assessing the room to see if there was anything else she needed me to do before leaving. Harriet, Sally, and I exchanged glances, awaiting the verdict. "You are free to go Nurse Wilson."

Sister Mary's scrutiny held me back from getting myself ready for the afternoon. Yet Sally and Harriet still insisted on me changing into the dress before making my way to the bus stop. The lilac material danced around my ankles as the breeze spun the dust from the pavement. The sunlight elongated the shadow of the man my heart yearned for as I approached the bus stop. Edward stood with his back against the wall, a white rose dangling from his hand, as he awaited me. My breath caught in my throat as the white petals tried to bring my mind back to the night of the dance in the village hall when Michael presented me with a white rose too. It was the same night Ross and I argued about joining the war effort, resulting in both of us being in this situation now.

I regained my composure and took a deep breath before stepping forward. My heels clacking against the pavement drew his attention, turning his gaze towards me. A smile pulled at the edges of his lips as I approached. "Hello," I greeted him. The sapphire blue of the hospital uniform still made him as handsome as the day I left him at the Officers' Hospital. His hair seemed to have been cut as his curls were far shorter than I remembered them. But those eyes… I couldn't possibly forget them. As his orbs mixed with mine in a sea of autumn hue, I knew his love would remain the bane of my existence – the desire to wake up every single morning just to love him once more.

"Belle," he breathed out, blinking rapidly. He stepped forward as his smile grew into a beaming grin. "I thought you weren't coming."

"I got held up at the hospital; you know how Sister Mary is. But I'm here now."

Edward handed me the rose with an outstretched hand, and I took it gracefully, examining the white petals. The bus pulled up as Edward opened his mouth to speak, ceasing his words before he could utter a syllable. He took my hand, helping me onto the bus, as we took a window seat. The stick he once relied on now rested over his arm as he used it less often than he had done. He started to tell me about his recovery as more people bustled onto the bus.

"I still never get used to it," Edward mumbled to me when men and women kept nodding at him. They recognised the hospital uniform and knew he had fought at the front – waiting to return after his recovery. "They're silently thanking me for fighting in a war that I not only got injured fighting in, but also one that I had no choice about joining."

"I'm glad you're safe though," I mumbled, not wanting to talk about the war if I didn't have to. He quickly caught on and talked of any other topic that came to mind; from the men we met in the hospitals to the difference in the gardens. Hearing the sweet melody of his voice fill the void my soul had hollowed out just for him created a peaceful paradise.

"The thing I miss most is you," he admitted, not breaking eye contact with me as he spoke. My cheeks burnt in a fiery red and I diverted my eyes away, down to the rose which rested on my lap. "I got that rose from the hospital gardens. They don't know I took it, but I did get some strange looks asking for a pair of scissors to walk around the gardens with."

"This is why I miss you – your humour and how you always make light of everything in this war."

He shrugged as our eyes met one final time with the rumbling of the bus driving off. The sunlight caught his face in a shadow of sorrow mixed with love. A unique combination of what this war had done to each of us. "What else can you do in a situation like this?"

We sat in silence the rest of the way to the coastline. Edward continually allowed his hand to brush against the back of mine, sending sparks flying through every vein in my body. The deep yearning for time alone with him grew stronger with each touch of his skin against mine. How did people cope with this love?

The unexplainable emotions tumbling into one large atom until it burst in an explosion of passion and love.

When the bus pulled to a stop near the coastline, we made our way off and towards the cliffs Edward directed me to. With the rose in one hand and Edward's hand in my other, the world of daisy fields and broken promises seemed miles away from the future I wanted in that very moment. This was more than I ever wanted and desired in my wildest dreams. The path grew muddy as we walked, but if I fell, I didn't want to let go of what either of my hands held. Yet, if I had to pick one to drop, it would be the rose. It would forever be the rose to crash to the ground.

The climb to the top of the cliffs grew steeper with the further we reached, but the view was worth it. The long grass danced by my knees and stretched out before us laid the great expanse of the sea. The grey waves lapped against the rocks on the sand, mirroring the clouds above us. Sunlight tried to break through in rays of gold beaming from heaven itself. I couldn't quite believe that just across the expanse of waves laid a war unimaginable to the human mind. If I believed this was before the war, and we stood on a ground of peaceful means, then perhaps my shoulders would have lost the tension with the beauty spread out before my very eyes.

"This is beautiful," I commented, trying to push all thoughts of war from my mind. As much as I vowed to do so, I couldn't manage it. "How can something so beautiful still exist when the world is falling to pieces?"

Edward's grip on my hand tightened and then loosened. "There's beauty everywhere, even in times of trouble and distress." I turned to face him, but his eyes remained fixated on the view that it took him a while to realise I was watching him. The ray of sun hit off his orbs, sending them into a sparkling daze of summer fields. He glanced over at me and flashed a lop-sided smile. "If you stare at me much longer, I'll end up getting a complex." I stifled a laugh and let go of his hand for the first time since we climbed the cliffs. I walked over to a bank and pulled off my jacket to sit down. My feet hung off the ground, losing my toes in the grass as I swung them in the air. It didn't take Edward long to follow and sit down beside me on the bank. Without wasting another second longer, he took hold of my hand again, lacing our fingers in an unbreakable bond. "What are you thinking about?"

I smiled slightly as the memories of his lips against mine in the trees flooded back to me. Perhaps it was when we were in the trees in the pouring rain that I realised I loved him, but as I turned to speak to him and the sunlight caught his face in shards of passion and desire, I knew then that I loved him far longer than I could have thought possible. "I'm just remembering us in the trees that day in the rain."

A smile pulled at the edges of his mouth as he put his finger under my chin, pulling me closer to him. Our breath mingled together, forming a mist between us as our lips grazed. Gravity refused to give us what we desperately needed by the shoreline. Edward fought against every force parting us and kissed me gently. The taste of the salt air coated his lips, reminding me how far from home I truly was. But what if right here, in the salt air of the coastline with Edward, was home? What if home was wherever Edward and I were?

Waves lapped and crashed against the cliffs of the beach as we stayed there, embracing each other in the middle of a war tearing the whole world apart. I couldn't have asked for a more perfect moment with Edward. We pulled away, breathless, as I laid my head on his shoulder. He wrapped an arm around me, holding me close to his side. I fitted into the grooves of his body as though I had always meant to be there. Neither of us broke the quietness, fearing it might ruin the magic of this memory. I needed to speak to him about the war effort and my next steps, but not at that moment. Not when the whole world ceased to exist except for us.

When Edward began to discuss returning to the frontline again, I knew I had to take my chance to say what I needed to. My chest tightened as my body started to shake in anticipation of the reception that he would give me once he found out.

"I might be joining you out in France." I lifted my head from his shoulder as his furrowed brow and clouded eyes greeted me. I glanced away, watching the waves come in and out with a rhythm which soothed my tightening throat. "We've received a call up to go to France. They need some VADs over there in the field hospitals with the war getting worse."

"Are you signing up?" he questioned. His voice remained steady, but the undertones of caution seeped through, nonetheless.

I shrugged, letting out a deep sigh. "I haven't decided yet. Sally, Harriet, and I are really considering going. We know the men need us here, but the aid is desperately required over on the frontlines in Belgium and France. I wouldn't feel right staying here, knowing they need me over there."

I waited with baited breathed for Edward to protest and argue like Ross had. The anger in Ross' spat words remained imprinted in my memory from that night. His quivering chin and shaking hand as he flung accusations of a false affection for Michael outside the village hall. I bit my lip as Edward remained silent, anticipating the same reaction from him.

"I'd be worried about your safety," he started, stroking my back as though sensing how much my hands shook. "But if this is something that you feel like you need to do, then I would never discourage you from it."

My gaze shot straight to him as a beaming smile emerged on his face. He truly meant everything he said. He wanted me to help the men and join the war effort to my greatest ability. I wrapped my arms around him, breathing in his familiar scent as his arms made their way around my waist. He pecked my cheek as we broke away from the hug and he stood up, putting his hand out for me to take. We took a stroll through the grass with the sun beating its rays down on us, clearing the clouds which had once disturbed our view of the deep blue ocean. The salt air caressed my skin as we walked and my once tame hair now broke strands away from the bun, flying about in the breeze like kites of golden sheaths. As his fingers maintained their grip in mine, my thoughts remained miles away from Ross, the hospital, and even the war. Edward had the ability to take me to a whole different world just by being in his presence.

He tugged my hand, pulling me back to him, and pretended to dance with me. His hand wrapped around my waist as he kept his hand in mine. Humouring him, I put my other hand on his shoulder. I bit the inside of my cheek, trying to conceal my laughter. Edward started to hum a song which was so much out of tune that I didn't have a clue what it was supposed to resemble. I snorted as the bubbling laughter threatened to burst out of my body. Without waiting a moment longer, the cliffs echoed with my laughter as Edward continued to dance with me. The vibrations of his chest against mine would forever remind me of coming home.

"You do not have a single note in your head," I told him between splutters of laughter.

He chuckled, and I swore I imprinted that sound into my memory for the rest of my life. "I'm afraid I don't have musical flare in my body. But I shall keep trying." He held me close to him, ignoring the flying strands of my hair which brushed against his cheek. "The next time we meet, I'll be out of hospital and back home before returning to the front. I've written to my parents about you, and they'd like to meet you when I'm home."

Every colour in my body drained into the soil beneath our feet as my heart thudded in my ears. Edward's family had a higher class status than I did or would ever have in society. No matter how many times Edward had told me that it didn't matter, he never once spoke for the rest of his family. My skin grew clammy, and I prayed he wouldn't notice as he held me close. I cast my eyes away, afraid he could understand my thoughts from a single look at me. Yet, despite every logical reasoning in my mind, I accepted his offer, knowing it would be the last time we saw each other before he returned to the front.

"Of course. I'd love to meet your parents." My voice remained steady as I spoke, sweeping the clouds of doubt away from his eyes as I finally looked back at him.

A grin broke across his face as he planted his lips on mine. His hands cupped my face, allowing not even the salt air to come between us. When he pulled away, he picked me up and spun me around, replacing the memory of the daisy field with salt air and crashing waves. He set me down and kissed me once more with a passion and vigour I hadn't experienced from his lips before. Perhaps this was the most important step for him in understanding my feelings – if I accepted his offer, I meant every word of affection I ever spoke to him.

Edward reached for his stick as we made our way back to the bus. The slow walk helped Edward to regain the strength in his leg, although he would never admit he winced every now and again as we descended the cliffs. The bus waited by the stop as we approached; the driver clearly spotting us in the mirror with Edward in his hospital uniform. He nodded his thanks to the driver as we climbed into the bus towards the nearest seat.

Edward breathed heavily with beads of sweat forming on his forehead as he took his seat. I returned my head to his shoulder as the rumble of the bus engine drifted us into the reality of parting again. Edward's grip tightened on my hand, and we refused to let go of each other – neither wanting to part when we had just come together again.

"I'll have a few minutes before the bus comes to take me back to the hospital," he informed me as the engine slowed to a halt. I nodded, unable to form any words without tears blurring my vision. Crying would only make our parting more difficult for us.

We stepped off the bus and waited by the stop at the side of the road for Edward's next transport to his hospital. With a swift movement, he drew me into his arm in an embrace of longing and yearning beyond our own words. We needed to hold each other before we said goodbye; the next time we spoke those words, Edward would leave for the front. We wanted to make each second together count, to give us something to remember in our darkest hours away from each other. People didn't stare, knowing he was a soldier saying farewell to his sweetheart.

"I don't want to go," Edward mumbled into my hair. I shifted myself away from him to look into his eyes which were glazed with tears. I swallowed hard, trying to stop myself from crying. "I don't want to be parted from you from this day forward… I… I'll miss you."

My breath caught in my throat at his hesitation. Those weren't the words he desired to speak. "I don't want to part from you either. But we'll send letters and see each other very soon."

At that moment, the rumbling of the bus signalled its arrival to finally separate us. Edward kissed my cheek, and I savoured that single touch for the rest of the night. He dug into his pockets and produced an envelope with my name scrawled across it. I frowned, taking it with a cautious hand as though it were ready to jump out at me.

"Just like old times at the hospital," he said, grinning at me as he walked towards the bus.

I beamed at him, holding the envelope and rose against my chest. "I'll read it when I get inside – I promise."

He took one step into the bus and turned to smile at me before disappearing from my view. As it drove past, Edward stayed at the window, waving back at me. I refused to move until the bus faded into the busy streets completely out of sight. And, just like that, Edward fled from my life again by the war. The hollowness in my heart bore a pain which remained with me as I changed back into my uniform to complete the rest of my shift.

Before leaving for the hospital, I read his letter and couldn't remove the rose flush which coated my cheeks in an illuminated glow. When Sally and Harriet greeted me in the ward, they questioned if I was feeling fine. Using the excuse of a brisk walk to the hospital, they ceased their interrogation. It was a lie of course, but I couldn't tell them about the letter. Since Ross, I didn't believe in promises anymore. Despite Edward fulfilling many of his, I couldn't allow myself to believe in the possibility of the one proposed to me in his cursive handwriting.

My lovely Belle,
Thank you for an amazing day spent with you. I hope by now you will have agreed to meet my parents – if you have, I want you to know that there is a very specific reason as to why I have requested it.

I have completely fallen in love with you. You consume my every thought and dream in a day. You're the first thought at the dawning sun and the last thought at the dusk of starlight. Leaving you is always so difficult because I want to be with you forever. When this war ends, I would like to ask for your hand in marriage. I do not want your answer yet as this war changes much more than we could possibly comprehend. But, I promise, when we meet at the end of the war, if your feelings still match mine, I will hopefully make you mine if you say yes. You are everything to me Belle Wilson. You are the purpose of my very existence and the reason for every dream I have ever had in my lifetime.

I look forward to your letter and seeing you again when I get out of hospital for the final time.

All my love forever,

Edward.

Chapter Thirty

"Paul, you'll be the death of me," I said through gritted teeth as I washed his bleeding foot wound once again. Twice in one day had been his previous record. This now marked the third time in a single day. "You've been told time and time again not to walk on your foot. Yet you still insist on doing so."

He shrugged, keeping his eyes on his hands which sat on his lap in the bed. "They already think I'm a coward, so I can't lie in bed until it's better."

I applied the disinfectant and he winced, gripping the bedsheet. His eyes crinkled at the corners as he tried to wish away the pain. "That's all well and good to say Paul, but you'll make yourself worse. I dream of the day that I'll come to treat you and be told that you've recovered by doing what you're meant to."

As I wrapped his foot up, he stayed as silent as he had when he first came to the hospital. I allowed my mind to wander to thoughts of Edward. A week had passed since we last saw each other and, despite writing letters, my heart couldn't settle until I laid eyes on the man I loved. We had already agreed on our final meeting before he went off to war. Next week marked the day that caused the most nausea I had ever experienced – the day I had to meet his parents. I threw myself into my work in the hospital to cease all anxious thoughts about the meeting.

"All fixed. Now don't you be walking around," I warned him, wagging my finger at him in good humour.

He smiled slightly before glancing at his foot. "Do you think I'm a coward?"

My movements froze the second he finished speaking. I opened my mouth to respond but no answer formed itself. My lips shut once more as I weighed up my response in my mind, busying myself by tidying up the medical equipment from his bed. "Well, I have loved ones fighting. I do think they're very brave and the men I've treated here have become close friends of mine too. But… I've seen how this war is affecting every single man who crosses my path. I'm not sure I'll recognise my loved ones when they come back because of the horrors they've seen. To answer your question: no, you're not a coward. I'm not sure I would have done anything different in your situation."

Paul's eyes met mine as we smiled at each other in mutual understanding. His shoulders lost all the tension as the creases around his eyes deepened in a hopefulness of reassurance. I moved on to the next man, but I couldn't stop thinking about the words I spoke to Paul. *I'm not sure I'll recognise my loved ones when they come back because of the horrors they've seen.* Would I recognise Ross and Edward after the war? Or would this conflict forever change the men that I once knew and loved deeply? I didn't want to imagine how they would come back from the war, but I already knew they would be half the men they once were. If I looked deep enough inside myself, I knew I would return someone completely different to the person I once was in 1914.

I returned the medical equipment to the sluice room after attending to the men who needed aid before visiting hours. I disinfected the bowl, allowing the distinct aroma to fill the air. The door swung open, whacking off the wall behind it, making me jump and spin around. Harriet stood there, out of breath with her hair flying out of her headdress. I closed the cupboard from putting the bowl back and ran straight to her.

"What's the matter?" I asked, putting my hand on her shoulder. Her body shook beneath my touch.

She regained her breath before talking to me. "It's Sally. She just got a telegram."

My heart sunk to the pit of my stomach as I realised this was the moment that we had all dreaded. This was when the war came directly to one of us – threatening to ruin our lives with a single telegram. Everyone who received a telegram delivery knew it meant either the man was missing or killed in action. Sally's brother had been fighting, but she hadn't received a letter from him in the last week. We had tried to reassure her he was fine, but in this instance, there was little we could do to offer the same reassurance of his safety. It was only Sally and her brother in their family – their parents had died only a year apart from each other. Harriet and I sped to the corridor near the front door as Michael embraced Sally who sobbed uncontrollably into him. His eyes met mine and, as if he knew what I wanted to ask, he nodded to confirm our worst nightmares. Her brother had died in the war.

Tommy's death had marked the only war death I had experienced so far. Every day I dreaded receiving a letter from Mother or Margaret to tell me a telegram had reached the Mason household, stating that Ross had met his end on the battlefield. As I watched Sally cry her heart out against Michael, my chest tightened picturing myself in the same situation as Sally over Ross. I pushed all thoughts of Ross or Edward to the back of my mind, knowing I had to be there for Sally.

Michael returned to his duty when we approached as we took care of Sally until her sobs had settled to mere gasps of air. Harriet and I allowed Sally to cry into us, uncaring as to whether our uniform stained with tears or not. When she felt ready to speak to Sister Mary, we walked her to the ward, gripping her hands to keep her grounded in the reality outside of the loss. She needed to regain enough of her strength to tell Sister Mary about the death. We insisted that she wasn't able to work today after the shock was still so clear on her pale features, but she fought against us with all her might, even in front of Sister Mary.

"What use will sitting crying do?" she protested with bloodshot eyes. She sniffed and wiped away her tears with the back of her hand. "I need to help these men; it's what Jack would have wanted me to do. I shall take an hour off during visiting and, I will return to my duty before the visitors leave."

Sister Mary opened and closed her mouth, utterly speechless at Sally's comments, which was a rare occurrence. Sally had always been the quiet one; she gave everyone the impression that she wouldn't say boo to a fly. Now, in the face of grief itself, she grew a confidence I could only ever dream of mastering. We never know what way sorrow and grief will affect us until it happens without any warning. All that we could do was agree with her wishes as she walked off from the ward. As we watched her go, a nurse approached Sister Mary.

"Sister, Paul is wanting to go outside."

Sister Mary sighed and shook her head. "That man hates being in the ward… Right, get him a wheelchair. I'll need two nurses to take him out. He likes walking himself when one nurse's back is turned."

Harriet nudged me before speaking. "Sister, Nurse Wilson and I will take him out."

She stared at the two of us, mulling it over in her mind. "Yes, that would do. Thank you, Nurse Smith."

Once we managed to get Paul settled into the wheelchair, I pushed him outside to the gardens while Harriet kept pace beside us. We took him around the concrete pathways of the garden, admiring the flowers which had started to come up in the warmer weather of spring. Harriet tried talking to Paul to find out why he didn't like being in the ward out of mere conversation. I kept reaching over to give his shoulder a reassuring squeeze when he shook his head in refusal to tell her. It was a secret between us – the reasoning behind every sorrowful look he gave us when he laid in bed in the ward; trapped by his own thoughts and injury. He would never openly admit it to anyone else, but he thought every man in the ward viewed him as a coward. He didn't know if Harriet would understand why he shot himself in the foot. As much as I could try to tell him that she would, he wouldn't pay attention to it.

When we did a full circle of the gardens, Paul pointed to Tommy's bench as we passed it. We glanced over as Sally sat there, crying and holding the telegram in her fist with a handkerchief in her other hand. We made our way over to her, pushing Paul in the wheelchair despite his offer to walk across the grass. Sally gazed up at us when the pounding of the wheels drew her attention. She wiped away her tears with the silk handkerchief.

"What's wrong?" Paul asked her as we put the wheelchair at the end of the bench, allowing him to sit beside her. Sally gave him a tight, sad smile and told him about her brother's death. He sighed and reached out for her hand. "I'm sorry for your loss. You must know that you made him proud."

Sally nodded as a hiccup escaped her lips from her sobbing. "Thank you, Paul. But I could be helping more men to make him proud of me."

Harriet and I glanced at each other, knowing exactly what she meant. Sally wanted to sign up to go to France as a VAD. Her brother's death had changed her indecisive mind. "You're applying for France then?" I questioned, staring into the tree to spot the Blue Tit resting on the branch.

"Yes – Jack's death has changed everything. I've no one left to stay here for now that he's gone. I might as well continue the fight for him in whatever way I possibly can. Have you two decided yet?"

"I'm going too," Harriet immediately agreed with her. Not one ounce of hesitation filled her tone of voice as she spoke with confidence in her decision.

Silence descended upon us as they waited to hear what I had decided. None of them pushed me for an answer as I contemplated it. All I had left in Britain was memories of Ross and Tommy. Leaving the country felt like leaving them and everything they meant to me behind. But going to France for the war effort didn't feel like leaving Edward. It made my heart grow closer to him with each time I decided I just might go. I wanted to help more men in this war and help to save their lives. Was France the right answer for me too?

"I'm applying to leave for France too," I finally decided out loud. I looked to either side of me as Harriet and Sally grinned, knowing that we were going to be joining the work in France together. Part of me worried about what the men would think of me leaving. Would they presume I abandoned them? A hand landing on mine drew my attention to what truly did matter. I looked at the hand which strained in reaching me with veins coming to the forefront of the skin. My eyes gazed to the side until they met Paul's proud smile. He squeezed my hand, telling me I was doing the right thing despite the doubts in my mind.

As if on cue, the Blue Tit rang out its sweet melody into the spring air. Tommy agreed with my decision to go; he was never going to leave me, just like Mrs Felton had stated in her letters. He would always support me, no matter how far I travelled to do my duty. I hoped I would still feel close to him in France – away from where the birds sang, and the Blue Tits never appeared to grace the men. I didn't want to lose that part of him by leaving.

When it neared the end of visiting hours, we took Paul back inside to the ward. Sister Mary rushed over to Sally to speak with her as we put Paul back into his bed. Harriet stood by the bed as I settled Paul before pulling the blanket over him. His eyes darted to either side of him, but none of the men paid him attention, easing the tense clenching of his jaw. We walked back to Sister Mary as Sally asked if we could speak with her privately. Collectively, we knew this was what we wanted to do for our duty and the men who were fighting. Sister Mary walked the three of us to her office, instructing us to sit down as she took her seat behind the desk

"We would like to apply to go to France next year," Harriet told her, raising her chin as she spoke.

Sister Mary kept a neutral expression, evading all our expectations of surprise. "All three of you?" She raised an eyebrow as we nodded in response to her question. I swore, for a split second, I spotted a small smile pulling at the corners of her mouth. "It's about time. I thought you three would have been the first ones to sign up."

"We each had a lot to consider," I mumbled, swallowing hard at the memories of Tommy coming back to my mind.

Sister Mary made a hum of agreement, nodding in my direction. "I understand. Well, I'll get the papers to you as soon as possible."

We thanked her before leaving her office. The second we closed the door behind us, Sally pulled us into a hug in the corridor. I breathed a shaky sigh as I held them, knowing life would never be the same again. We made our way back to our wards to continue our duty until the nightshift came in. As we worked, we exchanged beaming smiles with twinkling eyes at the prospect of joining the war effort in France. All we desired to do was help more men who needed us, especially with the war getting worse. Now we had the chance to become part of something even greater than what we had already done.

When we got back to the boarding house and ready for bed, I lifted out Tommy's letters and notebook from my bedside drawer. I flicked through the pages and smiled at the sight of his familiar handwriting. My heart yearned just to receive one letter or note from Tommy, but it would never happen. He was gone and all that remained was a hollow in my soul in the shape of him. My fingertips instinctively traced the indents made by his pencil. The last remnants of a life lost too soon to a conflict where men tried to see how little their humanity meant.

"Are you sure you'll be able to leave everything behind?" Harriet asked me from her bed.

I chewed the inside of my cheek and glanced over at her. She sat cross-legged, waiting on my answer with a reassuring smile. "I'm not sure. I thought I wouldn't be able to go before, but I did. I don't have anything left here for me anymore."

"So, Edward is going back to the front again then?"

I nodded, trying to resist a rose blush creeping onto my cheeks at the thought of him. "Yes, once the hospital deems him fit to go. So, I won't have anything here once he goes. What about your husband? Is he alright?"

Harriet shrugged, playing with the lace on the hem of her nightdress. "He's still at the front, so I'm in the same position as you. But I hear it's worse in the hospitals over there. We'll have to find a way to cope with the things we will see."

As I held Tommy's notebook close to my chest, I realised what I had to do to try to cope when I left for France. The only thing that helped me with what I witnessed in the hospital in Poole was writing letters to Edward. When I left for France, I had to keep picking up the pen and writing to Edward, my parents, Mrs Felton, and Ross. Perhaps it led the way to healing my broken heart from Tommy too.

Chapter Thirty-One

Seeing Edward for the final time had plagued my thoughts and our letters for the last two weeks. The day had come around with little more than an anxious knotted stomach on my part. Sister Mary had moved us to the nightshift, so I had the day free to travel to see Edward's family. When I admitted to Sally and Harriet about meeting his family, they shared sly smiles between each other before telling me that our relationship must be verging on serious. I refused to speak of the promise Edward made in his letter and the proposal he set out for the rest of our lives. I didn't want anyone but us to know about his intentions in case they fell to little more than blank words.

The clock struck noon as Edward's car stopped outside the boarding house. I glanced out of the window, spotting a man behind the wheel. With the war bending our ideals into mere questionable morals, I had forgotten how improper it was for us to see each other without a chaperone present. This man must have fulfilled the chaperone role for Edward's parents. I wasn't sure if I could ever get used to being watched after spending so much time alone with Edward. But, for one day with him, I made an exception; I would have done anything to spend this one final day with him before he returned to the war.

"You look beautiful," Edward gushed as soon as I made my way down the boarding house steps towards him. He took my hand in his, uncaring to the prying eyes which watched us at all angles. "It's seven thirty you have to be back for, isn't it?"

I nodded, squinting in the sunlight beaming down on us. "Seven thirty at the latest – Sister Mary's orders, of course."

Edward let go of my hand to open the car door for me. I slid into the seat and fixed my dress as Edward got into the seat beside me. As the car rumbled to a start, driving off from the boarding house, Edward reached over and laced our fingers together. My eyes bulged in his direction as I jerked my head towards the driver. Edward bit his lip before busting out laughing at my reaction.

"Matt here is the groundskeeper. We've been good friends and I asked him to drive us so he could act as a chaperone – that way we could at least be our normal selves before reaching my house," he explained, smiling from ear-to-ear as his eyes twinkled in the mischievousness that I'd only ever witnessed that day in the trees.

"It's nice to meet you, Miss Wilson. Edward hasn't stopped talking about you since he got back home," Matt spoke over the raucous noise of the engine. He turned to flash a smile in greeting to me. "His father is thrilled at the prospect of Edward finding a sensible woman eventually."

I merely nodded before glancing out of the window, watching the world fly past us in streaks of emerald and azure. Only one thought ran through my mind: the difference in social status between me and Edward. His parents had to have known about it before Edward had suggested meeting. What if they didn't accept me or our courtship? Nausea overcame my senses, and I pressed my hand to my forehead, attempting to calm my increasing temperature.

As if he knew what I was thinking, Edward squeezed my hand, pulling my attention to him. "It will be fine, Belle – trust me. You'll be welcomed with open arms and accepted by my parents. Father and Mother see Matt as another son."

"Indeed, they do, Miss Wilson."

I turned to Edward and let the traces of a smile pull at the corners of my mouth. "Please, call me Belle, Matt. Miss Wilson makes me feel older than I am."

The drive to Edward's house had proved shorter than I perceived it. I expected us to travel for over an hour at the most. Perhaps it had been Edward and Matt's comforting words which eased the anxious drive. As Matt turned into the driveway, my mouth fell open at the sight before me. One glance at the house caused my palms to grow clammy, yet Edward never let go of my hand. The house stood in a grey silhouette against the azure sky, with bright white framed windows. I swallowed hard as I estimated the size to be twice that of Ross' farmhouse. If I had any idea of not fitting into Edward's lifestyle before this, then I definitely did now. The emerald gardens stretched the length of the driveway and beyond the house itself. Flowers of all shapes and colours lined the stones the car crunched over in a rainbow guard of honour. The sunlight glimmered off the lake at the bottom of the garden at the front of the house.

"T-This is your house?" I stuttered, trying to ignore the tingling erupting in my chest.

Out of the corner of my eye, I spotted Edward's Adam's apple bobbing in his throat as he nodded. "It's too big and empty for me. Ideally, I'd love a cottage in the countryside."

The car pulled to a stop outside the house itself, making it tower over me in a dark shadow. Edward left the car first to open my door and I couldn't help but let a small grin escape over my lips as I remembered his words. *'I'd love a cottage in the countryside.'* Edward desired what I had always dreamt of. His determined and passionate tone rested my soul's doubt to our compatibility. He wasn't saying it for my benefit; he truly wanted a cottage in the countryside like Mother and Father had back home.

As we approached the steps towards the house, the mahogany door flung open as a small woman with greying curled hair stood watching us. Beside her, a significantly taller man eyed the two of us with a twitch of his silver moustache. My throat and chest clenched as he smoothed his grey hair down which had caught the slight breeze.

"Welcome," the man greeted in a voice deeper than I had anticipated. Edward rested his hand on the small of my back and the heat of his touch settled my tense muscles. "You must be Belle; Edward has told us so much about you."

Their mannerisms made me want to give them a curtsey, as the two of them pushed their shoulders back, holding their heads high. Edward's reassuring hand on my back reminded me not to embarrass myself to do such a thing. Instead, I reached out and shook their hands before they brought us inside. Despite the outward appearance, the house didn't resemble the overall size inside, but I soon discovered that it was due to the Blackwell's love of mahogany. They used the wood for the furniture and the doors which, in turn, enclosed and darkened their home.

They took us into the living room and, as I walked behind them, Edward held on to a part of my dress between his fingertips – a small mark of affection which his parents didn't and couldn't possibly see. I took a seat beside Edward on the sofa as his parents sat across from us, parted only by a small table with teacups and a teapot. Mrs Blackwell poured us a cup each, proceeding to discover more about me when I finally took a sip of the warm liquid.

"It's lovely to finally meet you Belle," she said, taking a sip from her own cup. "Edward kept talking and writing about you. To be honest, we were beginning to think he made you up."

A hearty laugh escaped from Mr Blackwell's mouth. "How glad we are that you weren't made up unlike before."

"Has Edward made up women before?" I couldn't help asking, with a teasing smirk.

"Oh yes," his father chuckled. I diverted my eyes to Edward, but he refused to meet my gaze. "He told us that he was courting a woman called Sharon. The silly fool made the whole thing up. Why, the only person we knew by that name was the Vicar's wife!"

I choked on my tea, almost squirting it up my nose. Edward rubbed my back as I coughed to clear the liquid from my nasal passage. I remembered when Edward told me he had an affair with the Vicar's wife when I first admitted my affair with Ross to him. Edward and I locked eyes as a smirk coated his pale pink lips. We were the only two in the room who knew he wasn't making any of it up. For once, a secret felt good to hold between two people.

"Of course, it wouldn't be the Vicar's wife," I agreed, regaining my breath from choking. I grunted lightly to stop myself from letting out a giggle or a laugh.

"Just what we thought," his mother seconded, nodding at her husband. Edward's hand remained between my shoulder blades. The heat blazed through my clothes, tempting me beyond my own comprehension. Our time alone couldn't come quick enough.

After we drank our tea, Edward offered to show me around the gardens of the house, knowing how much I loved the gardens at the hospital. Our roles had reversed as I reminisced back to taking him around the hospital gardens when he had recovered enough to try to walk by himself. As we sauntered around the paths, between the beds of flowers, I leant over the rose bush to take in the scent of the white petaled flowers which had followed me for years. Edward's eyes followed every move I made with an indescribable twinkle to them. He took my hand and led me towards the lake at the bottom of the gardens as the sun started to elongate the shadows across the stones.

The sun glittered against the water of the lake as though it were a precious diamond yet to be discovered. I watched as the breeze rippled the surface of the water in small waves undistinguishable to the passer-by. Edward's arms wrapped around me from behind, pulling me into the comfort of his solid chest, and I leant myself against the warmth of his body. A satisfied sigh escaped my mouth as his fingers laced with mine.

"Are you sure we're allowed to do this?" I whispered, afraid to break this moment from the peacefulness it granted us.

He nodded, settling his chin against my shoulder. "They can't see us from here." I let out a laugh, jolting my body enough to make Edward pull away. He spun me around, greeting me with a furrowed brow. "What's funny?"

"Your father thinking you made up courting a woman called Sharon."

He stifled a laugh as he shook his head. The sun glinted off his curls, echoing the tones of grey in the strands. "If only he knew that it was the Vicar's wife."

We gazed into each other's eyes in nature's silence. I retraced every colour of the window to his soul – from the grey-green to the burst of golden brown. The most unique pattern I'd ever witnessed in my whole existence. The colours of autumn burned together as we refused to break each other's stare. Edward gripped my hands, pulling me into his chest once more, enough to lean his head towards me. His lips brushed against mine, as though unsure of the territory, before the passion fired in his veins. I wrapped my arms around his neck, deepening the kiss as we defied every expectation of this war. It didn't crumble our spirits; it rose them higher than ever before. In this war we found a new life – a new purpose to our existence. In that moment, our purpose on this Earth was each other.

Edward pulled away and leant his forehead against mine, letting our breath mix in a warmth of desire. The sunlight broke between the gap in an amber fire, creating a golden glow which lit up his beautiful orbs. He laid his hand against my cheek and, for a second, he opened his mouth as though to speak. As his lips closed, he placed a kiss on my forehead. I reached my hand to his against my cheek, interlocking our fingers against my skin.

"We don't belong here," he whispered as the bird sang around us. He let out a sigh as his jaw clenched for a moment. "We don't belong in the middle of a war."

"We may not belong, but we found each other against every odd this war put us under. It will soon be over though."

"Will we make it?"

Edward's hand trembled against my alabaster cheek, threatening to break his resolve. For the first time since I had known him, the sheer terror of returning to the front bore through his exterior. I laid my other hand against his own cheek, rubbing my thumb against his smooth skin. His eyes met mine as they clouded over with sorrow and terror which desired to break into rain.

"We will make it," I affirmed with a strong, firm tone. I swallowed hard, knowing how difficult it would be to make it through this war as the same people we were now. "We *will* survive this war because we… we need to. We have a promise to keep to each other."

The edges of his mouth twitched as he tried to smile despite the pain searing through his chest. I planted my lips against his, hoping a single kiss would reassure every doubt he had about us in the middle of this conflict. He engulfed me into his arms, so I didn't watch him cry, as the plunks of droplets pattered against my hair. I snuggled my head into his chest, listening to the melody of his heartbeat. If I found myself taking my dying breath, the echo of his heartbeat would be all I desired to listen to in those final moments of my life. As I stood there by the lake, wrapped in Edward's warm embrace, I had broken my own rule. The one promise I had made to myself after Ross and Tommy crumbled into a thousand pieces. I loved Edward Blackwell more than I would ever care to admit to myself, but I loved him more than any words in this world could do justice to. I loved him with every ounce of my soul and entire being.

Dinner with the Blackwell family descended into silence on my part. I tried to speak when someone spoke directly to me, but my mind remained on how much my chest tightened at the thought of loving Edward. My hand shook as I picked up a mouthful of food on a fork, trying to swallow despite how much my throat clenched. When Tommy died, it broke me too much and I swore I wouldn't allow myself to love again. I couldn't suffer the pain of losing someone I loved all over again. But one look in Edward's eyes removed every resolve I had and that terrified me to the depths of my bones.

Edward glanced over during the dinner, noticing my silence, but not wanting to draw attention to it in front of his parents. Once we finished, he glanced at his watch and declared he would drive me back to the hospital himself. Neither of his parents argued with him as they must have picked up on my silence too.

I tried to maintain my cheerfulness as I bid them farewell. The smile strained against my cheeks, crinkling the lines around my eyes in an almost painful expression. Nevertheless, Mrs Blackwell hugged me, promising to send me a small gift at Christmas to help me through the hardships at the hospital.

Edward helped me into the car before waving at his parents as he started the engine. The second we reached the bottom of the driveway he began bombarding me with questions over my silence. His hands tightened and slackened against the wheel with each question and evasive answer I gave him. The vein in his neck protruded the more he continued with the interrogation.

"Did I do something inappropriate at the lake?" he asked, pulling the car out into the main road, away from the house.

I shook my head, diverting my eyes away from him. "No Edward, you did nothing."

"Was it my parents?"

"No!" I exasperated, throwing my head back. Edward stopped the car at the side of the road, turning off the engine. His eyes bore into me, but I continued to glance anywhere away from him. "Shouldn't we be going back to the hospital?"

"Not until you tell me what is wrong."

Tears rolled down the curves of my cheekbones every time I blinked. I swallowed hard as a shaky breath left my lips. I had to tell him the truth; it would either make or break us. But he was worth every risk in this world. "I love you, Edward. I've tried to bury the feelings under every hurt in my heart because I swore that I wouldn't love another after losing Tommy. The pain was too much to bear. I couldn't risk loving you and losing you too. Against my better judgement, I completely, utterly, and catastrophically love you. I don't regret it one bit. You are the obsession of my heart, the missing piece my soul has sought to find for all these years. I have spent the last few hours in agony because of how much the fire inside me blazes and burns for you. If your feelings have changed since your letter, I will understand, but I will forever love you and let myself fall for you with every new dawn."

Edward reached forward, cupping my face in his hands, awaiting any sign of my own inclination. I stretched my head towards him, giving him every signal that he desired as his lips met mine. He pulled me into his body, moulding us into one being. My chest pressed against his as my arms wrapped around his neck. Each touch of his lips sparked fire through my veins, becoming the very reason my heart thumped against my breast. Every kiss before disintegrated to dust as passion and desire oozed from our lips, coursing through the other's body.

"You have no idea how long I've waited to hear those words from your lips," he breathed out, beaming at me. "I love you too; more than anything possible in this mess of a world. My feelings haven't changed since I first wrote those words to you. You are the reason my heart continues to believe in the goodness of man when humanity has fallen to the depths of hell. Belle, I love you with every ounce of my being – more than I myself could ever comprehend. I hated the sound of forever, until I met you. Forever is the most beautiful word I could imagine, and I see forever every time I look into your beautiful chestnut eyes. Belle, I would live a thousand lifetimes just to meet your soul in one of them."

He pecked my lips, leaving them in place for a single second. Perhaps if we held on longer, we would erase time itself and reach the forever we so desired with each other. He pulled away, knowing we had to return to the boarding house for my shift. We arrived with enough time for me to change into my uniform as the time ticked down to the start of my shift. The rain hammered against the car as Edward ran out to open my door for me. Despite the rain, he hugged me, embracing me into the warmth of his body. The water soaked through my dress to my skin, clinging to every part of my body, yet I didn't care. All I desired was to spend a second longer with Edward before the inevitable farewell. With clenched jaws and reluctant eyes, we let each other go in our separate ways.

I ascended the steps of the boarding house, lifting the bottom of my dress to run in the rain. Edward shouting my name over the echoes of water pattering the pavements made me freeze in place. I spun around as he sprinted up the steps after me. The rain cascaded over his face in patterns and designs which only nature could claim. He took my hands in his as the water flowed over the crevices of our bond.

"Will you see me off next week?" he asked as his eyes searched mine for an answer. His breath formed a mist between us, clouding his lips from my view.

I nodded, blinking away the rain drops which had fallen and rested on my eyelashes. My chest lightened as an adrenaline rush burst through my veins. Could he feel my pulse against his skin? Could he feel how much I yearned for him even in that moment? "Yes, of course I will."

"I love you," he breathed out with a beaming grin on his face. An unmistakable glow erupted over his cheeks even in the greying daylight of rainfall.

"I love you too, Edward."

I kissed his lips as the rain dripped over our skin. The tickling of the cascading water didn't deter us from each other. Every moment mattered in this war, and we weren't prepared to sacrifice any. The rain slid over our lips and into our mouths as we kissed each other, wishing to become one being. Loving someone and being loved was the greatest ability given to mankind. In a war, love would defeat every violence man inflicted upon each other.

He pecked my lips before letting me go into the boarding house to prepare for the nightshift. My mouth twisted into a permanent smile which refused to leave my face. I was utterly in love with Edward. Every tense muscle in my body ebbed away knowing I could finally admit my love for him without the stomach churning guilt I had lived with since falling for him. Not even the slowing pace and heaviness of my body towards the end of my shift altered my elated heart. Nothing would ever conflict the love I held for Edward… as long as I never saw Ross again until after the war ended.

Chapter Thirty-Two

"Give my best to Officer Blackwell and tell him that we don't want to see him in hospital until after the war is finished," Sister Mary instructed when I had requested the visiting hours off to see him to the front. It was the first time I'd spoken to her about my involvement with Edward. After her finding out so easily about me and Tommy, her raised eyebrows and tilted head at the mere mention of our courtship had stunned the stern Sister into momentary silence.

"Of course, Sister."

As I completed my duties with Sally, she quizzed me about the courtship and the next stages of advancing such a relationship. I couldn't help but question if she and Michael were considering advancing their own courtship from her excited, desperate tone as she asked me various questions. I had told Sally and Harriet about our confessions of love in the car and his request outside the boarding house. The secret of a possible engagement at the end of the war remained hidden between Edward and I – refusing to let itself slip to anyone we knew. We desired to keep it a secret; I more than Edward wanted it hidden. After Ross' broken promises, I didn't want the inevitable humiliation of having it flung back in my face if Edward never returned to me at the end of the war.

"What will you do about Ross?" Sally dared to ask as we dressed one of the beds lying in the corridor. We had just discharged one of the men and needed to ready the bed for the next patient coming from the front any day now.

I sighed and tried to ignore the grip around my heart at the mere mention of his name. "I love Edward and I won't possibly be seeing Ross until this whole war is over. So, he won't be able to conflict my feelings about Edward."

A chuckle resounded behind us as Sally opened her mouth to respond to me. We turned around as Paul hobbled towards us down the corridor. He wore a lop-sided smile as he spotted us watching him. "That never works, Nurse Wilson. You'll end up seeing Ross again and, when you do, you won't have a clue what to do about either man. I should know – I was engaged to a beautiful girl because I thought I wouldn't see my sweetheart again. And guess what? She bleedin' well turned up at the wedding."

Sally gasped as her hand flew to her mouth. Her eyes bulged as she became utterly enraptured by Paul's tale. "What did you do?"

"I called off the wedding and married my sweetheart a month later."

I rested my hand on Sally's shoulder to stop her from encouraging Paul any more than necessary. Stepping towards him, he put his hand against the wall as the smile fell from his face, knowing exactly what was coming. "You shouldn't be out of bed with your foot yet. You know that – now get back to bed, come on."

Paul tutted and rolled his eyes at me, but he didn't try arguing or putting up a fight when I walked him back to bed, arm in arm.

As we made our way through the corridors, he asked me who Edward and Ross were, showing me just how long he had stood in the corridor before we noticed him. Without thinking, I started to tell him everything from the affair at home to Tommy and Edward (minus the promise of a proposal after the war). He nodded, listening along to everything I said. A weight descended from my shoulders as I spilled my heart out to my most problematic patient. I helped him into bed, swinging his legs on top of the mattress, before tucking the blanket over him. He made noises of agreement as I spoke the final parts of the journey, nodding along when he felt necessary.

"You'll see this Ross fellow again," he stated, looking me deep in the eyes.

I shifted under his gaze, shuffling my feet on the floor as I tried to divert my eyes from the grey orbs boring into my skin. "How do you know?"

"Fate doesn't like people who have a set plan for their life," he replied. He took my hand, forcing my attention back to him. His eyes softened to a warmth which settled the unease in my fluttering stomach. "After all, where would the spontaneity in life be if nothing surprised you once in a while?"

I swallowed hard, knowing I couldn't possibly come up with a cohesive argument in response to him. The prospect of seeing Ross before the planned time made my stomach churn and a clammy perspiration built in my palms. Paul didn't seem to notice as he maintained his hold on my hand. "Why do you keep getting out of bed and walking around?"

"It's not to make my foot worse if that's what you're insinuating," he defended himself. Now, he diverted his gaze away from me with the acknowledgement that I had seen right through his plan. "I just want to try to make myself better quicker."

I sighed, taking his other hand in mine. He turned back to me with a quivering lip and chin; his eyes flooding with clouds of sorrow. "I know you do, Paul. But this isn't the way to do it. Resting will make it better; walking will make it worse. Promise me you'll stay in bed while I'm away today?"

"I promise."

The station in London bustled with people as the burning coal filled the atmosphere in an aroma which tingled my nose. Edward wrote to me, stating his officer uniform would make him stand out more than the others, but it didn't. The sea of khaki before my eyes drowned every man's face into oblivion as I tried to spot Edward among them. I had remembered the officer's uniform from when he ended up at the hospital. Yet the image in my mind did nothing to help me find him. I made my way over to a wall away from the crowds and pulled out the letter Edward had sent me stating where he would wait for me. The name of the café where I met with Ross stared back at me, flashing images I wished to forget from my mind.

The rustling of the paper fought for dominance against the chattering of the crowds as I folded the letter. I weaved my way between soldiers and their sweethearts towards the café where I last saw Ross. Flashes of his hand, still warm in mine, blurred my vision. I shook my head, trying to rid my thoughts of Ross, at least for this one day. The sun caused me to squint to try to spot Edward standing outside. I raised my hand to my forehead, shielding my eyes from the brightness of the afternoon. The aroma of cigarette smoke drifted into the air from soldiers who stood waiting for their train to call them to the front.

Finally, I laid my eyes upon Edward, standing with his back to the café, his chest puffed out as he displayed his uniform with a sense of pride all the men had. His gaze met mine as the entire world faded to a blur in a second. Time froze until he began to run towards me, ducking and dodging everyone until he scooped me into his arms. A laugh erupted from my lungs and my chest grew light as his embrace calmed every fear that I had ever possessed about us. He set me down, drawing me into him once more, before kissing me as he held me tight against his chest.

"I'm sorry I'm late," I apologised, glancing into his green orbs. "I was busy scolding one of the men for not doing what he's told."

Edward burst out laughing and I tried to memorise the sound for the lonely months, or years, I would have without him by my side. "That certainly sounds like my Belle."

A rose flush crept onto my cheeks as he spoke. *'My Belle.'* I swore I could listen to him calling me that for the rest of my life. Edward took my hand and led me towards the benches near the entrance of the train station. The noise descended to a dull roar with the further we walked towards the oak benches. No one stood around the entrance, all too eager to hop onboard a train heading to thc frontlines. If they knew what awaited them or their men would they so willingly rush at the shrill of the whistle?

The sunshine had warmed the oak as it beamed its rays onto the wood to soak its heat through our clothes when we sat down. I glanced at Edward who stared into the distance. He looked so different in his long coat and peak hat. I'd become so accustomed to his medical attire that I had almost forgotten he owned a uniform. The khaki green stood out against his sun-kissed skin, emphasising the curves of his face which I had memorised like the back of my hand. The high cheekbones stood to attention as he swallowed hard before his eyes met mine. A smile tugged at the corners of his mouth as he removed his hat to kiss me.

His lips traced mine in slow, passionate motions – the perfect goodbye kiss no one ever desired to receive. I had tried to convince myself this wasn't goodbye, but a mere farewell for a short time. His hands cupped my face as tears cascaded over my cheeks. We pulled away and Edward wiped away each damp trail with his calloused thumbs. His eyes glistened with the reality of the situation as he rested his forehead against mine.

"Don't cry Belle," he pleaded. He diverted his eyes to my lips before glancing back at me. "You'll just make this harder for me to leave."

"I wish you didn't have to go," I admitted, sniffing away the tears which were yet to pour. "Please stay safe and don't you dare go after any vicars' wives out in France or Belgium."

He chuckled as a single water droplet fell from his eye and travelled over his cheekbones. He pulled away for a split second to peck my forehead, as though it would distract my attention from the tears he sought to let out. "And don't go after any married men while I'm away. You're going to be my sweet fiancée when I come home from war."

"Promise?"

The colour of his eyes dimmed to a faded grey, echoing the sorrow and passion in his soul. A sincere smile coated his lips as my heart stopped for a single second. There was no doubt in my mind that Edward was the best thing to ever happen to me. Now, I had to say farewell to him and let the world try to take care of him in a conflict-struck humanity. His hands shifted against my cheeks, pulling me away from the thoughts of a farewell neither of us wanted to speak of.

"You're my Belle – the love of my life – and I cannot possibly break a promise to you."

We let the noises of the people surround us as we held each other, savouring every second we had together. He laid his lips gently against mine as we knew the time drew nearer to the parting we dreaded. I pulled him close to me as I wrapped my arms around his neck; not even the world could separate what destiny brought together. He broke away from my lips, taking his warm hands away from my face. A shivering chill caressed my cheeks, feeling the absence of his touch from my skin. Edward ruffled in his long coat until he produced an envelope.

"Don't open this until you are on the train back to the hospital," he instructed as I took it from him. My throat clenched, knowing this was the last letter I would receive from Edward face-to-face. Despite how much I hoped circumstances would change and I would see him once again before the end of this war, a doubtfulness clouded my inner being. "Are you joining me in France?"

I nodded and beamed at him as I remembered how supportive he had been to my desires. "The three of us – Harriet, Sally, and I – signed up, but it could be next year before we're called over."

"Well, let me know when you arrive if you can. I want to try to see you if it's possible when you get to France."

He took my face in his hands once more and pressed his lips to my forehead. My eyes closed as a sigh of satisfaction escaped from my mouth. "I can't believe I fell in love with you, Edward. You're all I want and more… In this war I managed to find you and love you. If that's all I'm able to say at the end of this, then I'll be more than happy."

Before I left the hospital, Paul had instructed me to tell Edward whatever was in my heart. It was his attempt to help me stay on the right path after confiding my conflictions between Ross and Edward. As I spoke the truth to Edward, the words slipped out effortlessly in a manner I was unaccustomed to. A peace settled in my thudding heart, easing the rate at which it beat underneath my breast. Edward's lips caressed mine in the only response I sought to know his true feelings before leaving. His tears slid down our cheeks in warm streaks of unsaid words and unspoken feelings.

Ross had never given an emotional response to leaving for the frontline. If I hadn't started working in the hospital, I wouldn't know why he portrayed a lack of emotion. But now I did. The romanticised image flooded Ross' mind as though it were a jolly holiday which granted him the heroic image to try to win my heart once more. Edward had witnessed the true frontline. He knew he could get killed or badly injured at any given second. Ross had no clue about any of the realities of the war. Now, he couldn't escape them. I didn't know who my heart felt more for – Ross and his romanticised war, or Edward and his horrifying war.

Edward took my hand as he stood up, leading me back towards the platform. We weaved our way between men covered in a fog of cigarette smoke, chattering men, and soldiers saying their final farewells to their sweethearts. Edward's fingers gripped mine, maintaining a strong hold on me until we reached the train itself. He flung open the red-wood door and helped me inside the train. He climbed in behind me, directing me towards an empty carriage with a hand on the small of my back. Even under the rush of farewells, the heat of his body radiated through to me, making me crave one final touch even more. He closed the carriage door behind us, rattling the small windowpane in the wood. I spun around to him as he stared into my eyes, searching them for something unknown.

"I'm not saying goodbye," he stated, shaking his head at me. "Saying goodbye means I'll never see you again. But I promise we will meet again when you get to France. I'm not letting you go Belle; not now and not ever."

Paul's voice telling me to admit my true feelings to Edward kept replaying in my mind as I readied myself to let him go. "Promise me one more thing?" I asked, taking his hands in mine. Edward nodded, awaiting my final request. "Promise me, when we meet again in France, that you'll make me yours."

A grin spread at an achingly slow pace across his face as he took in my words. "I promise."

Our lips met in a spark of passion as the whistle shrilled in our ears, piercing the moment we had shared. Edward held on to me for as long as he could before pulling away. He opened the door and led me into the corridor where crowds of women flocked out of the train. Edward tried to keep his grip on my hand, hooking our fingers together until the crowd pulled us apart. I lost myself in the sea of women as they stepped down from the train and stood waiting on their men to leave. I watched Edward as he stood at the window of the carriage; his palm rested against the glass as though he could touch me through the cold pane. As the train began to move, I followed along with the crowd as our eyes remained locked on each other until they couldn't any longer. The hollowness screamed in my heart, reminding me of the man who had left me once again with the other part of my soul.

The train journey home lulled me into a false reality, allowing me to believe in the possibilities of seeing Edward again before the end of the war. As the city turned to emerald and gold fields, I tore open his letter in the empty carriage. The loneliness I had found myself in became a sanctuary as I read one of Edward's most heartfelt letters. Teardrops stained the paper as I blinked, daring not to wipe them off for fear of smudging his beautiful cursive handwriting. For all I knew, it might have been the last part of Edward I held against my skin.

To my Belle,

By the time you're reading this, I'll be off to the frontline. Since meeting you, leaving has been the hardest decision I've had to make. It's my duty to go back, but please know I will do everything in my power to survive, for us – for you and the future we will have together when the war learns the meaning of peace and humanity again.

You have changed my whole world in such a short space of time. I truly never believed in love. I always perceived it as an old wives' tale. But the more I got to know you, I began to understand why people love and the beauty to be found in being loved in return. There wasn't a morning that I didn't wake up with a smile on my face with the mere thoughts of seeing you again. I will forever be grateful that you saved my life because now I get to spend the rest of it loving you.

You should be proud of yourself for the work you do because I'm so proud of you. I know every single man that you've cared for is grateful and blessed. My men have told me so when we spoke in the ward or the recreational areas in the hospital. Never doubt the impact you have on the lives of those around you and those you've helped.

Please write to me until we meet again Belle. I will keep all of my promises to you. Rest assured I will. Stay safe here and when you get to France.

I love you forever,

Edward.

Once I had replaced my dress with my uniform, I made my way back to the hospital to visit Paul before the staff served the men their dinner. He had voiced his concern for the day ahead; it was only right for me to let him know how it went. I walked towards the ward and opened the doors as Paul glanced at me. He sat up in bed, eagerly waiting the news of my day, as I took a seat on the edge of his bed.

"I'll tell you how it went, but only if you tell me the truth about whether you were walking around or not," I bargained, cocking an eyebrow at him. I already knew the answer before he gave me a response.

A sheepish smile spread over his face as he glanced away, before looking back at me. "I got up once. Now, tell me your news."

I shook my head at Paul before starting to tell him the details of me and Edward's departure. "I admitted everything in my heart, like you advised me to, and it seems like his feelings match mine. I've completely fallen for him, Paul. I've promised to keep writing to him while he's away."

"And what if he stops answering?" he quizzed, staring me dead in the eye. The hairs rose on the back of my neck as a lump formed in my throat. I descended into an easy silence as the same concern which Sally had over Ross came to the surface once again. Paul reached for my hand and gave it a comforting squeeze. "I'm not meaning to hurt you, Darling. But I've seen many a man ignoring their woman's letters at the front. Either because they don't want to be yearning for home or because they just can't mentally handle normal life."

I tried to swallow the lump away, but it didn't budge, reminding me of the possibility of Edward becoming a fleeting memory. "If that happens, I'll be fine. I'll understand."

"No feelings for the other fella?" he asked, ignoring my statement. He knew full well I wasn't going to be anywhere near fine if I never heard from Edward again. Nevertheless, I shook my head, puffing out my chest in response to him. It wasn't that I hadn't any feelings for Ross at all. Those affections I held for him liked to air themselves when I didn't want them to. But I hadn't thought about him due to preparing myself for Edward's farewell. In truth, I hadn't wanted Ross to confuse me, not when

I had fallen in love with Edward. "What happens if you see the other fella again?"

I stifled a laugh as my stomach knotted with the thought of it. "That'll never happen."

Paul patted my hand sympathetically at my naivety about Ross. The final words he spoke to me sent a shiver down my spine and my skin turned ice cold with each syllable he uttered. "I wouldn't be so sure, Darling. Crazier things have happened."

Chapter Thirty-Three

My dearest Belle,

Oh, how good it is to hear from you. Fighting is getting heavier here. But we are winning – I'm sure of it. I'm honoured that you told me about coming to France as a VAD. They will truly value you. Perhaps, we might meet again once you get here. Right now, I want nothing more than to see your face. I miss you so much; unbelievably so.

My friend got killed yesterday when we went over the top. The bullet just missed me. Just. How did I manage it? I should have been hit by it. Not him. I don't know why I was saved. The men tell me I'm lucky, but I don't feel it. I feel like I should be out there with his body, crying and apologising. As a man who has done people wrong in life, why did a man who did nothing to anyone leave this world so soon? I cannot explain the grief in my heart right now. Perhaps our lives are mapped out for us already. If they are, I'm not sure I want to see what's in store for me, especially not now when we're in the middle of a war.

Belle, I hope you know that you are doing an amazing job with the men in the hospital. After losing a friend, I know now why you joined up. If there was a small possibility of saving someone when the world is in turmoil, you would do it – anyone would. I'm sorry I didn't understand before. I try to resist the temptation to ask myself if only I had understood, would I be out on the frontline feeling like this? But I know I would still be here. I couldn't let you go to war alone. I care too much about you to let that happen.

Please stay safe Belle. I do not want to lose you. Even if we don't rekindle our love after the war, know that you mean the absolute world to me. You always will no matter what happens to us after this war.

All my love forever.

Ross.

Dear Ross,

I'm sorry about your friend. I know how difficult it must be for you. Please do not feel guilty for surviving the gunfire, Ross. *I know it's easier said than done, but it was meant for your friend. If there's one thing that I've learnt from this war is that everything happens for a reason. Although, I cannot give an answer as to why the good ones go before others. I still struggle to comprehend why Tommy would leave this world so soon when he did nothing to anyone. I was meant to go to war the way I did, so I had no attachment to home, and I could do my duty without homesickness plaguing me. Now that I'm preparing to go to France, I see this more than I did before. These men need me. So, I must thank you for leaving me the way you did last year. Without it, I wouldn't be who I am today.*

Another Christmas is about to pass without you again. While this is a new normal, I cannot seem to get used to it. Times when we would celebrate life now seem to be continuous periods of mourning for lives that should have been longer. Some of the shell-shocked men won't even know it's Christmas. That upsets me even more than I can put into words. The war is changing everyone and everything around us. I pray we don't experience another war like this again. I don't think our fragile hearts could take anymore.

In the spirit of Christmas, I sent you some socks. Yes, three pairs this time! Once of the nurses taught me how to knit, so I couldn't help but give you handmade socks. Two pairs I have knitted for you and one I bought with my earnings. Of course, I couldn't forget to include some cigarettes for you. Use them sparingly if you can.

Margaret sent me a Christmas card this year. She believes that by me nursing the men, I am somehow saving you. I really hope she's right Ross. While we may never rekindle the love we once had, I still care and have compassion for you. I want you to survive this. Everyone does. Mrs Felton sent me some writing materials that were once Tommy's for Christmas. I'm using them to write this to you. Mother and Father sent me biscuits and a new winter scarf. They ask me all the time if I have come across you yet. You truly have no idea just how many people care and need you to survive this war.

Please survive and come back home.

Belle.

To my Belle,

I have arrived in France, but I cannot say where. I'm not near the front yet – rest assured I am still safe. There is talk we could be moved to the frontlines after Christmas. It will be nice to experience a Christmas where I'm not at the front. It makes the war seem further away than what it is to us.

I keep replaying our final few meetings together over and over in my mind. It doesn't feel right being away from you, especially when those memories come together – us in the trees, the salt air on your lips, holding you in my arms by the lake, and the crowded train station. It's these memories which I hold on to forever. It's you that I will always think of when the burning sun rises and the golden sun sets. It's you that I will think of during the day when everything seems lost and at night when the silence screams in our ears. You're the one thing that always remains in my soul. I don't know where I'd be if I hadn't met you.

Give my best to Sally, Harriet, Dr Henry and, of course, Sister Mary. Wish them all a Merry Christmas from me. To you, my sweet Belle, for Christmas, I send in this letter some flower petals I picked in France.

Unfortunately, this is the best that I can do for you this year. I promise I will make it up to you when I return and every year after it. I will keep every promise I have made to you.

I cannot wait to be back in your arms Belle. I miss kissing your lips and seeing your smile lighting up a thousand stars. If only the war would be over for Christmas. If only.

I love you,

Edward.

To my darling Edward,

I'm glad to know that you arrived safely in France. To know you're not at the front yet eases my worries. I pray that you will be safe. I have never quite believed that God existed. There was always doubt in my mind. Now, I take hope that there is one. I take hope that He listens to my prayers and returns you safely to me. Desperate people who just want to believe that there is humanity in a war-torn world find faith and pray. I'm now one of those people. Please keep the memories of us close to you, especially when you feel like you're losing hope. Know and take comfort in the knowledge that you will return to me again.

I will give your best to the girls, Dr Henry, and Sister Mary. Unfortunately, Christmas didn't bring us celebrations. Christmas Day was the worst influx as we lost five men. I'm utterly speechless at the devastation of this war. Several nurses and VADs had to walk out with the destruction and upset we witnessed. I pray it doesn't get any worse than this. There is no way that it can possibly get worse.

Thank you for the beautiful petals. I have put them in my drawer alongside your photo. I hope the socks I have sent you will come in handy when you are moved to the front. I hope you will keep the photo of me in my VAD uniform which I have sent with this letter and that it will keep you positive in your darkest days, knowing we will be reunited once more.

I long to be back in your arms too; kissing you and knowing you are mine forever. It's not the same from afar, with only written words and photographs to hold on to. The memories will haunt me until you return to me. It's all we have to cling to in this war.

Please come back to me Edward. I cannot wait to be made yours.

I love you too,

Belle.

1916

Chapter Thirty-Four

The last time I heard form Edward was his letter before the new year, marking seven months ago. Between caring for the men and preparing to leave for France in a few months, my days became filled with checking the newspapers for Edward's name. No matter how much I searched or double checked the lists, his name never showed up. The dark cloud which descended over my mind every time a letter failed to come, or his name never emerged in the lists eventually faded as I gave up my search for him.

Word arrived to us through the men that a huge push had taken place in France, near the River Somme. None of us knew anything except what the newspapers fed us through their calm words – signalling the scale of it was more than anyone expected. Sister Mary attempted to put out as many beds in wards, corridors, or anywhere else she could think of. Only then did the full scale of the push hit us and the devastation it must have caused.

"Our men will need these," she muttered whenever we questioned the date of the next influx. She refused to give us a straight answer as to when the men from the push were due to arrive with us. We still received boats of soldiers to the hospital, but it wasn't from the push due to the lack of numbers. The quietness which covered the hospital drew an eery shiver over our bodies every day. Sally referred to it as 'the calm before the storm,' and we couldn't help but agree with her. We knew the push was soon to hit us with a full force. Now, it was just a matter of when it would come.

Sally, Harriet, and I made our way to the hospital for our dayshift. The sun beamed its warmth against the beautiful, crisp azure sky. If I'd ever imagined the perfect July morning, this was it. The bright, early morning made my heart light in my chest as though the day held promise for us. On mornings like this, I always questioned if the sun ever shone as bright in France, or if it remained black in mourning for the blood shed over the battlefields. What did the men see when they woke up at all hours of the day in the trenches? Did they ever feel the heat and dream of hope the way we did?

"Have you heard anything?" Sally questioned, opening the door to the hospital for us to walk in.

I shook my head, keeping my eyes on the tiles of the corridor. I didn't want them to witness the wrinkle between my eyebrows as I thought of the possibilities of what happened to Edward. "No… Perhaps he no longer wishes to be with me. If that is the case, then I must try to accept it."

"If there's a push, then that would explain his lack of correspondence," Harriet tried to reason. We formed a horizontal line as we walked to the ward, chatting as we dipped in and out of the nightshift making their way out of the hospital. The corridors remained in an eery silence only split by the clacking of heels and thudding of shoes. "He clearly loves you, don't give up hope."

I nodded, unable to respond knowing Harriet was right, but it did nothing to calm my knotted stomach. Edward never backed out of his promises. He had shown me that as much as he could before he left for the war. He wouldn't do it now, not when he swore with tears of desperation that he would come back to me. All I could do was hope and pray he was safe in France.

Once we completed our morning rounds in the two wards, Sister Mary called us out for a meeting in the corridor. The minute her request met my ears, my throat clenched as did my heart, tightening my chest as I tried to breathe. This was the day we had dreaded reaching our doorstep since the push happened. This was the day of the influx from the push at the River Somme. Despite every possible thought of what could greet us this afternoon, we knew we couldn't except anything less than a horror beyond our wildest imaginations.

"You must keep yourselves calm and alert," she informed us, staying stuck to the same spot in the corridor for a change. The vein in her neck pulsed as her eyes darted along the line of VADs which resembled the colour of the white wall behind them. I had no doubt mine grew a similar colour too as perspiration built on my forehead and palms. "This will be the greatest number of patients we have faced to date. These men will have seen horrible sights from what has been mentioned in the newspapers."

I frowned, raising my hand out of pure instinct. Sister Mary nodded towards me, telling me to speak. "Haven't all of them witnessed these sights?"

She let out a shaky breath as her eyes met the tiles below her feet. A sullen expression coated her features as she finally looked back at us. "There was a massive push in France to relieve the French forces at Verdun. The allied forces went over the top somewhere near the River Somme on the first of the month. A lot of men… were killed instantly while some were severely injured. It was a bloody sight – a massacre almost – so these men need our care and compassion today. They're on their way, so please go and prepare."

Nausea overcame me as I imagined Ross or Edward in the middle of such carnage. This war couldn't have gotten any worse than it already had. And yet, man proved us wrong in the worst possible way. My mind spun in a whirlwind of questions and emotions, causing me to place my hand on the cold wall behind me to keep myself grounded. Were Ross or Edward involved? If they were, did they survive or did they lose their lives instantly like so many? Sally and Harriet rested their hands on my back as if they knew what thoughts had gone through my mind. Tears clouded my vision as my heart hammered against my ribcage. I refused to blink out the tears which had graced my eyes – I couldn't let my emotions overcome me. Not when the men needed us.

The three of us made our way to the sluice room to prepare the equipment needed upon Sister Mary's instructions. They tried talking to reassure me nothing had happened to Ross or Edward, but their voices faded to white noise. No matter what anyone would tell me, I couldn't believe them until I heard from Ross or Edward. A pain seared through my chest as though someone had stood on top of it at the mere thought of losing one of them or both. I promised Margaret I would keep Ross safe no matter who his heart belonged to. Just like Edward, I never let my promises go unfulfilled. I needed to get Ross home at the end of this war; trying wouldn't be enough anymore to ensure his safety.

"Are you alright?" Harriet asked, laying a hand on my shoulder. I looked up at her from where I had placed towels and flannels in piles on the trolley. Her eyebrows knitted together, forming creases between them, as concern flooded her eyes, dimming their once vibrant colour.

I swallowed hard as I set down the final pile of towels with a shaking hand. "What if Ross or Edward have lost their lives in this push?"

Instead of providing an answer, Harriet wrapped me in her arms, unable to speak. Her body shook beneath mine as her heart thudded against her chest at an unbelievable rate. Harriet's husband still remained out in France and, unknown to us, he could have been part of the battle which took place. Neither of us knew how the men we loved were or where they happened to be when the push started.

"We'll be alright, and so will our men," Harriet whispered, her voice crackling as she spoke into my ear. We gripped on to each other, knowing we didn't believe a single word of comfort anyone could give us, even ourselves. The situation in France was grave and we couldn't deny it any longer. Our men had to survive because they needed to come home to us. Those promises of returning were the only comfort we could hold on to – a comfort which words could no longer provide for us.

The door flung open, banging off the wall behind it, as Harriet and I pulled away from the hug. A VAD stood there breathing heavily as she told us the influx had arrived. The bulging eyes and quivering lip of the VAD immediately told the three of us that we weren't prepared for what we had to face. Sally, Harriet, and I followed the VAD out of the sluice room as we met male orderlies carrying bloodied men straight to surgery. The stench of rotten flesh, sweat, and blood caused me to gag, but I held my stomach as we ran towards the entrance of the hospital. Outside, ten ambulances had stopped haphazardly with their doors wide open for the men to get treatment. Male orderlies yelled that more ambulances were on their way to the hospital. As I glanced around, everything became a blur of khaki, blood, and carnage beyond any human comprehension. If this was the way the men came to us in Britain, then what way were they after the battle?

Men and women bustled around us, pushing and shoving to help the men inside the hospital to receive treatment as swiftly as possible. The scream, yelling, and chattering created a raucous noise as the rumbling of ambulances in the distance grew closer to us. I understood why Sister Mary needed us to stay as calm as possible. Nothing could have ever prepared us for this. If we thought of the worst sight we had witnessed as a nurse to date, this wouldn't have come anywhere close to it.

A numbness washed over me as I watched, dumbfounded, as male orderlies carried two stretchers past me with blankets pulled over the whole body. The men hadn't made it back alive. They didn't even make it home. Nurses, VADs, and doctors passed by covered in blood, almost from head to toe. A soldier came towards me and gripped my sleeve, leaving a bloody handprint. If this was what Britain was like, what did the battlefield look like after the push took place?

I snapped myself back to the reality of performing my duty to save as many men as possible. We didn't want any more deaths than the two we had already experienced from this influx "What's wrong?" I asked the soldier, setting my hand on top of his to steady him. My voice was nothing short of a quiver as I swallowed back the bile which crept up my throat. How could men do this to each other? What had humanity become when this became the answer?

"My leg is bleeding again," he informed me, pointing to his leg which had dripped blood onto the stones below his feet. The blood had seeped through the uniform and created a dark stain over the khaki.

I instructed the soldier to wrap his arm around my neck and I helped him inside as best as I could without a stretcher. I didn't want to ask anyone else to help due to the masses we had received. They needed to help other soldiers while I aided this one. I managed to reach a corridor with a free bed, and he laid down upon my further instructions. I rushed over to the trolley and grabbed the last pair of scissors to cut his trouser leg to where the wound had happened. When I separated the uniform from his body, I examined the bandaged wound, but failed to spot what was bandage and what was his skin. The blood had seeped through so much that separating bandage and skin became near impossible. The stench coming off his wound made my stomach lurch as a gag readied to form into vomit. Nothing so putrid and so indescribably vile had ever greeted my nose.

"I need to cut the bandage off to see the wound," I informed him, trying to breathe through my mouth. He nodded and dug his teeth into his bottom lip as I peeled the bandage away from the wound. A groan resounded from his throat as I peeled away the final piece, taking some skin with it. My heart tore apart as I watched the man wince. He had been through enough without experiencing this pain. But there was nothing I could do to ease his pain when removing the bandage.

Once I cleaned the wound and his thigh, I examined the injury to see the stitching hadn't been done correctly, resulting in it opening all over again. Whoever did it had to have done the stitching in a hurry. With the state of the men, it wasn't much of a surprise to discover hurried medical surgeries and stitching. I ran to the trolley with the equipment to patch the wound up once more. I returned to the man as he laid in bed, breathing heavily from the pain, with perspiration dribbling down his temple. He glanced around at the other men lying near him in an equal amount of pain, if not more so, as I pulled out the stitches. The soldier didn't flinch until I disinfected the wound to ensure no infection had gotten in from the stitches bursting. Another heart wrenching groan escaped his throat as he gripped the sheets until the pain settled. His fingers unclenched from the white material as I stitched the wound. A shadow covered his body while I worked on him as a nurse came over to get his details.

"Thomas Johnson," he breathed out. The nurse jotted down the details as I finished the final stitch. But when she asked him his age, I almost dropped the needle. "Seventeen."

I dared a glance at his broken, weathered face, and noticed he looked much older than my own age. The nurse patted his shoulder, telling him the doctor would be along soon to double check everything. When she walked away, I couldn't tear my eyes away from the young man lying before me. Tears brimmed my eyes as I tried to swallow them away before they spilled over. A chill ran down my spine at the mere thought of what this war had done to the youth of our generation. This man shouldn't have looked this way. This war, no, humanity itself had done this to him.

I finally tore my eyes away and finished the stitch before taking the soldier's uniform off him. I fetched a clean flannel to wash the dirt and blood off him which seemingly stuck to every aspect of his body. The skin on his feet was red raw, blistering everywhere possible, from between his toes, to the heel of his foot. Was this war truly worth destroying every man who went to fight for our country? Only in the New Year had the government introduced conscription, ensuring every able bodied man would fight and end up like this. I gritted my teeth as I fetched the soldier pyjamas. This shouldn't have been the way our men came home… It shouldn't have been…

Michael came along to check on Thomas when I helped him on with his pyjamas. As I gazed at Michael, I noticed how exhausted the once vibrant doctor was. Underneath his eyes had coloured a purple-black shade which stood out against his pale skin. The smile which had once greeted anyone now fell short of the edges of his mouth twitching. The wrinkles started to form around his eyes and on his forehead as though he had aged in the space of a few hours. The horrific sights before us were taking their toll on everyone, even the strongest amongst us, and I didn't want to picture how much I would change too by the end of the night.

"What happened to this chap?" Michael asked, trying to maintain a chirpiness for the sake of the soldier.

"Wound to his upper leg, along his thigh. It looks like shrapnel has gone into it, but the doctors in France must have removed it before sending him back. The stitching burst though so I restitched the wound."

He nodded and met my eyes with a piercing stare which sent my blood running cold. "I'll check him over. But you need to find Harriet and Sally *now*."

I frowned, trying to ignore the knotting in my stomach and the nausea coming over me once again. "Where are they?"

"Outside," he stated, bending down to check the soldier. "I would have helped you, but I have to check the new patients."

I tripped over my own feet as I scrambled to try to find Harriet and Sally. There was little point in asking Michael any more questions; he couldn't answer them with having to perform his duty. An unexplainable heat overcame every inch of my body, prickling my skin, as my stomach knotted to a painful extent until nausea became one of the many things on my mind. I sprinted outside, searching for Sally and Harriet, as I spotted them standing with a piece of bloodied paper in their hands. Harriet pointed at it as she spoke to Sally about whatever it stated. A lump formed in my throat as I approached them.

"What's wrong?" I asked, hearing my own heavy breathing as I spoke to them. Their eyes darted to each other before looking back at me. "Michael told me to come and find you."

Without speaking, Harriet handed me the bloodied page and I took it with a cautious hand. I glanced at it, making out the remnants of a letter between the blood and chalk. My eyebrows knitted together as I looked back at her. She sighed and bit her lip for a second, reluctant to tell me about it. "You need to find out who brought this with them, Belle."

"Why?"

Sally pointed to the letter with a firm finger. "Read it."

For the first time since Harriet handed me it, I caught the name of whom it was addressed to, and every part of my body flooded with a cold unaccustomed to a July day. This couldn't be what I thought it was… but I knew I had to read it despite the fear which stopped my heart, freezing out the world around me.

Dear Belle,

Tomorrow there is big push and we're to go over the top. We are scared for our lives and, if I make it, I will tell you why some day. But I cannot possibly write it here in case they find it. If I don't make it, I hope this letter will reach you somehow. Maybe one of the men who discover it will deliver my words to you.

Please know that I love you beyond comprehension. You are my one and only, despite everything that happened to us. If you don't feel the same way towards me, know that that never changed my feelings towards you. I am a fool for loving you so much, but a fool I will remain for my heart will forever be yours Belle. If I don't get a chance to tell you after tomorrow, I'm sorry for what I did to you. I was trying to protect us both against Margaret and her schemes. Now, I wish I never did it.

I'm scared Belle. My hands shake as I write this to you, but if people ask, tell them I was brave. I don't want people to think less of me.

I will love you forever. I will love you until my dying breath.

Ross.

Dizziness flooded my senses as I gripped the paper in my hand, creasing it beneath my touch. Harriet and Sally tried talking to me, telling me they discovered the letter on the ground, but I wasn't listening. Without another moment of hesitation, I ran back into the hospital, yelling for Ross until my throat grew raw. Either he had come in with the influx or someone he knew had been sent to us. Deep in my being, my soul sparked with the fire I had once felt around Ross. I dared to believe he was here with me in this hospital. All I had to do was find him, even if it took me the rest of my shift.

"Ross!" I yelled, uncaring of the looks I received from the soldiers and nurses as I sprinted past them. I took in every face but none of them were Ross' hazel-green eyes I'd known and loved in another life. Strands of hair fell out of my headdress, and I brushed them away as I kept running. I wouldn't find peace until I found him; my soul wouldn't let me rest until it met with Ross again.

As I reached the fifth corridor filled with men, some of the soldiers joined in, calling and yelling for Ross with me. I hurdled over nurses, jumped over medical equipment, and dodged male orderlies. My heart started to sink in my chest as the faces blended into one another – never showing me the one I craved the most. Tears blurred my vision, cascading down my cheeks enough to clear my sight to spot the faces. A pain tore through my heart, slowing me down to a walk.

"Ross!" I called as my voice cracked and broke with unimaginable sorrow.

"Belle!"

I ran towards the voice which grew louder with each step I took. We called for each other as the warm tears of hope streamed over the curves of my face. Staff and soldiers spread to the sides of the corridor, clearing a path for me to run to the voice I would recognise amongst a million strangers. As they split like the Red Sea, a figure emerged in the middle of the corridor. Clad in hospital pyjamas and limping towards me, Ross' face came into focus, freezing the world. My heart thudded in my ears as it hammered against my rib cage. If it wasn't for the echoing sound of its beats, I would have presumed I stood in a dream. Was this truly the man I had once loved coming back to me?

With the back of my hand, I swiped away my tears before running towards him. Despite my heavy limbs and drooping eyelids, I found the strength to keep running, refusing to stop until I could touch him to limit the possibility of an illusion or daydream. He hobbled towards me until we met halfway in the corridor. Without any hesitation, he took me into his arms and spun me around like he did in the daisy field. I cupped his face in my hands and stared deep into those hazel-green eyes I had dreamt of so many times.

The soldiers in the corridor cheered, clapped, and some even whistled as they watched our reunion. He set me down gently before he made his injuries worse, but he never lost his grip on me. I couldn't prise my hands away from his face. His touch, warm beneath my snow hands, removed every doubt I had as to whether this was a dream. Ross being here with me was the most real thing this war could give me after the sorrow it made me suffer.

Against every odd in this mess of a world, Ross came back to me. In that moment, his return was all that mattered. He finally kept a promise he made and came back to me once more.

Chapter Thirty-Five

Despite the influx which ensued our every waking moment in the ward that morning, visiting hours still took place. Every fibre in my body tingled in anticipation of seeing Paul once again. Before leaving the hospital, Michael had to amputate Paul's foot because it wouldn't heal. Yet Paul continued to contribute to the war effort by visiting the men and buying things for them from his own money. We knew his guilt was slowly making him bankrupt. After the war, we discovered Paul had in fact gone bankrupt, resulting in him putting a pistol in his mouth over it. I never understood if it was the guilt or the bankruptcy. Deep down in my heart I knew his death had ensued from the guilt, especially when he had found out that many men were court-martialled for 'cowardice.' He always claimed he should have been too. I always remembered him for his kindness and generosity, always giving with a smile on his face. The men never should have felt guilty or a coward for not being able to face the horrors of the war. Never.

"Belle," Paul greeted me with a beaming smile. I made my way over to him and hugged him, feeling his weight against my body. "You look a frightful mess, Darling."

I stifled a laugh as I gazed down at myself. Blood stains decorated my once white apron, matching the red cross on the front of it, and, in the elongated shadows against the wall, I could see strands of my hair hanging out of my headdress. "I'm still going though; we got some new arrivals which probably explains the mess I look."

"Edward?"

I shook my head, but the edges of my mouth started to curve into a smile. "Ross."

Paul refused to believe me until I explained the full story to him. I reached into my pocket and produced the blood splattered letter from Ross which I had kept close to me since the influx. We made our way to the ward that Paul was visiting as we spoke of Ross' return. He nodded along as I carried his belongings to ease the weight that he had to carry on his walking sticks.

"Unbelievable," he gasped, shaking his head. His eyes met mine and an unmistakable glint caught my attention. "I told you you'd see him again. I said crazier things have happened."

I stifled a laugh and nodded, remembering his words well. "Indeed, you did."

"I've not seen you this happy since Edward's letter. It's nice to see you smile." We approached the ward and Paul turned to me before I opened the doors for him. A warmth radiated off his features as he watched me basking in a newfound glow. "Go and see him. I'll find you when I'm finished visiting."

I held the door open for Paul to go inside. He hobbled in on his walking sticks as one of the ward nurses rushed over to me to take his bag. I handed it to her and bid Paul goodbye before travelling to the corridor where Ross had been placed since the influx. The corridors had become a tight squeeze with the narrow space left available to us with beds on either side. The men grinned up at me from their beds; maintaining their spirits despite all they had gone through in this war. I shook some of their hands as I passed and ruffled the hairs of the younger men, earning winks from them as they beamed at me.

When I approached Ross' corridor, I spotted a figure crouching down as they spoke to Ross who sat up on the bed. The closer I came to them, the more the figure merged into that of Michael. The two of them laughed as they spoke, earning raised eyebrows from me. I looked several times to make sure I had definitely spotted them laughing together. It wasn't a sight I thought I would see, especially after knowing Ross warned, or somewhat threatened, Michael over courting me back home. *Two years ago.* Two years had never felt like such a long time until I watched the two of them jesting with each other. Michael stood up as the echo of my approaching footsteps drew his attention. He smiled at me, but my eyes travelled to Ross who winked to tell me our past still remained a secret to Michael. My shoulders slumped as the tension left them knowing my mistakes hadn't coloured my future.

"You two caused quite a stir earlier," Michael informed me, pulling my attention back to him. He grinned at me, sparkling with the same amicability I had grown with in the two years since moving to Poole with him. "It certainly made the soldiers a bit happier and hopeful after what they had been through."

The memories of finding the blood splattered letter tore through my mind and I desired to ask Ross what had happened to him in the push. But I needed to wait until Michael left, knowing Ross' desire for privacy. Most of the men didn't like talking about their injuries at the best of times, let alone describing what they had witnessed before arriving with us at the hospital. None of them wanted an audience to see them break. Some of the men refused to talk about it at all; no one could possibly blame them for their silence. In this war, we had witnessed many sights none of us could ever speak about. Those sights remained incomprehensible to us. The men who had returned from the push in France didn't want to bring the war back home with them.

"I'll leave you two alone," Michael said, sensing my silence. He turned around and shook Ross' hand. Before he walked away, he laid a hand on my shoulder, squeezing it in a comfort he knew I would need when I heard Ross' story.

Once Michael made his way back down the corridor, Ross moved over on the bed to allow me to sit beside him. Out of mere instinct, he reached for my hand and laced our fingers together; I didn't pull away from him this time. As I glanced down into those hazel-green reminders of home, my heart remained numb to any sign of affection towards him. All I appeared capable of feeling in that moment was peace in my bones, knowing he had returned safe and home. I sat down on the bed beside him and let him maintain his hold on my hand. His palm clammed beneath my touch, shaking the slightest bit.

"I understand," he announced out of nowhere. I turned to meet his gaze as he swallowed hard, bobbing his Adam's apple. "I understand why you ran. It was easier after what I did to you. You were good to me, and I wish I had been better to you."

I shook my head, glancing away from his intense stare. "None of that matters anymore."

"I just want you to know that I'm sorry. I won't hurt you anymore, Belle, despite what you think about me."

My lips pulled into a tight, straight line as I mulled over his words. What could I possibly respond to him without breaking him more? Ross' chain weighed against my neck, reminding me of everything that happened back home. I hadn't removed the necklace since Ross gave it to me. If I dared to believe in old wives' tales or folklore, I would believe it led him back to me. Instead of trying to lie to him, I pulled the letter from my pocket, drawing Ross' eyes to the blood splattered paper. He glanced at me with a forced smile over his lips.

"I meant every word I wrote; truly I did."

"I know you did," I agreed. If there was anything I had learnt from the men it was that when they were in a 'last letter' situation they always wrote their honest last words to the person. Every word Ross poured into his letter was honest and true. "When I first saw you, you were hobbling. I'm assuming you injured your leg in the attack, but how come there's blood on the letter?"

He sighed, dropping my hand for a second as he pulled back the blanket to lift his trouser leg. A bandage decorated the bottom of his leg, along his calf muscle. "Shrapnel… A shell exploded and the shrapnel from it went right through my leg. I only ended up with the leg injury after I was hit on the chest with a bullet. Thankfully, it went through my right side – saving my life."

My eyebrows pinched together as I listened to his words. "How did shrapnel hit you if you fell down from the wound?"

"The shells are fired in the air, and they explode, raining hot balls of shrapnel down. They're so warm it's like fire hitting your body, searing right through it. The whole bottom of my leg felt like it was on fire, but I couldn't do anything about it. I laid out in No Man's Land for hours until they came to get the injured."

"What happened out there… on the morning of the push?"

He winced, as though reliving the moments all over again. "We were told by the high command that the wires were cut in No Man's Land. For us, going over the top would be easy, and we shouldn't worry about it. So, we went to the trenches with the hope of a straightforward fight the next morning. When we arrived to go into the trenches, they handed us wire cutters. The men asked why we needed them if the wires were cut, but the officers couldn't answer. That night, when we had to write our letters home before the push, I overheard the officer in charge of us talking. The wires weren't cut, he'd looked over. They were as terrified as the rest of us because they had to go over the top too. Men got caught in the wire, screaming it wasn't cut, and the Germans just… they just fired on them. It was a massacre, Belle. So many men's lives lost – some who survived were badly injured or affected in their own minds by what they witnessed."

My mouth opened and closed, trying to form any sort of words which would suffice. I couldn't begin to imagine the pain he had suffered in the push. I swallowed hard, reaching out to stroke his hair. It had grown much longer and darker than I had remembered – the blonde highlights had faded, but the sunlight of the Somme had started to bring them out again. As my hand traced the curves of his face, the weight which had fallen from his body became all too obvious. His cheeks had sunken compared to the way he left me, emphasising his cheekbones more. He seemed half the man I once knew, but when I looked into his eyes once more, I spotted the world I had left. A tear escaped from my eyes as I blinked, cascading over my cheeks. Ross laid his calloused thumb across my face as he wiped away the damp trail of heartache. His own eyes darkened and watered at remembering the fateful day which brought so many men to their deaths or to our hospital.

"I'll be okay," he reassured me. He didn't move his hand from my cheek and the heat radiated through my skin from his touch. "I have seen you again and that's what's keeping me strong right now."

I sniffed and tried to find my voice, but it came out as a raspy whisper. "But I almost lost you Ross." I swallowed the sour tasting bile which made its way up my throat in a mixture of guilt and regret. My stomach knotted as I shook my head at my behaviour. "I was meant to keep you safe."

"This isn't your fault," he reassured me, cupping my face in his hands.

Before I could respond, the heels clacking drew his hands away from me. The coldness from the absence of his touch sent a shiver down my spine. I glanced over my shoulder as a nurse approached us, telling me that Paul was leaving in a few minutes. The nurse turned around and left us alone as she made her way back up the corridor. I stood up, straightening my uniform, before leaning down to kiss the top of Ross' head. My lips lingered for longer than they should have, relishing in the knowledge Ross had come back. If I closed my eyes tight enough, shutting out the rest of the world, I could picture us in the daisy field once more, with the amber sunset behind us.

By the time I arrived at the ward, Paul already stood at the door, leaning against the wall as he waited for me. A soldier clothed in hospital pyjamas held Paul's bag while talking to him. I walked over and the two of them turned to smile at me. The soldier handed me Paul's bag before bidding him farewell with a strong handshake only accustomed to those men who had fought together on the frontlines. We made our way to the entrance of the hospital as he chatted to me about the men he spoke to and what he brought for each of them. From oranges to newspapers, he gave them anything they needed. His bag had grown lighter from when he first came into the hospital a few hours earlier.

Paul gazed at me out of the corner of his eye and a small smile graced the corners of his lips. "How's your man?"

"He's well… but I cannot help feeling guilty about his injuries."

Paul frowned as creases spotted his forehead. "Why guilty?"

"I was meant to keep him safe, and he almost died in the push at the Somme," I mumbled. A lump formed in my throat as my grip tightened around the handles on his bag. Ross had gotten a lucky escape with the injuries he received; other men hadn't been dealt such a fate as the list of deaths became a testament to. "If it wasn't for me, he wouldn't even be in the war in the first place."

"You've nothing to feel guilty about Belle. You cannot possibly control the war and what takes place it in. If you could, you would make sure it ends today. This happening to him was nothing to do with you. Deep down, you must know that."

I bit my lip, refusing to say anything as I knew he was right. But I couldn't help living with the weight of blaming myself for Ross going to France in the first place. My stubborn heart wouldn't leave the past where it belonged. Neither Ross nor I had to enter this war and I could have stopped us from going. Yet I didn't. Even now, I knew Ross had to return to the frontlines when he had recovered. The cycle of blame and guilt caused a dizziness to blur my vision. The breeze coming through the front doors calmed my burning skin and eased the light-headedness which came over me. I poked my head through the doors to check on Paul's driver, but he hadn't arrived yet. We waited in the porch of the hospital entrance as Paul leant against the wall to take the pressure off his arms. His hands coloured a flaming red and he rubbed them to try to return them to their normal tint.

"How do you feel now that he's here?" Paul quizzed, raising an eyebrow at me. "I know Edward left. Before I visited today, you told me you hadn't got a response from him. I take it that's still the same?"

I nodded, ignoring the first part of the question. I couldn't answer my feelings about Ross, not when I didn't understand them myself. "There's still no response from Edward. If I'm being honest with myself, I don't think I'll get one again."

"That must impact how you feel about Ross though."

Paul knew something more was going on in my mind, but I couldn't process it. Not when Ross had just returned to my side after the most horrific battle known to man. Looking into Ross' eyes when I first saw him in the corridor made me remember everything we once had together. Every secret moment in crowded rooms, every touch, and every kiss… I remembered them all as though they only happened yesterday. Despite everything we had gone through, I still remembered how I felt about him two years ago and I couldn't help but question how far away my feelings were from those I once had for him.

"I don't know," I finally admitted in an almost inaudible whisper. "You plan for so much and it gets destroyed in a second. Things were meant to be different with Edward. Maybe all I had with Ross was lust and passion—a fulfilment of a fantasy we both had."

Paul burst out laughing, shaking his head. My brow furrowed as I stared at him, waiting for him to explain his outburst. "Belle, Darling, we both know that isn't true. Every love has passion. If it didn't, we wouldn't fall so much in love with someone."

"It was an affair. Nothing more."

Paul and I stared at each other, never breaking eye contact. I didn't want to be the first to look away when I had sought to defend my relationship with Ross. Paul cocked an eyebrow and flashed me a sympathetic smile. "You would lie to yourself a million times to convince yourself that you felt nothing for

Ross." I swallowed hard, casting my eyes to the ground as his words hit a raw nerve. "If you look deep in your heart, you'll find he showed you this life in a way that no one else ever could. The two of you almost spoke a different language. There was a bond there and always will be, no matter how much you try to say otherwise."

"What are you trying to tell me?" I dared to ask, glancing up at him through my eyelashes.

For once, no sympathy rested on his face. Instead, a beaming smile altered his features, creating an enigmatic glow. "I'm trying to tell you that we both know you two would ruin yourselves for each other. That's something you can never deny. You would ruin yourself for him a million more times to spend another day with each other."

As I watched Paul leave the hospital and drive away in the car which came to collect him, my mind had resigned itself to agree with him. I would ruin myself a million more times for Ross Mason. It was something I could not deny.

Chapter Thirty-Six

It had taken a week for the hospital staff to receive a response from Ross about who to contact for visiting. Every day his answer remained the same: no one. Margaret didn't have a clue about his injuries; she still presumed he was at the front in the middle of the push. While it wasn't up to me to tell her the truth, my heart ached for her. I had no doubt she would scan the list of names in newspapers to find his amongst the hundreds. For months, I had done the same thing over Edward. Any chance Sally and Harriet got, they asked me about Ross and his condition. They noticed my distance from everyone since chatting to Paul, but they never directly brought it up. Subtilty stayed firm in their behaviours, but I didn't quite know how to speak of everything Paul had said to me. I couldn't comprehend or fathom it myself. Ross still had a hold on me, whether I desired to admit it myself or not, and it was anybody's guess as to whether it would change. Perhaps if I received word from Edward things would be different. But I still hadn't.

"You need to talk to us," Sally pleaded as we put the supplies away in the sluice room. I tried to ignore the questioning, but my resolve started to shatter, allowing rays of hope and sunlight through in their golden forms. "We can tell that you're thinking about a lot. It won't get easier unless you speak to us and talk about it."

The sluice room was empty except for the three of us packing away the supplies. Whatever I said would remain secret, even from Michael despite Sally's courtship with him. I sighed, knowing I had to admit it to finally let my mind rest. "I chatted to Paul about Ross at his visit last week. He said some things that I couldn't possibly deny, and he knew it."

"Such as?" Harriet finished, handing me a pile of towels to put on the shelf.

I shoved the towels into the cupboard as Paul's words rang in my ears once again. They had been on replay for the last week without any silence. "He said I would lie to myself a million times to cover up how I felt about Ross." My mouth formed a tight line as a clamp seemed to seal itself over my throat, constricting with every swallow. It was the last thing Paul had said to me which plagued my thoughts the most. "Before he left, he told me that Ross and I would ruin ourselves over and over again for each other… That I would ruin myself for him a million times more than I already had."

We continued to work in silence, fixing and sorting the equipment with a passion for getting out of the room. The aroma of disinfectant made my eyes water as a piercing headache came on from the stench. We glanced around the room as we finished, ensuring there was nothing lying about which Sister Mary would feel the urge to complain about. Before I turned to walk away, Sally gripped my hands in hers, pulling me back. She gazed deep into my eyes as if searching for the answer to the question she was about to ask me.

"What did you reply to Paul?" she asked, refusing to lose eye contact. Harriet moved behind Sally, waiting to hear my response. The two of them stared at me, causing the hairs over my body to spring to life as I shifted my feet against the tiles.

"I didn't answer him. I never replied."

The firmness of my answer and my inability not to meet their stare told them that I wasn't lying. More importantly, it gave them the signal they needed to know that I didn't deny any of Paul's accusations. I couldn't deny anything he had said then or now – every word he spoke proved right in my own heart. Instead of the judgemental looks I had expected from the women, the corners of their mouths turned up into a smile.

"There's still something there," Harriet stated, stepping closer until she was beside Sally.

Sally nodded, turning to Harriet before glancing back at me. A mischievous glint shone in her eyes. "I attended to Ross this morning and he never stopped talking about you."

I pulled my hands away from her and sighed. I wanted to run my hands through my hair and pull at the curls until I could knock sense into my own mind. "Look, I still haven't made up my mind about him yet. I have Edward and I can't do anything wrong on him. He… he loves me more than I can even fathom. Please, just forget about this conversation. Actually, even better, forget an affair ever happened between Ross and I. Goodness knows that's what I do."

I weaved my way past them and flung open the door, stepping into the sunlight of the corridor. The visitors bustled into the hospital, ready to see the men they had loved so much. I swallowed hard as tears welled in my eyes, blurring my vision as I made my way to the gardens. I had to forget everything Ross and I had together; I needed to move on without thinking of what had come before. Edward was the man I needed to focus on and divert every bit of my attention to. I couldn't keep reliving the past for a passionate, lustrous affair with the man I had grown to love in the two years before we started any form of relationship. We had fallen so heavily in love with each other that we acted without thinking – we behaved as though we were insane fools in a world separate from the standards of society. That world couldn't exist in this war… that love couldn't survive anymore.

The minute the heat of the sun hit my face as I stepped outside, the Blue Tit sang its melody over by Tommy's bench. A small smile tugged at the corners of my lips as I made my way over, as though Tommy was beckoning me to him. A peacefulness washed over my troubled heart as I sat down and the tension in my muscles ebbed away into the atmosphere around me. The Blue Tit moved closer to the bench, continuing to sing its song for the world to listen to. I dared myself to think of how much easier things would have been if Tommy had survived his injuries. Perhaps I wouldn't have found myself in such a mess as this.

I glanced over towards the trees where Edward had led me to in the rainstorm. Those woods held the secrets of our first kiss together – the one intimacy I didn't allow myself to have, but the one my heart couldn't resist around Edward. Instinctively, my fingertips traced the curves of my lips, still feeling the pressure of his kiss. In this world, loving someone proved the greatest defiance in a war. Yet, I didn't know if I would ever feel his love or his lips on mine again. Had the war taken his love away from me just when it gave me it?

I tore my eyes away from the trees and set my hands on my lap, gazing down at them as they rested against my body. Ross' warm hand in mine as the daisies surrounded us flooded through my mind. I pictured us back in my room, in the dead of night, intertwined with each other as we tried to keep quiet. Under the sheets, Ross held my hand and interlocked his fingers with mine.

Back then, I swore that there wasn't another feeling like it. The indescribable feeling of falling in love with someone who I knew like the back of my hand. From memory I could trace their every flaw and scar – all of which became mine the second I loved him. There hadn't been another feeling like it... until I met Edward.

"I was told I'd find you here."

I gazed up through my eyelashes as Ross stood in front of me. I had become so lost in my own conflicted feelings, weighing heavy in my body, to spot him approaching. "Who told you?"

"Sally," he stated, sitting down beside me. A magnetic force rested between us, allowing me space to breath against the headache which had formed, but not enough room to forget the strength of his love for me. "Please don't be angry with me or Sally, but she told me everything." My body straightened itself and I turned to him, waiting on an explanation of 'everything.' Despite how much my eyes bore into the side of his face, he refused to look at me, focusing his attention on the grass beneath our feet. "She told me about Edward."

His voice cracked with the mere mention of Edward's name. His hurt seared through my soul as I tore my gaze from him, staring at the same emerald which had once brought us so much joy. But the world we left wasn't the one which existed here. The emerald and white paradise of the daisy field couldn't survive in this war. Ross thought I would sit waiting for him after what he did to me. I wanted anything other than that after the hurt he caused me only two years prior to this moment. He didn't seem to understand the pain or hurt he caused me. If he did, he would know I couldn't possibly have waited for him.

"What did you expect me to do?" I whispered into the air. The Blue Tit had ceased its song, witnessing the fire in our magnetic exchange. "You broke my heart into a million little pieces. I risked everything for you, and you dropped me in a matter of seconds."

"I've already apologised," Ross exasperated. My eyes shot straight to him to find his already watching me. A violent blaze burned in his hazel-green orbs, setting them alight in a way which I hadn't witnessed since the daisy field. "I know what I did was wrong. I was stupid enough to think you'd be waiting for me after everything we had been through." When I didn't respond, he asked the one question which we both knew would close and seal the door on the love we once had for each other. "Is it serious between you and Edward? I guess what I'm asking is: are you two… engaged?"

I glanced away from him, swallowing hard as I debated whether to lie to him or not. Breaking people wasn't something I ever relished in, and I tried to avoid the confrontation of doing so to the greatest of my abilities. But Ross had forced me into a corner where I had a choice to make. I let out a shaky breath, knowing my choice always remained the same. I couldn't lie to Ross. "Not quite. We discussed getting engaged after the war is over."

The breaking of Ross' heart screamed in my ears as it shattered to a thousand tiny pieces before I finished speaking. My eyelids fluttered closed as a warm tear of regret swirled down my cheek. Sobs erupted from my throat, and I could do little else but curl myself in two, clutching my stomach as though trying to hold myself together. If I didn't love Ross still, then why did my heart shatter as much as his? A warm hand reached for mine, and I let Ross take it, freeing my stomach from my clutching grasp. My free hand flew over my mouth, attempting to conceal the sobs which hiccupped out of me.

"I understand why you did it," Ross whispered, squeezing my hand for a brief second. "I'm hurt and heartbroken, but I understand, because you didn't think I wanted you anymore. Who could blame you after the way I treated you?"

I pulled away from his grasp as a coldness descended over me. A chill ran down my spine and my gaze shot straight for him. The embers of fire sparked in my veins as the memories of sobbing in the daisy field flooded back to me. "You don't understand, Ross. Edward loved me the way you're meant to love a person. He never hid the fact that he felt every sense of desire and passion towards me. We never *had* to hide away. That love and affection was what I needed from you. I never got it and I was never going to because we were nothing but an illicit affair. Yet, even when you hurt me, I still loved you because I loved *everything* about you. I wanted to shout the love I held for you from the top of the world. But when I stepped away, I realised what I deserved, and it wasn't the love you gave me."

Ross opened his mouth to respond, and I waited with clenched fists to hear what defence he could possibly give me for his actions. Before he could utter a word, a nurse called for him to come inside for his medication. I stared at the ground, waiting for him to leave me, but his feet remained static. His eyes bored into me, willing me to turn to look at him one final time. When I wouldn't meet his gaze, he stood up and walked away with his feet dragging behind him, as though desperate for me to call his name to let him run back to me.

I stayed outside for a while longer, soaking in the summer sunshine and dreaming of worlds miles away from this war. The heaviness of my heart persisted beneath my breast as I made my way inside. The cracking of Ross' voice at the mention of Edward's name replayed in my mind until tears blurred my vision and poured down my face in streams of painful heartbreak. The doors to the garden slammed behind me, but I didn't move. I had hurt the only soul to know me better than I knew myself. I had shattered Ross' heart and my own in one single sentence. How could I give someone that I once called home so much hurt? How could I have turned out such a horrible person to do that to Ross? My knees buckled and I thudded to the floor, pulling my knees tight to my chest. Sobs of anguish echoed against the empty hallway, resounding my own pain back to me. In the distance, someone called my name, but I didn't dare glance at them. Over my sobs, the pounding of footsteps ran towards me, and their shadow filled the tiles on the corridor.

"Belle, what's wrong?" Michael asked as he bent down beside me. I sniffed and glanced at him, making his face out of the blurs of tears. "Is it Edward?"

I shook my head, knowing I needed to confide everything to him. For so long, I had tried to protect Michael from the mess I had gotten myself into back home. But after two years, the time had come to admit the truth. "It's Ross."

"What about him?" Michael's head tilted to the side as he pursed his lips and his eyebrows squished together.

"I had an affair with Ross Mason."

Everything which had happened back home spilled out of my mouth. The words flowed out of me without a single hesitation in what I told him. Perhaps this was what my heart needed most; it desired to confide itself to the one person who wouldn't judge me. Michael wrapped an arm around my shaking frame, pulling me into his side as though nothing had ever changed between us. Despite the doubts I held over our friendship, this one act of kindness and compassion proved to me that nothing ever had to change between us, no matter what happened. I admitted everything to Michael, from the first kiss in the church and the confession in my living room, until our heated exchange outside on Tommy's bench. When my words ceased into silence, my entire body became lighter as if the burden of guilt and heartache had removed itself from me.

With his arm still wrapped around me, rubbing circles on the top of my arm, Michael spoke of his thoughts about everything I admitted to him. "Ross has hurt you deeply. But I know that you would still do anything for him. You need to decide whether that feeling is because of love or because of the guilt you harbour over him joining the war. If there's one thing you take away from everything, it's this: you need the love you deserve. If Edward gives you the love that you deserve, then that's where your focus should be. He loves you as much as you love him. Despite Ross' return, you need to remember that about Edward."

"He hasn't responded to my letter for months, Michael," I mumbled, wiping away my tears with the back of my hand. The coolness of my skin against my cheeks eased the temperature rising in my veins. "I'm growing tired of all of this… this indecision about two different people. I don't know how to feel anymore. All I know is that I don't want to be alone, but I'm not sure if love even exists anymore. People make me promises and they consistently never fulfil them."

"People make promises because they don't want to lose the person that they make them to. I will have a chat with Ross about everything for you, but I cannot tell you what to feel. Although, there is one thing I can tell you."

I glanced at Michael and nodded. "What's that?"

He smiled at me and brushed the stray hairs back into my headdress with his free hand. "Love will always hurt us, whether it's right or wrong. The ones we love will *always* hurt us and break promises to us. But it's who we forgive and who we learn to love again that matters. When the cards are on the table and the stakes are high, our hearts will push for what they want. You just have to keep holding on to whatever hope of love you have left in your heart."

Michael couldn't tell me what to do in my situation, despite how much I desired someone to. This was my mess and I had to sort it out myself. All I could do was hope for a miracle or pray for a letter from Edward to try to sort my feelings out. No matter how much I desired to hold on to the small element of hope which might have brought a letter to me, I knew I would never receive one. This situation could only be resolved by looking deep into my heart to know who to spend my forever with. As Michael said, I had to keep holding on to the small element of love which remained in my heart. Who deserved to have the love in my heart – Ross or Edward?

Chapter Thirty-Seven

Sister Mary had assigned us back over to nightshift for the last week, allowing for me to avoid Ross for most of the day. The only times I saw him was when I had to get the men ready for lights out and check on them during the night. Even then, Sally and Harriet volunteered to attend to Ross, so I didn't have to. My mind plagued me with questionable debates which I shouldn't have had to face until the end of the war. Part of me had hoped the war would have sorted out this mess before I had to do it on my own. Perhaps fate hated me as much as this war had taken away those I loved.

I woke with the shrill of my alarm and rolled over to face the framed photos of Edward and Tommy clad in their respective uniforms. Edward's eyes followed me no matter where I moved in the boarding house, as though he were watching over me from afar. But, if he loved me as he said he did, then why hadn't I heard from him? Did he already have a woman waiting on him in France? I shut my eyes tight, squeezing my eyelids until the thoughts of such frivolous intentions of the man I loved faded into the darkness of my own mind. The three men who each had my heart in the last two years had abandoned me during this war. It astonished me that I had anymore love left in my heart to give.

"Are you okay?" Sally's voice resounded towards to me.

I rolled over on my bed and met her face which stared at me from the bed next to mine. She smiled with a warmth I wished I could possess once again. "I don't know anymore. I'm confused about everything right now. All I really want is my Tommy back."

"Tommy was lovely," Sally agreed. My mouth instinctively formed a smile at the thoughts of Tommy. The man with the sapphire eyes and cheeky grin who left this Earth before his time. "But remember that Edward is a gentleman. He wouldn't ignore you without a good reason for doing so."

Our boarding room door flung open, springing against the wall with a thud which woke most of the women. Harriet sprinted into the room with her hair falling out of her headdress from rushing about. Sister Mary had assigned Harriet to a few more days on the dayshift before her switchover. When she stumbled to my bed, nausea overcame every sense in my body, threatening to make me vomit at any given moment. I swallowed the bitter taste of sickness and bile as she stopped at the foot of my bed, gripping the wood.

"Harriet, what is it?" I asked, sitting up in bed as fast as possible. I flung the blanket back and stood beside her. Her hot breath echoed in the room as she tried to regain enough air to speak to me.

"T-There's someone at the hospital. They've arrived early for visiting, but she wants to speak with you first."

Instead of asking anything further, Sally and I donned our uniforms with a swift precision only years of working as a VAD could give us. My brain tried to come up with every possible person who would visit one of the men but also want to speak with me. The numerous names which ran through my mind didn't add up. As we made our way to the hospital, I spotted Harriet whispering something to Sally. They kept darting their eyes towards me, making my skin crawl as the hairs rose on the back of my neck. My throat grew dry, and no amount of swallowing lubricated the airway enough to calm myself down. From the looks of the women beside me, whoever awaited me wasn't going to deliver any sort of good news.

We walked through the main doors and Harriet led the way to an empty corridor towards the end of the hospital. A dark cloud descended over the building as we walked, creating an eery silence around the place. The hospital had never been this silent since the day Tommy died and I tried not to presume Sister Mary stood waiting with a telegram with news on Edward. In that moment, I knew I would have happily accepted any visitor as long as they didn't hold a telegram in their hands for me. Harriet stopped at the empty corridor, allowing me to walk in first. The entire corridor remained deserted, except for one woman who stood with her back to us. From the back of the woman, I didn't recognise her; her black hair which she had tied in a bun and her plain blue coat resembled no one I knew.

"Here is Nurse Wilson," Harriet announced as we approached her.

The woman spun around, and my heart sank to the pit of my stomach. My mouth fell open ever so slightly as the entire world stopped spinning. There, standing in front of me, was Margaret. I closed my mouth and forced my legs to move forward, despite my heart screaming at me to run. Ross claimed he didn't want Margaret knowing he was here, let alone paying him a visit. But he had to have changed his mind about her visiting after our talk in the gardens. There was no other way she would have known he was here except from his own handwriting in a letter.

"Oh Belle," Margaret gushed, pulling me into a hug. My hands remained stiff by my side as nothing around me seemed real. Margaret held me at arm's distance as though surveying me for any ill feelings. My eyes must have appeared as numb as my entire body in that moment as she swiftly continued. "Thank you for keeping him safe. I knew you would."

I nodded, swallowing back my tears. I needed to compose myself as I had learnt to do every time Ross had disappointed me. "I promised I would."

"I hope there's no hard feelings," she said as she continued to search my eyes. I refused to look away from her, knowing it would tell her the truth of my soul. "Not just about what happened before, but also for now too. When Ross requested for me to visit him, I knew then he must have chosen to stay with me."

I forced a smile onto my lips as though I didn't give a damn about Ross' decision. My heart ached as it clenched in my chest. "There are no hard feelings at all. Besides, I've got a sweetheart fighting now."

Margaret asked me every possible question about Edward. I couldn't tell if she was merely testing me to see if I had told her a lie about Edward. To maintain my privacy, I only shared the minimal amount of details, not wanting to overshare with one of the village's top gossips. Ross had always hated Margaret's title as one of the best gossips in the village. If anyone wanted to know anything about someone, they just asked Margaret when she was out and about. Her mind only sought to fill itself with other's secrets as though it were the only way to win favour with people. I had written to my parents about Edward, but they promised they would never spread things about our courtship to the village or Margaret. Unlike Ross, they had kept their promise to me. Margaret gripped my hand and beamed at me with wide sparkling eyes; whether in deceitfulness, spite, or admiration, I wasn't sure which.

"I really thought he would choose you," she admitted in a whisper. "The man was utterly infatuated with you. Perhaps it was fate for you to leave for the war effort."

I willed myself not to let the searing pain in my chest affect my emotion in front of Margaret. She would love knowing her words hurt me. Instead, I took a deep breath and plastered a smile on my face. She blinked several times as she took in my appearance. "Ross told me he didn't want me. He informed me that he never loved me, just before I left to join the war effort." I could recall the moment in the daisy field better than I could remember anything in my lifetime. No matter how much I tried, I couldn't let that moment go.

"He may have said that, but it wasn't true. Yet none of that matters anymore. We have found love, Belle, and that should make you happy, for it certainly gives me joy."

But it didn't make me anywhere close to 'happy.' My ribs clenched and squeezed as a pulling sensation attacked my insides. Ross had completely abandoned me once again for Margaret. How much did I have to do to prove my love and worth to him? Part of me desired to tell Ross I was sorry for anything I ever did to him and that I forgave him for everything he did to me. But what would have been the point? Inviting Margaret to the hospital had showed me the truth of his affections towards me: he truly didn't want me anymore.

"I should take you to Ross now," I said, refusing to chitchat to her any longer than I had to. We made our way back down the corridor with Sally and Harriet following at a distance. "Due to the unexpected number of men that we had, we couldn't fit them in the wards so he's in a corridor. I can assure you he is being treated as well as the men in the wards."

My words remained as the same speech I gave all the visitors who arrived with us for the first time, especially those who had loved ones in corridor beds. I updated her about Ross' injury as we weaved between the beds in the corridors. Some men wandered about with people who had visited them or by themselves. They smiled at me as I walked past, greeting me with an affection I wished my heart would allow me to feel. Instead, a numbness overtook every part of me which once felt love for anyone. How could one person ruin me so much? As we approached Ross' bed, he glanced up and his face paled to a discolouration similar to the white walls behind him. His eyes darted between me and Margaret as though he didn't believe I was escorting her to him.

"Your wife is here to see you," I spat at him, refusing to let him walk over me again. I spun around on my heel and stormed away from them with Sally and Harriet. My entire being shook as every nerve in my body fired with the balling of my fists.

"Belle!"

Ross continued shouting up the corridor to me several times. I ignored him and let his voice shred into white noise which became the only saving grace to my resolve. I kept walking until I reached the front door where Sally and Harriet grabbed my arm to stop me.

"I'd like to go back to the boarding house," I mumbled before they could ask me anything. I tried to walk, but the girls stood in front of me, blocking my way. Harriet put her arms out against my shoulders to stop me moving forward and pushing past them. I sighed and bit my tongue to calm the buzzing in my ears.

"What's happened?" Harriet quizzed. They had to have stayed further back than I anticipated in the corridor. I didn't want to relive every moment of the encounter, but I had to for them.

I sighed, letting tears drift over my cheeks in a trickle. My voice shook as I tried to speak, clogging my throat with a sorrow I hadn't anticipated ever feeling. I swallowed it back and licked my lips to steady myself. "He picked Margaret. He has ended anything we ever had in the cruellest way."

Sally and Harriet ceased their questioning and brought me back to the boarding house, rubbing my back and arms to try to comfort me. Their comfort provided little ease to the breaking of my soul inside. My face remained in a grimace as we made our way to the room in the house, earning the glances of VADs who knew the first signs of hurt from a facial expression. They bowed their heads or turned their gaze away from me out of respect. How could I ever forgive Ross for picking someone else when he told me that his heart belonged to me? How many times would Ross keep breaking his promises to me? All I knew was that I wasn't ready to forgive him this time. Not after breaking me more times than I cared to ever count.

Once we arrived at the hospital for nightshift, Sally went straight to Ross' corridor to attend to him. I still couldn't face him or even look at him, especially not after what he did to me a mere few hours earlier. Paul had arrived at the hospital for visiting after we had left. Harriet informed him about what happened, and his driver took him to our boarding house to let him see me. Even though he told me how sorry he was for what Ross did, he helped me to rethink my priorities once again.

"Your focus needs to be on Edward," he reminded me, taking my hands in his. "Focusing on him and finding out where he is will help you to forget about Ross Mason."

It was Paul's advice which helped me to face the nightshift. I had to remove Ross from my mind to do my duty for the injured men. The night-time had been the best time to forget him because I never saw him. By the time I was likely to come across him, the morning duty had started. The darkness of the moon's dominance and glory was my saving grace. I knew I couldn't avoid him forever, but even for a little while, it was enough. I finished checking on the men in one of the corridors, letting them rest for the night in the shattered moonlight streaming through the windows. As I made my way back to the ward, I came across Michael, and he stopped me in the middle of an empty corridor. I was under no disillusion that Harriet had told him about Margaret turning up. If she said it to Paul, she would do the same with Michael.

"Sally's in the other corridor," I informed him, trying to move past him.

He put his hand out, catching my shoulder, as he shook his head. "I'm here to see you actually." He moved his grip from me and searched in his jacket pocket, producing an envelope. The moment I spotted my name on the front, I knew it was from Ross. I'd recognise his handwriting anywhere, even amongst a sea of others. "Ross and Harriet filled me in on what happened earlier. In fact, Harriet told me as soon as you left. When I went to talk to Ross about it, he handed me this letter, asking me to give you it."

"I don't want it," I stated, folding my arms across my chest. My lungs expanded as pride took over. I wouldn't accept a meagre apology or excuse from Ross again. "It will either be him begging for forgiveness or him telling me that he did pick Margaret. Either way I don't want it."

"Or it could be neither," Michael offered, shrugging nonchalantly. He thrusted it forward again. The white envelope shone in the silver light coming through the windows – a mixture of starlight and moonlight. "Just read it. No one is asking you to do anything but that. A lot has happened, and I think you need a few days to process it all. Perhaps the letter will help you do that."

I chewed the inside of my cheek, mulling over my choices, before I caved in and nodded. As I took the letter from his fingers, he pulled me into a hug. His warm arms wrapped around me, providing me with an element of comfort when every piece of me shattered into a million tiny shards. I never wanted to tell anyone how much I was hurting; it just wasn't in my nature. Yet, somehow since working with Michael, he always seemed to know when any part of me broke or hurt inside. Perhaps that was why I sought to continue our friendship no matter what happened. Why would anyone want to lose the one person who brought so much comfort to such a broken soul?

"Goodnight Belle," Michael whispered in my ear.

"Goodnight Michael."

Sally came along after we broke away from the hug. She smiled at me once she spotted the letter; obviously Ross had told her what he had given Michael. I left the two of them to talk and dragged my feet back to the ward Sister Mary had assigned me to. None of the other nurses or VADs spotted my appearance as they scribbled on pages to their sweethearts or husbands at the desk. I took a seat among them, looking at the envelope which still sat in my grip. From tracing Ross' handwriting with my finger to twirling the envelope on the smooth wooden surface of the desk. My fingers itched to open it and, after resisting for too long, I tore the paper seal to reveal what Ross wanted me to know. The ripping of the envelope and rustling of the paper unfolding filled the quiet ward, portraying the loudest scream in the universe. I glanced around to see if it had disturbed anyone, but it hadn't. The snores of the men continued despite my apparent raucousness. My stomach churned and the temperature rose in my veins, prickling my skin against the heat, as I began to read the letter.

To my Belle,

I'm sorry for betraying you. I keep hurting you and I hate myself for it. I invited Margaret to visit after you told me about Edward. I shouldn't have done it and I know you will never forgive me for it. I should have tried to fight for your love, instead of giving up. I see the mistake I made, and I hope you know I am truly sorry. I'm refusing to give up on you; I will fight for you until the end of my days. This I do truly promise you in sight of every witness who could ever bear notice to our love. I swore I wasn't going to hurt you anymore and that's just another promise I have broken. But I will make it up to you if it's the last thing I do.

When you walked away earlier, it was like I couldn't breathe without you. A part of me walked out the door with your heart and soul. I just need you and I don't know why. But when we're apart I feel an aching deep in my bones. I'm not the same without you Belle. I fear, if this is the end, that I will always give my heart to you. I can't let go of you and a part of me shall always be yours whether you choose to let us go or not. You touched my heart, body, and soul. How can you ever forget someone who does that?

I'm sorry for every mistake I have made between us. God knows it's too many to count or list in this letter. My biggest mistake was saying I didn't want you anymore that night in the daisy field. I will forever regret that for the rest of my life. Part of me was stupid enough to think that, when you left, you would one day be ready to come back home to me. But I didn't take the risk. I couldn't. I needed to find you and make it up to you. Now, I've ruined it again for I haven't seen you since this afternoon. I'm an idiotic fool. I suppose we do anything to feel a tiny bit of love from someone, even if it isn't the person who has our whole heart.

Perhaps you think that moving on is for the best. I know you may never forgive me, but what if we move on just for the moment, rather than forever? If we must speak in truth, you showed me a world full of colour that I know I cannot see with anyone else. I would ruin myself a million more times just to be with you. Belle, I know that you might not have been able to see a future with me, but I swear that I saw it every single time I looked into your beautiful brown eyes. We were happy back home with each other because we got everything we wanted—we got each other. Back then, that was all that mattered to us.

I never had anything real until I met you. I knew this love between us would hurt me eventually because I cannot let you go. I understand now that I will have to. But please know that I will spend every second of my life hoping that your heart is free. You mean the entire world to me and I'm sorry I never treated you like it. You were good to me, and I've let you down once again. I shouldn't ask you 'what if we're still meant to be?' because I know we may never be again. But I shall forever ask myself that question.

I'm so sorry.

Ross.

With the letter in my hand, I walked outside and into an empty corridor coated in starlight from the abyss of night. I sat on the ledge by an open window, listening to the pattering of the summer rain filling the void. A tear slipped down my face which captured the moonlight and reflected against the windowpane. Ross had hurt me so much and I couldn't forgive him, not again. Not when I had Edward and he had chosen Margaret over me. My chin quivered as I choked out sobs in the silence of the hospital. Despite every aching bone in my body, I kept repeating Ross' question in my mind. *'What if we were still meant to be?'* If we were, why did he pick Margaret and why did I give my love over to Edward? I didn't know what to feel about Ross before he arrived at the hospital. Even now, I still didn't know after seeing him again.

I sniffed and wiped away my tears with the back of my hand. My head and heart were a muddled enigma. "Look at this mess that you've made me, Ross Mason," I whispered to the empty corridor. "Just look at this mess..."

We made quite a unique combination: an utter mess and an idiotic fool. Yet, I promised myself I would never enter such a disastrous affair again with him. I couldn't trust him not to break my heart or his own promises. After everything in this war, I had learnt what I deserved, and I wouldn't fall for his charm again. My nails dug into the palms of my hands, matching the pain in my throat. Ross had betrayed me and sent me into a new hell all over again because no matter how much I gave him, it never seemed enough to win his love. Deep down, I knew I would ruin myself for him just once more. But not this time.

Chapter Thirty-Eight

"It's been a week since Michael gave you the letter and you haven't so much as glanced at Ross," Sally stated in the boarding house as we dressed in our uniforms. Sally and Harriet had grown tired of taking some of my duties for me to avoid Ross.

I fastened my headdress in the mirror. "I've been on nightshift."

She scoffed, shaking her head, and glancing over at Harriet who stood waiting for us. "Well today that changes. I'm not saying to forgive him, but at least talk to him. I know you, Belle; you find it impossible to hold grudges."

I bit my tongue, knowing I couldn't argue the facts with Sally. Michael had outed the past I had with him by accident to Sister Mary. I swore for the first day after it happened that I wasn't speaking to him, even though there wasn't a lot which took place between us. The next day, I returned to the ward and chatted to him as though nothing had happened. I learnt then that I couldn't hold grudges for very long. So far, a week had become a new record for me.

As we walked towards the hospital, I made a resolve to do something about Ross. I just didn't know what quite yet. Despite her lecture in the boarding house, Sally offered to give me a reprieve by taking the breakfast dishes to Ross' corridor, with a stern warning that it was the last time until I spoke to him again. I agreed, knowing all I needed was the morning to work out what to say to him.

While I handed out breakfast to the men in ward two, my thoughts drifted to the seething anger which had radiated through my veins when I saw Margaret standing in the corridor to visit Ross. In my best reasoning, I could understand why he invited her to see him. After all, I had told him about Edward's intentions after the war; the one piece of information no one but us knew. I hadn't even told my parents, yet I felt the need to spill the secret to Ross, knowing it would break his heart. But I hadn't heard from Edward for eight months now. No amount of encouragement or comfort could make me regain hope in the love Edward and I once had. After spending time alone in the corridor once I read Ross' letter, I wrote Edward a new letter, asking if he was okay on the frontline. To date, I still hadn't received a response. As I handed around the breakfast dishes, I decided to ask the men how long it took to get a letter from here to France.

"Two or three days, My Dear," one soldier told me in an Irish burr. The bandages around his head moved as he spoke. "If there's a holdup, it could take us a week to get it at the front – that's at the most."

I handed him his breakfast as I swallowed back the bile which crept up my throat. "So not long at all really."

He gazed at me with round, understanding azure eyes. "No response from your sweetheart?"

I shook my head, turning my eyes away from him so he didn't have to watch them water. "It's been eight months."

When the soldier remained silent for too long, I returned my gaze to him, and he swiftly tore his eyes away. I watched as his Adam's apple bobbed in his throat, knowing something I didn't. When I pushed him for an explanation, he sighed, and his azure eyes met mine once more. "That usually means that he may have lost his life, or he's missing in action, but presumed dead."

"I know. I just… want to keep hoping."

"We've got to keep hoping," he said, reaching over to pat my hand affectionately. "'Tis the only thing that will get us through this ruddy war."

I handed out the rest of the breakfast dishes and tried to block out the words he said, despite knowing the harsh truth behind them. *'He may have lost his life, or he's missing in action, but presumed dead.'* I took some element of comfort in the fact that if it was either situation, I had left Edward on good terms. He knew I loved him with every ounce of my being. But if it happened to Ross when he went back to the frontline, I couldn't say the same thing about him. Adrenaline spurred through my veins, pulsing around my body with every beat of my heart as I realised the motivation I needed to speak with Ross.

After I finished all the morning tasks assigned to me, Sister Mary asked for me to mingle and chat with the patients while they waited for their lunch. A lot of the patients who arrived at the same time as Ross were now on their feet and walking about the recreational areas of the hospital during their free time. Michael had updated me on Ross, telling me how he was now spending most of his free time in the recreational areas bonding with the other men in his regiment. I made my way to the first area, trying to find Ross amongst the men, but he wasn't there.

When I asked the soldiers if they knew where he was, none of them had seen him.

As I turned into the second recreational area, I spotted Ross sitting at one of the tables, playing cards with another two men. They had cigarettes placed in a discreet pile in the middle of the table as wagers for their card game. My eyebrows knitted together as I tip-toed up to them. Any sound I made became masked by the chattering of the men in the area. I stood behind Ross, but all three of them were utterly oblivious to my presence.

"I'm all in," Ross said, throwing two packets of cigarettes into the middle of their table, adding to the already growing pile.

"Same," the two other men chorused in strong Irish burrs. One threw in three packets and the other threw two in. Ross wrapped his hands around the pile, sorting it out to make it appear as though the men were merely placing the items from their pockets on the table.

"Sister wouldn't like you gambling." The three men jumped at the sound of my voice, causing them to drop their cards on the table with fumbling hands. Ross spun around and his hazel-green eyes lit up, sparkling at the mere sight of me. The other men grabbed their cards and tried to hide them under the table. I lifted the deck which sat face down on the surface and each of them gave me a sheepish look with a rose flush appearing on their cheeks.

I smirked at them and began to shuffle the cards as quickly as I could muster, much to the shock of the men. The cards blurred with the swift motion as they slipped into each other. The men stared at me with wide eyes and open mouths, watching each shuffle with precision. I set the deck back on the table and met their stares as they tried to fathom what they had watched. My lips pulled into my mouth as I tried to stop myself from laughing at their expressions.

"Where on earth did you learn to do that?" one of the Irish men asked.

I shrugged, smiling at the men who watched me so intensely as though they could pick up the skill from staring. "When you're bored on nightshift at the hospital, it would amaze you what skills you learn while sitting there." My eyes darted straight to Ross and the bubbling anger which filled my veins softened as I stared deep into his eyes, remembering the long nights and afternoons learning to shuffle cards with him. "Plus, I had a very good tutor back home who taught me everything I need to know."

Ross and I stared at each other for longer than we should have, letting our eyes mix together in the colours of summer. The remnants of sun shining through the branches and green leaves on a warm summer's day – the creation only our orbs could resemble. I tore my eyes away from his and bid the men farewell before walking back out to the corridor. Ross' heavy footsteps followed behind me and, at the echo of the door swinging open again, I knew my instincts were right.

"Belle," he called when the corridor deserted into the recreation area. I turned around and he made his way towards me. He didn't have as much of a limp as before, demonstrating how well he had recovered already. It wouldn't take long before the doctors would recommend his return to the frontlines. Even after everything we had gone through in the last few weeks, I didn't want him to go and put himself back in danger.

"Yes?"

The edges of his mouth twitched as he tried to suppress even the smallest smile from appearing on his lips. "I thought I wasn't going to see you again. I've been wanting to talk to you about everything that happened last week. It wasn't entirely what you thought."

"Which part? You hurting me or you picking Margaret?" I quizzed, folding my arms over my chest. I wasn't allowing my resolve to slip now, not after everything that had happened and the promises he had broken.

"Me picking Margaret," he stated. He glanced around as more people walked past us. I smiled politely at the staff who made their way down the corridor, knowing I had to keep up appearances in front of them. "Is there somewhere we can go to talk?"

The gardens had always been my sanctuary throughout my time at the hospital. It was the only place where I could find alone time to think or just breathe. Now, it became the place where Ross and I would hear each other out after everything we had went through. Despite the anger which bubbled inside me, I had agreed to hear him out, even if I was unwilling to forgive him. At least Sally and Harriet would celebrate the progress I had made with Ross today. The drama and utter chaos with Ross had taken my mind off worrying about Edward, even if it was only for a few hours each day. Checking in newspapers and black fingertips had become somewhat of an obsession of mine since the push. Still his name wasn't listed, and the black stains marked my skin as a reminder of his absence. Was he missing in action, dead, or ignoring me? I didn't know which one to think or believe without any discernible proof.

Ross and I took a seat on Tommy's bench in the silence of the garden. I smiled as I glanced at the trees, spotting the Blue Tit flying down onto the grass near us. No matter what, Tommy never left my side. A sorrow weighed against my chest as I realised how much I would miss him when I left for France. Part of me hoped that the Blue Tit, especially if it was Tommy like Mrs Felton said, would somehow follow me out to France too. As the Blue Tit cocked its head at Ross, I drew my attention back to the man sitting beside me. The magnetic field between us ebbed as though trying to pull us together once more.

"I was angry and hurt when you told me about Edward," Ross spoke. He kept his eyes focused on the hospital building in front of us. "So, I asked for Margaret to come and see me in the hospital. But before she came to see me, I realised what a mistake it was. When she got here, I told her that I didn't want our marriage anymore – perhaps we could just part ways amicably for the children. I know society would hate us for it and Margaret hated me too for suggesting it. She refused my suggestion, but Belle I tried for you."

I shook my head, curling my lip in disgust at Ross' suggestion to leave Margaret in such a way. Didn't he know the repercussions for Margaret and the children? "And I'm supposed to believe you? Don't you understand what you could do to the children especially if you suggest doing such a thing?"

He sat up straighter and ran his hands through his hair. A frustrated groan escaped from his lips, but he still wouldn't look near me. "I know this won't change anything in the grand scheme of things. Margaret won't leave me and you're right, I couldn't do it to the children. But how am I supposed to show you I love you anymore than I've already tried doing? I even tried to explain my feelings in the letter."

I nodded, fixing my eyes on the Blue Tit hopping about on the grass. "I read the letter when Michael gave me it and I've been rereading it every night since. Look Ross, what we had was an affair; a simple, lustrous affair. We're now two years on from when it first happened. Back then, I didn't need anything more than that. Wanting each other was enough. But I need something more now."

Ross crouched down in front of me as he took my hands in his, making me look at him. He stared deep into my eyes as our colours mixed in a fog of autumn sunshine. "You and I can be more than an affair. I can give you everything you need."

"No, you can't Ross! Can't you see that we're just living for the hope of a love that has reached the pinnacle of its possibility? There's nothing guaranteed because you aren't mine to love anymore and I'm not yours. I know Edward may have died or is missing in action. Until I know for sure, I cannot possibly entertain this thought."

I tore my hands away from his and stood up to walk away. I weaved my way around his body, but he gripped my hand, pulling me back into his chest. He might not have fought for me before, but he was determined to do it now. His grip remained firm on my hand, boring his eyes into mine as he silently pleaded to let me hear him out. Our warm breath mingled together as our chests pressed tight against each other's. The fire burned from our souls as a violent blaze of passion and frustration threatened to let its embers spark over into something uncontrollable.

"I have always been yours," he spoke through gritted teeth. I swallowed hard and willed the heat rising in my body to cease. "Before you even told me you felt the same way and before you knew my feelings, my heart was always yours. You were mine to lose and I am *still* yours to lose." He pulled me closer to him until not even the fresh air could possibly part us. Not a single gap of light shone between our bodies as I glanced up at him through my eyelashes. "Those memories of us haunt me every waking moment. The memories of being tangled in bedsheets, in the horse stables, the daisy field… your name is forever written over my 'what-ifs' because of those memories. Don't tell me that you don't think of them too. If you felt nothing for me and had no hope for us, then you wouldn't think of those and you wouldn't have the chain around your neck."

Ross hit every single truth which I had tried to keep hidden in my heart. The memories had come back to me in dreams of passion and lust in the darkness of night. I had thought about us tangled together more times than I cared to ever admit, even to myself. His eyes darted to my chest, as though seeing through the uniform to the chain which rested there with his initials on it – the initials of the soul who knew me better than I knew the back of my hand. His gaze turned back to mine, awaiting the truth of having never taken the necklace off since the day he gave me it in the daisy field. I had constantly pleaded with myself to forget him and the memories. But I couldn't. No matter what I did, I couldn't forget. How could I possibly ever forget a soul like Ross Mason?

"This is impossible Ross. I have a sweetheart and you have a wife," I tried to reason as much with myself as with him. I never tore my eyes from his, knowing he would see through every lie I had spoken to him. "We… you're just hoping for something to happen between us." Warm droplets of tears fell over the curves on my cheeks, and I gazed at the ground to hide them. Ross' grip left my hand, turning to my arm and rubbing small circles on it. Every touch he gave me sent electricity surging throughout my whole body; filling my veins with the passion I once had for him.

We descended into silence as I composed myself, swallowing away any tears which hadn't made an appearance yet. I couldn't surrender my heart to Ross, not when I needed to find Edward. Not when he had hurt me so much in the small space of two years. Yet every bone in my body and every vessel in my heart ached for Ross just once more. My very soul screamed his name in every language and colour this world possessed.

"If we don't stop, we'll ruin each other over and over again," I continued, finally wiping away my tears. I pushed my shoulders back and looked at the clouded concern in his eyes, dimming the vibrant colour I had fallen for. "We could have stopped this affair over a hundred times, and we never did. Can't you see how much this will burn us?"

The fog passed in his eyes as I finished speaking, returning the hazel-green to its full brightness. He pulled me closer to him by my hips and my hands instinctively went to his shoulders. Under my touch, his flesh scorched against mine. "You're worth every single burn I get. If we could have stopped a hundred times and didn't, then what is the point of stopping now?"

Before I could respond, he leant in, grazing his lips against mine as though waiting for permission to let gravity win. The magnetic force lured gravity away to let my lips meet his in a hunger I had forgotten I could experience. Flames engulfed us as I consciously kissed him back with every passion in my blood. I knew it was wrong, but I couldn't stop myself wanting Ross. The hunger, lust, and passion faded everything to oblivion when I rested in his arms. He moved his head to deepen the kiss as one face flashed before my closed eyes. *Edward.*

I pulled myself away from Ross and raised a hand to my lips, wiping away any trace of his presence from them. "I can't do this, Ross." I untangled myself from his arms and ran towards the hospital, refusing to glance back even once.

"Belle, I'm sorry!"

I had to keep running before the flames caught up to me once again. I couldn't let it happen, not after all this time and the hurt I had gone through. I held the matches as much as Ross did and I wasn't letting the flames spark against my skin, scoring the alabaster flesh in Ross' name.

Chapter Thirty-Nine

In the two weeks since Ross and I kissed in the gardens, he had recovered quicker than most people. I spent my days checking the newspapers, awaiting Edward's name to appear amongst the list of dead or missing in action. Finally, his name stood out against the white paper in black ink in the officers' column. *'Lieutenant Edward Blackwell: missing in action – presumed dead.'* As soon as I read it several times, making sure it was real, I burst into uncontrollable sobs in the middle of the corridor. My heart shattered to a million pieces beneath my breast as Sally ran towards me. The paper laid at my knees in a haphazard manner, maintaining the page where Edward's name had been listed. The one person who made their way to me after Sally was the man who had walked around the hospital with her: Ross. He fell to his knees with Sally, wrapping me in his arms. He rubbed my back in circles, trying to comfort me, as he assured me that it didn't mean he had lost his life. Edward could have been a Prisoner of War or still out on No Man's Land. Neither of those thoughts appealed for an alternative for Edward's life.

Every member of the hospital staff and the soldiers had been incredibly understanding to my situation. Edward's parents wrote to me, telling me they were trying to receive any morsel of information about what had happened to him as soon as possible. Every day I eagerly awaited some news from them. Yet again, nothing came. The war had become a never ending cycle of sorrow and heartache for me. All I desired was for it to end as soon as possible. I didn't know how much more grief my heart could take before it became irrevocably broken.

When morning came, I had to pick myself up as best as I could muster under the circumstances. Sister Mary had planned on discharging a few men in the next couple of days. She was the first to tell me that Ross would be one of the few. After how he helped me with Edward's news, I wanted to try to make his final days at the hospital as enjoyable and happy as possible. Every man needed some joy before leaving to return to the frontline once again. There was no doubt in my mind that most of them would have done anything to never return to the life of war again.

"Will you be sad to see Ross go?" Sally asked as we fastened our headdress in the mirrors in the room.

"I suppose," I mumbled, trying not to think about him leaving. The hollowness had already etched its place in my heart, awaiting his absence every single day. "He's been a great help with Edward the last week since we found out, but…"

"But?'

I sighed, pulling my lips into my mouth, debating as to whether sharing my true feelings would help me. I had swiftly learnt that it hadn't, but this was Sally. She had always been there for me through everything. "But it would be an even better help if he went home so I could get on with my life, without him confusing my thoughts, and he could patch up his."

Sally smiled at me as I turned to her, not saying anything more about Ross. We both knew I needed to fix things properly with him before he returned to the frontlines. Despite how much I tried, it hadn't worked to patch things up because the kiss in the gardens kept replaying in my mind, as though teasing me over my own mistake. Neither Ross nor I spoke about the kiss since it happened, but he needed an explanation as to why I ran. He needed to know it wasn't his fault.

Sally, Harriet, and I made our way to the hospital for the dayshift. Some men stood outside the entrance to the hospital as they waited for ambulance to take them to the train station where they would return home on leave or continue to the frontlines. Each man wore the sapphire hospital uniform, with the red tie poking out of the suit jacket. The last time I had witnessed anyone wearing the suit was when I first saw Edward in the cliffs overlooking the coast. Even now, the bitter taste of salt air came to my lips as I remembered everything about the day. I watched the men smiling at us; their eyes sparkled with the delight of getting away from the hospital and returning to their friends on the front or their families at home. How many of them would see the end of the war? How many wouldn't? I had already lost two men I loved to the war. The mere thought of losing Ross too clenched my heart, tightening my chest, at the reminder of having no one left if it ever happened.

Sister Mary assigned the three of us straight to corridor five to check wounds and replace bandages. It was Ross' corridor. I fetched everything we needed from the sluice room and placed it on our trolley while Sally and Harriet spoke to Sister Mary. The trolley clattered into the corridor as I tried to suppress the butterflies in my stomach, making my hands shake with the nerves of seeing him again. *'It's Ross for goodness sake, not Edward,'* I attempted to chastise myself. I shouldn't have had a fluttering in my stomach for Ross – those feelings should be reserved for Edward. That period of my life had ended the minute I arrived in Poole in 1914. I had to keep reminding myself of how much Ross' part in my life had ended.

Once Sally and Harriet joined me, we gathered at the bottom of the corridor to agree on the sections to take. Harriet smirked at me as she delegated our areas. "Right, I'll take the top of the corridor, Sally you take the end and Belle, you can take the middle."

I narrowed my eyes at her as my head tilted. "That's where Ross is."

Sally nodded, no longer trying to suppress the smile which now spread across her thin lips. "Exactly, it'll be the perfect time for you two to talk."

I opened my mouth to respond, but no words emerged as they walked away from me to their sections of the corridor. The two of them had it planned since they woke up this morning. Nothing would persuade them out of their plan, especially when they wouldn't allow me to protest. I clamped my lips shut and swallowed my pride, before striding my way forwards to the middle of the corridor. Stopping at the delegated section, I looked around to spot Ross just five beds away. From where I worked, taking the stitches out of one of the men, his laughter greeted my ears in a sweet melody of daisy fields and homemade scones – the faint reminders of home which haunted me every time his laughter echoed off the walls.

"Are you Nurse Wilson?" the soldier asked me as I finished removing the last stitch. I glanced up at him through my eyelashes and nodded as a smile graced my lips. The man's amber eyes shone as he realised who I was. "Ross Mason talks so much about you. *'The prettiest and kindest nurse in Britain'*, he says. I have to say I think he's right."

A rose flush spread over his cheeks as he recollected his own words to me. The hardness of my heart since Ross' hurt melted away at how shy and embarrassed the man was in front of me. "That's very sweet of you."

He didn't speak again as I cleaned up, but he continued to avoid eye contact with me until I left his bedside. My eyebrows pinched together as the man's words flowed in my ears over the sound of Ross' laughter. Why would Ross say those kind things about me after everything that happened between us? Every so often, as I worked my way through the men, I glanced at Ross. He threw his head back as the laughter escaped his lungs; the image of his happiness in the daisy field just two years ago. His eyes sparkled with contentment every time the sun glinted off them through the windowpanes of the hospital. Was it being here with me which made him like this? After all, he had desired nothing more than to see me again when he was on the frontline – at least, that was what he wrote to me.

As I watched him throwing his head back in pure joy, I realised he was the only man that I had loved which I knew was still alive. I didn't want to further complicate the mess, but who was I supposed to talk to or love, if Ross didn't survive this war? My chest tightened as I thought about having to live without anyone I had ever loved. My throat clenched and I tried to swallow to ease the pain, but it came to little effect. Ross' eyes met mine, shining brighter than I had ever witnessed before, as he gave me the goofiest lop-sided grin. His joy came from coming back to me. Since he arrived at the hospital, we had spent more time fighting than anything else. If he was to leave in a few days, I needed to change it.

Sally had talked to me about everything just last night. She claimed destiny brought us together and, therefore, everything in mine and Ross' life would always connect us. There would always be a force which would guide the two of us to each other, no matter how far apart we travelled or what the circumstances became. I wasn't sure if I believed in destiny or fate anymore. But I knew something was always going to connect me and Ross together – the universe wouldn't let me rest so easily.

"Hello," Ross greeted me when I reached his bed. I tried to crush the fluttering in my stomach and dismiss whatever tricks destiny wanted to play on me.

I smiled at him, keeping my attention focused on my duty. He watched my every move as he waited on me to speak about something, anything, to remove the suffocating tension between us. "Let's get a look at you."

"The doctor says the bandages come off," he explained, lifting the blanket off his legs to let me see the wound on his thigh. "I'm almost going back to the front."

A pang of pain rippled through my chest knowing he wasn't going to be here much longer. I pushed it away to the back of my mind and unwound the bandage around his calf. "When do you leave?"

"Tomorrow morning."

My heart plummeted to the pit of my stomach as the bandage slipped from my grasp. My hands shook as I realised that today was Ross' last day at the hospital. I didn't even know; neither him nor Sister Mary had informed me. I took a deep, pained breath as my eyelids fluttered closed for a brief second. The swiftness of his departure made me feel guiltier than I already was.

"I'll miss you," I admitted, taking off the bandage from his chest wound. My voice cracked as I tried to speak, willing myself to lighten the dark cloud which descended over us. "I'll miss giving you blanket baths."

He burst out laughing, causing a smile to come to my face in spite of my mood. His laughter would forever remind me of the life I left behind. "Don't worry, there'll be plenty more times when we get home."

I stifled a laugh but couldn't work through the overwhelming heaviness in my heart. I finished removing the bandages on Ross' wounds which had now fully healed, leaving only a raw scar on the surface of his skin. As I gathered the equipment to stand up, he took my hand, stopping every motion I needed to make. I glanced up at him as he stared deep into my eyes. The colours of autumn of our orbs mixed in a moment of understanding. The embers of the fire I had experienced in the gardens sparked into a dim blaze.

"My feelings haven't changed," he stated, rubbing small circles on the back of my hand. The calloused skin against mine sent shivers down my spine. "I understand if yours haven't from… from telling me that you didn't want us."

I sighed, knowing I couldn't keep my emotions in any longer. "They haven't changed because I still can't be with you. But I'd at least like for us to go back to the way we were."

Ross flashed me a gentle, warm smile, as he nodded in acknowledgement of what he could never change. "I'd like that."

Without hesitation, I pulled him into my arms and enveloped him in a hug I hadn't known I needed until then. He wrapped me in his embrace, holding me close to his chest. I rested my head on his shoulder, turning my mouth to his ear. "By the way, stop telling the other soldiers I'm pretty."

When we tore ourselves away from the hug, he beamed at me as a red glow appeared over his cheeks. I held his eyes for longer than I should have, knowing he couldn't deny it. Not once did he even try to. I stood up and attended to the other men until I met Sally coming towards me to aid her final few men. As I walked away towards the sluice room, with Sally and Harriet by my side, I glanced around to find Ross still beaming at me. I swore my stomach jumped again as our eyes locked in the autumnal colours of a life that we desired nothing more than to return to.

Visiting time wasn't the same that afternoon as it was the one day a week that Paul couldn't come to the hospital. Everyone missed his presence, from soldiers and male orderlies to the nurses and VADs. I aimlessly wandered about the corridors and recreational areas, smiling at the men I passed and conversed with those who spoke to me. When I reached the final recreational area, I spotted Ross sitting at one of the tables, playing cards with the two Irish men again. One of the men had told me they went over the top beside Ross on the first of July in the push at the Somme. When I approached them, Ross' eyes diverted straight to me, and I tried to hide the heat rising to my cheeks.

"Nurse," one of the men called in an Irish burr I'd become so accustomed to. I pulled my gaze away from Ross and looked at the man who grinned at me. "Would you shuffle the cards for us again?"

"As long as you promise there's no gambling going on," I joked, raising my eyebrows at them, as I tried to suppress a smile which desperately tugged at the corners of my mouth. The three men attempted to conceal the cigarettes on the table, shielding them with their hands as they glanced around to see if any other staff members spotted it.

"No promises," Ross stated, winking at me. The men began to laugh along with him, and the smile finally won against my own resistance as it beamed across my lips. Ross' eyes brightened at the mere sight of a smile on my face; reminding me of the love he still held for me.

Laughter erupted from my throat as a song long forgotten by the conflict of the war. I shook my head as I picked up the deck of cards from the table. They fitted into my alabaster hand with ease, readying itself to shuffle into the form the soldiers needed. As I lifted a couple of cards to shuffle, the doors to the recreational area flung against the wall, drawing everyone's attention to the person who had certainly left a marking on the walls. Michael's eyes darted around the room as he tried to find the person he needed. His gaze fell on me as my heart plummeted to the pit of my stomach. He made his way over to me as I rested the cards back on the table with a shaky hand. The entire area descended into silence, knowing something wasn't quite right.

"There's a telegram for you," Michael announced. Everyone's eyes glanced straight to me, but I only kept my focus on him, trying to understand what awaited me in the telegram. Whenever the telegram messenger arrived, they always brought bad news to the person involved. Now, it was my turn. As I walked away with Michael, I could sense every heart in the room breaking for me among the silence of respect. Was Edward the reason I had received the telegram?

"Do you want me to come with you?" Ross asked, taking my hand to stop my movements. I shrugged, not quite knowing what to feel in the middle of the numbness which presented itself to me. Perhaps this was the closure I had sought for eight months while awaiting word on Edward.

Michael led me towards the main entrance of the hospital as Ross held my hand, ignoring how clammy my palm had gotten on the short journey. Sally and Harriet stood waiting with the unopened telegram in their hands. Their heads turned at the echoes of our feet resounding off the walls. Even though visiting hours had created a bustling to the hospital, the entire pathway to this moment seemed deserted of any form of life. I couldn't tell if it was a good sign or an ominous imitation of the news awaiting me.

With a shaky hand, I took the telegram from their grasp and walked outside to read it in privacy. If Edward had passed, I wanted to experience it alone, knowing no one else would understand how much I loved him. I sat down on one of the benches near the main entrance and stared at the envelope in my hands. My name and the hospital address gazed back at me, making me question if I truly wanted the closure that I had sought for so long. The nausea which had gradually built up made me lightheaded and I gripped the bench to stop the world around me spinning out of control. The prospect of knowing Edward might not be alive anymore made my entire body weak. Life would have to go on without him, but I could never be okay with moving on and living without him by my side. Was that the definition of love? I wasn't sure what I believed in anymore, not when the universe had dealt me the worst hand of cards known to humanity. A deep, shaky breath escaped my pursed lips as I calmed myself down enough to open the envelope.

Belle, we received news that Edward has been recovered from No Man's Land and is now safe and alive in a hospital in France. He promises to write to you soon and apologises for any worries we had.

Mr. and Mrs. Blackwell

I dropped the page to the ground, as though it were the hottest element on this Earth. Edward was alive… My Edward. A smile pulled at the corners of my mouth as my heart jumped in my chest, reminding me how alive I felt with Edward in my life. Tears fell from my eyes as I picked up the paper from the ground. I swiped them away with the back of my hand as a giddiness overcame me. Yet, despite the joy radiating through my veins, something was wrong. Why was I not as happy as I should have been? The gravel crunched behind me and, as I turned around, I laid my eyes upon the reason. *Ross.*

He sat down beside me on the bench, maintaining a safe distance between us. "Well?"

I beamed at him as I clutched the news in my hand, afraid it might blow away in the breeze which ruffled Ross' hair. "He's safe and alive. His parents sent me the telegram; you were right, he was stuck out in No Man's Land. They retrieved him and he's recovering in hospital."

Ross forced a smile onto his lips, creating tension crinkles at the sides of his eyes. He thought I couldn't see through the pain of losing me. But his eyes had always been the window to his soul. The hazel-green dimmed to an indistinguishable colour, radiating the pain which drove straight for his heart. "I'm happy to hear that about him; really, I am."

I stifled a laugh, shaking my head at him. "No, you're not. I can see right through you."

He sighed, diverting his eyes away from me, as he figured out how I knew his pain. "I'm glad he's alive for your sake Belle. I've always told you I care deeply for you, and I mean it. But if things turned out differently…"

His words ceased in his throat as he pushed himself off the bench, knowing I couldn't hear him speak of us all over again. As he made to walk away, I flew off my seat and grabbed his hand, pulling him back to me. Our eyes locked for a brief second; enough time to picture us back in the daisy field with the sun glinting between us.

"Can we have a proper talk tonight before my shift ends? Somewhere quiet and private, just us," I asked, knowing I didn't have much time left with Ross before he returned to the frontlines. I needed to make everything up to him, especially now with the news I desired, but the result Ross had dreaded to the very depth of his being.

Ross' mouth twitched into a slight smile. "I'd like that."

Sally, Harriet, and Michael met me outside the doors as I let them read the telegram from Edward's parents. Their eyes scanned the words over and over until they realised the truth I had desperately desired to know. Sally glanced up at me with bright, shining eyes, and opened her mouth to speak. But her words froze as her gaze shot straight to my hand. I followed her stare until I noticed my hand still in Ross'; our fingers laced and interlocked as they formed the perfect puzzle piece coming together. I dropped his grasp and tried to behave as though it were a mere mistake. As much as I had convinced myself otherwise, I had missed Ross' touch. Something about him screamed dangerous, passionate, and addictive. Even though we celebrated the news of Edward, I kept glancing at Ross, hoping for something, anything, later to explain the unfathomable feelings I held about him in my heart. I just didn't know what that 'something' was quite yet.

~

For the rest of my shift, I jumped at every noise, darting my eyes around a room or ward, as every aspect of my body felt on edge. My stomach fluttered as I bit my lip, trying to work out everything that had happened between me and Ross. One minute he wanted me, the next he didn't. How was I supposed to know what to feel about someone as indecisive as Ross Mason? All I knew was that I needed to see him once more before tomorrow when he returned to the front.

Sister Mary assigned Sally and I to tidy the sluice room before the end of our shift. The mundane task provided the perfect way to escape the thoughts which made my head throb with every push of blood flowing through my veins. Sally was unusually chatty, trying to draw me into a conversation. Yet all I could muster were noises of agreement or one-line responses. When we reached the end of the items to tidy away, Sally slammed the door shut, causing my body to jolt, and she stared at me with a furrowed brow.

"What's wrong, Belle? I thought your mood would have changed when you heard that Edward was okay."

I sighed, moving my jaw from side to side as I contemplated whether she would understand or not. I didn't even comprehend my own feelings, let alone someone else trying to. "I'm so happy he's alive, but I'm also confused. I love Edward and yet I don't want to lose Ross. All this while, I thought he had been leading me on. He hasn't though and I genuinely think he loves me. What do you do when two men love you?"

Sally smiled and the creases in her brow eased with the softening of her eyes. "If I were you, I'd talk to Ross and see what happens. We both know there's no guarantee that Edward will come back to you, especially when he only contacted his parents. No one is expecting you to decide which one to love for the rest of your life now. We're in the middle of a war and everything can change in the blink of an eye. Go and find Ross, I'll speak with Sister Mary to tell her we've finished here. But when you get back to the boarding house, I want all the news."

She pulled me into a hug as we laughed at her constant desire for gossip. Every time I swore someone wouldn't understand my mess, they proved me wrong in the best possible way. Sally opened the door, allowing me out of the sluice room to find Ross. Luckily, I knew exactly where he would be this time of day

– gambling cigarettes in the recreational area. As suspected, he sat in the corner of the room at the table, playing cards with the men. Yet the gambling wasn't its usual ferocious self. The men fiddled with the edges of the cards in their hands as Ross' voice mentioned my name. The tension in my shoulders ebbed away, slackening as I stood there, knowing he was trying to work things out about us, just as I had with Sally.

Once I made my way over to the table, their voices ceased, and they turned to smile at me. Ross' eyes diverted back to the cards in his hand, and I watched as his Adam's apple bobbed in his throat in anticipation of what I could possibly speak to him about. The two men bid me goodnight before walking off to their beds, leaving me alone with Ross in a crowded room. His chair scraped against the floor as he rose from his seat, taking my hand to lead me out of the recreational area. I let Ross take us to wherever he found the most comfortable to hear me out. Our whole time together in the hospital had resulted in fights, dangerous kisses, and stolen stares. Perhaps we could bed all the tension and return ourselves to some form of normality – whatever 'normality' meant during a world war.

Ross led us to the backdoors of the hospital where the building led into the gardens. Many a night I spent standing listening to the rain in the corridor, wondering where he was in France or if he still thought of me. Edward and I had shared moments here, believing it would become our sacred sanctuary. Yet now those memories tainted a burning red as we stopped by the doors in the silence. Our breathing echoed against the walls, as though the two of us were trying to restrain ourselves from an outburst of anger or passion – whichever came out first.

Before either of us dared to speak, we stood by the doors, listening for anyone approaching the corridor. Ross' calloused fingertips traced circles on the back of my hand, making every fibre in my body tingle in anticipation of his touch. His eyes remained fixated on the end of the corridor, ensuring we were alone. As any approaching footsteps stopped miles from us, our bodies relaxed against the cold wall.

"I wish you didn't have to go." My voice came out as a mere whisper, cracking in the strain of maintaining my steady emotions. We glanced at each other at the same time, mixing the autumnal colours of a forbidden love together once more. His eyes clouded over with rain showers threatening to break with a single blink. He forced a smile onto his face, but it failed miserably to convey any signs of comfort for me.

"I wish I didn't have to leave you. I wanted this time to make up everything I did to you. But it didn't work. In fact, I think I made it worse."

We turned to face each other; our hands interconnected out of instinct. I stared down to observe how well they fitted together as though they had always belonged to each other's soul. Anyone I had confessed to about my affair with Ross never once stated we didn't belonged together. As I glanced back at him through my eyelashes, my heart weighed heavy beneath my breast, knowing that if I let Ross walk out of my life, I would spend the rest of it missing a part of my soul.

"I'm sorry, Ross. I'm sorry for loving you and trying to deny it."

A genuine smile formed on his face which let the tears he held inside fall over his cheekbones. "I love you too, Belle. Sometimes I love you so much I can't even comprehend it myself. But we need to admit the truth before I leave tomorrow. Your heart belongs in France with Edward; not with me. I thought I might be able to win your heart back and no matter what I tried, I couldn't. I burnt us into ashes and hurt you beyond repair. As much as I love you to the very depth of my desires and my soul, we can't keep doing this. I can't keep hurting you in this way."

It was the rehearsed speech which we had both planned out in our own minds. Not one part of what he said resembled our true feelings. Yet there was nothing I could say to try to change his mind. His stubborn heart had wanted me but knew he could never have it with Edward now in the picture. His hand fell from mine, sending a shiver through my whole body. He waited there for a few moments, stepping back from me as though waiting for a rebuke for telling me lies. When I couldn't form a coherent sentence, he walked away without a single word.

"Stop!" My voice rebounded off the walls as Ross stopped in the corridor. His shoulders rose and fell before he turned around. Tears streamed down his face as he stared at me with red, bloodshot eyes. "Just stop being so stubborn. We both know that's not what you damn well want from us. So just admit it!"

"Fine, I'll admit I love you and I will love you until my dying breath! You have become a part of me – another half to my soul. Letting you go will kill me. I know I made it clear before the war that I didn't want you, but I was an idiotic fool. Your heart belongs to Edward now, but I will never stop fighting for you. We were a mess, but it was the mess I wanted and always will want. I'm not asking you to decide about us until the war is over, like we agreed. All I'm asking is that you don't shut the possibility of us out of your heart forever."

His eyes blazed into mine, waiting for an answer. I strode over to him until there was a mere few inches between our bodies. "You made it clear so many times that you did not want me. I swore after you invited Margaret here that I would never forgive you. I don't know what is wrong with me, but my stupid heart still falls for you every single time. I can't make my mind up yet as to whether I want you until the end of the war. All I know right now is that if I let you walk out of my life, I shall spend the rest of it missing a part of me."

We stood in silence, facing each other as our breath mingled in a hot, angry mist. My gaze travelled from his lips to his eyes and back again. All I desired was the feel of the flames of his lips on mine and to never pull away from him. Ross' hand reached up to caress my face. I laid my cheek against his palm as he leant his forehead against mine. His breath lingered on my lips; the anger between us had dissipated, turning to heated passion and desire. A lust neither of us had experienced in so long… back in the daisy field. I craved nothing more than to let gravity win, allowing our lips to meet in the longing my heart screamed for.

"Forgive me if this is impertinent, but… will you let me have one more kiss? No expectations, no questions. Just one kiss," he whispered against my lips.

Without another word, we leant into each other, letting our lips meet in a crazed passion we had desired, as the flames burnt the corridor around us. In that single moment, we both knew we would be the ruin of each other. Yet neither of us wanted it any other way. My arms wrapped around his neck as his hands moulded against my hips, pulling us closer together until the flames engulfed us as one being. Every memory which flooded my mind as he tilted his head, deepening the kiss, became searing smoke – tangled in bedsheets, scratches down his back, spinning in the daisy field, and kissing in the vicar's room. We were a blazing inferno; a flaming mess of one being… one soul. It was a kiss without any expectations and that was how I need to try to keep it.

Chapter Forty

All night I had tossed and turned, unable to settle knowing Ross' departure loomed over me. I had lied to myself a million times during the darkness of night of how I felt about him. Did I truly love him? Did everything I said to him mean anything? The kiss… the violent blaze of a kiss which had inscribed its memory in my heart. By the time our morning wakeup call came, I knew I had to ready myself to say goodbye. With every step I made, the echoes of my heart breaking rattled in my soul.

I washed and dressed myself in silence, mulling over every decision I made in relation to Ross. As I pinned my hair into a bun and pulled on the headdress, Sally and Harriet's eyes boring into me sent a chill down my spine. I had admitted everything about what happened between Ross and I when we met last night. They thought I had done right by kissing him goodbye. But every time I remembered his lips against mine, a tightness came over my chest and a pain stung the back of my throat which didn't move, no matter how much I swallowed.

"How are you feeling?" Harriet cautiously asked as we made our way out of the boarding house. Her eyes searched mine to scan for any signs of my resolve breaking.

I gave her a tight smile; the force of which hurt my cheeks as I tried to maintain it. "Heartbroken at him leaving, but it has to happen so I'm trying to be as cheerful as possible."

Before I left the hospital last night, Sister Mary informed me that Ross would be leaving after the morning rounds. The doctor needed to check him to make sure he was fit to return to the frontline. As Ross hadn't asked for home leave to recover, his train was bound for the frontlines. For me, waiting until the morning rounds finished just prolonged the agony. The only aspect I remained grateful for was that I wouldn't have to worry about my duties while saying goodbye to him. I had requested to Sally and Harriet not to see Ross until it was his time to go. They agreed to take any duties which would cause me to encounter him. If I saw him before the time, it would make the goodbye even more difficult than it was already going to be.

When we reached the hospital, the ambulances sat outside waiting to deliver the men to the train stations. Sally squeezed my hand to try to comfort me, but it did little for the tearing pain in my chest. How much more could my heart handle in this war? Sister Mary waited for us outside the ward as we approached, motioning for me to come over to her. I glanced at Sally and Harriet who nodded before beginning their morning duties. I swallowed hard and walked over to Sister Mary, hoping Ross still maintained a good health.

"Nurse Wilson, Mr Mason will be waiting in the first recreational area with the other men leaving today once he has been seen to by the doctor. When you finish your morning duties, you may go to say your farewells."

"Thank you, Sister."

Sister Mary had given me a reprieve this morning, assigning me to only hand out the breakfast to the men. Harriet took the breakfast to the corridor where Ross had stayed in his time at the hospital, ensuring I wouldn't lay eyes on him until it was time. Sally and I agreed to dish out the breakfast to one corridor and two wards each. As I handed out the dishes to the men, I greeted them with cheerful smiles, hoping they couldn't see right through me to the pain which carried heavy on my soul. With each step I made, memories of last night with Ross flooded my mind in flashbacks burning in bright red. There was something about him which kept bringing me back into his arms. Perhaps it was destiny, or fate, or even my own stupidity. But whatever it happened to be, I knew we would always end up crossing paths in this life and the next.

At home everything had been easier – I didn't have Edward and a possible engagement to consider. All I had to worry about was getting caught with Ross and the next time we would see each other. It had been a simple life, but as much as I desired to turn back time, I could never replace Edward, especially with Ross forever changing his mind about me. I couldn't risk giving my whole heart to Ross with his indecisiveness and losing Edward in the process. There was one thing I needed to do, but doing it would become the issue, because it went against everything in my heart.

When the breakfasts had been handed out, tunnel vision took over my mind as I made my way to Sister Mary. She was the only person who could let me carry out what I needed to do. She stood in the corridor with a bundle of medical supplies in her hands. At the echo of my approaching footsteps, she turned around and smiled. I opened my mouth to ask her the one thing I needed to when she bundled the supplies into my arms, asking me to place the items in the sluice room on the appropriate shelves.

"Wilson," Sister Mary called as I walked into the sluice room. I spun around as she stood in the doorway; the light illuminating the corridor behind her as though heaven itself had stepped foot in Poole. "You may accompany the men to the station with the ambulance driver before they make their train journeys either home or to the frontlines."

My mouth twitched at the mention of the plan I had wanted to convince her of. I willed myself not to look as elated as the lightness of my body suggested. Instead, I merely nodded at her. "Yes Sister."

The second she left, I put everything in order as swiftly as I could muster, knowing I had to try to find Ross before meeting the men outside. The supplies stayed on the shelves, despite the speed I had placed them, as I slammed the cupboard doors closed. My shoes skidded on the tiles as I rushed out of the sluice room and towards the recreational area to find Ross. The doors swung open in a breeze as I stepped inside, spotting Ross and Michael chatting together. I stood back, waiting on them to finish, as Michael shook Ross hand and wished him well before leaving me with him. Each man in the recreational area wore his hospital uniform, except for those returning to the frontline. Their regiment had sent a supply of uniforms for the men to wear on their way to the frontlines, including Ross. It was as though I had witnessed him for the first time in his uniform all over again. My stomach fluttered as Ross laid his eyes on me, sending me back to last night; the fire and passion of his lips still tingled on mine.

"Sister Mary has informed me that I'll be going with you to the train station, but can we talk before we leave?" I questioned, fidgeting with my fingers which had grown clammy since stepping into Ross' presence. He nodded and rose from the chair he sat on, following me into the corridors until we came across the first empty one.

The temperature dropped in the corridor, as if people alone were the only source of heating in the hospital. We stopped halfway, standing near the window to soak in the heat from the sun streaming shards into the emptiness. I turned to face Ross as the weight of my heart became burdensome against my breast. My eyes darted to the white and black tiles beneath my feet, reminding me of the world I had left behind the minute I fell in love with Ross.

"I think it's best that we remain friends," I mumbled, knowing it was the one sentence I had to say. The train station wouldn't have been the right time to tell him, not when he was on his way to the frontlines. "You're a wonderful man and part of me still loves you. But I cannot get hurt by you again. Back home I was in a life that I hated and loving you made it more exciting. It gave me a reason to wake up every single morning and face the day ahead. But now I have Edward and he provides the love and security I always needed from you. He saved me from the life that I hated back home; you could never save me in that way. You made it perfectly clear before the war. Edward helped me to see the good in what I do, and he never once argued with me about joining the war effort."

I took a deep breath and dared a glance at Ross through my eyelashes. The fiery stare of blazing anger didn't meet mine. Instead, his hazel-green eyes softened to a gentleness I hadn't witnessed when chastising him before. They melted, blending the opposing colours of his orbs together, in understanding.

"Is there anything I can do to change your mind?"

I watched as his eyes watered, breaking my heart as much as his had shattered. I shook my head, swallowing back any words which threatened to contradict those I had just spoken. "No, I don't think so."

Ross leant down, laying a hand on the top of my arm, and pecked my cheek in a sweet tenderness. He pulled away from me, dropping his hand as I opened my mouth to apologise. The words caught in my throat as a tear rolled down my cheek. The driver's voice echoed in the corridor, making my body jolt with the reality of what I now had to live with. Ross waited for me to move before he walked to the recreational area. I fetched my coat while Ross and the other men grabbed their belongings to take with them. The driver allowed me to sit in the back with the men on their way to the station. Ross climbed in first before he reached his hands out to help me inside. He kept a hold of my hand, pulling me over to sit beside him. No one batted an eyelid at our behaviour as they knew by now about me and Ross.

At the time, the giddy happiness of sitting beside him felt like the perfect decision. Yet, the closer we came to the train station, the more the decision became an unconventional form of torture. The magnetic field between us heightened its force and intensity until I wanted to scream. Despite how much I had talked to myself, convincing my heart that I didn't feel anything towards him, my fingertips ached to touch him, and my lips desired nothing more than to kiss him once more. But I couldn't. I'd made my choice and I couldn't go back on it now.

Once we stopped at the station, I opened the doors to let the men out of the ambulance before I stepped down. Ross stood waiting to help me out of the back. The driver watched the interaction between me and Ross, his eyebrows raising ever so slightly. I approached him and asked if we could stay for a little while. I needed to see Ross off; I couldn't let him return to the frontlines alone, not after all we had gone through together. Before the driver could open his mouth to form a protest, I handed him enough money for tea, cigarettes, and a newspaper. He took the money and agreed straight away, saying I could stay for as long as I desired to. Ross grabbed my hand, and we checked the timetable to see when the train to the frontline was due to leave.

We made our way up the steps to the platform, knowing we wouldn't have enough time to go far before the train left. Ross found us an empty bench as we sat down waiting on the allotted time to creep up on us. I glanced around, noticing how quiet the train station appeared. Every time I had been here the hustle and bustle of soldiers standing on the platform would have made anyone lightheaded. There were half the number of soldiers as the time I had came with Edward to see him off. Yet the silence did nothing to ease the nausea in my stomach. The stench of the train smoke tingled my nose, distracting me for a few seconds.

I turned on the bench to face Ross as his hand remained in mine. The stubble which usually formed on his chin had been shaved by the male orderlies in the hospital. This way, he wouldn't have to shave it when he arrived in France. But, as I looked at him, I could still picture the russet bear which caught the sun the time we stood outside the church. He had only touched the small of my back then, but it was enough to set my heart on fire. Ross sensed my eyes watching him and he glanced around to me, bringing me back to the smoke-filled train station and the ache in my chest for the goodbye I never wanted to say.

"I know you said that there was nothing I could say to change your mind about me," he started. His hand grew clammy in mine as our eyes locked in an unbreakable bond. "But, please, hear me out… please." When I nodded, he took a deep, shaking breath and swallowed hard, trying to contain his emotions. "From the first moment that I met you, you captured my heart, with your deep brown eyes and golden curls. I tried my hardest to suppress every emotion inside me that wanted you in ways that I never should have. You have no idea how much I buried my feelings about you, until I couldn't any longer. I never needed anything more than us. You think I was only living for the hope of it all. But I wasn't. I truly loved you. When I knew you felt the same way about me, it was the best day of my life. You're right, Belle – wanting may have been enough for us back home but it isn't enough anymore. I understand if Edward has every single piece of your heart, but don't forget the memories of us. You have etched your name on my heart and imprinted your touch on my soul."

I tore my hand from his and flew off the bench, storming off into the slight crowd which started to take up the platform. Ross' pounding footsteps sprinted after me until he stood in front, preventing me from moving any further. "Ross, nothing can change my mind – I've already told you so."

"Then why walk off if you feel nothing for me?"

I couldn't tell him the truth about my actions: if I hadn't walked off, I would have ended up admitting my true feelings to him. I would have told him that he had my heart as much as Edward. My soul had his touch forever scored into it; irreplaceably and unchangeably so. The reality of how much my heart still desired Ross terrified me beyond belief. My hands balled at the sides of my body as I dug my nails into my palms, using the pain to calm myself down.

"You can't love me when you have a wife," I attempted to convince him as much as myself. His eyes bore a violent blaze into mine, threatening to melt away my resolve if I allowed it to. "It's impossible. We both know it is, Ross."

"It's only impossible if you make it so." He tore off his hat and ran a hand through his hair, which had shown the golden highlights through his brown locks from the times we sat in the gardens of the hospital. All those times I had tried to convince us this wouldn't last. Yet here we were once again. "The more I got to know you, the more I realised that I didn't fall in love with the woman in the veil that I married. I fell in love with the woman who understood me, the one who loved me back as much as I loved her. I still love that woman… I still love you, Belle."

"Look at the mess of us Ross!" I yelled over the hissing of the train waiting to whisk him away. My body shook as I argued with him, despite the stares of the few soldiers who stood close enough to us to hear everything. "We are a mess and you… you've made *me* into the most idiotic fool ever to grace this Earth."

"But I showed you amazing things too," he fought back. The gap between us closed and I willed myself not to draw into him again. A force pushed us together and I couldn't let it win this time. "At least, you did that for me. You showed me the colour in this black and white world. I cannot see that with anyone else; only you provide me with the colour in this world."

I shook my head, trying to block out every argument he presented me with, knowing I didn't have any retaliation. "Didn't you listen to anything I said before we left the hospital? I needed saved from this mess of my life. You didn't do that for me. You *can't* do it for me."

I manoeuvred myself around Ross and ran down the steps, pushing past the people who were making their way to the platform. The mutters of how rude I was reached my ears, but they became white noise as the rushing of my blood filled the void. Tears blurred my vision as I reached the last step. I blinked, sending them rushing down my face in waterfalls of sorrow, heartache, and a love lost once more. I leant against the wall, trying to regain my breath as the tears left warm trails over my skin.

As my breath came back, Ross reached me, pushing through the people to get to my side. My feet tried to take me away, running from the truth he told me with every word he spoke, but he grabbed my hands in his before I could move any further. My heart broke inside my chest as I persuaded myself to fight against every feeling that I ever possessed for the man I first loved. How could I forget the man who first took my heart and made it his?

"I can save you," he pleaded. My hands melted into his as I stared down at our interconnected fingers. "I have surrendered my whole heart and soul to you."

I didn't dare to look up at him, knowing I would fall for those eyes in a second. "You don't need to save me! You made that perfectly clear before the war."

"Listen to me!" Ross shouted over the crowd. He dropped my hands and placed his grip on my shoulders, forcing me to look at him. His eyes searched mine for a reaction to his protests before he dared to continue with his persuasion. My breath hitched in my throat as the fire he ignited in my soul sparked to life. "I know you still love me. You're trying to persuade yourself out of it. Let yourself admit it, just like you told me last night at the hospital." When I refused to say anything, he moved closer to me until our chests pressed against each other's. I didn't pull away from him, no matter how much the rational side of my brain screamed at me to back off. The fire between us would reignite as swiftly as it started if our eyes remained locked on each other's for much longer. We breathed in sync as not even a morsel of air could make its way between us. "When this war is over, will you run away with me?"

I opened and closed my mouth, trying to form a response to such an irrational idea. I had lied to myself a million times all night and this morning, telling myself I felt nothing for Ross Mason. Yet, as I stood there with my chest pressed against his, we became one being all over again. My heart thudded between us, and I knew he could feel it too, telling him my true feelings even if I wouldn't admit to him. Our breathing grew rapid and heavy as it created a warm mist of desire in the gap between our lips. As his eyes scanned mine for any inclination of an answer, my honest, truthful feelings about him boiled to the surface of my soul.

The sudden loudness of the noise of the station which had once grew quiet filled my ears, trying to distract me from the decision I had to make. Neither of us moved from the proximity of each other, desiring this final touch between us. For all we knew, it could be the last time we ever saw each other again. The temperature rose in my body with a headache which throbbed in my temple as I thought of how Ross had caught me lying about us many times since we reunited. He knew damn well that I would ruin myself as many as a million times for him.

That was when the one word of an answer escaped my lips…

"Yes."

And just like that, I was ready to ruin myself once more for Ross Mason.

TO BE CONTINUED

Continue Ross and Belle's story, through Ross' eyes, as the war rages through Europe in the next Daisy Field series instalment...

Poppy Field

Coming Soon

Read on for a preview of the first chapter...

Daisy Field

The war must stop soon. It has to; the guns… they have to cease. They're in my dreams. They're there when I wake up. Their echoes fill my ears every minute of the day. It all has to end. Please, God, let it end.

My footsteps echoed on the cobble stones as I made my way to the pub where everyone had gathered. The chattering and singing in half-drunken slurs travelled towards me as I walked closer to where the soldiers stood outside with pints in their hands. They nodded at me as I weaved my way through them and into the pub. My eyes squinted in the darkness as they tried to adjust to the lack of sunlight which had coated my whole journey back to France. The rooms bustled with Tommies, making it difficult to spot anyone who wore the same uniform. My eyes landed on the far corner where my men sipped at their beers in a table hidden out of the way. A warmth enveloped my insides as I realised how much I had missed them. If the war wasn't in my favour, then at least I knew I had enjoyed and revelled in the camaraderie the army granted me. Robert's eyes lit up against the darkness as he spotted me dodging the Tommies until I made my way to the table.

He shot up from his seat, drawing the attention of the other men sitting with him. "Ross Mason, I thought we'd seen the last of you," Robert greeted me, pulling me into a hug.

I chuckled as I thudded his back. "You couldn't get rid of me that easily."

During the Somme, Robert and I had gone over the top, side by side, in our darkest hour. Our feet tripped on the chalked mud as we desperately scrambled across the barbed wire and dead bodies. The high command had sworn the wire was cut, but we soon discovered that we were to meet our fate wrapped in the razors of our so-called protection. Men got tangled in the wire as they tried to cut it, letting them become sitting targets for the Huns who shot them. Their misery was over before they witnessed the true horrors and massacre of the battlefield. Either side of us, men's bodies laid on the ground or over the barbed wire. Their eyes wide, bulging in fear and their mouths open as if they were about to scream for help. I had to have tunnel vision despite the aching tightness in my chest to do something for the fallen men. If I didn't keep my eyes averted, I wouldn't have been able to move forward to try for my own survival. I would have joined the men tangled in the wire; the sitting targets of the Huns. The whistling of shells rained hot shrapnel down on us, searing through our helmets and uniforms until it met the flesh of those still living. The exploding grenades burst the chalk ground around us without any warning – sending us flying through the air or killing us upon detonation.

The men shuffled over at the table to give me room to squish in beside them. The second I sat down, my fingers drummed the table to drown out the whizzing and whistling in my ears which plagued my every waking second. I swallowed back the lump in my throat which did little to ease the discomfort. The noises wouldn't just fill my ears soon; they'd echo all around me on the frontline… inescapable.

"Ross," Robert called across the table, pulling me back to the dark French pub. My eyes shot up from the oak beneath my fingers to him. His eyebrows pinched together as he watched my behaviour, but I plastered a smile on my face to hide the thudding of my heart and the clamminess of my palms. "I asked if you saw your Belle when you went home?"

My eyes darted back to the knotted wood, tracing every dark spiral in the oak. Belle's face when I climbed onto the train replayed in my mind for most of my journey to France. Her tired, lifeless eyes watched me leaving until they couldn't anymore. A warm flush flooded my body as my stomach sank picturing it all over again. I glanced at Robert as he smiled, awaiting a hopeful answer. His amber eyes sparkled with the anticipation of lovers being reunited. Little did he know how much I had hurt Belle and drained her of life.

"Yeah… she was working in the hospital I was sent to. She saw me off on the train when I was leaving to come back."

"So, it's still love then?" Sam questioned, leaning over the table with a beaming grin. For a young lad who had witnessed the destruction of war, he was doing too well compared to the rest of us. Then again, unlike Sam, we had watched the war unfolding from near the start of the conflict; we had become known as old timers. There were very few of us left, as though we were a rare breed of animal close to extinction. Robert and I both feared Sam would end up snapping at some point throughout the war. It happened to every single man in the army, whether he admitted it or not. If it hadn't happened yet, then it was only a matter of time – a sealed fate of this war.

I stifled a laugh, not quite knowing how to answer without confessing the whole truth. The least I could do was help the men believe in happy endings after what they had gone through. "Who knows, Sam. War changes everyone."

"Here, here," Robert agreed, taking a drink from his pint glass as though it were a wedding toast. He motioned for a waitress, calling for her to bring a pint of beer over for me. She set the bubbling liquid in front of me, frothing the edges of the mug in an enticing manner. If it wasn't for the drink and cigarettes, half of the men would go insane. "Oh, by the way Ross, we're getting a new officer."

"A new officer? What happened to Officer Healy?" I quizzed, taking a sip of the beer. It warmed my veins as it travelled down my throat, reminding me of the second home I had found among my men.

Robert placed a cigarette between his cracked lips, searching for a lighter in his pocket. "Healy's only just gone off his ruddy rocker, hasn't he. Somme got to him. So, they're sending in someone else. No doubt another one who'll shout orders at us and expect us to do all the dirty work while he stares down his nose at us."

There was only ever one word to sum up Healy: devious. None of us liked him from the moment we set foot on the soil of France. His beady eyes watched as Sergeant Wilkins drilled and punished us until he couldn't anymore. There was nothing wrong with us except for Wilkins, who liked to see which one of us would crack first with him. Before we received the orders to go to the front for the Somme, Wilkins made our friend, Nicky, run with his rifle over his head until he told him to stop. But he never did. Nicky threw down the rifle, splashing mud across our uniforms as he sprinted for Wilkins. With tense fingers, bulging with the veins under the flesh, he grabbed Wilkins by the collar of his jacket and yelled into his face. Officer Healy had to pull them apart before delegating the punishment. He ordered Wilkins to strap Nicky to a cartwheel for six hours as the disciplinary measure; earning him his first criminal record for the army.

After we finished our pints, we made our way back to the base camp to meet our new officer. The men chatted about the type of man he would be, or if he would end up being the same kind of man as Healy. Would he be as slimy and devious as Healy had been? According to their predictions, that's exactly what he would be like. Walking back to base with Robert, Nicky, and Sam made every tense muscle in my body ebb away as though we hadn't been parted by the Somme. Since leaving Belle at the train station, my being personified stress with veins poking through my skin and pounding headaches. Something wasn't right between me and Belle. It hadn't been since that day in the daisy field. The men tried to take my mind off my distant thoughts as they caught me up with who was no longer with us. I had been in hospital in Poole while they had stared at the two walls of a trench. Robert informed me that Sergeant Wilkins had received the call for our regiment to return to the front within a few days. My hands shook and buds of sweat broke on my forehead as the words left his lips. All I desired was for the war to end soon. After witnessing the massacre of the Somme, I knew I couldn't face another slaughter of my friends again.

"Line up you slimy lot!" Wilkins yelled, sending spittle flying from his mouth. We pulled our caps onto our heads and joined the line-up, standing to attention and waiting for further orders. Wilkins patrolled the line, staring us up and down with beady eyes and an upturned lip of disgust. If he were a butcher, I had no doubt this was how he would decide which pig to send to the slaughter.

"He's one to talk, calling us slimy," Robert mumbled in a barely audible voice to me. I bit the inside of my lip to stop myself from smirking or sniggering.

"What did you say Private Hornsby?" Wilkins screamed as he stormed from the top of the line down to him. Their faces stood inches apart and Wilkins' nostrils flared as though he were ready to charge at the slightest flicker of red.

Robert stared straight ahead, pretending he wasn't blowing hot air into his face. "Nothing Sergeant."

Wilkins' moustache tickled his nose as he stepped closer to him. "I should bloody well hope not. You're not to speak unless spoken to Hornsby, or have you forgotten basic army etiquette after having a drink?"

Wilkins stepped away, not awaiting a reply, and Robert kept his eyes fixated on the horizon. The tiny droplets of Wilkins' spittle glistened on his nose. He dared not to even lift a hand to wipe it for fear of receiving a punishment. Wilkins' eyes darted down the line, meeting mine, and he marched back to me. I focused in front of me, refusing to give in to an egotistical little man. Out of the corner of my eye, I spotted the crumbs and spittle hanging on to the bristled hairs of Wilkins' black moustache.

"Private Mason, I never thought I'd see you back," he challenged.

I kept my facial expression and eyes neutral, pinching my blunt nails into the palms of my hand to ease the anger coursing through my veins. "I'm not a deserter Sergeant."

"No, because, from the talk of the men, your sweetheart nor your wife would respect you if you were," he stated through gritted teeth. I swallowed against the lump which had formed in my throat, unwilling to budge to ease my discomfort. My hands clenched and unclenched by my sides as the temperature in my body rose, prickling my skin in the woollen uniform.

Before I had the chance to retort, Wilkins turned around in a flash and stood beside me at attention. An officer walked across the front of the line, smiling at us in a genuine way which made the hairs on the back of my neck rise. His black, curly hair had started to grey at the sides, reminding us of his age, and somehow his status too. Alongside the mature sophistication he exemplified, he held himself better than any of us; he pushed his shoulders back, never once allowing them to droop, as he kept his back straight. The officer held his hands behind his back as he faced us.

"At ease men," he spoke in a relatively posh-sounding accent. Every officer held status; a world war still had every element of class and society dictating it. "I'm Officer Edward Blackwell and I'll be taking over from Officer Healy."

I watched him, cocking my head as he spoke, wondering why his name sounded so familiar to me. I hadn't come across him before in my two years in the army. At least not to my recollection. He began to tell us his military story so far and I listened intently, hoping to catch a place that the two of us might have fought in. While every place he fought in had been in France or Belgium, we had never crossed paths. But the minute he mentioned getting injured and being sent to a hospital in England, the breath in my body escaped in a single knock against my soul. My stomach sunk as I realised who the man standing in front of us was and why his name had become familiar to my ears. This officer was Belle's; he was Belle's Edward.

"I hope to get to know each of you as best as we can in the middle of war. We'll begin our move to the front in two days. Over this time, I want to supervise training, as I know from Sergeant Wilkins that some of you have spent time in hospital after the Somme. I want to help you get back on the path to returning to full speed in time to reach the frontlines," Edward explained, smiling at us before dismissing us with a simple nod of his head.

We stood idly chatting to each other at the rest camp as Officer Blackwell approached each group of men with Wilkins hot on his tail. I watched him talking with the gathering of men just behind our group and Wilkins leant his ear into the circle as though Edward's very presence had dismissed his authority over us. Had Belle told Edward about us? If she did, then what did she tell him or how much of our affair did she confess? Would he even know it was me when he approached? There was no doubt that Belle told him; she was the most honest person I had ever known in my life. Our relationship tested her strongest value and virtue. The minute she met Edward and fell in love with him, I knew she would have told him because she wouldn't let herself lose her honesty to another man ever again.

"Gentlemen, what are each of your names?" Edward questioned as he came over to us. His hands remained behind his back, portraying the appearance of an aristocrat to the rest of the ordinary soldiers; something I could never muster even if I tried.

"Robert Hornsby."

"Samuel, Sam, Fletcher."

"Nicholas, Nicky, Fenton."

Edward's eyes met mine and my chest tightened in anticipation of him discovering my identity in a second. But, instead, a glow of radiant amicability came from his smile as he awaited my response. I took a deep breath, knowing I couldn't give a fake name to protect Belle's love for him. If she had told him, I could never avoid him finding out it was me – not when he was now in charge of us.

"Ross Mason."

His eyebrows pinched together as though some part of his mind had recognised the name, in much the same way as I had with him. I willed myself to keep my face neutral and blank. Edward's eyes clouded over in the evening sunlight before he nodded, turning his face away from me without any indication of whether he knew me or not. "It's a pleasure to meet you all. Head over to get yourselves dinner and then you're free for the rest of the evening. You can go to the pub again, into the village, or just stay here. But remember, you need to be back early for training in the morning."

Almost half of the regiment were killed or wounded from the Somme, resulting in the dinner line to have significantly reduced. Those of us who were left became known as 'old soldiers'. It didn't necessarily mean we were battle-hardened despite everything we had lived through and somehow had managed to survive. The thought of returning to the trenches became every 'old soldier's' worst nightmare; at least, it was for me and Robert. After the Somme there was little that we hadn't seen, but the cold sweats and shaking limbs after a dark slumber plagued each of us. It was now our job to take the new recruits under our wing and help them through the hell of what was to come on the frontlines.

Sam arrived with us a month before the Somme, becoming the latest new soldier in our regiment. Wilkins assigned me and Robert to look after him, or in his words, to make sure he didn't run away or desert the front. Everything we did for Sam couldn't have prepared him for the massacre he witnessed. Yet he wasn't once terrified to fight for his friends and die alongside them. One thing I'd learnt by taking care of the new recruits was they could be mentally stronger than the rest of us. Officer Healy had left the regiment, yet Sam still stood tall despite the horrific punishments he inflicted on the young lad. If Sam survived the war, Robert and I had envisaged him continuing in the army, working his way through the ranks. Some people had been born for the army, and some just weren't; Sam had definitely been born for his duty.

As the war continued, the food became as bland as eating the chalk and mud of the trenches. The watery soup sloshed about in my bowl as I took the stale bread and mug of tea from those serving us our dinner. The food was never enough to keep us from going hungry or losing weight. Soldiers lined the long tables, savouring their food with slow spoonfuls and mouse-sized bites of bread. Our group took a seat at the end of a half-full table, devouring our penultimate dinner before heading to the trenches once more. I stared at the soup, trying to find the vegetables which were meant to linger in the bowl. Behind us, the sky formed the first signs of a sunset, erupting the camp in a golden glow.

"Is this seat free gentlemen?"

We glanced up from our bowls as Officer Blackwell stood there with Wilkins. They held their own dinner in their hands, expecting to sit with us. We shuffled down to allow them room to find space between us. I tried not to groan or roll my eyes when Wilkins took a seat beside me. Robert's eyes darted over to me with a smirk plastered over his lips at my new dinner partner. I glared back at him, but my skin grew cold as a shadow darkened my place at the table. If I hadn't suspected Edward recognised my name before, I did now as he chose to sit directly in front of me.

"It's a lovely evening," Edward commented, breaking a piece of his bread off to dip into his soup. Everyone mumbled noises of agreement before they chatted amongst themselves, trying to include the new officer when they could. Needless to say, no one spoke to Wilkins – the Devil's personal partner in crime.

I kept my eyes fixated on my soup, allowing the bland liquid to force the hard corner of the bread down my throat without getting stuck. Every time I dared to look up through my eyelashes, I found Edward already staring at me. Wrinkles formed at his eyes and across his forehead as though still trying to remember why my name sounded familiar. Whenever he caught me watching, he glanced away, pretending he had never done it. Behind Edward's head, the sky turned to a blazing amber the likes of which I'd only ever seen at home. My heart warmed as I remember all the times that I had watched the sunsets with Belle. As I let the amber blaze glint in my orbs, my mind wasn't in France anymore. Instead, I travelled back to the daisy field with Belle; the only person I had ever dared to call home.

The sun began to set as I made my way across the field to where she stood behind the trees in the shade of the leaves. The sun still streamed its rays through the branches, echoing its golden shards against her alabaster skin. The daisies danced around her in the shadow of the trees as though they too were pleased to see her. My heart lifted in my chest as a smile spread across my lips at the mere sight of Belle. Her white dress flowed in the gentle breeze as some blonde curls descended from the bun at the back of her head. The pounding of my feet drew her attention to me as she spun around. Within seconds, her solemn expression vanished, and her eyes twinkled, matching the beaming grin which completely altered her face. My feet picked up their pace, running towards her, until I pulled her into my arms.

"How did you get away?" Belle asked me, searching my eyes with sparkling orbs. Every time she looked at me like that, time slowed until it didn't exist anymore.

"Margaret had a headache and didn't want to go for a walk this evening." It was the perfect getaway to see the one person who made my heart sing a different tune every time our eyes met. Belle let out a sigh as her shoulders slumped in my arms. The weight of her body seemed to press against my chest as though a burden had lifted from her heart.

"I was worried you weren't coming."

My eyebrows pinched together, forming a small crease between them, as I shook my head. "I would never do that on you."

I took her soft, delicate hand in mine as we made our way to the highest point in the field. In the dimming light of day, the horizon blazed with amber, causing the light to catch Belle's hair like a halo. Despite the warmth of the smile on her face, something niggled at me. Whenever her eyes met mine, a mist flooded her chestnut orbs. I never asked her what was wrong, regardless of the pain in my chest as I watched her. Perhaps I should have…

The emerald grass crunched in the heat as we sat down, and Belle reached out to pluck a daisy from the mud below. The flower twirled in her fingertips, dancing in the remaining sunlight of the day. Belle moved herself to lie with her head in my lap, taking her hair out of her bun. Her curls blanketed my thighs in golden threads of satin. She wasn't looking at me or the twirling daisy. Instead, her eyes remained fixated on the clouds above us which burnt with the horizon. My fingers traced her curls which fell into place effortlessly. The orange clouds reflected in her brown eyes, turning them to an amber chasm. The birds sang in the trees around us to nest down for the night, creating the only sound nature possessed. The world didn't exist when I was in the daisy field with Belle.

"Do you truly love me?" Belle mumbled. My gaze shot straight to her and only then did her eyes meet mine. I never once hesitated in my answer to her.

"Of course I do."

She sat up to face me and the light illuminated her hair in gold crested streaks. The daisy remained between her fingers as the amber sky blanketed every aspect of nature. My throat clenched as though waiting for her to tell me she didn't love me anymore. "I wish things were different. I wish we could court properly, but we'll never be able to."

"Don't say that. We will be, I promise you Belle. Someday we'll be given a chance to run, and we'll do it. We'll leave everybody behind, and I'll come back to see Eliza and Arthur when we get settled."

A smile pulled at the edges of his lips as she lifted herself up to sit on my lap. I wrapped my arms around her, holding her close and wishing I never had to let her go. She leant against my chest as I embraced the way her body curved into mine. "We'll have a little cottage and live the life we always wanted to," she continued, twirling the daisy as she spoke. I craned my neck and kissed her soft, alabaster cheek. Sparks erupted against my lips as the single touch of her flesh against mine drew a magnetic force around us, always pulling us together no matter how far we parted from each other. She turned to face me and held the daisy out for me to take. "Dry it and keep it with you. That way you'll always have a piece of me wherever you go."

The blazing sky behind her faded as did the vivid memory of home. The laughing and chattering of the men brought me back to the harsh reality I wish I could have left behind. I pushed away my empty bowl and made my way over to the trees to light a cigarette. The whooshing of the lit match drowned out the noise in my mind for a split second – silencing the guns and shells which rang out in my ears. As I put the matchbox back into my jacket pocket, the soft fabric of the handkerchief brushed against my calloused fingertips. I pulled it out as slow as I could muster and, in the palm of my hand, I unfolded it to reveal the dried daisy Belle gave me. It had become so brittle that even picking it up with bare hands would make it crumble to pieces. I couldn't lose the last piece of her that I had left. Deep down, part of me knew I needed to accept that her heart wasn't mine anymore. If the daisy was all I would have left of her love for me, then I wanted to keep it intact.

I placed the handkerchief into my jacket pocket with a careful and cautious hand, making sure the daisy wasn't going to crumble in the material. Footsteps echoed behind me, coming closer with every thud, and I spun around to see Edward. He smiled at me as I swallowed back every feeling and love I had towards Belle until he stood beside me.

"Ross, I was wondering if you and Robert would take a new recruit under your wing for training? Sergeant Wilkins told me that you two did a fantastic job helping Samuel and Nicholas," he requested. I stared into his eyes, watching for any single trace of trickery because of my affair with Belle. If he knew about it, he showed no signs of acknowledgement.

"That's not a problem, Sir."

"Thanks Chap." He patted my shoulder and walked away, but he froze in mid-step. My throat clenched, making it difficult to swallow or breathe. The world stopped spinning as he turned back at an agonising pace, wagging his finger at me. "Tell me Ross, have we met before? Your name sounds very familiar."

"No Sir, we've never met as far as I can recall."

At that moment, the daisy in my pocket became even more delicate, threatening to disintegrate into dust at any given second.

Sign up for Gabrielle McMaster's mailing list to be notified when Poppy Field is available for pre-order:

www.authorgabriellemcmaster.wordpress.com/email-list

Also, by Gabrielle McMaster

Not Always Blu Skyes

Twist in the Wind

The Wonders of Life List

Always Look Down

Social Media for Gabrielle McMaster:

Instagram: @authorgabriellemcmaster
Facebook: www.facebook.com/authorgabriellemcmaster

Historical Note

Thank you so much for reading Daisy Field. Even though it's a work of fiction, I have tried to keep as close to historical fact as possible. While none of the characters are based on real people, some events in this book did happen during the First World War. First off, the hardtack biscuit photograph which Tommy gave to Belle did take place. It was given to a nurse from Northern Ireland by her soldier sweetheart during the First World War. I absolutely loved this story when I first heard it, and this was how Tommy and Belle's relationship came about in the book.

The shell-shock of the men during the First World War features heavily in this book. Unfortunately, many men did suffer mentally during the war after witnessing sights they had never dreamt of before. The horrific nature of the war had a long-lasting effect on the men. Shell-shock was named after the shock and reverberation of sounds men would experience after shells exploded on the battlefield. When they first came to hospitals, it became a new phenomenon for hospital staff to care for and deal with alongside other injuries never witnessed before, such as the effects of gas. Eventually hospitals were formed specifically for shell-shocked men. However, by this stage many of them had suffered badly, including some of the men being terrified of their own uniform or shaking uncontrollably. Later, shell-shock would become known as PTSD.

The Battle of the Somme has been written about many times and, needless to say, I knew I had to feature it here too. I wanted to take a different angle on it. Rather than focusing on the frontlines, I wanted to look at the effects of the hospital staff back home in Britain. The Battle of the Somme became known as the darkest hour in British military history and still to this day we read and learn about it. This important battle had to feature and bringing Ross into the battle was vital for me. It allowed Belle to feel a personal connection to this horrific massacre which took place after the failings of the higher command in the British Army to recognise the dangers of their attack to their own men.

Despite the Battle of the Somme becoming Britain's darkest hour, the use of gas in 1915 caused many problems for the men. The two gases used were Chlorine and Mustard. These gas shells would have been painted yellow for the men to see in the darkness of the night in France or Belgium. In 1915, the Germans used gas for the first time on the French as discussed in the book. This caused a turn in the war to something far more horrific than any man had anticipated. The gas masks designed for the men were not adequate in the First World War with many suffering from the effects of gas despite wearing them. Gas would seep in through the eyehole linings, through the bottom of the gas mask, and many soldiers had to urinate on the masks to get them to become more affective for them. Depending on the exposure to the gas, the men would have suffered differently with some being temporarily or permanently blinded, as well as the lungs of the men being affected. The effects of gas in the book and Belle hearing of when the gas was first used was accurate to the time, including the newspaper statement on the result of the attack on the men.

The greatest amount of research which took place was on the routines and lifestyles of a VAD (Voluntary Aid Detachment) nurse during the First World War. VAD nurses had twelve hour shifts from eight in the morning until eight at night or vice-versa depending on the night or day shift. During this time, they would care for the men and take on various duties which Belle herself did throughout the narrative. Growing close to the men was inevitable and many soldiers took a shine to the nurses caring for them in the hospitals. The possibilities of sweethearts forming from these friendships fired my imagination as I came up with Daisy Field. The different past times of nurses, including sitting with the men and helping them write home, were accurate to what was expected from VADs at the time. Daisy Field highlighted the emotional and mental toll that injuries and death took on VADs during the First World War.

For five years I have worked on this novel and since then I have completed my BA Theology and History and my MA History degrees which had fuelled my love for historical fiction writing. Blending fact and fiction has always appealed to me, especially with my love of reading historical fiction. Finally, I hold in my hand the first historical fiction I came up with and it will certainly not be the last historical fiction novel I will write.

ABOUT THE AUTHOR

Gabrielle McMaster hails from Northern Ireland. She is an author and historian, best known for contemporary and historical fiction.

Gabrielle is the author of Not Always Blu Skyes (2020), Twist in the Wind (2021), The Wonders of Life List (2021), and Always Look Down (2021). She has a passion for history which led her to complete her BA in Theology and History and her MA in History with Queen's University Belfast. She specialised in cultural, social and European history throughout her two degrees.

Instagram | @authorgabriellemcmaster
Facebook | Author Gabrielle McMaster

Acknowledgements

Thank you to God for giving me this ability to write and produce stories that help people feel less alone in the world. Thank you for the opportunities you endlessly give to me to share my work with the world.

Thank you to my family who encouraged me with my writing for five years since starting Daisy Field. You have all supported me and my writing endlessly. I will be forever grateful for that. Historical fiction books were the first full length novels I read from the encouragement of my mumma. Now, I have finally published my first one.

To everyone who has read my books and supported me in one way or another (whether by social media or in person). Thank you for always supporting my work.

Thank you to my amazing editor and proof-reader, Siobhan O'Brien. I have loved working with you on this book! Thank you also to the people who have beta-read this book and gave me helpful advice. I hope you enjoy the final version of the book you read in its very early days!

Finally, to myself, who always wanted to write an historical fiction novel someday like the first author I fell in love with, Michael Morpurgo. This is the book of my heart and dreams. From 2017 until now, this book has become the best version possible. Even though this started as a simple scene – the village hall dance – it has become such a wonderful adventure. To finally hold it in my hands is utterly unbelievable. The years of work and research have been worth it. My eight year old self would be so proud and happy of me right now to see her historical fiction dream a reality.

Printed in Great Britain
by Amazon